A Legion
of Honor

A LEGION

A NOVEL

David Horton

VICTOR BOOKS

A DIVISION OF SCRIPTURE PRESS PUBLICATIONS INC.
USA CANADA ENGLAND

Designer: Paul Higdon
Editors: Susan Reck; Barbara Williams
Cover Illustration: Kazuhiko Sano
Maps: Daniel van Loon

Library of Congress Cataloging-in-Publication Data
Horton, David E.
    A legion of honor / by David E. Horton.
        p.   cm.
    ISBN 1-56476-540-7
    I. Title.
PS3558'.06978L44   1995
813'.54--dc20   95-25037
                                                           CIP

To Jennifer

"All that is necessary for evil to triumph is for good men to do nothing."

—*Edmund Burke*

Acknowledgments

I am convinced that no worthwhile book reflects
the efforts of the author alone, and this is no
exception. And so I offer my heartfelt thanks to
the people who played a part in the birth of
A Legion of Honor:

To Frank Ley, Del Linderman, Steve Lake,
and Mark Weinert, who believed in my
dream—even before I did;

To Greg Clouse, who saw the novel lurking
behind my short story and gently coaxed it out of
hiding;

To Penny Stokes and Sigmund Brouwer,
whose tactful critiques and timely coaching
proved invaluable;

To Beth Knox and Michael and Sandy
Redding for their research help;

To Serge Audisio, whose encouragement
and research assistance in France helped a great
deal;

To my friends in Domène, whose stories
inspired me;

To Sue Reck, whose deft editorial touch
rescued me from many a faux pas;

To Paul Higdon, Barb Williams, Dan van
Loon, and the rest of the team that put all the
pieces in place;

And finally, to my family, Jennifer, Ryan,
and Melissa, who cheerfully endured my long
hours at the computer and my preoccupation
with a story from another time and place.
Merci mille fois!

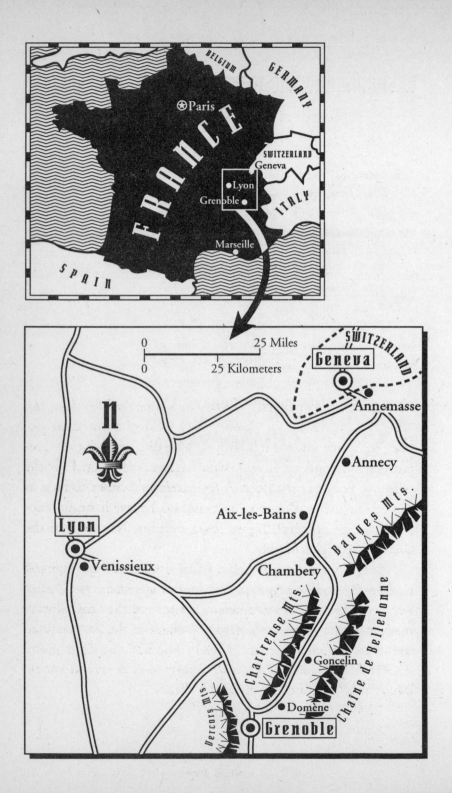

Prologue

Paris, July 16, 1942

Rumors of a massive roundup had circulated for days, but few residents in the Rue des Rosiers seemed to pay much attention. Of those who did, some merely prepared for the inevitable and, with bags packed, waited for the ominous knock at the door. A few attempted either to hide or to flee the ghetto. But most just couldn't believe it would happen. Not to peaceful, law-abiding citizens. Not here in the land of the "rights of man."

When three French police officers mounted the stairs at number 23 and knocked on the door of apartment 4-C, there was no answer. It was just before 5 A.M. and they had already made several arrests on the street. A check of the list reassured the officer in charge that, indeed, they had the right place. *KARMAZIN, Isabelle, 23 Rue des Rosiers, 4-C.* A second knock, louder this time, was also met with silence.

"Police! Open up immediately!"

Again nothing.

"They're probably gone, Sergeant," offered the youngest of the three. Officer Eugène Dumas had been on the Paris police force less than three years. Beads of perspiration formed on his forehead in spite of the cool morning air.

The officer in charge, a sour-looking man in his mid-forties, scowled at his young subordinate and resumed his vocal barrage.

"Open up or we'll break down the door!"

Without waiting further for a response, the sergeant turned and nodded as if giving an order. Without a moment's hesitation the third officer, a husky sort in his late twenties, removed his *képi*, lowered his shoulder, and rammed his way through the sagging door and into the empty room beyond. Service revolvers drawn, young Dumas and his sergeant followed close behind and began searching the tiny, unlit apartment as carefully as their flashlights would allow.

It didn't take long, as the apartment consisted of only one room. Against the far wall stood a neatly made bed and an ancient armoire half-filled with clothes; along the left wall, a small gas stove, a sink, a single wooden cabinet, and an oak table with two chairs; on the right, in front of the only window, a homely wooden bookcase flanked by two chairs.

"The shutters are unlatched." Eugène Dumas gave a nervous, boyish laugh. "Maybe she jumped." The other two glared at him but continued poking about.

"I'll make a note for the next shift," the sergeant said absently as he scribbled on the notepad he had pulled from his pocket. "They can check again later to see if anyone returns."

"Sergeant! Look what I found." The officer who had so eagerly smashed through the door held a photograph in the beam of his flashlight. "I was looking behind these books and this fell out. Is it the woman we're after?"

"Give it to me." The sergeant reached out and snatched the photo, quickly examining it under his own light. Eugène waited expectantly for his turn to have a look. Instead, the sergeant cast the photo aside, and turned abruptly toward the splintered front door.

"Let's get on with it," he said. "We've got a lot more Jews to round up before the day's over."

Eugène lagged behind until the others were outside, then quickly scooped up the fallen photograph. A demure young couple in wedding garb smiled up at him. The sharp-featured, bespectacled groom appeared to be in his mid-twenties. The bride, dark-haired and beautiful, seemed hardly more than a teenager. "It's a good thing you weren't home," he whispered, then tucked the photo inside his uniform and hurried outside.

Chapter 1

Near Grenoble, September 1942

The warm evening air felt unseasonably thick as Marcel Boussant peered at the cluster of men in the village square. If they noticed that the cooling breeze that swept down out of the Belledonne range most September nights was arriving later than usual, they gave no sign. Their attention was fixed on the two contestants in their midst, as it had been for the past two hours. There was virtually no conversation, not even about the week's news, which as usual had been discouraging. But these were discouraging times. The world would have to wait while the game was decided.

Only the two men on the fringe of the group seemed at all distracted. They spoke in hushed tones, their voices barely carrying to where Marcel stood partially hidden among the plane trees behind them. His attention diverted from the action, Marcel edged his way closer to the pair, straining to hear their conversation.

"Do you really think he can win?" Marcel was close enough to recognize the voice of Emile Bonet, the village butcher.

His companion, René Carlini, a produce distributor, had been influential in local politics before the war. "You needn't worry," he replied with a sinister smile. "I know very well what I'm doing. He'll be sorry he ever interfered."

Marcel exhaled slowly, suddenly aware that he had been holding his breath. Carlini's words had him puzzled—and a little nervous. The contest was still in doubt, and it was plain from the mood of the onlookers that the stakes were high—far higher than the usual handful of francs. And as much as he wanted to see who won, the lanky nineteen-year-old entertained a moment of doubt about the wisdom of remaining uninvited.

Unsteadily, he leaned back against the stately bulk of a plane tree and cast a quick glance around. Standing like sentries in parallel ranks, the square's aged trees kept a silent watch. They needn't have bothered, for the men in the square were captives of their contest. Even the surrounding village of Domène lay silent and shuttered, hunkered down for the night. Marcel mopped an already damp sleeve across his sweaty face and wondered anxiously how it would end.

❧   ❧   ❧

René Carlini wished he were as confident as he sounded. A businessman and sometime politician, he was used to having his way. When an employee was insubordinate, he simply fired him. When an aspiring party member questioned his leadership, he could unseat him by merely withholding his support. But he was finding that presiding over a local resistance network was a lot more complicated. The men were volunteers, of course, which made strict discipline next to impossible. Many of them were armed, making diplomacy extremely important.

Challenges to his authority had to be dealt with, however carefully, or the future—his future—would be compromised.

Earlier in the evening, he had sensed such a challenge taking shape. Not that it was the first. Forced to form a leadership "council" of sorts to satisfy a previous dispute with one of the old-timers, Carlini had bided his time, waiting for the right opportunity to reassert himself. Now, he needed to nip this new challenge in the bud.

The young upstart had claimed to speak on behalf of General de Gaulle. But in his effort to impress the men, he had laid claim to being the *boules* champion of Marseilles as well. *Hardly likely at his age.* So Carlini had proposed a contest as a way to establish the newcomer's credibility. If it all went as planned, the newcomer would be discredited—and Carlini would be back in control.

Of the dozen or so men who made up his clandestine network, none could be relied on as completely as Emile Bonet. A powerful fireplug of a man with massive shoulders and thick forearms, he was as raw as Carlini was refined. The only weapons he ever carried were his fists, but he was committed to a France free of foreign influence. And though he didn't always comprehend the significance of his orders, he carried them out thoroughly.

"And if he loses—" began Bonet, turning his head so as not to be overheard by the others. Perhaps it was just the moonshadows, but his usually placid face seemed clouded with apprehension. Perhaps he too had been seduced by the newcomer's charm and promises. All the more reason to move quickly and decisively.

"He will lose, my friend," interrupted Carlini, "and then you'll take him out near the Gypsy camp. Make sure he won't be easily found by passersby." Carlini moved toward the others then, pausing just for a moment to light a fresh cigarette.

❦   ❦   ❦

A harvest moon hung full and bright, illuminating the square and its occupants. In spite of the soft light, no one seemed to be aware of Marcel's existence—no one but Antoine LeBoeuf, that is. Not that he acknowledged Marcel in any way. But Marcel had found LeBoeuf to be very observant. Not clairvoyant or a genius. He just noticed things. And spoke his mind. Marcel had reason to expect that the old man would ask about his presence at the game the next time they met.

Not surprisingly, Antoine was one of the two contestants. He spent a lot of time playing *boules*. His thick, snowy hair and leathery hands and face belied a youthful enthusiasm for the game and a keenly competitive spirit. He seldom lost, and then not by much. Marcel recalled how the few who could boast of having bested the old-timer did so with a sort of reverence, knowing it was a feat unlikely to be repeated. But on a night like this, when the light was dim and Antoine was no longer young, anything was possible.

LeBoeuf's opponent this stifling Friday night was a man Marcel didn't recognize. His speech gave him away as a southerner, probably from Marseilles or Aix or thereabout. But he spoke so little it was hard to say for sure. He looked to be in his early twenties, tall, with a narrow face and jet-black hair swept straight back. His face, gleaming with a thin film of sweat, was all seriousness and concentration.

He had an air of confidence about him that wasn't swaggering or punctuated by coarse boasts, and that suggested he was older than he looked. So far, his confidence didn't appear to be misplaced. But he was up against a local legend, and unless Carlini was bluffing, he might need more than confidence to see him through the night.

He'll be sorry he ever interfered, Carlini had said. Marcel didn't like the sound of it. *Interfered with what, exactly? Carlini's business?* If not, why would he threaten a complete stranger over a game of *boules*—if he really were a complete stranger? It just didn't make sense.

To his surprise, Marcel found that he had begun to harbor a flicker of hope that the stranger would win—even against Antoine LeBoeuf.

The game seemed innocent enough, and not unlike the *boules* tournaments played regularly on Friday and Saturday nights in villages all across France. But ever since the humiliating surrender to the Germans, Marcel had mustered little enthusiasm for *boules*, or any other game for that matter. Tonight, however, he had felt the need for a little diversion and had wandered down the hill from his house only to find the village square empty but for these few men. Curiosity, more than anything else, had kept him from returning home just yet.

Of course, like all other activities, *boules* tournaments were subject to the curfew, but depending on geography, it was possible to skirt such rules—sometimes by guile, other times by simply ignoring them. This night the latter method prevailed, and the local *gendarmes* were apparently occupied elsewhere.

While civil laws could sometimes be ignored with impunity, Marcel knew very well that the rules of the game of *boules* could not. Rigorously enforced during the course of a match, they were simple enough that he and his friends had become adept at the game by the time they started school. The gritty, pebbly surface of the *boules* court became familiar territory, and lofting or rolling a steel ball, or *boule*, weighing about a pound and a half, as close as possible to the round wooden *but*, quickly became second nature.

The drifting haze from a dozen unfiltered cigarettes added to the unusual heat, casting its pall over the little band of onlookers and curling its sluggish way toward where Marcel stood half-hidden. He squinted his eyes against the irritating fumes and watched as the dark young southerner slowly approached the tiny circle scribed into the dusty surface of the plaza. The stranger clutched his third and last *boule* in his right hand. Four steel balls already formed a ragged circle around the tiny wooden *but*. LeBoeuf held the advantage. In fact, two of his *boules* lay slightly closer than his opponent's nearest one. The best the younger man could hope for was a tie, while Antoine could win outright if he could maintain the position he currently held. Cautiously, not wishing to attract attention, but not wanting to miss anything either, Marcel began to edge closer.

The southerner stepped into the circle and prepared to launch his final attempt. He bent slightly forward and peered at his target with determined, unblinking eyes. He drew his arm back deliberately as though cocking a gun. Unconsciously, Marcel held his breath again, the pulse in his ears the only sound he heard. No one moved. Then, like a viper, the stranger's arm uncoiled, making his strike.

Marcel's heart lurched against his ribcage, and he was barely able to stifle the disappointed groan that rose in his throat. *How could he throw it all away so foolishly? He will never win like that!* But astonishment quickly replaced his anguish as the sharp sound of steel on steel broke the stillness. There, spinning to a stop within inches of the *but*, lay the southerner's *boule*. Dislodged, Antoine's *boule* rolled harmlessly off the court. Marcel checked himself in time to prevent a relieved smile from crossing his face. Accompanied by murmurs of approval, the challenger strode from the circle to await the outcome. He brushed away the rivulet of sweat making its way across his high cheekbone and stood stony-faced and silent.

The setback didn't seem to have unnerved LeBoeuf. In fact, he seemed completely unfazed. *"Bien joué!"* he said to no one in particular as he approached the sandy circle. "Well played."

By now Marcel was nearly among the onlookers, having lost his concern with being seen. He knew many of these men—several of them had even been to his family's farm—and he held them in awe. Their respective occupations were ordinary enough. Laborers, merchants, and peasant farmers mostly. But their much-rumored yet vague exploits of resistance were the stuff of a young man's fantasies. He was certainly not the first to entertain visions of becoming one of their number, though precisely what that entailed was unclear to him.

Now, silence once again. No one so much as twitched an eyelid. Even the cigarette smoke seemed to hang motionless in the leaden air. LeBoeuf scrutinized the tiny *but* and crouched low to almost kneeling. He brought his arm back smoothly and, with little hesitation, swung it forward again, releasing his final throw just inches above the ground. The steel ball met the ground quickly and whispered its way across the gritty surface on a straight line—wide right of the wooden goal. Marcel's mind flashed to occasions when he had witnessed Antoine's largesse. Perhaps he was giving the stranger a break, another chance. Or maybe, just maybe, there were limits to the old gentleman's abilities. Marcel had his doubts.

As if to confirm those doubts, the rolling *boule* dipped into a slight hollow and curved to the left, a scant three feet from the *but*. Its momentum, however, would surely carry it past the tiny wooden goal even if it came close. But as Marcel watched in absolute disbelief, the *boule* curved directly into the *but* and pushed it backward, away from the stranger's *boule*. As if to add insult to injury, the roller came to rest not more than an inch from Antoine's second *boule* with the *but* nestled neatly between them! Game, set, match. In spite of the younger man's skill, the wily veteran had prevailed.

Will Carlini carry out his threat? Marcel felt a pang of

remorse as he looked to where the defeated stranger stood. For a moment so good, so confident, there he now stood, unmoving, appearing numb, seeming not to fully grasp his loss. He couldn't possibly have known what he was up against, Marcel decided as he tried to imagine what the young stranger must be thinking. Then he crept silently behind the nearest plane tree to watch and wait from the shadows.

One by one the other men extended a congratulatory hand to the white-haired LeBoeuf. In victory, he looked like a beardless, benevolent Father Christmas, although in the stifling late summer heat the comparison seemed ridiculous. With characteristic grace, he kept his voice low and nodded with a half-smile as he shook hands all around. At last he moved toward the benumbed stranger, clasped his shoulder with a leathery hand, and said something softly before moving on.

Out of the corner of his eye, Marcel caught sight of Bonet the butcher twitching nervously, trying to make eye contact with René Carlini. Carlini glanced briefly in his direction, then calmly dropped his still-smoldering cigarette to the ground and crushed it under his heel.

Antoine LeBoeuf, René Carlini, and the others soon abandoned the square and faded into the night, while Bonet and two husky laborers converged warily on the southerner. Marcel shuddered involuntarily as he watched them lead the stranger away.

❦   ❦   ❦

For years Gypsies had encamped on a large tree-sheltered field just beyond the Rue des Contamines, the last street at the north end of town. The location of their camp was as certain as their arrivals and departures were unpredictable. Even when unoccupied, everyone referred to the field as "the Gypsy camp," and for the most part, the *Domenois,* as the village residents were called, kept their distance.

The prevailing local wisdom held that, whatever else they might be, Gypsies were trouble. True, people admired their ability to trade shrewdly in the *marché*. And the dark-eyed beauty of young Gypsy girls was legendary. Add to that the colorful caravans and storied travel to romantic places, and these nomads took on an exotic air. But their transient lifestyle made them susceptible to accusations of rather less-admired activities. That they were guilty of petty thievery, vandalism, and other assorted crimes was routinely assumed—especially in the absence of proof to the contrary.

Of course, most could point to experiences that proved the conventional wisdom. There was the time Marcel caught two young Gypsy boys trying to steal eggs from his father's produce stand at the *marché*, or two summers ago, when a young man from the camp had made amorous advances toward Marcel's then-fifteen-year-old sister Françoise. A puffy black eye would remind him for some time to come that French flowers would not be easily plucked by such as he.

Tonight, however, the Gypsies did not figure prominently in Marcel's thoughts as he approached their camp. And he was only vaguely aware of the soft strains of guitar and mandolin, of laughter and singing that floated toward him on the gentle breeze.

For what seemed like eons he had remained frozen in the square, staring dumbly into the dim night in the direction of the departing men who had wasted little time disappearing down the nearest side street, evidently headed toward the camp. The spell was eventually broken by the toll of the church bell across the street, sounding eleven o'clock. It was as if an alarm had gone off in his brain, jolting him back into the here and now. And he felt compelled to see if his fears for the stranger were well-founded.

By the time the bell had struck four, he was moving at a

slow trot across the square to where he had last seen the stranger and his escorts. As the bell fell silent again, he stopped to unlace and remove his shoes, fearing that the sound of his footfalls might alert the others to his pursuit. The last thing he wanted was to be caught sneaking up on men who might easily include him in whatever plans they had devised for the southerner. And whatever their plans, there were three of them and only one of him.

The streets were unlit, save for the moon and a scattering of stars that winked in casual disregard of the night's events—and of the war itself. It wasn't the first time that Marcel had wondered how heaven could be so placid in the face of France's humiliation. The chaos that reigned here below seemed unable to penetrate the skies, and he found that thought more confusing than comforting. But, unlike so many, he was not yet ready to give up hope. He jogged ahead, not at all sure of what he could or should do about the dilemma facing the country or the plight of the stranger, but certain he wanted to do something.

When he reached the Rue des Contamines, he slowed to a stop and replaced his shoes. There was no point in continuing to run. He had only to turn right and walk a hundred yards or so up the lane to where the camp lay on the left behind some oak trees. Creeping along the stone wall that bordered the right side of the lane, he kept as low a profile as possible. Even with the moon casting its pale glow through the overhanging tree branches, he could make out no shapes that resembled men or anything else out of the ordinary. Only the shadows of an occasional gateway broke the dingy gray of the stone wall.

As he crept past the second such gateway, he felt something strike his shin hard. He exhaled a startled grunt and promptly lost his balance, pitching forward awkwardly. He managed to break his fall only at the last instant with his outstretched arms. The shock of the hard landing was greater than the pain, and he pounded his open right palm angrily on the warm paving stones, upset by his clumsiness.

Muttering to himself, he clambered to his feet. But the instant he straightened up, a meaty fist smashed into his jaw, snapping his head back and sending him sprawling again—this time onto his back.

Momentarily stunned and unable to move, he stared lazily up at the sky. The moon seemed so close he could almost touch it. Voices came from silhouetted shapes weaving slowly overhead, partially blocking his view. But the voices sounded strangely distant. And cold as ice.

"Who is he?" The first voice sounded unfamiliar.

"It's the Boussant kid. What's he doing here?"

"How should I know?" That hoarse whisper might have belonged to Emile Bonet, but Marcel couldn't be sure. "He was watching in the square, I think, but he's probably harmless."

Marcel worked his lips in an effort to tell them just how harmless he was, but no sound came out.

"Allez! Come on. I doubt if he saw us. Anyway, if he says anything we can take care of him later."

They were gone then, but as he tried to roll gingerly onto his side, Marcel didn't care. Full awareness was flooding his senses, and his jaw was pounding the beat of a parade drum. A tingling numbness had settled over much of his back, and his left sleeve was torn and damp where his arm had struck the paving stones as he fell. A twinge of pain accompanied every move he made.

Rising onto all fours, he was once more aware of the soft music coming from the Gypsy camp, and he found it suddenly irritating. *Why can't they sleep at night like everyone else?* he fumed. But it occurred to him that the continuing serenade meant that the camp must be unaware of his presence—or that of his assailants—and he preferred it that way. This hardly seemed the time to make acquaintances, least of all with Gypsies.

Marcel crawled to the side of the lane opposite the stone wall, and with some effort, managed to stand. His jaw hurt so badly he could barely purse his lips to spit out the blood he was tasting. He walked forward tenuously, afraid of what might lie ahead, but not willing to retrace his steps and risk running into Bonet and his toughs again.

He found Bonet's other victim a few yards away—or at least he found someone. Even the man's own family, if he had one, would have had difficulty recognizing him. His face was swollen and bleeding, and his left arm was twisted into an unnatural position. Marcel was pretty sure he recognized the shirt the man was wearing, but even in the dark he could see that it was badly soiled and torn across the front. The stranger wasn't moving, nor did he appear to be breathing.

Marcel sank painfully, dejectedly to the ground beside the body. He had come too late. A new kind of numbness enveloped him, pushing aside his physical pain. He shed no tears for the stranger, but he ached for all the craziness that war had brought to France and its people. Having failed to defend their borders, they had apparently been reduced to killing each other.

The darkness seemed to deepen around him and the music stopped. That's when he heard the dogs.

Chapter 2

The notion that dog is man's best friend had always struck Marcel as a bit naïve. Not that he disliked dogs. On the contrary, he was quite fond of Léo, the Boussant's five-year-old German shepherd (though since the war broke out, all reference to Léo's unfortunate ancestry had been dropped). Léo was practically a part of the family, and as such had proved to be dependable, predictable, and even gentle. But since he was a small boy, Marcel had felt a certain reserve toward other people's dogs, a reserve he was unable to trace to any particular trauma, yet which persisted even into young adulthood. The baying he heard at present sounded neither familiar nor particularly friendly, and the rise of the hair at the base of his neck signaled that it was time to move.

The aches and pains which had temporarily subsided as he sat beside the stranger's battered body returned in waves as Marcel struggled to his feet. He immediately felt lightheaded and had to steady himself against the nearest oak tree to keep from falling down. In a few seconds his head cleared, and he angled back onto the lane in the direction opposite the way he had come, casting a glance back over his shoulder, unsure what to do about the stranger.

The unsettling sounds of the as-yet-unseen dogs weren't far off now, and Marcel quickened his pace to a hobbling trot in spite of the pain in his shin and his pounding jaw. This time he took care to stay clear of the gray stone wall with its dark, gated, hiding places.

The Rue des Contamines ended abruptly at the two-lane highway that hugged the eastern edge of the Gresivaudan Valley, connecting Grenoble and Pontcharra over a distance of some twenty-four miles. Normally, it was somewhat less traveled than the *route nationale* on the opposite side of the valley. Now, in the middle of the night, the road was completely deserted as Marcel turned right and headed up the incline toward the center of Domène. He could still hear the dogs, though it was difficult to tell just by listening if they were gaining on him.

Marcel slowed his pace slightly in an effort to relieve his throbbing head and aching body. It didn't seem to help, and fifty yards after turning the corner he was wondering if he could make it another fifty. But stopping was out of the question. The curfew had long since passed, and he really couldn't afford to flout it indefinitely. Besides which, Maman would be furious if she discovered he had crept out again at night. And he didn't want another encounter with Emile Bonet and his pals, though he figured that by now they were home in their beds. He certainly hoped so. Of course, there was still the matter of the dogs. He picked up his pace again.

Twin beams of light crested the hill at the center of town, still a good three hundred yards to the south, just an instant before Marcel heard the growl of the car's engine. Even in a small town like Domène, it was hard to imagine anyone who would disregard the curfew so blatantly. Just five miles from Grenoble, Domène was subject to more than an occasional police patrol. And though the Germans only occupied the northern three-fifths of the country, the government for the unoccupied zone, headquartered in the resort town of Vichy, seemed filled with eager surrogates. Arrests and seizures by the Vichy police were not uncommon.

The idea that this was a cocky *paysan,* thumbing his nose at the world and its rules, was dispelled almost immediately. Brazenly, the rapidly approaching car straddled the center line. Clearly, whoever it was, was not expecting to encounter anyone this late at night. And just as clearly, Marcel realized that there was a good chance that whoever this was worked for the government or the police. Worse, he also realized that in a matter of seconds he would be trapped in the glare of the headlights. He needed a place to hide. The dogs, whose insistent baying was now all but swallowed by the rumble of the advancing car, suddenly seemed less frightening than armed men.

The garden wall to Marcel's right was higher than his head, offering no hint as to what might lie on the other side. Still, he had little choice. The nearest open space, a small lane, was too far ahead. To cross the road to more protective surroundings would be foolhardy. So, leaping as high as his aches and bruises would allow, he grasped the wall's flat top with both hands, inched his fingers to the far edge, and began to haul himself up. He dug into the wall with his toes to speed his climb, but the outside surface had been plastered smooth and he failed to gain a good foothold. With shoulders and arms straining, he pulled himself to where he could prop his elbows atop the wall and throw his bruised right leg over. His breath coming in ragged bursts, his tired limbs protesting every movement, he scrambled over the top—and immediately lost his grip. The last sound he heard before crashing into the hard ground six feet below was the roar of the passing automobile.

※   ※   ※

The dogs were circling warily, baring their teeth and growling, looking for a weak spot to attack. How they had been able to follow him over the wall, Marcel couldn't fathom. Numb from head to toe, he felt the hair on his neck rise again as the mangy hounds paced 'round and 'round. Each dog moved in on him in turn, in a menacing feint, only to retreat at the last second to be replaced by another. Just how many there were Marcel couldn't tell. They seemed to dart in and out of his hazy field of vision as he lay paralyzed on his back.

"*Allez,* you mangy devils! Go on." He tried to punctuate his epithets with a wave of his arms, but they were like lead. Emboldened by his inability to move, the beasts crept closer and closer. Marcel could feel the heat emanating from their bodies, smell the stench of their breath. He knew it wouldn't be long before they would overcome what little fear remained.

As if on cue, the largest dog moved in purposefully, alternately growling and whining, baring its teeth. Marcel steeled himself, then began thrashing his head from side to side to fend off the inevitable.

"Well, what do we have here, Bayard?" Marcel's whole body jerked at the sound of the voice. "He doesn't look too well, does he?"

Marcel wanted to open his eyes, but he was almost afraid to. The rank smell of dog breath dominated his senses, and the low growling kept him from trying to move. Ever so slowly he raised an eyelid. The sky overhead was the deep blue of early morning.

"I think his eyes are opening, old boy. Well, at least he's not dead."

Not yet, Marcel mused, unsure as to where he was or what was happening to him. The voice, however, sounded vaguely familiar.

"Ah, Bayard. By all the saints, it's young Monsieur Boussant! What's he doing in my garden? And in such a state! Marcel, are you all right? Marcel?"

By now Marcel had both eyes open, and he recognized the voice and leathery face of Antoine LeBoeuf. The old man knelt down carefully and cradled Marcel's neck in his right hand, helping him to sit.

"Are you all right?" Antoine repeated. He continued to maintain a hand behind Marcel as if he were afraid he would fall back onto the ground.

"I . . . I think . . . I'm not sure." Marcel's throat was parched and his voice sounded strange to his own ears. His jaw hurt when he spoke, and the right side of his face felt swollen when he touched it.

It was just now dawning on him that he hadn't actually been attacked by bloodthirsty hounds. The only dog to be seen was Antoine's aging collie, Bayard, who was still growling and sniffing about. Marcel pulled away from the dog and looked anxiously about, half-expecting the hounds to reappear.

"Where did they go? Where am I?"

"Did you hear that, Bayard? He wants to know where he is." Antoine seemed momentarily amused. Turning a more serious look toward Marcel, he added, "You're in my garden, young man. How did you get in here? What happened to you? And where did *who* go? No one's here but me and old Bayard. And now you, of course."

"What time is it?"

"Six thirty. But, you haven't answered my questions, my friend. What happened to you?"

"After you beat that man last night at *boules...*" Marcel's voice trailed off as he tried to force his mind to work. Then, as though a dam had burst, it all came rushing out. "I think he's dead. . . . They ambushed me and there was a pack of hounds and then—"

"Dead? Whoa, slow down. Perhaps you'd better come inside and clean up, and then you can tell me everything—slowly." Antoine helped Marcel to his feet, put an arm around him, and half-carried him into the house. The old collie, still sniffing and growling his displeasure, followed them.

Inside, the house was dark, the only light coming from the open door through which the two men entered. The shutters had not yet been opened to welcome the day, and not a single light bulb illuminated their way. Antoine, however, moved about with a deft assurance borne of decades of living in the same house. The doorway opened into a corner of the *salon*. A quick turn to the right brought them past the stairway and into a room which apparently served as both kitchen and dining room.

Once Marcel was more or less comfortably settled in a straightback chair at the kitchen table, the old man filled an ivory-colored ceramic washbasin half-full of water from a matching pitcher. Both pitcher and basin sat on a sagging, cluttered table, pushed against the back wall. Pulling a small towel from a hook on the wall and laying it gently over his arm as though he were a waiter at Maxim's, Antoine carefully lifted the basin and brought it to the table, placing it in front of Marcel.

"Wash up," he prodded, handing Marcel the towel. "You'll feel better. I'm sure of it. Then we'll talk." And with that he left the room and headed up the stairs.

Marcel took hold of the towel and dipped it gingerly into the water, barely bothering to wring it out. Ever so gently he pressed the dripping cloth to his swollen face. And while it hurt to have anything touch the puffy flesh at first, he was quickly rewarded by the coolness of the water. He didn't care so much that he was probably filthy; the cool relief was all that mattered for the moment. Little by little, however, he wiped the rest of his face free of blood and grime, and had even removed his shirt to begin swabbing his arms and torso when Antoine descended the stairs and closed the front door. In his left hand he held a kerosene lantern aloft. In his right, he clutched a pistol.

Marcel, his eyes fastened on the gun, laid the towel aside slowly. He watched as the old man walked casually around the end of the table where he deposited the lantern, giving the room an eerie glow. Seating himself directly opposite Marcel, Antoine placed the revolver carefully on the table between them.

"Now, then," he began slowly, leaning back slightly in his chair. "What's all this about a dead man?"

Chapter 3

Marcel couldn't take his eyes off the revolver. "What's this talk about a dead man, Marcel?" The old man repeated the question after a long silence.

"The man you beat at *boules* last night?" It was more a statement than a question. "I found him dead. He'd been beaten over on the Rue des Contamines, near the Gypsy camp."

"Are you sure it was the same guy?"

"Yeah . . . well, I'm almost sure. I got a pretty good look at him." Marcel shuddered as he recalled how the stranger's body had looked, battered and crumpled next to the road.

"Did you see who did it? Was it the Gypsies?"

"I didn't see any Gypsies. And it didn't sound like them, either."

"Sound like them? Then you didn't really see anyone?" Marcel couldn't tell if Antoine sounded more hopeful or apprehensive.

"Not really. I mean, I didn't actually see anyone beat him

up. But didn't Emile Bonet and his two buddies take the guy out there? It had to be them!"

"What makes you so sure Bonet wasn't already gone when this guy was attacked? Perhaps he just took him out there to meet someone." Antoine sounded as though he were defending Bonet.

Marcel looked up from the table and straight into Antoine's cool gray eyes. "It was Bonet. I'm sure it wasn't just my imagination." He reached his hand up to gingerly touch the swelling along his jawline. "I know I didn't imagine this," he added emphatically.

"You saw him?" Antoine still seemed disbelieving.

"Not clearly. But I heard his voice. And he recognized me. Said they would 'take care of me later' if I made trouble." Just thinking about it again made Marcel angry. "Who was this guy, anyway? I mean, why play a game of *boules* with someone and then send Bonet out to beat him to death?"

"I swear to you, Marcel, I knew nothing about any plans for a beating. If I had, I would never have agreed to be a party to it. To my knowledge, the game was simply a way of checking out his story; that's all. No one really knew him."

Neither of them said anything for several minutes. They just stared down at the tabletop, thinking. Finally, Antoine raised his eyes and spoke again, his voice softer than before.

"What were you doing there, anyway, Marcel? In fact, why were you in the square last night?"

So, the old-timer *had* seen him. Marcel wasn't surprised.

"I don't know. I was bored, I guess. And curious. People talk, you know, and I thought that if I hung around, perhaps somehow I could join you."

"Join what, exactly?"

"You know what I mean!" The idea that Antoine was toying with him irritated Marcel. "Resisting the *boches* and the traitors in Vichy! I know you and Carlini and the others are part of it. I want to do something too. I love France too much to just sit by while she crumbles."

"So, you want to get involved." A faint smile played at the corners of Antoine's mouth. "It looks to me like you're involved already. Is this what you had in mind?" He gestured toward Marcel's bruised, swollen face.

Marcel frowned his annoyance and looked down at his hands.

"I'm sorry, Marcel," Antoine continued. "I really don't mean to mock you. It's just that it's not that simple. What a few of us are doing requires more than patriotism. 'Joining,' as you call it, carries a price that few can afford to pay—that fewer still are willing to pay. You cannot expect to merely present yourself and be accepted. There is far too much at stake. First, you've got to prove yourself.

"Unfortunately, because of your gaffe last night, you are involved whether you like it or not—whether *anyone* likes it or not. Take my advice, my friend. Show that you can be trusted with what you already know, and perhaps there will be opportunities. Otherwise. . . ."

These last words were spoken with such foreboding that Marcel realized, perhaps for the first time, that he might live to regret his impulsiveness.

Antoine continued in a fatherly tone. "If you can be trusted, and if your help is needed, someone will call for you. Understood?"

"Yes, I think so." Marcel wasn't quite as sure as he sounded. Nor was he sure he still wanted to join Carlini's group.

"Now, then, you still haven't told me why you followed the men out to the Gypsy camp!"

So Marcel described the previous night's activities in detail, beginning with the conversation he had overheard between René Carlini and Emile Bonet. Antoine raised his eyebrows at that, but remained silent. Marcel left out nothing that he could remember, right up to the point where he had clambered over the wall and fallen into Antoine's garden. When Marcel finished, Antoine rose from his chair without a word and lit the stove under an old brass teapot.

"I'll make some *tisane,*" he offered. "It'll do us both good." Then he sat down again while he waited for the water to boil. "I'm sorry I don't have any bread in the house," he winked, "but I was interrupted on my way to the bakery this morning."

While he was drinking his *tisane,* it occurred to Marcel that he would have some explaining to do when he got home. At nineteen, running the farm had largely become his responsibility. And though he was fairly free to come and go, staying out all night was a different matter. Not that he had stayed out intentionally. But his family had no way of knowing that.

He drained his cup and stood to go. "I can't stay any longer, Monsieur LeBoeuf," he said. "Maman will be worried, and besides, I've got work to do today."

"Of course, of course." Antoine rose from his chair. "But first, show me where this dead body is. It's very important."

"All right, but we'll have to hurry."

"Marcel?"

Marcel turned just as Antoine reached down and picked up the revolver. He grasped it by the barrel and extended it, butt-first, toward Marcel. Marcel took an involuntary step back.

"Take it," the older man said firmly. "I'm afraid you may need it."

"I . . . I don't understand."

"Something strange is going on, and you're a witness to it. I think it would be wise for you to be able to defend yourself."

Marcel grasped the pistol's checked wooden handle and stared at it as though it were the first gun he had ever seen. "Where did you get it?" he asked.

"Try not to ask too many questions," Antoine replied. "You may not like the answers.

"By the way," he added, "it's loaded, so keep the safety on until you need to use it."

Marcel tucked the gun into the waistband of his trousers, put his shirt back on, and led the way out the front door.

Antoine extinguished the lantern and called to the dog. "Come on, Bayard," he said aloud, then added under his breath, "let's keep an eye on our young friend." The dog, which had curled up on a small rug in the far corner of the kitchen, rose obediently and joined the two men.

❧   ❧   ❧

The gun felt uncomfortable as Marcel walked, and he paused several times to adjust it, looking around to make sure no one was watching. He wasn't at all sure he liked this idea, but he guessed he would have to get used to it. Maybe it would be different in the winter when he could carry it in an inside pocket of his heavy wool coat. It would be easier to hide, and he was sure it would be more comfortable. Then again, maybe this would blow over and he wouldn't need it at all.

When they reached the spot where Marcel had last seen the stranger's body, it was gone. And there was not a trace of it anywhere.

Antoine looked quizzically at Marcel. "Well? Are you sure this is the right place?"

Marcel looked around carefully. "I'm positive. He was lying right at the edge of the road under those oak trees. Who could have moved him?"

"Maybe nobody moved him. Maybe he wasn't dead after all," Antoine suggested. "Maybe he just *looked* like he wasn't breathing."

Marcel felt insulted, but said nothing in reply. He knew what he had seen, but the fact remained that the stranger's body was nowhere to be found. He racked his brain trying to think of anything he might have overlooked that would help them find it. Then he remembered the baying hounds that had run him off just a few hours before. They had come from the direction of the Gypsy camp.

"Hey, what about the Gypsies? Maybe we should ask them if they saw anything."

"All right," said Antoine, "but let's not go too near their camp. They're not particularly sympathetic to strangers, and they have a lot of unfriendly dogs."

"I was just thinking about that myself." Marcel swallowed nervously as he recalled the previous night's chase.

They had only traveled a few dozen yards down the narrow dirt track leading to the camp when three Gypsy youths appeared and began to walk toward them. Bayard immediately went to stand between his master and the three boys and growled as if to warn them not to come any closer.

"Let me do the talking," Antoine warned Marcel out of the side of his mouth. Marcel started to protest, then thought better of it.

"*Bonjour, messieurs,*" Antoine began with characteristic formality. "We're wondering if you would be so kind as to render us a small service."

"And what would that be?" asked the tallest youth stiffly.

"Did you see or hear anything unusual around here last night?"

"Just a couple of men in a shiny black Renault," replied the Gypsy. The car had obviously made a favorable impression on him.

So, at least that much is true, thought Marcel.

"You didn't see a man get beat up?" Antoine probed.

"I thought you were interested in something unusual. People get beat up all the time—sometimes even Gypsies." The boy's companions smirked at his last remark.

"There was a dead body," Marcel blurted out, "right over there!" He turned to point back the way they had come.

Antoine scowled at Marcel, then turned back to the boys. "A dead body is a bit unusual, isn't it?"

"He wasn't dead," the tall boy said with assurance.

Marcel started to say something, but felt Antoine's restraining hand on his shoulder.

"How do you know?"

"Because I heard him cry out when the other men dragged him into the back of the Renault!" He was beginning to sound irritated. "Is that all?"

"Yes, thank you. You've been very helpful."

Without another word, the Gypsy boys retreated back in the direction of their camp. Marcel waited a long moment after they were gone before turning to face Antoine.

"How could that be?" He was mystified. "He wasn't breathing. I was sure he was dead!"

"Things aren't always as they appear," Antoine said thoughtfully. Then he added, "Someone has a lot of explaining to do."

❧   ❧   ❧

The two-mile walk back to the Boussant farm seemed much longer than usual, and the fact that it was all uphill didn't help. The road rose steeply from where the village crowded the base of the hill and only flattened out slightly over the four miles to the tiny hamlet of Revel. A break in the trees a half mile up afforded a spectacular panorama of Domène and beyond. Marcel seldom passed this point without stopping to take in the inspiring view.

Immediately below him lay the red tiled roofs of Domène in a maze of twisting streets and alleyways, spreading out into the near reaches of the valley floor. The village traced its roots back over a thousand years, though only the ruins of an eleventh-century *prieuré* remained to attest to the richness of its history. The surging Domenon Creek cut a swath through the center of town on its way to the Isère River. The town square, where the *boules* game had been played, lay straight ahead. On market day it would swarm with color and conversation as people from all over the valley converged to gossip and to buy and sell what they could.

To the left of the square the Catholic church thrust its steeple skyward. At the far edge of the square stood the stately town hall, and on its left a high-walled schoolyard. Bordering the winding main street were a profusion of shops, bars, and restaurants. Looking to the right, Marcel could see Antoine's house along the northbound highway, and farther still, the Gypsy camp.

In the distance across the valley, the Chartreuse mountains rose sharply to form a line of steep cliffs. Grenoble sprawled in front of the Vercors range to the far left. And off to the right, dominating the valley, loomed the majestic Dent de Crolles mountain, high above the cliffs of the Chartreuse.

Marcel never tired of the scene that lay before him. Its beauty changed, but did not diminish, with each passing season. And lately, he took comfort in its reminder that there are some things beyond the control of governments, armies, and ambitious men.

A tiny emerald hollow, dotted by oak trees and sliced through by the lively Domenon Creek on its descent from Revel, had been home to the Boussant family for years. The old stone and stucco house with its tiled roof looked only slightly better than the similarly constructed barn.

It was after 9 A.M. when Marcel finally trudged into the yard to the welcoming bark of an exuberant Léo. Marcel stroked the shepherd's thick fur absently, wondering what his mother would say about his unexplained absence. He didn't have to wait long. She appeared in the doorway, hands on her hips, just as he ascended the first of the four front steps.

"Where—" she began, then stopped, the color draining from her face as her gaze settled on his bruises. "What happened to you? Are you all right? Let me have a look at you."

"I'm okay, Maman. Really. And I'm sorry about not coming home sooner. I can explain, but it's kind of a long story."

"It must be," she said, looking reproachfully at her son. "Otherwise it wouldn't have kept you out all night."

Evelyne Boussant was a handsome woman by all accounts. At forty, she showed few ill effects of life on a farm. In spite of having borne three children, the active country life had enabled her to maintain her pleasing shape. Her shoulder-length brown hair was pulled back away from her face, making the tiny crow's-feet at the corners of her eyes more obvious. Today, however, she looked tired, and Marcel didn't wonder why.

He was her eldest child, having just turned nineteen in June. Physically, everyone told him that he took after his lanky, though muscular, father, Albert. Albert, who would be forty-two, had been gone for more than two years. He had traveled to Alsace at the outset of the war to evacuate his sister and her family and had not been heard from since. He had never been listed among the casualties, and since the Germans had effectively annexed Alsace and Lorraine, it was impossible to go look for him or to obtain any reliable information. Marcel had stepped into his father's shoes with little prodding, helping to run the farm and hoping to make ends meet until Albert returned—*if* he returned.

By lunchtime Marcel had washed up, changed clothes,

and been thoroughly grilled about his absence. Not that he gave his mother all the details. He didn't want to alarm her any more than necessary, so he left out the part about finding the stranger and thinking he was dead. And the part about knowing that it was Emile Bonet who had hit him. He also failed to mention the revolver, which was now safely hidden in his bureau drawer.

Françoise, who was seventeen, and nine-year-old Luc came in from doing chores, and Marcel was forced to tell his story all over again. Luc was fascinated, of course. He couldn't wait to grow up so he could have real adventures of his own. When he wasn't reading books about knights and soldiers, he was waging imaginary war in the woods, spying on invisible Germans, or rescuing unseen maidens.

Françoise was all seriousness as she listened to Marcel. She said little, but worry lined her tanned face. She resembled the photographs of their mother at the same age, though she wore her brown hair plain and long, and it seemed to Marcel that her hazel eyes were sadder.

Late that afternoon, Françoise tagged along as Marcel, accompanied by Léo, made his way to the barn to feed and milk the cows. She stood quietly as he milked first one brown Swiss and then the other. Marcel guessed that something was on her mind, but he decided not to say anything until she was ready to talk about it. She cleared her throat nervously just as he hoisted the milk pails to return to the house. He set them down on the flagstone barn floor and turned to face her.

"What is it, Françoise?" he asked. "What's troubling you? It's not my banged-up face now, is it?"

A little smile crept across her face. "Hardly," she said. "I could have done more damage myself."

They both laughed at the memory of the black eye she had given the amorous young Gypsy a couple of summers back.

Françoise looked at her shoe tops and her face became serious again. "It's just that I'm worried," she said. "And Maman's worried, too, though she probably wouldn't say so."

"I'll be okay. There's nothing to worry about."

"But this is only the beginning, isn't it? I know you didn't tell Maman everything, you know. And it's what you didn't say that bothers me."

Marcel wanted to defend himself. "I told her enough," he said. "If I had told her everything, she would worry even more."

"And what about us, Marcel?" She looked him in the eye. "What about Maman and Luc and me? This is no time to play commando games. It's just too dangerous. And with Papa gone—"

"I don't propose to play games, Françoise," Marcel said, feeling his temperature begin to rise, "but I can't sit idly by while our country, our way of life, is trampled by the *boches*. The Nazis may have killed Papa for all we know. At the very least they've kept us from finding out where he is. And Marshal Pétain and his pitiful government are doing nothing to stop Hitler from destroying the rest of us, piece by starving piece. Is that what you want? Well, it's sure not what I want, and I'm going to do something about it. I just don't know what yet."

"Is that what this is about—getting even for what's happened to Papa? It won't bring him back, Marcel."

"It's not that simple, Françoise. I've done nothing for two years—"

"Nothing but provide for your family," she interjected.

"Well, last night I saw a man—a Frenchman—badly beaten, maybe even killed. And it wasn't the Germans who did it. It was other Frenchmen! People I thought I respected. And the worst part is I felt helpless to stop it. I don't want to feel that way again."

Françoise said nothing for several moments. When she

finally spoke there was a quaver in her voice.

"Do what you have to do, Marcel," she said. "Just don't forget the people who need you."

Chapter 4

Near Lyons, September 1942

As the sleek black sedan sped through the darkened streets toward the highway, Isabelle Karmazin couldn't stop trembling. The temperature was unusually warm for late September, yet even the woolen blanket around her shoulders didn't seem to help. She kept her jaw clamped shut for fear that her chattering teeth would be audible to the others, but in such close quarters it would have been difficult not to notice.

On her left, a short stocky man of forty-five or so sat silently on the edge of the back seat, turning halfway around from time to time to peer apprehensively out the rear window at the road behind. An equally silent woman, about the same age as the man, sat on her right and seemed only slightly more relaxed. In the dark, Isabelle couldn't make out the features of either. The driver and his companion in the front seat kept their eyes glued to the road ahead, now and then exchanging a few muffled words. The men wore hats pulled down low as if to shade their eyes, in spite of the fact that it was just past 3 A.M.

Isabelle had only the vaguest idea of where she was being taken. She had overheard the name of a village but, as she was unfamiliar with the region, it meant nothing to her. And since the moment she had been thrust into the backseat of the black sedan, no one had said much of anything to her. In the midst of her trembling, she silently cursed herself for her naïveté. She might never have been in such danger in the first place had she been more careful about trusting Gentiles. And now here she was making the same mistake again.

Her mind drifted back to Paris, where Ginette Dumas, from a middle-class Catholic family, had become a friend shortly after the two met at Madame de la Court's in the garment district. She worked as a seamstress, as did Isabelle, in order to learn the trade. Her parents hoped to one day establish her in her own dress shop.

On the eve of the massive July roundup of foreign-born Jews in the French capital, Ginette's brother Eugène, a young police officer, had warned his sister of the impending arrests, and she had in turn offered shelter to her Jewish friend. Isabelle had been frightened by the news, but she was grateful for the protection, even if it were to be temporary. She had felt safe with the Dumas family—that is, until the next afternoon when Eugène returned from work. The sense of betrayal she felt after learning he had been part of the roundup had left that afternoon seared into her mind.

"Where will you go, Isabelle?" her friend had asked as they stood at the apartment door, "and how do you expect to survive?"

"I don't know, but I can't stay here. Not anymore." *Not when your brother considers his job more important than his conscience,* she had wanted to add. She couldn't believe that he had helped with the arrests, that he had even been to *her* apartment! How could he knowingly participate in such a crime against humanity—against her neighbors?

"He's just trying to survive like everyone else," Ginette had said apologetically, nodding toward where her brother sat alone in the *salon*.

"I'm sure he'll survive just fine." Isabelle's cynicism hadn't been very well disguised.

Ginette had ignored the remark. "Write and let me know you're all right, won't you? I'll say a prayer for you every day."

It must be comforting to be so superstitious—and so shallow, Isabelle remembered thinking, but had only nodded. She had leaned forward and kissed Ginette softly on both cheeks. Then she had turned and hurried away before hot tears could begin to flow.

It seemed like such a long time ago, now.

The black Renault hit a deep pothole just as it rounded a corner, throwing Isabelle against the woman beside her. She swiped with the back of her hand at the tears that had suddenly squeezed from her eyes, glad for the cover of darkness. She still felt as tight as a watch spring, but at least the trembling had begun to subside. Her anonymous companions were no more relaxed than before, leading her to believe that they were still in danger, though from whom she couldn't be sure.

"Look! Straight ahead," the man in the front passenger seat blurted. He pointed to a pair of uniformed figures standing near a makeshift barricade seventy-five yards ahead in the middle of the street. Immediately the driver began slowing the car, shifting into a lower gear.

"Can we make a run for it down one of the side streets?" asked the woman.

"They'll all be blocked off," said the driver. "We'll just have to take our chances."

The last time Isabelle had seen such a checkpoint was a month earlier when she had attempted to pass into the unoccupied zone with the help of a professional *passeur*. Fabien, he had been called, and he had promised her safe passage from Dijon to Lyons where she had heard the conditions for Jews were much better. It had taken everything she had—the few gold coins that remained from her father's wedding gift—to pay what Fabien demanded.

Fabien, however, hadn't been very satisfied with her meager offering. So when the free zone border was reached, he had simply turned her over to the French authorities and collected the reward offered for the capture of Jews crossing into the zone illegally. The only view Isabelle had glimpsed of Lyons had been from the back of a military transport truck on her way to the detention camp at Vénissieux. Her stomach knotted and the taste of bile rose in her throat at the thought of repeating that experience.

The stocky man on Isabelle's left had pulled a semi-automatic pistol from somewhere in the folds of his clothing and was busy checking to see that the magazine was full. He cocked the gun and then slid it under the edge of Isabelle's blanket. She could feel the cold steel against her thigh, even through her skirt, but she didn't dare move. She glanced at the woman beside her, who looked as though she were praying. Isabelle stared at her for a moment, then turned to look out the front window again.

No one spoke as the Renault continued its slow approach. All eyes were fixed on the two *gendarmes* as the near one unslung his automatic rifle. The second one manned the barricade. Then, as the car rolled to within fifty feet of the barrier, a sudden look of recognition appeared to cross the face of the first *gendarme*. He barked out something and signaled his partner who immediately raised the red and white bar. Both men stood at attention as the black sedan rolled past.

"It sure helps to drive a government car," the driver

remarked casually as he turned onto the highway heading toward Grenoble. The passengers exhaled their pent-up anxiety—all except Isabelle, who was beginning to wonder if her troubles weren't just beginning.

❦   ❦   ❦

The first glow of dawn was still a couple of hours away as the black sedan approached the sleeping St. Egrève, whose shops and houses sprawled comfortably in the shadows of the steep Chartreuse hills northwest of Grenoble. The fog that shrouded the nearby Isère River curled long, lazy fingers over the highway, toying with the beam of the car's headlights and causing the driver to slacken the pace. Within moments he steered onto a darkened street that wound its way through the heart of the village, leaving the fog behind as it climbed into the hills beyond.

The stocky man said nothing to anyone. His sidearm was once again out of sight, but he continued to glance nervously out the rear window every mile or two, as though he expected to be followed. Several times, the woman had touched Isabelle's arm gently and asked if she were feeling all right. Each time Isabelle had nodded affirmatively without speaking, and had avoided the woman's attempts to engage her in small talk.

She was exhausted but dared not close her eyes. No one had told her where they were taking her, yet she couldn't help feeling that they must be nearing their destination as the car crawled slowly upward along the winding track. The driver, after a long silence, had renewed his conversation with the man beside him, though Isabelle, over the growl of the engine, could make out little of it besides the fact that this was apparently not the driver's first trip of the night.

Isabelle shivered in spite of the warmth radiated by five

bodies in the close confines of the car. A cold cloud of fear seemed to envelop her as she contemplated what awaited her when the car finally stopped. The thought wouldn't leave her. She had no idea who these people were. *What if they're just like the others?* Desperate, she had entrusted herself to the first people who offered help. And now, as had happened before, she wondered if she would live to regret such a rash decision. But her only alternative had been to remain incarcerated in the detention camp, and she knew there was no future in that.

So, here she was, reliant upon four complete strangers. True, they had helped her escape from the hellish camp, along with a sympathetic doctor who treated the detainees. But, with the exception of a few efforts by the woman, they hadn't really spoken to her much. She could understand their desire to remain anonymous, whatever their intentions toward her. She had assumed their intentions were good, for they stood to be in danger from the authorities for helping her escape. If not, well, she tried not to think too much about that possibility. But try as she might, she couldn't shake the nagging sense that the worst was coming true all over again.

Whether from her delicate condition, the constant swaying of the Renault on the twisting climb, or simply the fear that gripped her, she wasn't sure, but Isabelle felt increasingly ill. She had been trying for miles to ignore the way she felt, but that was no longer possible. *Surely they'll stop soon,* she thought. *If I can just hang on a few more minutes.* Squirming in her seat, she shifted from one position to another, trying to stave off the wave of nausea that rose in her throat. She looked plaintively toward the woman sitting beside her, who, unaware of Isabelle's discomfort, was gazing out the window into the darkness.

"Please, stop the car!" Isabelle finally pleaded. It was the first time she had spoken aloud since being helped into the backseat in Vénissieux, and her plea cut the stillness like a knife. The woman turned quickly at the first sound of Isabelle's voice, and instant recognition animated her face and eyes.

"Pull over! She's not well."

The driver stopped without pulling over. The chances of another car passing by at this early hour were slim. Without a word, the woman helped Isabelle out of the car and over to the side of the road near the edge of the shallow ravine, lowering her to her knees to keep her from falling. She stayed with Isabelle a while, holding the younger woman tightly about the shoulders like no one had done in a long, long while.

"I'll get some water, Isabelle," the woman said after a few minutes had passed. "Will you be all right by yourself?"

Isabelle turned to stare at the woman but said nothing, puzzled by the sound of her name. *How does she know who I am?* she wanted to know. The woman stroked Isabelle's back softly, then rose and walked to the car. She reached inside, retrieved a small container, then disappeared toward the gurgling, splashing sounds of the stream that coursed through the ravine.

As soon as the woman was out of sight, Isabelle straightened up cautiously. Weakness born of hunger, fatigue, and now sickness enveloped her body, but her mind raced, fueled by fear. *I won't let anyone betray me again,* she told herself, *no matter what they've done for me.* She couldn't. So, casting a glance over her shoulder toward the car, she plunged unsteadily down the hill into the predawn darkness.

With only stars to light her way, Isabelle was forced to go more slowly than she wanted. The brook churned out a noisy alarm, warning her away from the ravine to her left, but the road twisted unexpectedly and she couldn't always tell how close she was to the edge. Still, she forged ahead, stumbling over the uneven surface in her haste to put distance between herself and the others.

She froze momentarily when she heard the woman's voice

calling out softly, then more insistently. "Isabelle. Isabelle! Where are you? Hervé, she's gone!"

The car engine jumped to life and Isabelle could hear its tires claw at the roadside gravel as the driver turned it around and started back down the road in her direction. Heedless of the danger she faced in the darkened roadway, she bolted like a frightened deer, adrenaline fueling her headlong flight. But even the surge of adrenaline wasn't enough to overcome her depleted physical condition for long, and she found herself slowing to little more than a walk. The twin beams of light from the rapidly approaching car soon caught and held her from behind.

She collapsed in the middle of the track with her sides heaving; she felt completely spent. The black Renault rolled to a stop just yards away, headlights still trained on her. All four passengers got out, but it was the woman who appeared first at Isabelle's side.

"Isabelle," she said, reaching out to take hold of her hand, "please don't run from us. We're trying to help you. Don't you understand that?"

Isabelle was too weary even to withdraw her hand from the woman's grasp. She surrendered numbly as the woman and her stocky companion helped her up and practically carried her back to the car. Once more seated in the back seat, the woman offered a few more soothing words, but Isabelle made no reply.

Less than ten minutes later the driver pulled off the road into a wooded area, turned off the engine, and extinguished the lights. Obviously bleary-eyed, he remained with the car while the others struck out along the narrow road with the two men leading the way. The woman walked with a steadying arm around Isabelle, who was feeling in no condition to walk very fast. The mountain air was thin, and though the others paused at short intervals to let her catch her breath, no one spoke.

After a short climb, the terrain flattened out and Isabelle could just make out a few buildings directly in front of them. The stocky man motioned for her and the woman to stay close to the first building, a barn of some sort, while he and his partner went on ahead. Isabelle noticed with alarm that his automatic pistol was once more in his hand as he disappeared around the corner of the barn. The women crouched down and waited.

"Who are you?" Isabelle asked the woman when the men had been gone several minutes, her voice a hoarse whisper. "I don't even know your name."

"Sometimes it's best that way," said the woman. "The less you know, the less you have to worry about."

Isabelle wasn't at all sure why she should worry about knowing this woman's name, but for the moment, she lacked the strength to push it further. Neither woman said anything more.

After what seemed like forever, the men returned and signaled for Isabelle and the woman to follow. Isabelle hesitated for an instant, but the woman took her arm and led her a short distance to where a gate opened on a small courtyard fronting an ancient stone farmhouse. The house was shuttered and dark as they passed through the gate, but as they came closer, Isabelle could see a faint sliver of light where the front door stood slightly ajar. The stocky man held the door partway open but remained outside as the two women entered.

Isabelle squinted against the light as the door closed softly behind her. When she could clearly see again, she discovered that the inside of the house looked almost as ancient as the exterior, with its rude furnishings and stone floors. There didn't appear to be any electric lights, but the amber glow from the coal-oil lamp was soft and warm. Standing at the edge of the halo cast by the lamp were two old women. One was tall and slender, almost elegant in appearance in a well-worn blue silk dressing gown. Her counterpart, much shorter, stout, and with an ample bosom, wore an ordinary rose-colored cotton house-dress. Both had hair as white as snow, pulled straight back into tight little buns. They smiled as they moved toward her in unison, but neither said a word.

"This is Isabelle," said the anonymous woman to the older pair. "She hasn't been feeling very well, I'm afraid."

"Oh, my!" said the tall one.

"Come and sit," offered the short one. "You must be exhausted."

Isabelle turned to her companion, wanting desperately to ask what she should do next, but she never got the chance.

"Au revoir, Isabelle," the woman said as she leaned forward and kissed her lightly on both cheeks. Her voice was barely more than a whisper. "God bless you."

For a moment a tear formed in the woman's eye and threatened to spill over, but she turned quickly and walked back out the door, leaving Isabelle speechless and alone with the two old ladies.

Chapter 5

The past two months had been spent with strangers—nameless faces for the most part—who departed Isabelle's life as quickly as they entered. And some, like the *passeur* Fabien, had not departed empty-handed. Numbly, she turned to face her hostesses and prepared to let them know that she had nothing to give in exchange for their shelter. But the short round woman spoke before she could open her mouth.

"Isabelle is such a lovely name," she said without a trace of insincerity. "Please call me Tante Marthe," she added and then gestured toward her taller companion, "and this is my little sister Tante Solange."

Isabelle nearly smiled in spite of her fatigue at this last remark as Tante Solange was a good four inches taller than her older sister.

"They say it's best not to use one's surname in this sort of work," Tante Solange said with a serious air. She seemed oblivious to the annoyed glance Tante Marthe shot in her direction.

"And just what sort of work is that?" asked Isabelle, not comprehending entirely.

"Why, hiding Jews from the authorities, dear girl." Tante Solange looked slightly perplexed. "You *are* a Jew, aren't you?"

"Of course she's a Jew, sister," Tante Marthe rebuked the taller woman. "And she's obviously very tired and hungry, too." She motioned Isabelle to a large, cushioned armchair. "Sit, child," she said, "and don't you worry about a thing. We'll fix you a little something to eat and then you can rest as long as you like." And with that the two women scurried off to the kitchen.

Isabelle removed her dirty shoes and pulled her feet up under her in the big armchair. The offer of food was the best thing she had heard in a long time. Hunger had become something to stave off, not something she expected to satisfy, even temporarily.

The rationing of food had kept satisfaction out of the reach of all but those wealthy enough to shop the black market. The last really good meal she had eaten had been two months earlier in the home of her friend Ginette. Served at a long, gleaming, walnut table set with the Dumas' everyday china, it had tasted better than any meal Isabelle could remember since before the war. She hadn't realized how hungry she could get, and only her slightly queasy stomach had kept her from gorging herself. The generous portions of roast duck, pâté, and Camembert were obviously not purchased with ration coupons. Even *with* coupons, she had always had to stand in line for hours to purchase tiny quantities of bread, meat, cheese, butter, and the like. Life apparently wasn't so difficult for Ginette and her family.

But life had become increasingly difficult—even dangerous—for the Jews in occupied France. The German-instituted "Jewish statutes," aimed first at diminishing their influence, then at restricting their movements, had not come as a complete surprise since the anti-Semitism of the Nazi party was well known. But what had astonished Isabelle was the often enthusiastic enforcement of these laws by French officials, and the ease with which so many Gentiles turned a blind eye. People seemed far more concerned with eating and surviving than with justice.

The fact that Ginette's brother was a police officer, and her father a mid-level functionary in the Paris city administration, kept the Dumas family well-informed, well-connected, and well-fed. But for Isabelle, the meal she had eaten at Ginette's house on the eve of the July roundup had marked the beginning of a long famine.

❧   ❧   ❧

When Tante Marthe and Tante Solange returned from the kitchen with a pot of hot coffee and a tray of food, they found Isabelle curled up in the big chair, sound asleep.

"Poor dear," said Tante Solange as she placed the tray on the low table beside the cushioned chair. "She doesn't look well at all."

"Is it any wonder?" asked Tante Marthe. "She's escaped after several weeks in that awful prison camp near Lyons. It's practically a miracle that she survived at all." And with that she turned and carried the brass coffeepot back into the kitchen.

❧   ❧   ❧

When Isabelle awoke, the room was flooded with light. A soft breeze carried the aroma of rosemary through the two open windows across from where she sat curled in the cushioned armchair. For just a moment she forgot where she was. It felt so good to sleep—even in a chair—that she was reluctant to stir.

She searched the room with her eyes for signs of the old sisters, but she found only a huge gray cat curled up on the stone floor in a pool of sunlight. Next to her chair sat a low table on which lay a wooden tray covered with bread, butter, jam, and cheese. The cat seemed oblivious, both to Isabelle and to the food beside her. Except for the distant symphony of cowbells and the purring of the big gray, the house was quiet.

When Tante Marthe appeared in the doorway a few minutes later, Isabelle had consumed half the bread on the serving tray and was busily devouring the cheese. She blushed involuntarily when she realized she was no longer alone. Tante Marthe spoke before Isabelle had a chance to swallow.

"Would you like some hot coffee to go with that?" she asked, smiling pleasantly. "I didn't want to leave it out for fear that it would grow cold while you slept."

"I—uh, how long have I been asleep?"

"It's about 2 in the afternoon," Marthe said as she glanced at the wall clock behind Isabelle, "and you arrived just before 5 o'clock this morning. You must be starving, dear. Now how about that coffee?"

Isabelle looked down at what was left of the tray of food and blushed again. It was humiliating to be in such obvious need. She nodded yes to the offer of coffee, but she didn't touch another bite of food while Tante Marthe went to get it.

"Isabelle," began Tante Marthe when she returned with a brimming cup, then paused suddenly. "May I call you Isabelle?"

Isabelle looked up quickly, surprised at the courtesy the old woman offered her. "Why, yes," she said softly. "Yes, of course."

"Well then, Isabelle," the old woman began again, "you must do here in our home just as you would do in your own."

"Why are you doing this?" Isabelle asked. She set the cup of coffee down, not knowing whether to be suspicious or just surprised. "I can offer you nothing in return. I have nothing left to give."

"I don't expect you to understand this, Isabelle," said Tante Marthe as she sat down on the faded blue settee across from her young guest, "but we wish nothing in return for what little we have to offer. God has been good to us, and the very least we can do in return is to offer a small kindness to one of Abraham's daughters."

"I see," was all Isabelle could say in reply. Inside she had to admit that she really didn't see at all. In her experience—especially of late—*everyone* wanted something in return. And as for God—well, even if He existed, He hadn't seemed particularly good to *her* lately. He was apparently more interested in people like Ginette and her family. *They* weren't suffering much. *They* hadn't gone to bed hungry every night for months. Nor had they been forced to sleep in barns, alleys, and open fields. They were probably still living as though life were more or less normal.

No, Isabelle decided, if a good God were paying attention, her husband and her father—perhaps even her mother—would still be alive. And He would have protected her from the likes of Fabien, whose offer of help was motivated by personal greed.

During her detention at Vénissieux, she had heard plenty of talk about God: from guards who cursed the Jews as "Christ-killers," to fellow Jews who suddenly rediscovered religious rites they had spent a lifetime ignoring. She found it pathetic, mostly, and so hypocritical.

Rather than risk seeming ungrateful by challenging Marthe, however, she changed the subject. "Was your husband in the war?" she asked.

"My, no." A wistful smile crept over Marthe's face as she spoke. "I never married. Papa was not well for many years, and I had to stay on the farm and look after him. When he died it was too late for thoughts of love. Besides, what man would want a plump old woman when he could have a pretty young one?"

"I'm sorry, I didn't think—"

"You needn't apologize, child. I'm quite used to the idea, though perhaps it would be best not to talk of such things with my sister. She was a beauty, you know, and had many suitors in her time. For some reason, Papa never approved of a single one. She finally ran off to Paris with the most handsome of them all, but he broke her heart. Papa died while she was gone and she's never quite gotten over it."

"How sad," Isabelle said. She could relate to the broken heart. It had been less than five months since she had lost her own husband. Adam Karmazin had been a twenty-four-year-old law student and she barely eighteen when they married. Those first weeks of marriage had been blissful in spite of the occupation of Paris. They rented a tiny apartment, Isabelle found work as a seamstress in Madame de la Court's dress shop, and Adam prepared to reenter classes in September. They took long walks in the park and talked of life, love, and a happy, prosperous future.

In the fall of 1941, Adam was informed by the university administration that he was not among the tiny handful of Jews who were to be allowed to continue studying law. No longer a student and unable to find any work, he began to write for a communist underground paper. His scathing editorials denounced capitalism, racism, fascism, and the seeming apathy of most Parisians—Jews and non-Jews alike. To Isabelle's dismay, however, the more involved he became in political action, the more distant he seemed from her. He talked little of his activities, probably because he knew she detested politics. And since he was increasingly consumed by politics, there was little to talk about.

Toward the end of March, however, after months of decline

in their relationship, Adam ceased all his activity. Without explanation he stopped writing, attending communist party rallies, and being involved in other pursuits Isabelle had previously only guessed at. He seldom left the apartment, and never without Isabelle. Isabelle was elated. So elated, in fact, that she had simply accepted the change without question. She wasn't sure she wanted to know why he had changed. He was home and that was all that mattered to her. She reveled in his presence and lavished him with affection.

But when she returned home from work on May Day, Adam was gone. The note on the table said that he had gone out briefly and would return before nightfall. A secret meeting, she supposed.

He never came back. Two days later Isabelle learned of his fate from propaganda posters hung throughout the Jewish neighborhoods of Paris' fourth arrondissement. Adam and several others had been summarily executed before a German firing squad for subversion. She wasn't even allowed to claim his body for burial.

Had he lived another month, they would have celebrated their second wedding anniversary. And although there had been some stormy days over the course of their brief life together, a day didn't go by that she didn't think about him. Some days she was overcome with sadness, other days with anger. But every day she missed him terribly.

"Is your family . . . all right?" Tante Marthe interrupted Isabelle's thoughts hesitantly.

"I'm an only child," Isabelle replied, "and both my parents are dead. My mother died of tuberculosis in Poland when I was just a girl." She felt safe talking about her mother. It had happened years ago and the pain had long since subsided. Her father, however, was another matter.

Professor Alexander Rayski had brought his young daughter to Paris where he had accepted a faculty position at the Sorbonne. He had hoped that she too would one day pursue an academic career, but he had been gracious enough not to stand in the way when she announced her desire to marry a bright young law student. Professor Rayski loved teaching and had given himself to it with a vengeance after his wife died. Then when his daughter married, his teaching consumed him—a fact Isabelle had found herself resenting, but one which his students seemed to appreciate immensely.

The "Jewish statutes," however, made no allowances for student opinion, and the previous fall, Professor Rayski had been dismissed from his faculty position simply because he was a Jew. Though Isabelle and Adam had done their best to comfort him, he was inconsolable. A few weeks after his dismissal, his body was found floating in the Seine River. It had been nearly a year, and still Isabelle fought back angry tears every time she thought of the injustice of it all.

Tante Marthe stepped close and put a reassuring arm about her shoulders. "I'm so sorry, Isabelle," she said softly. "It must have been painful to lose both your maman and papa, and to find yourself all alone in the world."

Isabelle struggled to maintain her composure. "But surely you too have suffered such pain," she said finally.

"Yes, that's true. But Maman died giving birth to Solange, so I hardly knew her. And I was already so old when Papa died. Besides, I still have my sister. And God is only a prayer away, so I never feel completely alone."

There it was again—*God. Why do so many people find it hard to accept just what they can see and touch?* Isabelle wondered. *Why must they always turn to fairy tales and superstitious rituals for comfort?*

Since her father had not attended synagogue to speak of, nor had he compelled her to go, Isabelle freely admitted that there was a whole dimension—the religious side—of her Jewishness that she did not understand. Even after the enactment of the "Jewish statutes," she had resisted identifying with the religious element. It wasn't that she was ashamed of her heritage, though she had sometimes found it socially inconvenient. She had simply adopted her father's view that there was no place in a scientific world for anything that wasn't, well, scientific.

She glanced quickly around the room, expecting to see a crucifix or a smiling likeness of Jesus or Mary—or both—as she had seen in other Gentiles' homes. Finding none, she decided that they were probably kept in another room. She had never understood how people could revere a symbol of torture and death. Or why they insisted on treating as alive a person who had supposedly lived and died centuries ago. Jews might have their weaknesses, she mused, but Gentiles were a study in contradiction.

"Are you feeling all right, dear?" asked Tante Marthe. "You seem so—well, preoccupied."

"I'm sorry," replied Isabelle. "It's just that so much has happened lately. I'm feeling much better, really, what with the food and coffee and all." She uncurled her long legs and prepared to rise out of the comfortable old chair. "I'd love to get cleaned up, though," she added. She couldn't remember just how long it had been since she had felt clean, and she imagined that her tidy hostesses were rather disgusted by her dirty, unkempt appearance. "Do you suppose that I might—"

"Take a bath?" Tante Marthe finished the question for her. "Of course, my dear. And perhaps we can find you some clean things to wear, too."

Isabelle looked down at the plain blue cotton dress which she had worn daily for weeks. At first she had managed to keep it fairly clean. But her stay in the camp had made that impossible, and now it was not only soiled, but also torn in several places. She couldn't help but wonder, though, at just what sort of clothing the elderly sisters might provide. She wasn't in much of a position to object in any case.

"Now help yourself to more food and then rest a bit while I draw you a nice hot bath," Marthe was saying as she withdrew to the kitchen to begin heating the water on the wood stove.

The water enveloped Isabelle in its warm embrace as she lowered herself slowly into the copper tub an hour later. The lavender scented soap felt luxurious on her dry skin and her soft, clean hair squeaked as she ran her fingers through it. When she had finished washing, she lay back, hugging her arms tightly about her, basking for long minutes in the rare pleasure.

Isabelle exited the bath just as the water was turning tepid. On the straightback chair beside the tub she found a large towel and a tortoise shell hairbrush. A green silk dressing gown—from Tante Solange's wardrobe by the look of it—was draped over the back of the chair. She dried herself quickly as the mountain air had begun to turn cool in the late afternoon.

Leaning over to reach for the dressing gown, she caught a glimpse of a reflection in the floor-length cheval glass. Clutching the gown in her right hand, she straightened and stared in disbelief into the first mirror she had seen in weeks. She knew that the reflection was her own, but it shocked her to see what had become of her. Her eyes looked more deep-set than usual, and her cheeks were hollow. Her shoulders seemed to sag as though weighed down with some immense burden. She could number her ribs with ease. Her arms and legs looked so thin she wondered if they didn't belong to someone else.

But what captured her attention was the sight of a delicate swell in her once-slender belly—visible evidence of what she had known since the end of April and had begun to feel weeks ago. The secret she had been unable to share with anyone— not even Ginette—would soon be public knowledge.

As a single tear spilled onto her cheek, she turned from the mirror and donned the silk dressing gown. The tear, quickly followed by others, was partly for herself. How she missed Adam, and how she longed to turn back the pages of the calendar. But mostly, she wept for the innocent child she would soon bring into a world gone mad.

Chapter 6

Without opening his eyes, Armand Moreau listened intently to the half-whispered conversation between the two men who stood somewhere near the foot of his bed.

"I want a man—someone I can trust—watching him around the clock, Sergeant. Understood?"

"As you wish, Inspector. I'll have someone here within the hour."

"And I want a doctor who won't give us any problems. Our terrorist friend Pascal here is in pretty bad shape, and I need whatever information he has as soon as possible. I can't have anyone interfering—especially not some leftist physician. See if we don't perhaps have a file on some of the medical staff here."

"I'll check on it right away, monsieur."

The sound of shoe soles on the tiled floor was followed by the sharp click of a light switch, the metallic clank of a door latch, and then silence. Carefully, Moreau opened his right eye. He saw no one. He tried his left eye, but it refused to open and the effort made him wince in pain. He turned his head slightly to look toward his left. More pain. In fact, everything he tried to move hurt miserably—everything but his left arm, which he couldn't feel at all. By probing about with his right hand, which he found sore but mobile, he discovered that his left arm was all there and apparently unbroken, but completely numb. He couldn't quite decide whether he should be worried at the lack of feeling or grateful that at least it gave him no pain. To his great relief, he could wriggle his toes even though his legs felt like heavy stumps.

The fact that he had not yet been seen by a doctor—at least not while he was conscious—did worry him a little. The room—what he could see of it in the dark with only one eye—looked like a hospital room. There was even a faint medicinal odor in the air. But he wondered if it were a civilian hospital or a prison infirmary. In a regular hospital, he imagined that he would have been attended immediately by a doctor, or at least a nurse or two. But no one came, and little by little Armand Moreau drifted off to sleep once more.

Hours later, he reawoke to the sound of voices, though not the same voices he had heard before. This time the voices spoke out loud. And this time one of the voices belonged to a woman. Armand opened his good eye and immediately blinked and squinted at the brightness of the room.

"He's awake, Dr. Billot." The woman's voice was smooth as silk.

"Yes, I see. But in his condition, he'd be a lot better off asleep." The voice belonged to a man already past middle age. His once jet-black hair was thinning ever-so-slightly and was generously dusted with gray. He carried himself with a military bearing in spite of his five-foot five-inch frame. He walked slowly around the side of Armand's bed while the nurse remained at the foot.

Armand could see now that the bright light was coming from the window to his right. Daylight. So, he had been here for several hours.

"You've had quite a fall, young man," the doctor said almost amiably. "Next time you'll have to be more careful."

Armand tried to tell him that his injuries had nothing to do with a fall, but he could barely move his lips and only succeeded in uttering an indistinct grunting sound.

"Don't try to talk just yet," the doctor warned. "I don't think anything is broken, but you've got some pretty deep bruises to your jaw and cheekbones. You've also got some nasty lacerations inside your mouth. I've sutured the worst of them, but talking and eating are going to be difficult for several days at least, maybe as much as a couple of weeks. Can you understand what I'm saying?"

Armand nodded as best he could.

"Your left shoulder was badly dislocated, but I've pulled it back into place. It should heal just fine if you can keep it in the sling. All in all you're going to have to limit your activities for a while, I'm afraid."

Armand attempted another weak nod. The irony of the situation wasn't lost on him. He was under guard and barely able to move, and the doctor was requesting that he limit his activities! Maybe the inspector hadn't gotten to the doctor yet. Maybe the doctor didn't realize that he was a prisoner. Or maybe it was just a flimsy attempt to cheer him up.

"He's probably hungry," the doctor was saying to the nurse. "See if you can get him some nourishment he can take through a straw. A little broth is probably just the thing."

"Of course, Dr. Billot," she replied as she turned toward the door. She was young, a pretty brunette. Armand saw her just long enough with his one good eye to hope she would come back—with or without food.

When she had gone, the doctor moved close to the side of the bed and leaned over until his face was only a few inches from Armand's. "I don't know what you've done, young man," he whispered, "but it's clear to me that you took a beating. Am I right?"

Armand nodded. The remark about taking a fall must have been for the nurse's benefit.

"I'll do what I can," continued Billot, "but I can only help you so much. I've got problems of my own or they wouldn't have dragged me here to treat you. Threats, intimidation, blackmail—that's the way our police work these days."

Dr. Billot continued without waiting for a response. "I'll tell Inspector Malfaire that you won't be able to talk for several days yet. I hope that will buy you enough time to regain your strength. Beyond that I can promise you nothing. Nothing at all."

Armand grasped Billot's arm with his right hand and offered his thanks with a solid squeeze. The doctor rose and prepared to leave. "One more thing," he said softly, though no longer in a whisper. "The nurse, Mademoiselle Previn, was also assigned to look after you. I'd be careful if I were you."

Armand lay quietly for several minutes after the doctor exited the room. The fact that Inspector Malfaire himself was apparently handling his case did not bode well. Malfaire had referred to him as Pascal, which could only mean one thing— he had been "burned" by some Judas inside the Resistance! Now, the doctor's warning about the pretty young nurse had his mind on alert. *Maybe the doctor wants to confuse me,* he thought, *so I'll confide in him. Or maybe they're all working together.* He would have to be careful not to confide in anyone.

He wondered how, or if, he could have avoided this entire

mess. In Armand's mind, the men who had beaten him senseless were nothing but buffoons, small-town toughs. The problem was that there had been three of them. And regardless of intellect, three to one odds are hard to beat. He had battled long odds before, but it had never ended so badly.

❦   ❦   ❦

It had begun well enough. At the beginning of April, Lieutenant Armand Moreau was dispatched back to France from London by General de Gaulle himself. He was to assist Jean Moulin, a talented civil servant who, when the war broke out, had been the country's youngest prefect at the age of forty. Moulin had eventually fled to London via Spain and Portugal, and had hooked up with de Gaulle and the Free French. He had returned to France on New Year's Day past on a mission many thought impossible—to organize and unify the Resistance throughout France under de Gaulle's banner. Armand was delighted at the opportunity to work with such a man.

After flying from London to Algiers, Armand had then embarked for the southern French coast by fishing vessel, landing on the beach near Palavas-les-Flots at night. Using the code name Pascal, he had proceeded to make contact with one group after another, beginning in Montpellier. He had slowly worked his way north through Nîmes, Avignon, and Valence, before turning eastward toward Grenoble and the Alps.

The going had been slow—even discouraging—and progress slight. His information had been surprisingly good, and contacting dissidents was relatively easy. But the difficulties had usually begun once contact was made. By the time he had reached Grenoble and its surrounding towns, he could only count a small handful of groups willing to work together under the banner of de Gaulle's French Forces of the Interior, or F.F.I.

What all the resistance groups had in common was a passionate desire to be rid of their German occupiers, and an intense disgust for the French government's decision, under Marshal Pétain, to enter into "the way of collaboration" with the Nazis. But not all were yet willing to lay aside ego or ideology to fight side by side in their common struggle.

Some of the local groups, particularly the communists, had political motivations and ambitions that made cooperation with non-communists or anti-communists problematic. Some were led by men whose tenuous grip on power did not permit them to share it with anyone. Others were simply opposed to submitting to the leadership of Charles de Gaulle, whom they considered an upstart general with too much personal ambition and too little real authority. Many found the very idea of central accountability an intolerable threat.

But Armand had managed to convince some that there was strength in numbers, power in collective action. Some he had coaxed by invoking his connections to Moulin and the general. Some had been won over by the logic of his arguments in the face of their isolation and general ineffectiveness. Some had had to be persuaded by promises of arms, ammunition, shortwave radios, and even money—promises Armand desperately hoped he could keep.

When he had arrived in Domène, a small bustling town northeast of Grenoble, Armand was tired—tired from months of travel, and tired of the endless and often unfruitful negotiations that his mission required. Too tired, perhaps, to be fully alert to the dangers of forging an alliance with an unknown group. But he had been anxious to move quickly on the recent information he had received—information suggesting that this group, though relatively small, was armed and ready to march to de Gaulle's orders.

Armand's first encounter with the Domène group had

come through the person of Emile Bonet. After having taken a bus to the village, he had made his way down the winding, narrow main street and entered Bonet's butcher shop. From behind the counter, Bonet had been helping a lone customer, an elderly woman accompanied by her dog, a small white bichon. Armand had nodded a polite but silent greeting in the direction of both proprietor and client, and had then begun looking about at the few items displayed, waiting for the old woman to leave. Her purchase made, she had taken her small package from the counter, bent and scooped up the little dog with her free hand, and bid Bonet *adieu* on her way out the door.

"I hope you'll share some with Grandmère, Mimi," she cooed to the dog as she stepped into the street.

The door closed noisily before either man could hear the dog's reply. Armand shook his head in disbelief and looked at the butcher for an explanation. Bonet held up what remained of the woman's ration coupon as proof that she had the right to make the purchase—even if it were for her canine friend—but Armand thought he detected a little embarrassment in the burly man's flushed face.

"Good morning, monsieur," offered the butcher. "How may I be of service?"

"Good morning," replied Armand. "Do you by chance have any *boudain* for sale?"

Just then another woman entered the front door, setting the bell above the doorway to ringing cheerfully. *"Bonjour, messieurs."*

Bonet looked from Armand to the woman and smiled pleasantly.

"Bonjour, Madame Boussant. I'll be with you in a moment."

"I'm very sorry, monsieur," he said, turning back to Armand, "but we've been out of *boudain* for some time. Perhaps monsieur would like some cooked ham instead? I prepared it myself only yesterday."

"Just seven ounces, please," Armand replied.

The butcher made no move to get the ham, but continued to stare at Armand expectantly. *Did I get the message wrong?* Armand wondered. *No, I'm sure it was to be boudain and seven ounces of cooked ham. Maybe he didn't hear me.*

"Seven ounces of cooked ham will be fine," he repeated.

The butcher almost looked irritated. "I need to see your ration coupon, monsieur."

"Ah, yes, of course." Armand felt sheepish as he dug into his pocket for the required coupon that entitled the bearer to twelve ounces of meat per week. The one he handed to Bonet was a clever forgery, given to him only the day before by members of a clandestine group in Grenoble. He wasn't able to get one by legal means. He had forfeited all such rights when he signed on with de Gaulle in London. In the eyes of the Vichy government, he was an outlaw—a terrorist.

Emile Bonet wasn't particularly concerned about Armand's legal status, or even the validity of his ration coupon. The password had been correct. Now he needed to get a message to this stranger without raising the suspicions of Madame Boussant or any other client who might walk in. He wrapped the ham with the ease of many years of practice, and handed it to Armand.

"I'm sure you'll enjoy it," said Bonet. "It's the best ham around."

Armand paid and thanked him, nodded politely to Madame Boussant, and left the shop. He headed immediately for the seclusion of the tree-covered hills above the village.

Bonet had been right. The ham was superb. And inside the wrapping he found a tersely worded note.

"7 P.M., Le Dauphin, double pastis, Ninety-Three."

He looked it over carefully, then tore the small strip of paper into tiny bits and chewed and swallowed them. They didn't taste nearly as good as the ham.

At 7 o'clock that evening, Armand entered Le Dauphin, a café-bar on the edge of the town square, and took a table toward the back. He sat facing the front door, as was his habit, where he could see all who came and went. The place wasn't crowded, but it was far from empty. Three men stood at the bar, smoking filterless cigarettes and talking casually, while four more huddled intently over a game of cards at a nearby table. A well-dressed man sat by himself near the front, reading a newspaper.

The proprietor, a trim, bespectacled man in his fifties, put away the last of a dozen glasses he had been polishing, circled around from behind the bar, and approached Armand's table.

"*A pastis,*" Armand said when asked what he would like. "Double."

When the owner returned with the anise-flavored drink, he took a seat across the table from Armand, careful not to block his view of the front.

"I've been doing a lot of reading lately," he said without introducing himself. "Do you find much time for books?"

"From time to time," Armand replied, "especially when I find a good one."

"Have you read any of Victor Hugo's fine work?"

"Yes, as a matter of fact. My favorite is his novel *Ninety-Three.*"

The man in the glasses leaned forward in his chair and lowered his voice. "Pay for your drink and walk out the front door. Once you are sure no one is watching, turn left into the alley and go all the way to the end. Take the stairs on the right to the second landing. Knock twice and someone will let you in. Understand?"

"I understand." Armand had been through this countless times before. He tired of it at times, but he understood that more often than not it was absolutely necessary to the security of the local resisters. They couldn't meet openly, nor could they take chances with meeting places that were known to too many or too far in advance. Besides, as an emissary of Moulin and de Gaulle, Armand felt he had to go along with whatever instructions he was given—within reason, of course—in an effort to establish the bridge of trust on which his mission depended.

Once outside, he stood casually against the front of Le Dauphin, glancing about unhurriedly, before slipping around the corner and down the alley. He climbed the two flights of creaky wooden stairs, hoping he would never need to sneak down the same way in the dark. At the landing he knocked, then knocked again.

A full minute went by before the door opened to reveal a roomful of men, perhaps a dozen in all. It was hard to tell how many were there because of the dim light and the pall of smoke from several cigarettes. Armand entered the room slowly to give his eyes a chance to adjust. The white-haired old man who had opened the door shut it behind him, and ushered him to the far end of the room where he was offered a chair. Two of the men he recognized. One was Bonet, the muscular butcher, whom he had met that morning. The other was the well-dressed man he had seen reading his newspaper in the front of Le Dauphin only moments before. *Obviously,* Armand reflected, *there is more than one way into this apartment.*

"Sit, young man," said the old man almost casually. "Can we get you anything? Some food? A drink perhaps?"

"Thank you," Armand replied, "but I've already had some good cooked ham today."

Several of the men chuckled at this, indicating that they knew how the meeting had been set up. The old man smiled broadly. "Then perhaps you won't mind that we're eating lightly tonight." And with that one of the younger men produced a basket filled with bread, cheese, and three bottles of local wine, which he served as though it were a social occasion.

"So," began the old man after everyone had been served, "what brings you to our humble village?"

The others sat quietly while Armand explained his mission. Their participation in the F.F.I., under General de Gaulle's direction, was critical to the eventual liberation of France, he told them. Such cooperation would hold many benefits for them, not the least of which would be money and weapons, but also a secure place in the France of the future.

"We already have weapons," said one of the men proudly.

"So I've heard," replied Armand. "Are they powerful enough for frontal assaults on the *boches?*"

"Perhaps not," said the well-dressed man, "but I can assure you that they are adequate for our immediate needs."

"What can de Gaulle know about our needs here in the provinces when he remains in London?" asked a younger man.

"The general has many men and women throughout France who serve as his eyes and ears."

"Men such as you, no doubt," suggested the white-haired old man. "But you are not from the Gresivaudan Valley, nor from the Isère at all. All you can report is what you see, what you hear. You cannot hope to understand who we are or how we feel after a brief visit. Marseilles is a world away from Grenoble."

Armand felt himself blushing slightly at the mention of his birthplace. He realized that his distinctly southern accent gave him away whenever he traveled, but few had made it an issue. He would have to deal with it as best he could.

"We're not so different, you and I," he replied, "in spite of our speech. Deep down, we want the same things—for France and for ourselves."

"And what would that be?" asked the well-dressed man.

"We want a France governed by patriotic Frenchmen with no foreign interference. A France restored to her former glory and her rightful place among the leading nations of the world. A France where we can raise our families free from fear and hunger."

He paused, and then with just a hint of a smile added, "We want a France where we can eat, drink, and love to our hearts' content. And of course, where we can play *boules* all day instead of working."

The men all laughed at this and immediately the conversation turned less serious.

"Do you play?" asked Bonet. He'd been quiet up until this point, deferring to the older men.

"Quite well, actually," replied Armand matter-of-factly. "I won the Marseilles city championship in the fall of '39."

That wasn't quite true, though it seemed harmless enough since he had participated in such tournaments. But the statement set the room abuzz. It seemed to break the ice, especially with the younger men. They were passionate about sports, and they crowded around to hear of the exploits of a champion—and a young one at that. Perhaps he would at least win some of them over.

In the background, three men, including the white-haired old man and the well-dressed man, huddled together, talking quietly among themselves.

⚜   ⚜   ⚜

From his hospital bed, the previous evening's events still baffled Armand. What had begun with such promise had ended so badly he could hardly believe it—that is, until he tried to move. The pain reminded him that it was all too true.

Nurse Previn returned with a glass of water and a steaming bowl of broth on a wooden tray.

"I'll help you sit up a little so you can eat," she said cheerily.

Armand tried unsuccessfully to smile. The prospect of her touch eased any doubts he had about the possibility of changing positions. He only hoped she would find it necessary to help him eat too.

Once she had propped him up with pillows, she seated herself on the edge of the bed and held the water glass to his swollen lips.

"Now then," she said quietly as she lowered the glass. "I know you're in some kind of trouble—"

Armand tried to form the words to say that it was actually worse than it looked, but she stopped him.

"Shh!" She laid her forefinger gently across his lips. "Don't try to talk now. There'll be time for that later. Just remember I'm here to help you any way I can."

Chapter 7

M alfaïre here." The inspector's voice betrayed his irritation with being telephoned at his office on a Saturday afternoon. The pile of unfinished reports on his spacious walnut desk seemed to be mounting out of control, and Saturday was often his only chance—however remote—to catch up. On top of that, he had been out until nearly 2 o'clock in the morning following up a tip from an informant. The tip had led to a surprisingly easy arrest, but the prisoner, an outlaw known only as Pascal, was unable to talk for the moment, which added to Malfaïre's irritation.

"Ah, *Commissaire.*" Malfaïre sat up straight in his leather chair. "No, monsieur, it's no problem. Not at all. What can I do for you?"

There was a long silence, during which Police Inspector Jean-Claude Malfaïre scratched furiously with an ornate fountain pen on a sheet of paper hastily pulled from the desk drawer. He listened and wrote for two full minutes before speaking again.

"I agree completely, *Commissaire*. We can't allow this sort of thing to get out of hand. Sends all the wrong signals to the rest of them. I'll get on it right away. *Au revoir, Commissaire,* and thank you."

He replaced the phone in its cradle and reread his notes. Then he picked up the phone again and dialed out.

"Dominique?" he said after a few seconds, "it's Malfaire. Listen. I know it's your day off, but the commissioner just called and wants me over at Vénissieux this afternoon. Would you bring the car around? Right away, if you don't mind."

He knew Dominique wouldn't mind. Not really. Dominique had been his driver for nearly five years now, and he knew him pretty well. He seldom had much to say, though when he did it was usually worth listening to. And Malfaire trusted him implicitly. Dominique was an excellent driver and a brilliant mechanic. His was an enviable position—especially for a man who loved cars.

The inspector bent once again over his reports while he waited for Dominique to arrive with the car. Normally, he would have begun making notes in preparation for the assignment the commissioner had given him, but today, he reasoned, there would be time for that on the drive to Vénissieux. Having a driver afforded him the luxury of concentrating exclusively on the task at hand, even while traveling.

The fact that he'd had a car and driver for five years was a sore point with many of his colleagues. But his uncanny ability to ferret out information and run criminal suspects to ground had made him something of a law-and-order celebrity in Lyons. He liked to think that one day all of France would come to appreciate his skills. The defeat by the Germans had temporarily sidetracked his plans for advancement, but the Nazis, he had discovered, appreciated efficient police work too. For the moment, however, he had few direct dealings with the invaders since Lyons lay in the unoccupied zone.

Dominique arrived fifteen minutes later in the official black Renault sedan, and they sped off toward Vénissieux and the detention camp for which it had gained notoriety. The camp was used by the Vichy government primarily as a holding pen for Jews, but it also housed a few Freemasons, homosexuals, and common criminals. From there the detainees, as they were called, were periodically sent by train to the camp at Drancy, near Paris, and from there to points east, among them Auschwitz, though details were sketchy at best.

Once they were underway, Malfaire briefed Dominique on the assignment the commissioner had given him. "There's been another escape from the camp," he said. "The commissioner claims it was a woman this time—alone."

Dominique looked quizzically at his boss in the rearview mirror. "A woman? Alone? Excuse me for saying so, Inspector, but that doesn't sound very likely."

"Maybe not," replied Malfaire, "but it's apparently true. And to make matters worse, she's a Jew. They've increased security at the camp, but the commissioner is afraid that more of them will try to break out if we don't catch this woman and make an example of her."

"That may not be easy."

"How's that? I figure she can't have gone far alone. And most people aren't going to risk arrest to help a lousy Jew, even if she is a woman."

"But the fact that she's a woman can make it pretty hard to tell that she's a Jew, especially if she's not full-blooded. It'd be a lot simpler if she were a man, if you know what I mean."

"I'm well aware of Jewish customs, Dominique," Malfaire said brusquely. "It's just one more reason to track her down quickly before she worms her way into the embrace of some blind fool and spawns another little Jew."

"I beg your pardon, Inspector?"

"It's bad enough that these Jews become wealthy on the backs of the honest, hardworking French. But more and more they conspire to intermarry as well. In the eyes of some, a child of such a union is only half Jewish. But, in my view, half a Jew is a still more dangerous Jew."

"Dangerous in what way, monsieur?"

"Don't you see, Dominique?" Malfaire was becoming impatient. "The more they are able to integrate into French society, the more difficult it becomes to recognize them. The leeches are corrupting our culture. Only when France is pure will she ever regain her greatness. We can't allow this fugitive, or others like her, to threaten our future. Especially not now when we're on the verge of solving the whole Jewish problem."

The inspector marveled at his driver's density at times, especially when it came to political or cultural issues. But of course, Dominique didn't have the benefit of his education, nor of his vast experience.

"Do you really think she acted alone?" Dominique asked.

"Not for a minute. She may well have been the only one to escape, but she most certainly had help—perhaps even help from the inside as we suspected in last month's escapes. Most of these Jews have money. She probably bribed someone."

Dominique made no reply, and they drove the rest of the way to the camp in silence.

❧   ❧   ❧

Inspector Malfaire leafed through the contents of a file folder as he sat in an upholstered armchair across the desk from Pierre LeFevre, commandant of the detention camp. For several minutes Malfaire had said nothing, choosing silence over conversation with a man he considered incompetent. It was clear to

Malfaire that a capable commandant would not be in the embarrassing position of requiring outside help to track down an escaped prisoner—or "detainee" as LeFevre and his kind preferred to call them—for the second time in just over a month.

Finally, Malfaire finished his reading and looked across at LeFevre.

"I'll need a room in which to conduct my interrogations," he said. "I'm sure you'll have no trouble finding me something suitable, Commandant."

LeFevre reddened noticeably, and his thin smile was forced. "Whatever you need will be provided, Inspector." He obviously disliked Malfaire, but he would cooperate, of course. There was little else he could do under the circumstances—even less that he could say—and Malfaire knew it. In spite of his political connections, the commandant's job was in jeopardy.

"I know I can count on your assistance, Commandant," Malfaire said matter-of-factly. "I'll want to begin by questioning everyone who occupied the barracks where our young fugitive was housed."

"But we've already done that, Inspector," sputtered LeFevre. "The reports are right there in the file, as you can see." His face had turned a deeper shade of red and a vein in his neck was bulging.

"What I can see, Commandant LeFevre," hissed Malfaire as he rose to his feet, "is that some Jew woman named Isabelle Karmazin has managed to escape from your camp, and she's still at large. If your reports were of any great value I wouldn't be here! Now, bring in the prisoners I asked for, one at a time, and then stay out of my way."

LeFevre had gone white. "And where would you like to question them, Inspector?" he asked meekly. He would have to be a fool to make things any worse than they already were.

"I'm sure your office will do just fine, Commandant."

Chapter 8

Woe to those who make unjust laws, to those who issue oppressive decrees—

Marcel admired the dramatic way Charles Westphal read the Scriptures. The pastor paused and looked defiantly out over his congregation as though challenging anyone to rebut the words of the Prophet Isaiah. The Sunday worshipers who filled Grenoble's *temple protestant* seemed to hold their collective breath as the animated reading continued.

—to deprive the poor of their rights
and withhold justice from the oppressed of
my people—

Marcel sat next to the aisle, halfway between the rear of the church and the massive carved pulpit from which the passionate pastor hurled his biblical missiles. An often intense man, even under normal circumstances, Westphal was as agitated as Marcel had ever seen him. Now he raised his fist to punctuate his indictment.

> —*making widows their prey*
> *and robbing the fatherless.*

Marcel glanced along the hard oak pew to his left where his mother sat motionless, staring straight ahead. He wondered how she felt inside whenever she heard the word widow. It was hard enough for him with his father gone, but he couldn't begin to imagine what she must be going through. True, they didn't know for sure that Albert Boussant was dead, but after two years—well, two years was a long time to be without a husband and a father.

Françoise, seated next to Marcel, was riveted as usual to Pastor Westphal's sermon. She had become increasingly quiet since Papa's disappearance, and it worried Marcel. It wasn't that she was sullen. She just seemed sad much of the time. Maybe it was the combination of the war *and* losing Papa. It was hard to say. But in any case, her faith seemed strong and Marcel took some hope in that.

Luc, on the other hand, who sat restlessly next to Maman, seemed only vaguely aware of the hazards of war—and probably only vaguely aware of the sermon too. He seldom talked of their father anymore. It was hard to tell if he were beginning to forget, or if he simply tried not to think about it. He seemed enamored with war, but in a fairy-tale sort of way. In his mind, men fought for noble causes and justice always prevailed. Evil men met with certain death or disaster. Marcel often envied his little brother's innocent perspective. For him, reality was decidedly more difficult to live with.

When he turned his attention back toward the front of the church, Marcel realized that Pastor Westphal had completed his reading of Isaiah and had launched into a fiery sermon denouncing the evils of racism and anti-Semitism, even reading an official letter from the National Council of the Reformed Church. Westphal was a persuasive man and Marcel admired his courage. He was proud that the pastor was using his position to lash out at the Vichy government. Someone needed to, he reasoned.

Ever since Marshal Pétain's government had sued for peace, it seemed to Marcel that they had engaged in one act of betrayal after another. While it was true that Pétain had managed to keep nearly forty percent of France free from German occupation, he had not substantially improved their lot in the eyes of many. And some of his initiatives had seemed downright provocative.

The Boussants and their Protestant friends had been outraged when the old marshal, as one of his first official acts, dedicated the country to the Virgin Mary. He was undoubtedly appealing to the traditional Catholic majority, but some feared a return to the days when the bloody persecution of the Protestant Huguenots was officially sanctioned. Then the announcement of the government's policy of collaboration with the Nazis sent shockwaves throughout Catholic and Protestant communities alike, as did Pétain's public handshake with Hitler himself.

Yes, Marcel reasoned, it was high time someone stood up to this puppet regime and denounced its offenses. And he was gratified that Pastor Westphal had the courage—no, the audacity—to do just that.

At the close of the service, Marcel headed back up the aisle and out the main doors without waiting for his family. The glare from the noon sun made him squint as he stepped out onto the sidewalk and strode up the narrow street.

"Hey, Marcel! Wait up." Marcel turned to see his friend Gilles Théron jogging to catch up with him. Gilles, whose

father had turned a modest inheritance into a burgeoning
import-export business, had befriended Marcel when the two
were young boys. The Protestant community was close-knit, if
not large, and the boys had built a solid friendship, based in
large part on their shared heritage.

The Thérons, like many others, attended church primarily
as a means of reaffirming their cultural roots. It was not that
they were insincere. They simply saw no reason to make more
of their proud heritage than it was. But young Gilles had often
expressed his admiration for the way Marcel's family openly
embraced both the history and the simple faith of their
Huguenot ancestors.

"What happened to your face?" was the first thing Gilles
said when he caught up to Marcel, "and why the hurry?"

"The hurry," Marcel replied dryly, "is to avoid dumb
questions about what happened to my face."

"So, did you get hit by a truck?" his friend laughed lightly.
"Or were you just caught trying to kiss one of those Gypsy
girls again?"

"Don't make me laugh, Gilles," pleaded Marcel. "It makes
my face hurt worse." Then he gave Gilles the condensed ver-
sion of his weekend adventure as the two friends strolled to
where the Boussant family car was parked.

The dark green Peugeot 183 was in remarkable condition,
considering its thirteen years of service. Albert Boussant had
purchased the six-cylinder sedan second-hand in 1936 and, as
he did with everything he owned, had taken meticulous care of
it. Marcel had done his best to follow suit since his father's disappearance. He kept it under blankets in a corner of the barn,
and used it little except for the weekly trek into Grenoble to
attend church. Of course, his caution was partly due to the
rationing of fuel, but since the war, the family rarely ventured
far from home anyway. His mother had never learned to drive,

leaving the responsibility entirely to him.

"So, what are you going to do?" asked Gilles as they reached the car.

"I'm not sure yet." Marcel checked to see that the gas cap was securely in place. It was. He had not lost gas to any siphon-hose bandits yet, but it was such a common practice that it was probably only a matter of time.

"What about the gun?"

"It's at home. I'm certainly not going to carry it to church."

"Well, I wouldn't carry one of those antique Lebel revolvers anywhere, if I were you."

"What, then? The army—or what's left of it—still uses them."

"My point exactly. And look what happened to them. Let's face it. The *boches* are better equipped than we French ever were. Maybe we just need to steal some of their weapons."

"I don't know," said Marcel, shaking his head, "but guns or no guns, we can't just sit on our hands while France disintegrates."

"I agree."

"Then what do we do?"

"There's talk at the university of some groups forming to sabotage trains and factories—anything to disrupt the *boches*. I have some friends—"

"Shhh!" Marcel interrupted when he saw his mother and Françoise approaching, with Luc trailing behind. "I'd rather they didn't hear this. We'll talk later."

"*Bonjour*, Gilles," Evelyne Boussant said pleasantly as she leaned toward him. "How nice to see you."

Gilles obliged her with a kiss on each cheek. "It's always a pleasure to see you, Madame Boussant. You're well, I trust?"

"Very well, thank you."

"Hi, Gilles!" blurted Luc, looking up admiringly at his

brother's handsome, fair-haired friend. "How's everything at the university?"

"Just fine, Luc," chuckled Gilles, clapping the nine-year-old on the shoulder. "Just fine."

Gilles turned his steel-blue eyes toward Françoise who hung back a few feet behind her mother. "Hello, Françoise," he said simply, taking a step toward her.

Françoise politely held out her hand. *"Bonjour,* Gilles," she replied without meeting his eyes. Several seconds passed in silence as her hand lingered in his grasp. Marcel thought he noticed fresh color infuse his sister's cheeks. *What a strange way to act now,* he mused. *You two have known each other since you were kids.*

"Marcel." His mother's voice broke the awkward silence. "Madame Lambert has invited us to lunch with them. We really ought to be going soon. She'll be expecting us."

Marcel made a conscious effort not to change his expression. He genuinely admired Professor Maurice Lambert and his wife, but the prospect of spending Sunday afternoon with them and their noisy brood did not appeal to him. He would have to field a dozen more questions about his bruised face, and he really just wanted some time alone to think—and to heal.

"Well, I'll be going then," said Gilles, turning to walk back toward the church. "I hope to see you all next week." Marcel could have sworn that his friend's last words were directed at Françoise.

Moments later, the Peugeot glided to a stop at the curb in front of the aging stone home of Maurice and Claudette Lambert and their four children. Matthieu, the most reserved of the four, was Luc's age, and the two got along famously. The precocious twins, Miryam and Madeleine, were seven, and liked nothing better than to badger their older brother. Marc was a three-year-old whirlwind of unbridled sound and motion.

Claudette Lambert served a soup of potatoes and leeks in the large but plain dining room. The meal, like her home, reflected the unadorned lifestyle to which she and the professor seemed accustomed. It was clear that she had chosen—every bit as much as her husband, who was one of the elders of the congregation—a life of ministry and service to others, and there was a quiet grace reflected in the way she attended her guests.

There was, however, little else that was quiet about the meal. Maurice Lambert, seated at the head of the table, invoked the Lord's blessing on the food. But at the exact moment of his concluding "amen," complete pandemonium broke out and continued well into the afternoon. Luc and Matthieu compared notes on the merits of their respective school teachers. Miryam and Madeleine vied loudly for the attention of the older Françoise, whom they adored. Claudette filled Evelyne in on several parish families who were in great need, while little Marc talked loudly to whomever would listen. The professor entered each conversation as the need arose—sometimes mediating, often informing, always affirming.

Marcel, seated at the far end of the table, listened but said little. No one had yet asked about his face, though the twins looked from time to time as though they might. His opinion was occasionally asked by the boys or by the other adults, but he limited his response to a few words. He liked the Lamberts well enough. It was just that he would rather have been elsewhere that afternoon—anywhere else.

Finally, when the women rose to clear the table just before 3 o'clock, Lambert pushed back his chair.

"Marcel," he said as he rose to his feet, "would you care to join me in my study? Perhaps we can catch a bit of the news from the BBC."

The professor led the way from the dining room, through the *salon,* and into his cluttered study. The sunlight from a sin-

gle window spilled into the room and illuminated a small tres-
tle table that faced the door and served as a desk. Its top was
nearly invisible under the assorted piles of books and papers. A
single brass lamp, perched at one end of the table, appeared to
provide the room's only light when daylight failed. A large
chair made of nondescript wood and sporting a worn leather
seat and back sat at an odd angle behind the desk.

Floor-to-ceiling bookshelves nearly hid the two side walls,
giving the room the look of a library and the smell of leather
and old paper. A chair, similar to the one behind the desk, sat
in the middle of the room on an oval rug that covered a small
patch of the dark hardwood floor.

Marcel was staring in awe at the collection of books on the
shelves when he heard the crackle of the radio. Professor
Lambert had seated himself behind his table-desk and was fid-
dling with the dial of the cabinet radio that sat on a low shelf
beside the window. He motioned Marcel to the remaining chair
as the crackle became a clearly distinguishable French voice.

News of the war was mixed, according to the report. While
the German army reinforced its stranglehold on Stalingrad, it
was bogging down in the sands of North Africa. American and
British bombs continued to inflict damage on military and
industrial targets inside Germany, but there was little cause for
new hope of a major Allied breakthrough.

As the news summary ended, Marcel started to say that he
hoped the next day's news would be more encouraging, but
Lambert raised his hand to silence him.

"Pierre wishes Martine a happy anniversary," intoned the
announcer. "Is Père Noël coming to Mâcon before Christmas?
The leaves have fallen from the maples, but not from the oaks."

The professor clicked off the receiver and turned to
Marcel. "Any of those coded messages for you," he asked with
a grin, "or are they as mysterious to you as they are to me?"

"Sometimes I wish they were for me," replied Marcel seriously. "Then perhaps I could do something about the mess we're in."

"And just what would you like to do?" asked Lambert.

"Anything that would rid us of the Germans, and the collaborators and traitors in Vichy."

"Anything?"

"Well, nearly anything."

"What's stopping you?"

Marcel was silent for a few moments. "I'm not sure," he said finally. "I guess I don't know *what* to do."

"Marcel," began the professor gently, "perhaps you should be more careful in your criticism of the Vichy government. After all, many in the government are just like you: young and idealistic. But not knowing for sure what to do, they choose to do nothing. And doing nothing is often as treacherous as open collaboration because it allows our enemies to have free rein in our country.

"It's true that certain officials have actively promoted laws and regulations which Christians should find intolerable. And we should actively oppose them and their laws. But we should pray for all who tolerate oppressive policies, that they will no longer give their tacit support. Without support, the government will have to change. I'm convinced that when enough people cease to cooperate, even the German occupation will fail—perhaps not right away, but in time it will."

"But how are we—how am I—supposed to actively oppose the government's policies? I thought about joining a local *maquis,* but after this," Marcel pointed to his discolored cheek, "I'm not so sure. They seemed less interested in combating the Nazis and fascists than in fighting each other."

"Armed resistance is not always the answer, Marcel. Have you seen the response to the communists' assassinations of

German officers? The Germans kill scores of civilians in revenge! Where does that get us? Our side kills one or two; their side kills twenty, or fifty, or maybe even a hundred. The communists may accept such an equation, but I cannot.

"I prefer to resist government oppression and *save* lives at the same time. Somehow, I believe God prefers that too. And I could use your help, Marcel."

"What do you mean?"

"How much do you know about the government's Jewish policies?"

"Not very much, I guess. I've heard that they have to wear a yellow Star of David everywhere in the occupied zone, and I've read about some camps where homeless Jews are temporarily housed. And, like everyone else, I guess I've known all along that the Nazis and Fascists haven't much use for them."

Professor Lambert rose from his chair and circled around to the front of the desk. Sitting on the edge, hands gripping the wood on either side of him, he leaned toward his young visitor. "Unfortunately, Marcel, most people either don't know or they choose to ignore that the policies of our own government are nearly as restrictive as those of the Germans. It is true that Jews are being temporarily housed in camps, as you say. But what many people don't know is that most foreign Jews are only housed temporarily because their property has been confiscated and our officials are preparing to hand them over to the Nazis! We can't prove it yet, but we have reason to believe that Hitler is systematically killing them off by the thousands. You see, some people will never be satisfied until all the Jews are destroyed. So, along with some others, I've determined to save as many as possible from destruction."

Marcel was stunned. He stared at the professor, trying to grasp what he was hearing. This was new information—unthinkable information. Yet he still didn't understand how he could do anything. He was just one man, armed only with an outdated revolver. It just didn't make sense. And Lambert had made it pretty clear that armed resistance was not part of his plan.

"I could use your help, Marcel," Lambert repeated himself, "but I won't lie to you. It is dangerous and exhausting and you won't be able to talk about it. The results aren't visible to others like they are when you blow up a bridge. Few will understand what you're doing, and fewer still will care. People you'd think would offer assistance, won't. Some you'd never think of asking, will. But I believe it's the right thing to do. The Jews are God's chosen people and they need our help escaping this persecution. Besides, if we don't act to save them now, we may be next."

"I don't understand."

"We Protestants are a small minority in this country, Marcel. If we stand by while the government disposes of three hundred thousand Jews, who will defend us if they decide that eight hundred thousand Protestants are undesirable? It happened before. It could happen again."

Marcel looked into the earnest eyes of the taller man. This was not the sort of thing he had envisioned when he had determined to act on his frustrations. He had entertained thoughts of hiding out in the forest by day and attacking German installations and supply convoys at night. It had seemed so glorious and satisfying in his mind. But this—well, this didn't seem glorious at all. How could he help bearded old men and their dowdy wives and somber children? He couldn't fathom how it could succeed, let alone how it would help France or harm her enemies.

"I don't know, Professor." His voice was subdued. "It all sounds, well, kind of foolish, if you want the truth."

"Think it over, Marcel. The right thing to do is not always easy—or obvious. You know, sometimes God uses seemingly foolish things to confound the wise.

"Come to lunch on Tuesday." Lambert smiled as he stood and offered his hand. "We'll talk more then." He walked to the door and prepared to usher Marcel back into the *salon*. "By the way, Marcel," he added impishly, "just what *did* happen to your face?"

Chapter 9

J ean-Claude Malfaire crossed himself, knelt stiffly at the rail and, head erect, prepared to receive the sacrament. His glare failed to penetrate the implacable expression on Father Benoit's face as the old priest slowly dipped the host into the chalice. Malfaire opened his mouth automatically and tasted the sweetness of the wine as Father Benoit placed the wafer on his tongue.

"Corpus Christi." Malfaire squeezed his eyes shut for an instant, momentarily lulled by the comforting familiarity of the sacrament and the priest's Latin. But the words that followed were unmistakably French. "Do not take lightly the gift of grace, my son."

Malfaire looked up in stark surprise, only to find that the priest had already turned toward the altar. Jean-Claude rose to his feet and returned to sit beside his wife and son, but not another sound penetrated his awareness until after the final benediction. He had received the sacrament hundreds—no, thousands—of times, and no one, not even Cardinal Gerlier, had ever spoken to him apart from what the liturgy required. Who did this man, this aging excuse for a priest, think he was?

Malfaire's anger had been mounting all morning. Instead of his usual simple homily, Benoit had had the audacity to read one of the so-called pastoral letters that had begun circulating from church to church. This one had supposedly come from Monsignor Théas of Montauban who claimed that . . . *Jews are being treated in the most barbarous, the most savage way.* What nonsense! And, as if that were not enough, the letter went on to denounce . . . *families being torn apart, men and women abused, penned up, and sent to unknown destinations of extreme danger.* Obviously, some of the clergy simply did not fully understand reality. *The indignant protest of the Christian conscience will be heard,* the monsignor's letter declared. *I proclaim that all men and women, Aryans or otherwise, are brothers because they were created by God . . . and have the right to be respected. . . .*

By the end of the reading, Malfaire was grinding his teeth. Monsignor Théas and his ilk had clearly gone beyond the bounds of religion and were beginning to meddle in the affairs of state. There were laws about that, he fumed to himself, and without such laws France risked a return to the days when kings and cardinals vied for power. No, the church should stick to religion, he reasoned, and leave matters such as the Jewish question to the proper authorities.

A tug on his coat sleeve interrupted his thoughts. Suddenly aware that the mass had concluded and that people were filing out, Malfaire looked down into the wide eyes of five-year-old André.

"Papa," André said, continuing to pull at his father's sleeve, "can we go to the park today? You promised!"

"Yes, André," Malfaire replied with an indulgent smile.

His tension and anger dissipated quickly under the gaze of his only son. "We're going to eat a nice lunch and then we'll go walk in the park."

He glanced at Marie, his bride of fifteen years, and gave a wink. "I hope you don't mind dining out again, *chérie.*"

"You know I don't, darling," she replied sweetly, "but there's really no need to spoil me so."

"Don't worry yourself about that," said Malfaire as he guided his family out into the sunlight. "There's a little restaurant nearby whose owner owes me a favor." He smirked to himself. *A lot of careless people owe me favors, my dear.*

⚜   ⚜   ⚜

Armand Moreau shifted uncomfortably in his bed. Since Dr. Billot had realigned his dislocated shoulder the day before, the numbness had gone away, only to be replaced by a throbbing ache. Unable to speak as of yet, his attempts to communicate the pain had been fruitless. Even Nurse Previn, as attentive as she was, hadn't seemed to comprehend. Of course, there was always the chance that she understood very well and simply chose to ignore it. After all, he was not one of the paying guests.

He had spent the night drifting in and out of consciousness, and though he felt utterly exhausted, the pain kept him from enjoying any profound sleep. He had taken advantage of what little sleep he could manage, but during his waking hours he had racked his brain trying to decide who might have betrayed him.

Since he had heard the police inspector refer to him as Pascal, he decided that it was probably someone who only knew him by his code name. That immediately eliminated anyone from his old army unit. It also pointed away from Jean Moulin and the two or three de Gaulle operatives who actually knew his real identity. No, it was more likely someone from inside one of the networks; someone who had it in for him, or perhaps someone who had been arrested and had purchased freedom with information.

But the possibility that troubled him most was that someone in one of the networks was a plant—a spy. Engaging in active resistance, especially armed resistance, was a dangerous game under the best of conditions. But if a network were to be infiltrated by Nazi—or even Vichy—sympathizers, it could be deadly. He shuddered at that thought.

What favored the spy theory was the fact that the police had found him on an obscure street in a small town like Domène. He had heard just enough snatches of conversation in the car to know that he had been taken to Lyons. And only someone with inside information about the hastily arranged *boules* game could have led this police inspector from Lyons to Domène, nearly two hours away.

After the beating he had received at the hands of Emile Bonet and his thugs, it seemed logical that they were also responsible for arranging his arrest. As far as Armand knew, they were the only ones who had exact knowledge as to where he could be found. And more than likely, the well-dressed man was in on it too. He was probably the head of the operation, and Bonet the one who carried out the orders. But considering the extent of his injuries, Armand couldn't shake the nagging thought that perhaps Bonet had not intended that he should live long enough to be arrested.

His thoughts were abruptly interrupted by the sound of voices outside in the hall. The sight of Nurse Previn was something Armand had eagerly anticipated since yesterday's visit, though she had yet to put in another appearance. His aches and pains seemed strangely diminished, as if the healing process had suddenly accelerated at the thought of the pretty young nurse. But when the door swung open to reveal the same frowning, pasty-faced, old crone who had been storming in to tend him at odd intervals all day, the pain rushed back in with the realization that Nurse Previn was probably off-duty on Sundays.

The old nurse never entered the room unless accompanied by a uniformed guard. The guard apparently changed from time to time, but the old woman's expression did not. Armand read in her eyes a combination of fear and disgust, and he wondered what she must have heard about him. She had not spoken to him all day except to reproach him for his inability to rise and tend himself.

The one thing the old nurse's presence allowed, however, was a close look at the police guards. Most of them were young, alert, and armed with semiautomatic pistols, Armand noted with chagrin. That, and the fact that he could barely move, put escape out of the question for the moment. But he also knew that the longer he had to wait, the more remote his chances for freedom became.

Dr. Billot returned just after sundown. The guard, apparently at ease to permit him to examine his patient alone, remained out in the hall. The doctor smiled pleasantly as he approached the bed.

"*Bon soir, mon ami,*" he said. "Feeling any better yet?"

Armand shrugged.

"That doesn't surprise me. Our good inspector doesn't wish you to have any pain medication. Perhaps he's afraid that if you do, you might not have the proper motivation to cooperate."

While he talked, Dr. Billot poked and prodded here and there on Armand's body, provoking predictable, if painful, reactions. Armand could only grunt his responses.

"He'll be in to check on you tomorrow, you know," said the doctor. "Of course, I'll tell him that you won't be able to help him just yet. But he can be quite impatient. If I were you, *mon ami,* I would pray to God that the inspector becomes entangled in another investigation—or perhaps that he gets struck by lightning!"

❧ ❧ ❧

Inspector Malfaire drummed a fountain pen on the leather top of the commandant's desk, and glared at the woman who had been seated across from him for the past ten minutes. Her file said she was twenty-nine, but her appearance said at least twice that. "Let me be certain I have this right," he said, glancing once more at the file. "You occupied the bed next to the Karmazin woman."

She nodded timidly, fear in her eyes.

"And yet you expect me to believe that you know nothing about her?"

"Nothing that could be important, Inspector."

Perhaps he should have waited until Monday, he thought. After a memorable lunch and a pleasant stroll in the park with Marie and André, he had telephoned for his car. Dominique, whose sense of duty rivaled his own, had driven him to the camp and was even now waiting patiently in an outer office. Maybe he should have enjoyed the day with his family, and let Dominique do the same. But he really wanted to make some progress before the trail of the escaped Jew turned cold.

"Do you know what can happen to you if you do not tell me the truth, madame?"

The woman looked down at her feet and shook her head. It looked as though she were on the verge of tears.

"Would you like to find out?"

Again she shook her head, more vigorously this time.

"Then you will start telling me what I wish to know!" Malfaire shouted and slammed the pen down with such force that it shattered. He cursed and drew back his hand, dripping blood and India ink. He hesitated for a moment, torn between easing the pain and containing the ink spill. Doing neither, he scooped up the remains of the pen and hurled it at the startled prisoner. Her reactions were slow, and he watched with a furious glee as dark splotches materialized on her ashen face and tattered dress.

Malfaire bounded around the desk and grabbed the still-stunned woman roughly by the arm. "I will not tolerate your lies, Jew," he hissed, his face just inches from hers. He pulled her up toward him and then released her arm, sending her crashing back against the wooden chair and into the wall, forcing the air from her lungs. She gasped repeatedly, struggling to catch her breath, her eyes dilated in terror.

"You will tell me everything I wish to know," he said, once he had regained his composure, "and you will start by telling me who helped this woman to escape." Sooner or later, he knew he would have the answers he needed. Then he would simply rearrest the Karmazin woman and bring her back to the camp. *Unless*—he smiled to himself at the thought—*unless she were to have an unfortunate accident!*

Chapter 10

The morning train to Geneva was much more crowded than Marcel had expected. Unable to find an empty seat, he stood from the time he boarded in Domène until the train reached Goncellin, twenty minutes later. Fortunately, more people got off than on at the tiny station, and Marcel found a window seat toward the rear of the car.

"*Pardon,* madame," he said as he squeezed past the middle-aged woman occupying the aisle seat. He clutched a tan leather valise tightly, resting it on his lap as he sat down. The middle-aged woman did not reply or even divert her attention from the tatting she worked at on her lap. The man in the seat facing Marcel looked up from his newspaper and nodded politely as their eyes made brief contact. Dressed in a well-tailored suit, he had the look of a prosperous businessman. The woman on his right, obviously much younger and wearing a cashmere coat, was equally polite. His mistress, Marcel supposed, given the way she looked at the man and clung to his side. He had barely enough time to get comfortable before the train pulled out of the station.

The fall scenery was spectacular. October and its cooler weather had arrived, and the trees that lined the valley were a festival of color. Small farms dotted the landscape on either side of the tracks, adding their patchwork of fields and fences to the scene. The light frost still clung to the grass in the corners not yet penetrated by the warming sunlight. On another day Marcel would have reveled in such beauty, but today his mind was filled with other thoughts.

He shifted slightly in his seat and felt the bulge of the Lebel revolver against his ribs. He had stuck it into the inside pocket of his wool coat at the last minute, but now found it uncomfortable—in more ways than one. He glanced self-consciously at the couple facing him, hoping they had not noticed his uneasiness. The man had raised his newspaper, his face hidden from Marcel's view. The woman smiled but quickly averted her eyes as Marcel looked in her direction. The middle-aged woman beside him seemed oblivious to everyone.

As Marcel turned back toward the window, the newspaper caught his eye. There was something strange—it was German! The man was reading a German newspaper. Marcel felt suddenly warm and a single drop of sweat trickled down his neck inside his shirt collar. He scolded himself silently for not having remained standing at the front of the car. Of course, if he got back up now he'd only draw more attention to himself, and then "Franz"—as Marcel had named him—would know he was up to something. He would just have to remain seated and try to stay calm.

Professor Lambert had warned him that this job might not be easy. He just hadn't expected trouble to find him so soon. Perhaps the man and his companion would get off at the next stop. Or perhaps when he got off in Aix-les-Bains the couple would stay aboard and continue on out of his life forever. He tried to think through Lambert's instructions just in case neither happened.

On Sunday, when the professor first approached him about joining his efforts to aid Jewish refugees, Marcel had been skeptical. Though it was true that he hadn't yet decided what he wanted to do for France, he had been pretty sure that wasn't it. It didn't seem as though one person could make much of a difference in this kind of effort, and it certainly lacked the glamour of joining one of the bands of armed *maquisards.*

Marcel had spent much of the next day alone in the hills above the farm, mulling over his options. Antoine LeBoeuf had held out little hope of any meaningful involvement with the local *maquis. "If your help is needed, someone will call for you."* Wasn't that what he had said? It just didn't sound very promising. And after what he had seen and heard—and felt— the night of the *boules* game, Marcel wasn't sure he could actually trust men like Emile Bonet and René Carlini, no matter how much he looked up to Antoine.

For the first time he began to wonder just how LeBoeuf fit into such a group. Obviously, there were many things about the group Marcel didn't know. And maybe the old man knew what he was doing. He hoped so. But in spite of his friend's apparent key role in the *maquis,* Marcel couldn't see himself as part of it. At least not without some strong reservations.

Doing nothing, of course, was out of the question. He had already decided that. It would sure be a lot easier. And it was the path most people chose to walk. But he felt he had spent the past two years doing nothing—in spite of what Françoise thought—and now it was time for action.

Aiding Jewish refugees, however, was something he had never even contemplated. It sounded harmless enough. And after hearing the details of the persecution of Jews in France, he knew it was important. But Professor Lambert had spoken of more than just need and Christian duty. He had warned of danger—danger in acting, certainly—but even greater danger in failing to act. Marcel had decided to hear the professor out.

Lost in his own thoughts and gazing blankly out the window at the passing countryside, Marcel didn't notice that the man across from him had folded his newspaper in his lap and was looking at him.

"It is far to Geneva, *ja?*"

Marcel jerked his head around to face the man he thought of as Franz, who beamed his pleasure at his own halting effort to speak French. Marcel's eyes darted from Franz to his girlfriend. She too smiled, as though it were perfectly natural for conqueror and conquered to have a friendly chat on the train. He forced a thin smile, but said nothing in reply.

"You go maybe to Geneva to make business?" Franz asked, motioning toward Marcel's valise.

"*N-n-non,*" Marcel stammered and tightened his grip on the tan case. *Why all the questions?* he wondered. Was the German simply making small talk, or did he suspect that Marcel was carrying false documents? If the contents of the valise were discovered, a lot of refugees' hopes for survival would be dashed, and the aid network would be seriously compromised. Marcel didn't want to think about the personal consequences if he were caught. He hadn't actually considered that possibility—that is, until now.

"Ah, you have maybe the family in Geneva, *ja?*" Franz seemed to enjoy the one-sided conversation.

"*Non,*" Marcel replied, hoping the conversation was about to end. "I'm not going to Geneva." There. He had ended it. Now, perhaps Franz would stop interrogating him. He turned back to the window just as the Chambery station came into view. After a two-minute stop and a scramble of passengers to exit and others to board, the train was once again underway.

"So, where do you go today?" Franz was obviously not going to give up on the conversation easily.

Marcel thought for a moment before offering a reply. "Aix-les-Bains," he said finally. It was partly true. He had to change trains there before going on to Annecy to deliver the valise. In fact, he would have an hour or so to kill before the next train, and since he'd not been to Aix before, he hoped to walk down to the lake. He doubted that he would have the time to see the thermal spas that had made the town famous. Maybe on the way back.

"It is very nice, Aix-les-Bains," the German said. "I go there with my parents when I am a boy. It is before—" He turned to the woman at his side and said something in German.

"*La Grande Guerre,*" she replied with a flawless Parisian accent.

"*Ja,*" he said, turning back to face Marcel, "before the Great War."

The middle-aged woman seated next to Marcel had ceased her tatting and was staring at the young woman. "Where are you from, mademoiselle?" she asked, her voice husky with emotion.

"Paris," she replied. "Why do you ask?"

"Life in Paris must be worse than I thought," the woman said as she collected her things and stood. "In my village we keep pigs in the garden, but we don't sleep with them!" And without another word she stormed down the swaying aisle and through the exit doors to the next car.

A hush fell over the entire train car. Only the clacking of the wheels on the rails could be heard. The departing woman had spoken loud enough for all to hear, and now all eyes were focused on Franz and his friend. The young woman's face had turned crimson but her eyes flashed defiance. Franz continued smiling, but the words he muttered aloud sounded a lot like expletives to Marcel.

Eventually the buzz of conversation returned to its previous level. This time, however, Franz remained silent, and once more unfolded his newspaper. Marcel returned to gazing out the window, and presently the train began to slow for its arrival at the Aix-les-Bains station.

Marcel rose to make his way to the exit doors. With the valise held firmly in one hand, he smoothed his coat with the other to assure himself that the revolver wasn't noticeable. Satisfied, he nodded politely to his seatmates and headed down the aisle, glad to finally be free of their scrutiny.

Once outside, Marcel walked quickly away from the station. A block away he found a small café, and decided to stop and buy a cup of coffee before touring the lakefront. *Just act natural,* Professor Lambert had said. Sitting in a café was natural enough, and besides, he figured a cup of strong black coffee would be just the right prescription for the tension he had been feeling this whole trip. The sun had dispelled the early morning chill, and Marcel chose a seat outside at the edge of a small plaza.

Waiting for his coffee to be brought out, Marcel cast a glance back in the direction of the train station. So unprepared was he for what met his eyes that he nearly bolted from his seat. It was Franz from the train, unaccompanied by his mistress, striding up the street in the direction of the café. He was not alone, however. Flanking him were two local police officers. Marcel felt his stomach sink into his shoes.

As the three men approached the café, one of the policemen broke off and jogged down a side alley toward the rear of the building. The stylish Franz and the remaining officer headed directly toward Marcel, who sat motionless, frozen except for his pounding heart and racing thoughts. Then without even looking at him, the pair walked past him and through the front door of the tiny café. The policeman's revolver was in his hand as he entered.

From inside the café came the sounds of men shouting, followed by the scraping of furniture and breaking glass. Marcel could hear a woman screaming, and then he heard a loud noise, like the splintering of a door. What sounded like a scuffle ensued, followed by more shouting and screaming. And then the two policemen burst through the front door into the sunshine, half-dragging, half-wrestling a man in handcuffs between them. Franz followed at a safe distance. Behind him the old proprietor and his wife were still screaming and shouting insults and curses.

As the police dragged their prisoner past Marcel, the handcuffed man lunged sideways, knocking one of the officers into the table and sending Marcel, chair, and table crashing to the paving stones. The officers began beating the man to subdue him while Franz stepped toward the sprawling Marcel. Recognition lit his eyes.

"Ah, my young friend from the train." He smiled and reached out his hand. "You are healthy, *ja?*"

"I'm fine, *merci,*" Marcel replied as the man helped him to his feet.

"*Sehr gut,*" said the German, "but you are much more careful in the future, I think." And with that he turned and followed the policemen and their still-struggling prisoner down the street.

"Monsieur?" The voice came from behind Marcel. He turned to see that the old couple had begun to right the table and chair he had so recently occupied.

"I believe this belongs to you." The café's proprietor was nervously holding the Lebel revolver along with the tan valise.

"The table fell on top of it, monsieur. I don't think anyone saw it."

Marcel looked quickly around before making a move. Then, his hand trembling, he grabbed the pistol and shoved it quickly back into his inside coat pocket. He dusted off his coat and reached for the valise. *"Merci bien,"* he said and turned to go.

"Your coffee?" asked the proprietor's wife.

Marcel turned to stare at the forlorn faces of the old couple. After a moment he shook his head and retreated toward the lake.

❧   ❧   ❧

By the time the train pulled into the station in the ancient lakeside town of Annecy, Marcel was tired and hungry. Hungry, because breakfast had been hours ago. Tired, because he had been on edge all morning—at least since he had encountered Franz and his friends. What if Franz saw the gun? What if he were following him? Or having him followed? He had looked over his shoulder ever since leaving the café in Aix-les-Bains.

Now, however, he would have to be even more careful. He didn't know who would be meeting him. He only knew that he was to go to the Café des Amours in the old part of the city, near the mouth of the Thiou River. There he was to eat lunch and wait for a messenger.

Marcel had long since removed his coat. The cool autumn nights and chill, frosty mornings usually gave way to warm, sunny afternoons, and today was no exception. Even the sweater he wore felt too warm to Marcel, but it was the blue and red sweater by which his unknown contact was to identify him, so he had to leave it on for the moment. He bundled up his coat carefully so that the revolver would remain safely inside, and trudged from the train station toward the unusual rose, ocher, and rust-colored façades of the old city that lined the banks of the Thiou.

Midway through his soup, Marcel looked up to see a young woman approaching his table. To his astonishment, she walked directly up to him, leaned over, and planted a kiss on each unsuspecting cheek. Then she smiled and sat down across the table from him.

"I like your sweater," she said simply.

She was pretty, he thought. Shoulder-length brown hair, big brown eyes, smooth olive skin. Very pretty. So this was his contact. Perhaps this work *could* be interesting. "I'm glad you weren't looking for my coat," he replied, and smiled broadly for the first time all morning. "Won't you join me for lunch?"

"No, thank you. But please finish your own. Then we'll go."

Lunch was decidedly less interesting just now, especially with the feel of her soft cheeks still lingering in his mind. But he finished as quickly as good manners would allow and paid the proprietor. As he rose to leave, the young woman slipped her hand into the crook of his elbow and guided him up the street and onto a small bridge. Marcel was not as surprised as at her kiss, but he wondered why he hadn't considered this kind of work before. Once on the bridge, she tugged his arm for him to follow her over to the railing. There he followed her gaze out to where the river entered the lake, the beautiful Lac d'Annecy.

"Relax," she said when no one was within earshot. "It looks much less conspicuous if we appear to be lovers out for a noontime stroll. And it will give us time to make sure you weren't followed."

An hour later, the two entered the *temple protestant* through a narrow alley at the back. Inside it seemed dark after having strolled so long in the bright sun. The woman ushered Marcel to a pew near the front of the church and motioned for him to take a seat.

"Wait here," she whispered, and then she disappeared through a side door. Moments later she returned with a tall young man wearing small, round glasses. Marcel stood to his feet as they approached his pew.

"This is Pastor Soulain," she announced softly. "He's the assistant pastor here in Annecy."

Marcel reached out his hand, and the pastor returned his strong handshake. He seemed rather young for a pastor, Marcel thought, even for an assistant. Aloud he said, "I believe I have something for you, Pastor."

"Please call me Jean," said Soulain. "I'm not that much older than you, and besides, we're all doing God's work, aren't we?"

Marcel nodded agreement, but he had to admit to himself that he wasn't thinking of it in that way. He handed the valise to Jean Soulain.

Soulain took the valise and reached inside to pull out a sheaf of official-looking documents. He smiled. "Babette is going to be very happy to see these," he said.

"Babette?"

"Babette is a remarkable woman who has helped hundreds of Jewish refugees escape to Switzerland. She is sometimes able to do so whether or not the Jews have proper documentation, but it's much simpler and quicker when she is able to obtain papers like these." The young pastor turned as if to leave. "Come," he said over his shoulder, "I've got some things for you to take back to Grenoble. Then Anne will see you safely back to the train."

So her name was Anne. He followed the pastor, but his mind was already on the long walk back to the train station. He hoped Professor Lambert had many more such trips planned for him.

Young Pastor Soulain took the forged identity papers out of the valise and laid several pieces of paper in their place. "You needn't worry about getting caught with these," he said with a wink. "They're monthly reports on the church youth activities, baptisms and such, and they are of no value to anyone else. But they are extremely important. Your friend Lambert will understand."

The shadows were beginning to lengthen by the time Anne walked Marcel back to the train station. They sat in the park and chatted, and strolled down by the lake on the way. Marcel loved being close to Anne, her softness constantly at his side. He hated the thought of getting back on the train.

"Perhaps I can come back soon," he suggested hopefully as they stood waiting for his boarding call.

"I hope so," she said brightly. "I'm sure Jean would like that too."

"Do you know Jean well, then?" he asked.

"Quite well," she replied with a sweet smile. "We're to be married in the spring."

Marcel barely noticed as Anne stood on tiptoe to kiss his cheeks. At the sound of the conductor's voice, he plodded up the steps onto the train and found a seat by the window. When he looked out onto the platform, she was gone.

❦   ❦   ❦

It was late when Marcel returned home. Maman was surprisingly silent. Naturally, she had no way of knowing where he had been all day, but Marcel expected a bit of concerned prying, or at least a few curious questions. Instead, she warmed his dinner on the kitchen stove without a word and sat down across from him at the table, watching while he ate. Luc, and even Françoise, had already retired for the evening and the house was silent, except for the crackling of the fire in the stove.

Then, in a soft, almost wistful voice, Maman began to

reminisce aloud about Papa—how they met, their wedding, the early years together, Marcel's birth. She looked at Marcel as she spoke, and yet he had the impression she was looking right through him—beyond him. He had heard her tell it all before, but never quite like this.

"I miss him terribly, you know," she said finally, her eyes glistening.

"I know, Maman," Marcel replied hoarsely. "Me too."

Again the house fell silent. Maman rose from the table, gathered the empty dishes in her hands, and began to wash them in the basin. Then, turning back to Marcel, she spoke in a low, strained voice. "Don't make me any promises you can't keep, son," she said, "but please be careful. I couldn't bear to lose you too."

Chapter 11

Isabelle sat straight up, her wide eyes searching the inky blackness, her ears straining for the slightest sound. Her pulse throbbed in her temples and her whole body felt taut and damp. Instinctively, she drew her feet up under her, leaned forward, and reached her hands tentatively out into the dark to get her bearings.

Her muscles relaxed the instant she touched the pillows and blankets, and she let out a long, slow breath. She had been dreaming again, the same awful dream she'd had before. Just thinking about it made her shudder, for this time the rats had come close—too close. She shook her head angrily, trying to clear her mind of the fear that always accompanied the dream, then lay back against the feather pillows.

What a contrast this bed was to the one she had occupied just a week ago. This one was soft and clean, warm and dry—everything her last bed was not. It had been just an old straw mattress thrown on the cold, dirty, concrete floor or, when she was lucky, on a makeshift wooden bunk. The bunk was better only because it was farther from the rats and cockroaches and human filth. But the barracks-like room had been crowded much of the time, and there weren't enough bunks. She had stayed outside as much as possible to avoid the stench and the almost contagious depression of the room.

Isabelle tried once more to put those thoughts out of her mind. She hated the dark dreams that haunted her sleep. And she musn't allow the same fearful images to invade her waking hours. She tried to think of something more pleasant. It wasn't easy. Not much good had happened to her in recent months. Softly, she began to hum a little lullaby her mother had sung to her as a child. It helped, as it always had, to keep the dark thoughts at bay, and little by little the tension melted away. Her eyes, however, remained open for a long time.

❧   ❧   ❧

Before dawn, Isabelle was awakened by the sound of a car in the courtyard, just outside her window. Her heart was in her throat as she crept to the window and peered through a crack in the shutter. She could see nothing at all in the dark. A car door creaked open and closed, and then there was a sharp knock at the front door of the old farmhouse.

Moments later she could hear the old sisters talking in animated tones with a man. With trembling hands she donned her robe and opened the door to her room just a sliver to try to hear what was going on, but it was to no avail. The voices were still too low to make out what was being said, and they were all talking at once. Was it the police again? she wondered. Now she could hear footsteps coming in her direction. She shut the door as quickly and silently as she could and tiptoed toward the window.

As she unlatched the shutters and swung the window outward, she heard the door open behind her. Light flooded the room just as she was about to climb over the sill and out into the courtyard. The sound of her name stopped her.

"Isabelle, dear, it's only me." It was the half-whispered voice of Tante Solange.

Isabelle turned to see the tall woman, clad in her aging but elegant dressing gown, holding a lantern aloft and smiling sadly.

"What is it? Who's here?" she asked, her voice suddenly hoarse.

"It's our dear friend, the pastor," Tante Solange replied softly. "You musn't be afraid. I'm sure he'll see that you are kept quite safe."

Isabelle's thoughts tumbled over one another as she tried to make sense of Solange's words. Pastor? What did a pastor have to do with this? And what did Solange mean that he would keep her safe? Conversations with Tante Solange often puzzled her. "What are you trying to say?" she finally asked. "Do you mean that I am going to have to leave?"

In the few days since she had arrived at the sisters' house, she had come to appreciate both Solange and Marthe. They had treated her with respect, and they had seen to her comfort, often at the expense of their own. For the first time in months she had felt almost safe—almost. Now, fear flooded back into her mind at the thought of leaving.

Tante Marthe appeared just then behind Solange, and it was she who answered the question. "There is a rather good chance that the police know where you are, Isabelle. You won't be safe here anymore, so our friend has come to take you somewhere else—somewhere safe."

"But I don't want to—"

"Isabelle." Marthe's voice was low but firm. "They may be

here soon. You've got to go with him now, unless you want to run the risk of being sent back to that dreadful camp."

The thought of the camp—especially after last night's dream—was more than enough to jolt Isabelle. And although she was still afraid to leave the peace and comfort of the old sisters' farm, she was horrified at the prospect of being rearrested and sent back to Vénissieux.

"But what about you?" she asked the two sisters. "What if they find out I was here—that you hid me? What will happen to you?"

"Oh, don't you worry about us, child," Marthe said quickly. "We'll be fine. God has been watching over us for years. I'm sure He hasn't forgotten us now."

Isabelle looked at the older woman reproachfully. She had become accustomed to such talk, especially from Tante Marthe, but she really hoped someone with flesh and blood would look after her two elderly friends—just in case their God didn't come through.

❦ ❦ ❦

Jean-Claude Malfaire sat fuming in the back seat of the big black Renault as Dominique turned off the highway and into the foothills village of St. Egrève. After several days of investigating the Jew's escape, the inspector was about to bring this case to a close. It had not been easy, of course, or there would have been little need to call in a man of his talents. But there had been some rather annoying complications and delays.

He had called Dominique at midnight, wanting to make the arrest in the wee hours of the morning when it would be least expected. Dominique, however, had not answered the phone. Instead, his wife had picked up the receiver, saying that Dominique was not well. Could her husband call the inspector in a couple of hours if he were feeling better? Malfaire was furious, but could do little other than agree since Dominique had the car. And when Dominique finally did arrive, he hadn't looked all that ill, though in the dark it was difficult to tell.

Malfaire said little except to give directions. He knew he really couldn't blame Dominique. After all, if the man were ill, he was ill. It was just that this whole investigation had dragged on several days longer than he had expected, and he wanted to be done with it. He had other matters to attend to, not the least of which was the young terrorist, Pascal. If the information he had gathered about the Jew was reliable, he would soon be able to focus his energy on encouraging this Pascal fellow to tell what he knew about the Resistance.

Malfaire was pretty sure of his information. He smiled to himself as he recalled how freely the woman at the camp had talked once he lost his temper. She had become so frightened that she had told him things he hadn't even asked about, like the fact that the Karmazin woman was carrying a baby—another little Jew! And then he discovered that some high-minded doctor had requested that she be exempted from deportation to Drancy because of her pregnancy.

What the doctor had no way of knowing, of course, was that the exemption rules had been recently amended. It was now necessary to be *visibly* pregnant to avoid the train ride north. And since "visibly" was a term far less precise than "pregnant," the new rule could be interpreted to suit the needs of the authorities.

The fact that the doctor had argued so vigorously for an exemption hadn't apparently aroused the suspicions of Commandant LeFevre. But LeFevre was a fool. He had allowed Amitié Chrétienne, a group of religious do-gooders, to bring medical and material aid to the detainees on a regular basis. It had, he claimed, kept him from having to spend his meager budget on medicine and other items for people he was just going to deport anyway. But allowing such meddling was something Malfaire would never have permitted, had he been in charge.

Once he had established the link, however, between the doctor and the A.C., and figured out who the doctor was, it wasn't long before he figured out where the woman would likely be hiding.

"*Allez!*" he said to Dominique. "Can't you go any faster?"

"There's a car coming, Inspector," replied the driver. "I don't want to take a chance on hitting it—or going over the side."

The winding lane they were traveling in the hills outside St. Egrève hugged a high embankment on one side. On the other, only the narrow ribbon of the shoulder separated the roadbed from a ten-foot drop into a rushing stream. The car Dominique referred to was approaching rapidly, and appeared to be straddling the center of the road.

"Flash your high beams. He'll kill us, the fool!"

Dominique complied, and the car bearing down on them edged toward the embankment and squeezed past at the last possible moment. The driver looked straight ahead, almost as though he were alone on the road. Dominique let out a sigh of relief. Inspector Malfaire began cursing peasant motorists and didn't stop until the other car was out of sight.

⚜   ⚜   ⚜

"I think it's safe now, mademoiselle. You can sit up if you like."

Isabelle had been huddled on the floorboards of the pastor's ancient touring car since the moment they had seen the headlights coming up the hill toward them. The seat, though it wasn't all that comfortable, felt wonderful compared to the floor. The pastor, who had not yet volunteered his name, drove so furiously down the winding road that she had almost welcomed his request to duck out of sight. But in her condition, the cramped space quickly became almost unbearable.

"I'm sorry that was necessary," said the pastor without taking his eyes from the road, "but I'm pretty sure that the car we just passed belongs to the police. No one else would be out here before dawn. They're going to be surprised to find the tantes all alone, and they may come after us if they suspect that you were there. We need to put as much distance as possible between us and them. And quickly."

"Will they be all right?" Isabelle glanced nervously at the twisting road ahead.

"Tante Marthe and Tante Solange? I don't think they're in any great danger, now that you're gone."

"But they're old, and Tante Solange—well, she's rather—"

"Peculiar?" A grin erupted on the pastor's face. "Yes, I suppose you could say that. And she occasionally says things better left unsaid. But, all in all, she and Tante Marthe are utterly reliable. And amazingly resourceful for their age. You needn't worry about them."

"I can't help it. They are, as you say, resourceful. But also quite simple, don't you think?" her voice began to rise. "Tante Marthe thinks that God will help her, but she doesn't understand that the Nazis and the police are not concerned about this God. They do as they please. I know. I have seen it too often. And if you ask me, a God who allows such evil must be either pitiless or very weak. Or perhaps He's not there at all."

Isabelle was glad it was dark. The flush of anger she felt was immediately replaced by embarrassment at having spoken so to a total stranger. She wondered if he too felt the sting of her candor, being a pastor and all. She kept her eyes to the front, unwilling to look at him, expecting antipathy, or at least condescension. Instead, he let several moments pass in silence.

"I can understand why you might question God," he said finally, his voice calm. "Perhaps I would do the same if I were in your situation. I don't know. But I can assure you that Tante Marthe's view of God is shaped more by experience than naïveté. We French pride ourselves on being rational and scientific, and yet we do not find it the least bit naïve to believe in the wind, which we cannot see, or even describe satisfactorily. It is enough for us to feel its coolness against our faces, or to see tree boughs bend in silent witness to its passing. And our inability to adequately explain or understand the wind does not keep it from blowing. In many ways, I believe God is like that. We cannot see Him, but often we can feel His presence, and in a sense, if we look carefully, we can sometimes see where He has been."

It was Isabelle's turn to be silent. She had never heard such an analogy, and she wasn't sure she was prepared to accept it. The wind in her life seemed too much like a hurricane—leaving nothing but debris in its wake. No, there was a lot that still needed explaining. But it would have to wait. Right now she wanted to be safe more than she wanted to be right.

❦ ❦ ❦

The first rays of sunlight were inching their way over the peaks of the Belledone range as Pastor Charles Westphal coaxed his old touring car along Grenoble's riverside quay and up the hill toward the suburban village of Corenc. High above on the left, the fortress of the Bastille kept watch as it had for centuries. The warming light of the sunrise bathed the ancient stone walls and flowed slowly, relentlessly down the hillside toward the waking city.

Westphal shot a quick glance at the young woman who

sat silently on the seat beside him. In the light of day, dim as it yet was, she looked beautiful—even to a married, middle-aged minister. She was too thin, perhaps, but that was easily explained by the recent months of hardship and hunger. Even the clothes she wore, the faded hand-me-downs of two elderly sisters, did little to diminish the natural beauty of young Isabelle Karmazin. If she had been Protestant instead of Jewish, he mused, he would have had little trouble finding her a husband among the young men of his parish.

He urged the car up the winding street for about half a mile and then pulled onto a small, flat patch of grass lined with fir trees. The shadows were still deep, as the sunlight that spread down the hillside had not yet reached this point. Isabelle, silent for some time now, gave Charles Westphal a startled look.

"Why are we stopping here?" she asked. "I thought you were taking me somewhere safe."

"And that is exactly what I intend to do," replied Westphal, "but first we must make certain that 'somewhere' *is* indeed safe." As he spoke, he reached under the seat and drew out a leather case from which he pulled an old hand-held telescope.

"My grandfather gave this to me when I was just a little boy," Westphal said in response to Isabelle's apparent puzzlement. "He showed me how to use it to see the moon, the stars, and other planets. This morning, however, I'm hoping it will permit me to see something a bit closer to home."

He exited the car and motioned for Isabelle to follow, which she did, though at a short distance. The frost-encrusted grass crunched lightly under their shoes. They advanced as far as the row of fir trees that marked the end of the tiny plateau and the beginning of the steep descent to the valley floor. Charles turned to see Isabelle standing motionless, her eyes wide with wonder as she looked out over the city and beyond.

He couldn't suppress a little smile. The view from this spot never failed to inspire awe, even to one accustomed to it. But for this young woman from Paris, it must have seemed unimaginably beautiful.

Directly below lay the ancient Roman garrison city of Grenoble, built at the meeting place of the Drac and Isère rivers. Narrow streets and broad boulevards spread out across the plain in every direction. And yet, as a celebrated visitor once remarked, every lane, every avenue ended at the foot of a mountain. From this vantage point, as from below, it didn't seem too exaggerated a claim.

The sunlight, creeping out from beyond the Belledonne range, now spilled down the Chartreuse hillside where they stood, making both Charles and Isabelle squint in its brightness. Just a few more minutes, Charles remarked to himself, and the light would flood the valley floor and the city. He waited quietly, knowing he would need all the help he could get if the old telescope were to do him any good.

As sunshine seeped between the buildings and into the streets below, Charles Westphal began to scan the near quarter of the city with the telescope. The tiny magnified circle roamed the streets and plazas, pausing here and there until it finally came to rest on the entrance to the old stone *temple protestant*. He took a deep, slow breath and steadied the telescope.

"What do you see?" asked Isabelle. She was standing close behind him.

"Nothing, yet," he replied without moving. *Nothing at all, I pray,* he added silently.

Moments later, however, a slow movement caught his eye. A familiar-looking black sedan rounded the corner and braked to a stop in front of the church. Westphal's pulse quickened as he watched the driver emerge, walk around to the rear passenger door, and open it. A second man exited and strode purposefully toward the building while the driver leaned casually against the car. Charles, almost afraid to blink, continued to watch as the driver toyed idly with the car's outside mirror, causing it to reflect the morning sun intermittently.

Knowing that the church was locked up tight at this hour of the morning, Westphal was not surprised when the second man returned after only a few minutes and the car sped out of sight. But his heart sank as he realized that it was headed in the direction of the presbytery. He lowered the telescope slowly and turned to Isabelle.

"We'll have to change our plans," he said grimly. "The police are closer than I thought."

Chapter 12

Marcel Boussant sat alone on a bench across from Le Dauphin, the dingy little café-bar that faced the tree-lined Place de la Mairie, Domène's main square. He had risen early, fed the animals, then walked down the hill into the village to await the bus to Grenoble. According to the clock atop the church, it would be along in just a few minutes. He drummed his fingers on the tan valise which lay on the bench beside him and stared absently at the still-shuttered entrance to the bar.

His thoughts had been a jumble from the moment he awoke. Foremost in his mind was the need to get Jean Soulain's reports to Maurice Lambert as soon as possible. Lambert had instructed him to come to the regional art museum at ten for the exchange, since it would no longer be prudent to meet at the professor's home. Marcel wanted to make sure he wasn't late. The idea of holding on to the documents, whatever they signified, made him anxious.

Heightening his anxiety were his recollections of the peculiar German man he had met on the train. Who was he? Had he suspected anything? Why was he accompanying the police in Aix-les-Bains? Marcel had looked over his shoulder, figuratively as well as literally, for the entire return trip, fearing that somehow the man might be following.

And then there were the bittersweet thoughts of Anne. Posing as her lover had been the highlight of the trip: her warmth and softness close to his side, the sweetness of her mint-tinged breath as she kissed his cheek lightly. But the disillusionment of learning she was unattainable was mingled with the shame of knowing that he had let his feelings compete with his mission. He vowed to guard his heart more closely in the future.

Maman, of course, wanted him to guard more than just his heart, though she couldn't possibly know what he was doing. Much to his relief, she hadn't dared to ask, because he wouldn't have been able to lie to her. She knew that. Yet somehow, she apparently sensed he was taking risks with which she was uncomfortable. He couldn't decide if it were just the maternal instinct to protect, or something more. But he hated to see her hurt again.

The rumble of a diesel engine and the squeal of well-worn brakes combined to startle Marcel. He jerked upright just as the bus pulled to a stop in front of him. As the doors opened and the half-dozen early morning passengers descended the steps to the sidewalk, Marcel heard his name and felt a hand on his shoulder. He spun around to find Antoine LeBoeuf cheerfully holding up the tan valise.

"You weren't planning to leave this behind, were you?" said the old man, his eyes twinkling playfully.

Marcel went pale. "I, uh—I didn't see you standing there, Monsieur LeBoeuf." He reached out and took the valise, then clutched it tightly under one arm. "I guess I wasn't paying much attention."

"Well, we'd better get on the bus now, or it will leave us both behind."

Marcel swallowed hard. "You're taking the bus into Grenoble too?" He hoped he wouldn't have to field any questions about the valise, or what he had been up to lately.

"Do you think there'll be room?" Antoine teased as he followed Marcel up the steps into the empty bus. "Perhaps I should wait for the next one."

"I—I didn't mean—"

"Relax, my friend. I'm only joking. Why don't we find a seat near the back where we can talk?"

Marcel paid the fare and moved quickly toward the rear of the bus, finding a seat that wasn't too tattered. Buses to the outlying villages were always less well-maintained than those in the city center. Of course, since the invasion, little money had been spent on anything but the most necessary repairs, even in the city. He sat down next to a window and waited for his old friend.

As Antoine LeBoeuf made his way slowly down the aisle, Marcel watched several more people board, but they all sat near the front.

"So, how is your dear mother?" began LeBoeuf as he eased himself into the seat next to Marcel. "Is she well?"

The bus lurched into motion and Marcel relaxed a little. Perhaps talking to Antoine would do him good. It usually did. He would just have to be careful to avoid talking about his errands for Maurice Lambert. "She's in good health," he answered, then added hesitantly, "but I'm a little worried about her. Last night she seemed more discouraged about Papa than she has been in quite a while."

"Well, I should think that would be quite natural. Losing

someone you love is never easy, you know, and it sometimes takes years to come to terms with the idea. Besides, these are discouraging times. And with a son who's out looking for adventure—"

"Adventure? What do you mean by that?"

"I saw you board the train yesterday morning."

"Yes, well, I'm grown now. I can take the train if I like, can't I?" Marcel suddenly felt irritated. Sometimes Antoine knew too much.

"Of course you can, my friend. But people have eyes, you know. If they see you coming and going on the Geneva train, they'll assume you're up to something other than farming—maybe something they won't like."

"I can't help what people think."

"Perhaps not. But if our friend Carlini finds out, he may begin to wonder if you are working for another network—or for Vichy. That could mean more trouble for you than a bruise on your jaw."

"But that's ridiculous!" Marcel spoke so loudly that other passengers turned to stare. He raised his hand reflexively to his face, his fingers gently probing the diminishing tenderness. He lowered his voice again. "You know I don't like the Vichy government any more than you do. And what makes it any of Carlini's business where I go or what I do?"

"It's just the way he is."

"Well, I don't like it. First he has a man beaten—killed for all I know—and now you say he might make trouble for me too? Is he crazy?"

Antoine didn't answer right away, for by now the bus had reached the village of Gières where the driver pulled over to take on more passengers. Three women climbed the steps, paid the fare, and sat among the others near the front. Almost before they were seated, the bus accelerated carelessly onto the main road again.

"He's not crazy, Marcel," Antoine replied once the engine noises had risen to cloak his voice, "just power hungry. He wants control of the network so he can control the area. That's what the *boules* game and the beating were all about, as it turns out. I think Carlini saw the young stranger as a threat. He used the game—and me, obviously—to discredit him, and then he turned Bonet loose on him to make sure he never raised a challenge again."

"What are you going to do?"

"Do? I'm not sure I can do anything but try to minimize the damage he's likely to cause. He can't get rid of me easily, because I know too many people. But I'll have to be very careful from now on. And so will you."

"But I'm not really part of your network. You said as much yourself."

"That's true. But you were in the square the night of the *boules* game, and Carlini knows it. He also knows you followed Bonet when he beat up the stranger. He won't take any chances if he thinks you know too much. He'll have someone keep an eye on you. You can count on that."

Marcel felt his stomach start to churn slowly. His forehead beaded with sweat in spite of the fact that the bus was unheated. It had never occurred to him that his decision to cast his lot with Maurice Lambert might be compromised by the curiosity that had led to his midnight encounter with Emile Bonet's fist. And to think he had wanted to join Carlini's network as recently as last week!

He had to admit that he really hadn't known much about Carlini beyond what was public: son of immigrants, successful businessman, active in politics. Now, however, he felt as though he might know more than he wanted to know. Or perhaps he didn't yet know enough.

"What is Carlini really after?" he asked finally. "Does he really intend to strike at Vichy or the Germans?"

"In the beginning I thought so," replied LeBoeuf, "but now I'm not so sure. The reason the stranger came to us in the first place was to propose linking up with those networks loyal to General de Gaulle. He even promised money and weapons if we joined. But it would have meant submitting to a higher authority, and I don't think that sat well with Carlini. He wants to come out on top no matter which way things go, so he's not going to commit himself to anyone just yet."

"Well, if I stay out of his way I certainly can't be much of a threat to his plans, whatever they are." Marcel hoped he sounded more confident than he felt.

"Don't be too sure, my young friend," said Antoine as the bus slowed for city traffic. "Don't be too sure."

Both men were silent for several minutes. The throb of the diesel engine intensified Marcel's anxiety over Antoine's warning. Was the old man right? Should he rethink his commitment to Lambert and the rescuing of Jews? After all, he didn't actually know any Jews. And besides, there were plenty of others willing to help, weren't there?

Antoine interrupted his thoughts. "Whatever happened to joining our network?" he asked. "I seem to recall you being quite anxious to be a part of it, to strike a blow for the glory of France. Have things gotten a little too complicated for you?"

Marcel looked at his friend and wondered why Antoine seemed so confusing at times. Was this all a test of some sort? He hesitated before answering. "I—I think your way is—well, maybe not the only way to frustrate the Nazis and their fascist friends."

"And you've found another way?"

"Perhaps."

"A less dangerous way?"

Marcel didn't respond. The bus had reached his stop near

the prefecture on the Place de Verdun. He nodded good-bye to Antoine LeBoeuf and exited the bus, still clutching the tan valise. Crossing against the traffic to the center of the square, he entered a small park, an oasis of greenery and tranquility in the shadow of the imposing gray stone prefecture. He would wait there, alone with his thoughts and fears, until ten o'clock.

⚜   ⚜   ⚜

"I'm sorry," Isabelle said. "What did you say?" She shivered as the cool breeze tugged at the hem of the outdated dress she wore. So mesmerized had she been by the sight of the sunrise spilling over the mountains and down through the city streets that until now, she hadn't noticed the morning chill.

"The police," said Pastor Westphal. "Either they forced the tantes to tell them something, or they already knew where to come looking. They just left the church and headed in the direction of the presbytery, as near as I can tell."

"The presbytery?" Isabelle didn't understand.

"My home," he replied quietly. The muscle in his jaw twitched. "My wife is alone there with our children."

Isabelle felt a stab of pain in her stomach. She had never thought of the pastor's family—hadn't even considered that he might have one. And the poor tantes. *How frightened they must be,* she thought. She had come to know the feeling well, and she wondered if Pastor Westphal did too. She knew he must if he loved his wife the way she had loved Adam. And the children—did they have any idea that their father was in danger? That *they* were in danger?

Her hand reached instinctively for her belly, as if to comfort the tiny life inside. She couldn't help but notice the change in just the last week or so. Already her abdomen was more than faintly round, at least in her own eyes, the result of recent days of eating well.

"Are you all right?"

Isabelle blushed as she realized that the pastor was watching her, his expression a mixture of puzzlement and concern. "I'm fine," she said, letting her hand drop to her side. "Really, I am."

"Well, we can't stay here any longer, mademoiselle," he said. "But I think I know someplace where you'll be safe—at least for a while."

Isabelle followed along in silence as Charles Westphal led the way back to the car. *Safe.* She wondered if she would ever really feel safe again. Oh, there were safe moments, certainly. Ginette's apartment in Paris had been safe—for a night. And the tantes' house had been safe, if only for several days. But each time the safety had come to an abrupt end. And now, even this man of faith seemed to concede that perhaps permanent safety was beyond reach. A corner of her mouth curled cynically as she thought back to what he had said about the wind. She wondered if he knew which way it was blowing this time.

⚜   ⚜   ⚜

The regional art museum on the Rue de la Liberté, just off the Place de Verdun, opened at ten o'clock. Marcel entered as soon as the doors were unlocked. He wandered through the lower galleries, from one painting to another, finally coming to a halt before an enormous Rubens tableau. Gazing silently at the larger-than-life scene in the huge gilded frame, he wondered if Maurice Lambert had forgotten their appointment.

He was about to abandon hope when the sounds of restive children reached his ears, mingled with a distinctly adult shushing. He smiled to himself, imagining monsieur the curator trying to drive off a gaggle of unruly street urchins.

The smile disappeared, however, as he turned in the direction of the sounds. There, approaching him from across the gallery was Claudette Lambert, her energetic flock in tow.

"*Bonjour,* madame," Marcel greeted her as she drew close. Over her shoulder he could see the scowling curator, who had followed the Lambert clan into the gallery, standing with arms folded across his chest in the entry. Marcel lowered his voice to a whisper. "I was expecting your husband."

"Something has happened, Marcel." Madame Lambert also whispered, in deference to the curator. "The police came to the church early this morning."

"To the church? Why?"

"Pastor Westphal is part of the network. He helps us hide a number of Jews in the church basement."

Marcel was not surprised to learn that his outspoken pastor was doing more to help the Jews than just talk about their plight from his pulpit. "Was there trouble?"

"It was early enough that the doors were still locked. But Maurice was on his way over to check on the Jews in the basement when he saw what he thinks was a police car pulling away from the church. He's busy trying to make arrangements to move the refugees quickly before the police return. He asked me to come warn you—and to give you this." She glanced over her shoulder to find that the curator had disappeared, then handed Marcel a small white envelope. "Read it later," she said, and turned to go.

"Madame, wait. I almost forgot." Marcel reached into the valise and pulled out the pages that Jean Soulain had entrusted to him. "These are from Annecy," he said. "I guess your husband will know what they mean."

"Yes, of course." Claudette Lambert tucked the papers inside her coat and once again turned to leave. The children, wandering about the gallery, gathered at her whispered command and left just as noisily as they had entered.

⚜   ⚜   ⚜

Isabelle pressed her hand against her stomach, hoping that the growling noises she heard weren't audible to the pastor. He didn't seem to notice, or at least pretended not to. They had been sitting in his old touring car for hours, waiting in the woods for dusk to settle over the hills. There had been nothing to eat all day, and what water there was had long since grown warm and stale.

When she left the tantes' house in the predawn hours, Isabelle assumed that she was being taken directly to another hiding place. And judging from their intermittent conversations, that is what the pastor had thought too. Instead, once they had watched the sunrise over Grenoble, he had driven her to a remote wooded area to wait for nightfall. He felt it would be safer that way, he had said.

She chided herself for thinking so much about food. Until recently, hunger had seemed her constant companion. But the tantes had changed all that. *How quickly one can get used to having enough food,* she mused. Even before her narrow escape in July, having enough had gone from difficult to impossible. With all the shortages caused by the occupation and requisitions for the German war effort she, like everyone else, had been obliged to obtain coupons in order to buy food legally. From the outset, the daily ration of certain staples—twelve ounces of bread, an ounce and a half of meat, a half-ounce of sugar, a third-ounce of coffee, a quarter-ounce of cheese— seemed outrageous. And it had gotten worse as time went on. Now, as a fugitive, she had no way of obtaining the coupons.

"Getting hungry, mademoiselle?" asked the pastor suddenly.

Isabelle felt her face grow warm. Had he heard the growling? She nodded without looking at him. *"Oui,* a little."

"Then perhaps we should get started," he offered. "The sun has gone down. It will be dark soon."

The old car shuddered as the engine sprang to life. Isabelle shuddered too, partly from the chill evening air, but mostly because she was headed once more for an unfamiliar destination.

Within half an hour, the pastor turned the car off the rising mountain road and onto a narrow gravel track. A tightly shuttered stone house and ancient barn were visible in the glare of the headlights as he braked to a stop. When he extinguished the lights, however, they were plunged into near-total darkness.

"Wait here," he said quietly as he opened his door. "I'll be right back."

Isabelle strained to follow him with her eyes as he disappeared into the night, leaving her alone. *What if*—she didn't dare finish the thought. The growling hunger in her stomach was quickly becoming a twisting lump as bony fingers of fear tightened their grip. The car seemed to close in on her, and her breathing became labored.

Air! She was frantic for fresh air. Clutching at the door handle, she shouldered the door open and nearly tumbled to the ground in her rush to freedom.

Reaching out to break her fall, her hand brushed heavily across something warm and furry. The growl that followed seemed to come from deep inside the earth, a fearful sound that made her heart stop. Was it a dog or a wolf? Instinctively, she backed a few halting steps over the uneven ground, away from the rumbling beast that faced her.

"Léo! Enough!" The man's stern voice came from behind her, frightening her nearly as much as the growling. She spun around to face this new threat, but as she did so her right foot landed on the side of a loose stone. Her ankle rolled, she gave a startled little cry, and she lost her balance. Then, just when she expected to slam into the unforgiving ground, strong arms gathered her in and held her tight.

❧   ❧   ❧

Marcel had been standing in the doorway of the barn gazing at the night sky when the car pulled up beside the house. It was too dark to tell from that distance, but it looked like Pastor Westphal's old touring car. So when the driver got out and walked straight for the house, Marcel reached down for the milk bucket and the lantern he had extinguished, clucked for Léo to follow, and made his unhurried way over the familiar ground toward the house. He had been caught completely off guard by the woman tumbling from the car just as he approached.

"Are—are you all right, madame, er—uh, mademoiselle?" he stammered. He was glad it was dark. He had no idea who she was and he had never held a woman before.

"You gave me a fright!" Her tone made it sound more like an accusation than a statement of fact. "Put me down, monsieur, if you please."

Marcel understood—even shared—her embarrassment at the awkward situation. "Can you stand?" he asked as he lowered her to her feet.

"Why, of course—" her assertion was cut short by a gasp of pain as she attempted to put her weight on her right ankle.

"Perhaps I'd better carry you into the house," he offered, and tightened his grip around her.

"But, this man—the pastor—said to wait—" she began.

So, it *was* Pastor Westphal. Why would he bring a woman out to the house late at night, unless—"I'm sure he wouldn't want to see you injured," Marcel interrupted. He had cut his own thoughts short as well, not sure he was ready for the answer. He climbed the steps and pushed open the front door, careful not to jolt his soft, warm cargo in the process.

Everyone in the room turned and gaped as Marcel entered and headed for the settee. He deposited the woman carefully to avoid further injury to her ankle, then turned to greet Pastor Westphal. Four pairs of eyes bored into him, leaving him speechless.

Westphal was the first to speak. "So, Marcel, I see you've met our friend." He winked and added, "I didn't expect you to carry her into the house, you know."

Marcel felt his face grow warm. "I—that is, she—I think Léo frightened her and she nearly fell and hurt herself," he blurted. "She couldn't walk and I was just trying to help."

Maman and Françoise rushed immediately to Isabelle. "Are you all right, mademoiselle?" asked Maman. "Where does it hurt?"

Marcel looked on as mother and sister worked to make the young woman comfortable. Seeing her for the first time in the light, he couldn't help but stare. Straight brown hair, intense gray-green eyes, full lips. And she was young. Too young for the strangely antique coat and dress she wore. They looked as though they had been borrowed from her grandmother's closet. But even the strange clothes could not diminish the fact that she was undeniably beautiful.

"Who is she?" he asked softly, turning to the pastor, "and what is she doing here?"

Westphal put his finger to his lips and nodded toward Luc, who stood transfixed by the sight of the newcomer. Then the pastor motioned for Marcel to follow him into the kitchen.

"So, who is she, Pastor?" Marcel asked again when he had closed the door behind them.

"Her name is Isabelle Karmazin," he said. "Our people helped her escape from the camp at Vénissieux recently, and she's been hiding out with Tante Marthe and her sister."

Marcel smiled. That explained where the clothes had come from.

"Unfortunately," Pastor Westphal continued, "the police somehow got wind of things and I had to move her during the night. I thought perhaps this would be a good place to hide her for a while."

The smile faded from Marcel's face. So this was why they had come after dark. The woman was a Jew on the run, and that meant danger—not only for her, but now also for his family. "I'm sorry, Pastor," he said, "but I'm not sure that's such a good idea. I'm more than willing to do my part to help the Jews, but when it comes to my family—well, you understand, don't you? Can't you find some other place to hide her?"

"Perhaps you should let us decide what risks we're willing to take, Marcel."

Neither Marcel nor Charles Westphal had heard the door open. Evelyne Boussant, quickly joined by Françoise and young Luc, had a look of calm determination in her eyes. "I know you only mean to protect us," she continued, "but we're not helpless, you know."

"But, Maman," Marcel began. "Last night you said—"

"Last night I was feeling melancholy about losing your father, and I was thinking mostly of myself. But Marcel, I can't bring him back by holding on to you any more than you can take his place by protecting us. If Papa were here, you know what he would say, don't you?"

Marcel looked at the floor and said nothing. He knew very well what Papa would say, and yet it didn't quell his rising fear— fear that they would all regret the choice they were making.

Chapter 13

L'Argentine was full to overflowing when Inspector Jean-Claude Malfaire arrived around 8 o'clock. He shouldered his way past the patrons who lined the foyer waiting for an available table, and hailed the maître d'.

"A quiet table for two, if you please," he said more loudly than necessary, "and quickly!"

Stunned by the impoliteness of the request, the diminutive maître d' nonetheless maintained his dignity. "One moment, monsieur," he said. "If monsieur would be so kind as to give me his name, I would be most happy to accommodate him as quickly as possible. Your name, monsieur?"

Malfaire was in no mood to be trifled with by someone's employee. He had spent an unpleasant day in Grenoble, searching in vain for the elusive Mademoiselle Karmazin. He was tired, hungry, and in need of a few glasses of good wine. "I do not wish to wait until all these people have eaten," he sputtered, turning to indicate the waiting patrons behind him with a sweep of his hand. "Where's Ricard? I want to see Ricard."

"Monsieur Ricard is in the kitchen at this hour, as usual, monsieur."

"Get him." Malfaire's glare was meant to intimidate the little man. "Tell him Inspector Malfaire would like a table. Now."

The maître d' scurried off to the kitchen and returned almost immediately, followed by Pierre Ricard who removed his apron as he walked. Ricard's L'Argentine had become one of the more prominent dining spots along the Boulevard Gambetta, and he gave the appearance of a man who was prospering in spite of the times. Tall and dark, he moved with ballroom grace.

"*Cher* Inspector, what a pleasure to see you." The words fairly oozed from his thin smile as he extended his hand. "What good fortune brings you to our humble city?"

"Nothing you'd care about, Ricard." Malfaire halfheartedly received the hand that was offered. "Now, how about that table?"

"But of course, Inspector. Right this way." Chef Ricard ignored the insulting behavior, spun on his heel, and led the inspector through the maze of tables, amid a chorus of muffled complaints and curses. Several of the waiting patrons gathered their wraps and stormed out of the restaurant.

When the maître d' came to the table a few moments later, he was accompanied by another man, well-dressed, and a bit older than Malfaire.

"He said you would wish to see him, *monsieur l'inspecteur,*" the little man said, polite to a fault.

Malfaire, his glass to his lips, waived the maître d' away and the newcomer to a chair with his free hand. Not until the man had been seated did he lower the glass and speak. "Grenoble, the walnut capital of France," he said in mock admiration. "I'm familiar with the cakes and candies, but I had no idea you could make such good wine from nuts, Carlini."

"Careful, Inspector," the man smiled, indicating the bottle on the table. "It doesn't take much walnut wine to make your head spin."

"Oh, let's not exaggerate," Malfaire scoffed as he drained the dark liquid from his glass "A little wine never harmed anyone—least of all me." He reached for a menu. "Order whatever you like," he said. "It's on the house."

"On the house, Inspector? Are you a friend of Chef Ricard?"

"Pierre Ricard is a crook. I caught him laundering money when he owned a restaurant in Lyons. He was never officially arrested and he's always shown the proper gratitude, if you know what I mean. But this is the first time I've been to see him since he came to Grenoble. I hope he can still cook." He chuckled at that, and René Carlini joined in politely.

When they had ordered, Malfaire glanced around and then leaned forward, his elbows on the table. "I need some information," he said in a low voice, "and I'm willing to pay handsomely to get it."

Carlini pulled a pack of filterless cigarettes from his pocket and offered one to Jean-Claude Malfaire. When Malfaire declined, he took a cigarette, placed it between his lips, and leaned forward until the end touched the flame of the candle on the table. Once it was lit, he sat back, exhaled a thin cloud into the air, and smiled. "Was the last information I gave you of any value?"

Malfaire nodded slowly but did not return the smile. He reached for his wine glass again and took a drink before speaking. "This Pascal fellow was just where you said he'd be, Carlini. But I have to say I thought he would be in better condition. He was so badly beaten he was unable to talk for a few days. And I've been too occupied with another case to deal with him properly. I'm sure he'll cooperate when I get around to him, though. They usually do, sooner or later." He smiled again. *This wine really is very good,* he reflected silently. *I'm beginning to feel better already.*

"So how can I help you this time, Inspector?"

"Tell me how you knew where to find Pascal." He wondered if the dapper businessman had inflicted Pascal's injuries personally, but saw no point in asking. He knew Carlini was no match for him, and that was all that mattered.

"Well, I make it my business to know people who know things," Carlini said, tapping the cinders from his cigarette on the edge of the ash tray, "and they tell me things I want to know. I don't remember exactly, but someone who saw what happened must have told me about it, and as you know, I told you."

The inspector had danced this dance before and knew that it could go on all evening. If it weren't for the wine and his need for more information, he would have had the man thrown out into the street. Of course, he had no jurisdiction in Grenoble and Carlini knew it. So he decided to explain himself clearly—as clearly as he could at this point.

"I have reason to believe that someone in this area may be harboring or assisting fugitive Jews," he began. "There have been a couple of escapes from the detention camp at Vénissieux lately, one in August and one just about a week ago. This last time they claimed that a woman escaped by herself, something I find hard to believe. I'm sure she had help, and I want to find out from whom."

"What makes you think I could help you here in Grenoble, Inspector? Isn't Lyons a more likely lair for the foxes you're hunting?"

"We're checking leads everywhere, of course. But something we found in a Lyons doctor's office tipped us off to the possibility that there may be a connection here."

"What did you find?"

Malfaire's anger flared briefly at the idea that a snitch like Carlini should be asking *him* questions. He was the Inspector. *He* should be *asking* the questions, not answering them! But then again, maybe he stood a better chance of getting what he wanted if he yielded a bit of harmless information. What could it hurt? The wine was working its calming magic and he decided to answer.

"Two scribbled addresses that didn't match any of his patient files."

"And why is that so curious?"

"Because this doctor has been to Vénissieux recently to examine the prison—er, I mean, detainees. And within forty-eight hours of each of his last two visits an escape has occurred. That alone makes everything about him curious, Monsieur Carlini."

"Have you arrested him?"

Malfaire gave a short laugh. "Arrest him? He's a prominent doctor and I don't have enough evidence—at least not yet. But, I find anyone willing to help these pathetic Jews more than a little suspicious. If I watch him carefully, sooner or later I'll catch him doing something illegal. In the meantime, if he's free to come and go, I believe he can help me."

"Help you in what way?"

"I've requested that he attend this Pascal fellow." Malfaire smiled with satisfaction at his cleverness. *At least I have some power in Lyons,* he thought. Reaching for the bottle, he refilled his glass, then raised it in a salute before downing at least half of its contents. "That way," he continued after swiping the back of his sleeve across his mouth, "I can keep an eye on them both. And if I'm right, and the doctor is engaged in some sort of subversion, he won't be able to resist telling our friend Pascal all about it. And maybe Pascal will divulge information to the doctor. Then I'll have them both, you see, and the proof I need to get rid of them." He clutched his throat with his hand.

"Very clever, Inspector. You simply eavesdrop on their conversations until they incriminate themselves. *Chapeaux bas!* No wonder you are the inspector of choice in such difficult cases."

Malfaire exulted in such praise. The man might be a snitch, but he obviously recognized talent. Perhaps he had underestimated Carlini's potential usefulness. After all, he hadn't become successful in business by being stupid.

The waiter returned with a plate of *crudités* for each of them, and half a *baguette* which had been sliced into diagonal pieces. Neither man spoke until the waiter had moved on to another table.

"So then, Inspector, what exactly do you wish me to discover for you?"

"Yes, of course." Malfaire was feeling more and more tired. He had momentarily forgotten where all this talk was leading. "These addresses we found in the doctor's office—one was a farmhouse in the mountains near here where two old spinsters live. Either it was a mistake or these old crones are very clever. In any case, we found nothing.

"The other address was the *temple protestant* here in the city. I tried to speak to the pastor today, but he was neither at the *temple* nor the presbytery all day. His wife said he was out for the day but wouldn't say where. As it turns out, our good doctor is also Protestant. And since many of their pastors speak out against Marshal Pétain's policies (may God preserve him) I think there might be some connection." He raised his glass again at the mention of Pétain's name.

"You know of course that many Catholics are also opposed to the government policies, Inspector," said Carlini as he stubbed out his cigarette and attacked his plate of *crudités*.

"Yes, I'm aware of that," replied Malfaire, "but I think it's because they do not truly appreciate the situation France is in. When they understand, they'll support the marshal. I'm sure of it. The Protestants, on the other hand, don't wish to understand. They're belligerent. They always have been."

"I see. And if I find out who is hiding these escaped Jews?"

"I'll pay you double what I paid you last time."

Carlini looked thoughtful for a few moments. "Perhaps you could do something else for me instead," he said.

"Something other than money?" Malfaire's surprise at the idea registered easily on his face. "And what would that be?"

"Well, I was thinking that you might use your influence with the local *gendarmes*. They, uh—they seem to want to restrict my ability to buy and sell freely."

"The black market, eh?" Malfaire grinned wickedly. "You just find me the Jews and I'll see to it that no one bothers you again."

René Carlini reached his hand across the table. "You can count on it, Inspector," he said as he clasped Malfaire's hand. "I won't let you down."

"No, Monsieur Carlini," replied the inspector, "I'm sure you won't."

Chapter 14

An uncertain edginess gnawed at Isabelle as she sat at the Boussant family table, awaiting the start of the late evening meal. The pastor had gone, declining a hasty dinner invitation. He had seemed preoccupied with thoughts of his family throughout the day, and Isabelle wasn't surprised when he hurried off soon after learning that the Boussants were willing to keep her. He had been more than kind, and she hoped his wife and children wouldn't suffer on account of her.

Her uneasiness wasn't really due to the pastor's departure. She had expected that. But she had overheard just enough of the discussion in the kitchen to know that the decision to hide her here on the Boussant farm wasn't unanimous. Evelyne Boussant had assured her that they would do everything in their power to ensure her safety, then had busied herself with dinner preparations. Françoise had tended carefully to Isabelle's swollen ankle, trying to make her comfortable. Young Luc had just stared at her, mostly. She couldn't help but notice, however, that Marcel had kept his distance after having carried her so gallantly into the house. She felt strangely disappointed by that.

The smell of food reminded her of just how hungry she had been all day, and she was relieved when Madame Boussant and Françoise announced that everything was ready. The bread, cheese, and vegetable soup were simple fare, but there appeared to be more than enough for the five of them. Evelyne and Françoise sat on one side of the table facing the two boys. Isabelle sat at the end nearest Marcel and his sister, and tried to keep her sore ankle out of the way of table legs and human feet.

"Maman," asked Luc when they were all seated, "may I pray?"

"Yes, Luc," his mother replied, "go ahead."

Isabelle rolled her eyes as the whole family bowed reverently, waiting for little Luc to begin.

"God," he said, his eyes scrunched tightly shut, "it sounds like this nice Jewish lady is in a lot of trouble. I hope You can do something about that, because we sure don't want anything bad to happen to her like it did to our Papa. Please bring him home safe, if You can. Oh, and thank You for the good food we're going to eat. Amen."

Isabelle daubed quickly at her moist eyes as a chorus of "amens" echoed around the table. Somehow, the boy's prayer was not at all what she had expected. It had seemed so simple, as if he were talking to someone, yet the words did not seem at all childish. And it was the first time she had ever heard anyone mention her name in a prayer—at least in her presence—though she suspected the tantes prayed for her every day. For the first time since leaving Paris, she wondered if Ginette Dumas did too. She flashed Luc a weak smile and the boy beamed in return.

Conversation was light and sporadic during dinner. Perhaps the Boussants were just as nervous as Isabelle. Or perhaps they were just sensitive to her uneasiness. Whatever the reason, little was said beyond talk of the weather and the food on the table until everyone had nearly finished. It was Luc, unsurprisingly, who could no longer contain himself.

"Who are you hiding from, mademoiselle?" he asked, bursting the bubble of near-silence that had enveloped the table.

"Luc! What an awful question!" Evelyne Boussant's gaze was nearly as stern as her tone. Françoise colored with embarrassment, and even Marcel was unable to mask his dismay at his little brother's impertinence.

"It's all right, madame," Isabelle said, rescuing Luc from his mother's indignation. She had decided not to volunteer the fact that she was no longer "mademoiselle" in spite of her youth. There would be time for that later. She turned to the eager young boy. "Not everyone in France likes people like me," she began.

"Do you mean Jews?"

"Yes, Luc. And some of them want to send us away so there will be no more Jews in France. If they find me, I'll have to go away too."

"Like Jean Calvin?" Luc asked.

Isabelle looked at Madame Boussant. "I—I'm afraid I don't understand," she said.

"In the sixteenth century there were those who wished to reform the church. People were often hounded from their homes, and some were even tortured and killed for their beliefs. Many, including Jean Calvin, one of the early Protestant leaders, fled to Switzerland."

"So, Protestants too know what it is to be persecuted," said Isabelle slowly. "Is that why you are helping me, madame?"

"I suppose that's part of it. But for us it's more basic than that. As Christians, we have a duty to help those in need, especially the descendants of Abraham. And although we're happy to do so, we're only doing what we believe is required of us."

"I don't mean to insult you, madame," Isabelle said as calmly as she could, "but I have seen far too much suffering to put much faith in Christian charity. Especially when there are some who use religion to justify their hatred."

"I won't deny that what you say is true. But not everyone who is religious is a Christian. We all have to answer for our own sins."

Isabelle didn't respond aloud, for she knew that even among the Jews there were those who followed few of the teachings of the rabbis, yet laid vigorous claim, as she herself did, to being Jewish. *Perhaps,* she thought self-consciously, *Christians and Jews are not so different in that respect.*

Marcel excused himself and went outside, taking his jacket from a peg on the wall on his way out the door. Evelyne rose to begin clearing the dishes from the table. "Françoise," she said, "perhaps you should show Mademoiselle Karmazin where she'll be sleeping. I imagine she must be very tired after such a long day."

"You can sleep in my room," said Françoise cheerfully. She had said little up until now, though she had not seemed unfriendly. "If you like," she added with an awkward glance at Isabelle's borrowed dress, "you can wear some of my clothes, mademoiselle."

Isabelle looked down at the floppy yellow dress the tantes had given her. It had been stylish once, she was sure. Probably before she was born. It suddenly struck her how ridiculous it must have made her look. She put her hand to her mouth in an unsuccessful attempt to suppress a giggle. Françoise's puzzled look gave way to a soft chuckle, and then she too was giggling. Luc and Evelyne joined in a moment later, and soon all four were swept away in gales of laughter. Their mirth was like a dam bursting, washing away the pent-up tension in its flood.

In the midst of it all, Isabelle realized that she hadn't really let go since she lost Adam. It was refreshing while it lasted.

❧   ❧   ❧

Marcel leaned back against the outer stone wall of the old barn, chewing on the stalk of a wild reed and staring through the frosty darkness at the house. Two tiny slivers of light escaped through the shuttered windows, visible only when viewed from precisely where he stood. Anyone passing by on the road to Revel would have missed the farm altogether on this moonless, cloudy October night.

Léo lay resting nearby, ears pricking at every sound. Though he never strayed from the confines of the farm, he was seldom far from Marcel as he performed his daily chores with the animals. Tonight, the cows had been milked and fed along with the goats, rabbits, and chickens. Yet Marcel remained outdoors, and Léo stayed with him.

Marcel pulled his collar up against the chill autumn breeze and remarked to himself how dramatically the weather had changed in just a matter of days. Winter would be along soon enough, and there were still too many things to do to prepare for it. Far too little wood was split, and he had put off the final mowing of the lower field for too long. Perhaps he would make a start tomorrow. It would have to be soon in any case, for it seemed likely to be a long winter—especially with another mouth to feed.

Maman was right of course to take in the girl. But it was hard not to be disappointed by her decision. In Papa's absence, it was up to Marcel to provide for, and to protect, the family. Granted, Maman had always participated in managing the farm. She had run it almost single-handedly a time or two when Papa had taken temporary work down at the paper mill in Domène. And she had managed successfully and without complaint, just as she did now that Papa was gone.

But it had never been Marcel's intent that his family should even know about his covert assistance to Professor Lambert, let alone that they should become his accomplices. When he rode the train to Annecy, he had been afraid; there was no doubt about that. But his fear had been for his own safety—neat and uncomplicated. He had considered his family perfectly safe. Next time—if there were a next time—he would have much more to worry about, including this beautiful intruder.

That she was beautiful, he couldn't deny. She seemed undernourished to be sure, and oddly dressed, but striking nonetheless. He found himself comparing her to Anne, but quickly dismissed such thoughts. The moments spent in Anne's presence had stirred feelings that shouldn't exist for a total stranger, no matter her beauty.

If this woman were other than a Jew, or if she were somehow less attractive, perhaps things could have continued as before—the way he had planned. But her Jewish blood put the family at increased risk. And as for her beauty—well, he would just have to stop thinking about that.

Dear God, why does everything have to be so complicated?

❧   ❧   ❧

"I hope your mother wasn't offended," Isabelle told Françoise when the two had retired for the evening. She had declined Evelyne's invitation to join the Boussants for their customary evening prayers. Marcel had not returned to the house since dinner, but Françoise and Luc had sat with their mother in the *salon* for a brief reading of the Scriptures, after which Evelyne had offered an earnest prayer. Isabelle had listened to every word from the safety of Françoise's tiny bedroom.

"Of course not, mademoiselle," Françoise replied. "She just wanted you to know that you are welcome to join us any time. But if it makes you feel uncomfortable—well, that's up to you."

Isabelle had to admit that it made her very uncomfortable. It wasn't so much the Scripture reading. She had heard something similar before—one of the ancient Hebrew prophets, she guessed—on one of the rare occasions when she had accompanied Papa to the synagogue. But when she overheard the family's matter-of-fact prayers for her protection and well-being, she felt confused and embarrassed: confused as to why they would ask for the protection they were in fact providing; embarrassed at the thought that, having just met, they already cared for her.

"Listen, Françoise," she said, anxious to change the subject, "would you mind calling me Isabelle? I'm really not much older than you are, and, well, I'd like it if you would." She paused and took a slow breath. "Besides," she added, "I'm really not a mademoiselle anyway. I was married for nearly two years."

There. She had said it. But somehow, Françoise didn't look as surprised as she'd expected.

"I thought so," said Françoise, "but I didn't want to say anything."

"But how—how could you tell?" Isabelle frowned. She had told no one—not the pastor, nor the tantes, nor anyone else.

"You have a mark on your finger where you once wore a ring. I just assumed it was a wedding ring."

Isabelle looked immediately at her left hand. There on her ring finger was the scar left by the guard at Vénissieux who had taken by force the last object of value she owned. He had threatened to take *her* if she didn't give up the gold band, and he had finished by impatiently tearing it from her finger. She had avoided looking at her hand for more than a month in an attempt to forget. And now, Françoise had innocently dredged it up again.

"Yes," Isabelle said finally, still staring at the scar, "my husband gave me a beautiful gold ring." Then half-aloud, half to herself, she added, "Now it's gone . . . and so is he."

They were both silent for a long moment.

"Dead?" Françoise asked, her voice little more than a whisper.

Isabelle nodded, her eyes on the floor. "Since May. The Nazis—in Paris."

"I'm so sorry, Isabelle." Françoise paused. "And your baby?"

Isabelle's eyebrows arched in surprise as she looked up.

A wan smile crept across Françoise's face. "You can't hide it forever, you know. Maman said she could tell the minute my brother carried you into the house."

Isabelle blushed at the memory. *Had he too noticed?*

"Even the boys will notice eventually," Françoise added with a conspiratorial wink, as if she had read Isabelle's thoughts. "But things like that usually take them a while."

❧ ❧ ❧

Lying on her back on one side of the large double bed, Isabelle was unable to sleep. Soft, slow breathing came from the unconscious Françoise who lay facing away from her. Sharing such close quarters with someone she had only just met put her in mind of the cramped room she had been obliged to share at Vénissieux. There, darkness was often accompanied by a cacophony of disquieting sounds, which added to the constant assault of foul odors. Yet somehow, sleep had nearly always come for at least a few hours each night. Here, in the quiet and simple comfort of this country home, sleep seemed far away, exhausted though she was.

Sliding from beneath the covers and out of the creaking four-poster bed, Isabelle shrugged into the soft cotton robe Françoise had laid out for her. Perhaps a cool drink of water would help her fall asleep. Careful not to make any unnecessary sound, she opened the door and padded barefoot down the worn oak stairs to the *salon*. A soft glow illuminated the corner of the room just beyond the front door. A kerosene lamp burned dimly as if on the verge of going out altogether. Grateful for the light, Isabelle began crossing the cold tiles toward the kitchen, then pulled up short, her breath catching in her throat.

She hadn't heard a sound from upstairs, and had expected to find the downstairs dark and deserted. But there, sprawled on the settee, his eyes closed and an open book lying tent-like on his chest, lay Marcel. A blanket, unused, lay folded at his feet. His right arm hung limply over the edge of the cushion, fingertips brushing the braided oval rug.

Isabelle didn't take another step. Instead, she folded her arms and gazed at the man—looking hardly more than a youth as he slept—who apparently preferred that she not stay in this house. His dark, unruly hair framed a boyishly handsome face, and his lanky frame belied the strength she had felt when he had saved her from falling and carried her easily in his arms.

But there was something else—the book. Yes, the book. How many nights had Adam fallen asleep in a chair with an open book, studying until his eyelids sagged shut? She would wake him gently, and taking him by the hand, lead him to bed. Or sometimes she would cover him with a blanket where he was, kiss him gently on the forehead, and leave his slumber undisturbed. If she could only race back to Paris, climb the stairs to their apartment two at a time, find Adam waiting, and know that this had all been a very bad dream—

A tear spilled onto her cheek and rolled nearly to the corner of her mouth before she realized it had fallen. She closed her eyes tightly in an effort to hold back the flood—and to keep from looking at this unsettling man. Unsuccessful, she buried her face in her hands and sobbed, silently cursing Marcel Boussant for reminding her of Adam Karmazin.

When her emotions had subsided, Isabelle swiped haphazardly at her tear-stained face with the sleeve of her robe. Fatigue was rapidly overtaking her, and she longed to sleep. In the end, she forgot why she had come downstairs in the first place. But before she left the *salon,* she walked slowly to the settee and unfolded the blanket that lay at Marcel's feet. Careful not to wake him, she covered him with it. Then she extinguished the flickering lamp and tiptoed up the stairs to bed.

Chapter 15

It was nearly noon by the time Marcel reached Lyons' *temple protestant* in the Rue Lanterne. He passed through the main entrance into the nearly empty sanctuary, and headed straight to the third row of pews from the back. Taking a seat along the right side aisle, he waited, shifting nervously on the hard oak seat, unsure of what, if anything, he should do next.

The envelope given him by Madame Lambert in the art museum the week before, had contained a second, smaller sealed envelope he was to deliver to Pastor de Pury, as well as the details for his arrival at this meeting. Beyond that, the instructions had been vague.

He was anxious to meet Roland de Pury, not just because he was curious as to the nature of this mission. He had heard a lot about de Pury and his work. Like Pastor Westphal, de Pury had decided early on that resistance to the official anti-Semitism was a necessity. In order to be as effective as possible, he and several other Protestant leaders joined forces with some prominent Catholics in an effort known as Amitié Chrétienne. Believing that impassivity in the face of the suffering of the Jews was a denial of Christian faith, pastors, priests, and laymen alike set out to give witness to their faith by offering assistance to the Jews.

Pastor Westphal was actively involved in CIMADE, an organization of Protestant youth movements with goals similar to Amitié Chrétienne, and the two groups cooperated freely. Both groups had official status, recognized by the Vichy government as providers of social services to Jewish refugees. But both operated clandestine operations as well, hiding Jews and providing escape routes wherever possible.

Maurice Lambert, though an active CIMADE participant, had suggested that Marcel remain free of organizational ties, at least for the time being. With the recent escapes from various detention camps, including Vénissieux, he explained, the relief agencies were coming under increasing scrutiny and official criticism. Lambert felt it might be wiser for Marcel to keep his participation unannounced and unofficial, particularly since his opportunities for involvement in the officially sanctioned social services would be limited at best. Marcel had readily agreed.

The church bells tolled twelve noon, and still no one appeared to direct Marcel to Pastor Roland de Pury. He scanned the sanctuary, noting the half-dozen scattered parishioners, none of whom seemed aware of his presence. Most were older women who appeared either lost in thought or bowed in prayer. Marcel wondered how many were mourning the loss of a son or a brother, or pleading for their safe return. Bowing his head, he silently reminded the Almighty of his own father, hoping against hope that after all this time, Albert Boussant was only missing and not dead.

Marcel's eyes snapped open at the sound of hard-soled

shoes clomping oddly in a slow, muffled rhythm on the hard floor tiles behind him. He held his breath as the footsteps neared where he sat, then shuffled into the pew behind him. Silence—and the permeating odor of garlic. *What now?* he wondered, almost afraid to move. *Do I wait, or do I say something?* He reproached Maurice Lambert for not being more explicit in his instructions. He would feel like a complete fool if he said something only to find that this unknown person had no idea what he was talking about—or worse, was sent by someone other than de Pury.

"Don't turn around."

His mind had been racing so fast, trying to decide what to do, that Marcel nearly missed the whispered command, carried on garlic-laden breath.

"Come to the side alley at quarter past noon. *Et faite très attention.*"

Marcel nodded stiffly but said nothing. He wasn't sure he liked the tone of the last words, whispered or not, and he nearly turned to face the stranger in spite of the request not to do so. He wasn't a child, after all, he fumed to himself. And he was well aware of the need to be careful.

A light rustle of clothing interrupted his riled thoughts, followed by the same soft, rhythmic clomping fading away toward the main entrance to the church.

When the church bells rang the quarter hour, Marcel rose and strode quickly out into the bright midday sun. The fall air was comfortably warm at this time of day, unlike the often frosty mornings and chill evenings, and Marcel carried his winter coat under his arm. He squinted as he looked the length of the Rue Lanterne, first one way and then the other, to ensure that he wasn't being watched or followed. Garlic-breath was right, of course, to be concerned about safety, but it still galled Marcel that his youthfulness gave the impression that he was careless. But for now, he decided, he needed his wits about him, and he really couldn't afford the luxury of whining—even if he had cause.

He peered cautiously around the corner of the *temple* and into the narrow passageway where the interplay of sun and shadows made instant, opposing demands on his still-squinting eyes. He felt the rough cobblestones beneath his feet as he ventured tentatively into the alley. As far as he could see, no one awaited him. The farther he went the more he wondered if he had gotten the wrong alley, or if someone were simply toying with him.

The scraping sound of a boot or shoe on stone startled Marcel, and he froze in his tracks. Then slowly, he turned to see who was behind him. He could see no one. Taking a step or two back in the direction of the Rue Lanterne, he peered apprehensively into each shadow, each doorway, but saw nothing. He took another couple of steps and stopped, willing someone to appear. Still nothing. *Maybe I'm imagining things,* he grumped to himself, *or maybe it's only a cat.* Still, just to be safe, he reached into the coat he had been carrying and wrapped his fingers around the cool metal of the Lebel revolver, making sure the safety was off. A momentary surge of power pushed back the nagging cloud of fear. Pistol in hand, he pressed forward again, this time a little more boldly, but with an occasional glance over his shoulder just in case.

When at one such glance he caught a slight movement out of the corner of his eye, Marcel whirled about and found himself facing a man not more than fifteen feet away. The man froze at the sight of the pistol, which Marcel had instinctively leveled at his chest.

"What's going on here? Why are you following me?" Even Marcel was surprised by the intensity in his voice.

The man, his eyes wide and round, raised his hands slowly above his head, but said nothing. Marcel took two deliberate paces forward. The man's eyes widened, his hands stretched higher.

"Who are you? What do you wmmpphh—"

The air was hammered from Marcel's lungs by huge arms that encircled him from behind, cutting him off in mid-sentence and lifting him off the ground. His upper arms were pinned to his sides, and he could feel the hot, labored breath on the back of his neck and head. The pungent odor of garlic left little doubt as to who this faceless assailant might be. He wanted to cry out for help, to invoke Pastor de Pury's name, but he couldn't catch his breath.

Just as Marcel was sure he would be crushed, the man in front of him lunged for the gun. Marcel had maintained his grip on it, but in the few seconds since the attack began, hadn't thought to use it. Now, in desperation, he flexed his wrist and raised the muzzle to point directly into the chest of the onrushing stranger, squeezing the trigger just as the man clawed at the barrel of the gun.

Thrown violently sideways, Marcel slammed into a wooden door along one side of the alley, shoulder first, sending splinters of pain up and down his arm and into his neck. Off-balance, he tottered away from the door only to fall into the opposite wall. Half-dazed, he slid straight down to sit on the ground.

The man he had faced was sprawled headlong on the cobblestones just a few feet away, still clutching the gun, barrel first, in hands that had begun to ooze blood. *So,* Marcel's thoughts ground much too slowly, *I must have hit him! But the report—I don't remember hearing the gun fire!* He didn't have long to dwell on it, as the fallen man's companion, a giant in peasant clothes and wearing a farmer's wooden *sabots* on his feet, knelt beside his friend and gently turned him onto his back.

The prone man smiled. "Ooh-la! That was too close," he said, shaking his head slowly as he sat up unassisted. "I thought for sure he had me."

The big man playfully cuffed him. "Eh, well, you had me going there, Hugue. I thought you were really hurt. What's all the blood from?"

"Must have snagged the front sight on the gun when I grabbed it," the one called Hugue replied. "Cut my hand pretty good. Lucky for me I got to him before he had a chance to fire. Otherwise, I'd be bleeding a good bit more."

So the gun didn't fire after all? Marcel was sure he had pulled the trigger.

"Ha! Lucky for you I grabbed him when I did, or you might be dead."

"Let's not exaggerate now, Pepin," said Hugue. "I think he was just scared. I don't mind telling you that I sure was. But I don't really think he was planning to shoot me—not at first, anyway."

"We'll see, my friend. We'll see." Having said that, Pepin the giant stood up and walked over to the still-seated Marcel. Reaching down, he grabbed hold of Marcel's shirt with his huge, fleshy hands, pulled him effortlessly to his feet, and leaned him against the wall.

"So. Are you all right, *petit?*" he asked as he released his grip on Marcel's shirt.

Marcel, still reeling from being slammed into the door, stared at the biggest man he had ever seen and wanted to run as fast and as far away as he could. But when he turned his head slowly toward the Rue Lanterne, Hugue had risen to his feet, blocking any possible escape. And Hugue was holding the gun. Marcel blinked hard, trying to unscramble his thoughts. Finally, he turned back to the giant.

"I—I'm okay," he said softly, and without much conviction. He didn't really know whether it were true or not, but he didn't know what else to say.

"Eh, well, you gave us quite a scare," Pepin chuckled, and clapped him on the shoulder. "What are you doing with a gun, anyway, *petit?*"

Marcel winced. His shoulder had nearly splintered a door only moments ago, and already the big clown was pounding on it. And calling him *petit,* of all things! Marcel could feel his face and neck grow warm as he groped for an answer he wouldn't regret giving.

"Trying to protect myself," he said, a bitter edge in his voice. "And apparently with good reason." He turned to point an accusing finger at Hugue. "Why was he sneaking up behind me?"

Pepin glared at the suddenly sheepish Hugue before turning back to Marcel. He had a strange expression on his face. "You'd better come with me," he said flatly. "Pastor de Pury is expecting you, *petit.* This," he shook his head and indicated the alley and a forlorn Hugue with a broad sweep of his massive arm, "this was not supposed to happen." With that, he spun on his wooden-soled heel and strode off down the alley.

Marcel started after him, his thoughts racing, his temperature rising. *So, this wasn't supposed to happen, was it? Was that all he could say? Not, "I'm sorry you nearly shot my stupid friend"? Or how about "excuse me for crushing your ribcage"?* Aloud he blurted, "And you can stop calling me *'petit'!*"

The man called Pepin only chuckled.

Marcel followed the giant through a side door near the end of the alley. Once inside, they took a narrow set of stairs down into the dank basement of the *temple protestant.* A door opened to the right at the foot of the stairs, and here the big man ushered Marcel into a dimly lit and sparsely furnished gray room. A solitary man sat across the room behind a long table.

"Ah, there you are," said the lone man, standing to his

feet. "I was beginning to think you weren't coming."

"We, uh—there was a little problem," began Pepin. Seeing the man's suddenly furrowed brow, he hurried on. "Nothing serious, Pastor. I'm sure he wasn't followed."

Marcel rolled his eyes, then caught himself. So, this was Roland de Pury. He hardly looked like the type to employ ruffians. Too intellectual.

"I'm Pastor de Pury," the man said, extending his hand.

Marcel grasped his hand firmly, nodded politely, but said nothing.

"Are you all right, young man?" asked the pastor. "You look as if you've been in a wrestling match."

Marcel looked down at his rumpled clothes, straightening them self-consciously and tucking his shirt back into his trousers. A button was missing, but he couldn't do anything about that for the moment. He cast a sideways glance at the towering Pepin. "I'm fine, monsieur *le pasteur,*" he replied at length. "Please pardon my appearance."

"Well then," said de Pury, motioning to one of the straightback wooden chairs at the table, "sit while I explain what I need from you. Have you been to Lyons before?"

Marcel shook his head, though he didn't see why it mattered. He wasn't planning on spending time in town. He figured he would deliver his message and bring back some additional forged papers. Lyons was reported to be the center for that sort of thing.

"Perfect," de Pury went on. "Most of our people are becoming too easily recognized. Professor Lambert was very kind to send you." Looking up he added, "Pepin, see if you can't find this young man some decent clothes. He's going to need them."

Pepin left without a word. Marcel listened as carefully as he could while Pastor de Pury laid out his plans.

He hadn't really known what to expect on this trip, but so far it was nothing like his first mission. The trip to Annecy had been perfectly simple: deliver false papers, return with reports. Sure, there had been some tense moments, thanks to Franz the friendly German. And as for complications, well, there was Anne, to be sure. But next time, he would know better than to let his feelings interfere with his work.

❧   ❧   ❧

Two hours later, Marcel walked out of the alley into the Rue Lanterne, wearing a charcoal wool suit and white shirt, and pushing a green bicycle. In addition to the fifty francs Pastor de Pury had supplied, his pocket contained a forged ID card in the name of Pierre Roux, a twenty-two-year-old student. Though he had expected to transport false papers from time to time as necessary, the idea of actually *using* a phony document was unnerving. He hoped he wouldn't need it.

A hundred yards from the alley and the church, Marcel mounted the bike and unhurriedly pedaled through the busy streets of Lyons. The capital of the French silk and textile trade, the sprawling city dated to before the birth of Christ. Like Grenoble, it had been built at the meeting of two rivers, the Saône and the Rhône, and bridges abounded. But Marcel's eyes were captivated by the stately basilica of Notre Dame de Fourvière, high atop the hill which overlooked the city center, and by the nearby Tour Métallique, a scaled-down replica of the Eiffel Tower.

Lyons' size alone was enough to hold Marcel's interest. Never had he visited a city so large, teeming with people of every sort. The Jewish population in particular had burgeoned since the debacle of 1940, in part because the city lay in the unoccupied zone. But virtually every nationality was represented in this bustling, colorful city.

Unfortunately, on this day Marcel had more to think about than the splendors of France's third largest city. Along with the money and forged ID, Pastor de Pury had given him explicit instructions for a rendezvous with a certain doctor. The doctor, it seemed, had some critical information for the pastor and his friends in the Resistance, but he was being watched so closely that he dared not meet anyone with known ties to de Pury or official links to groups like Amitié Chrétienne.

Not wanting to carry written directions to the doctor's office, and being unfamiliar with the city, Marcel had been told the address and the simplest route there. He in turn had repeated each detail back to the pastor to ensure that he hadn't missed anything. Even so, recalling each turn, each intersection, with all the fascinating distractions of a strange, big city, took a great deal of effort.

Finally, at 14 Rue Saint Georges, he parked his bicycle inside the gate and climbed the steps to the front door of what appeared to be a combination residence/office. The small metal plaque on the door read *Dr. R. Billot, médecin.* He rang the bell and waited.

A moment later the door was opened by a slender woman who looked to Marcel to be about fifty. She arched her eyebrows quizzically, but said nothing.

"*Bonjour,* madame," he said when he realized she was waiting for him to speak. "I have an appointment with Dr. Billot at three-thirty. Is he in?"

"Please come in," she said, smiling politely.

Marcel couldn't decide if the woman were the doctor's receptionist, housekeeper, or wife, by the almost plain way she dressed. Whoever she was, she shut the door carefully behind him, and stepped to where an appointment book lay open on a nearby table. She traced half the length of a page with her forefinger.

"Your name?"

"Roux. Pierre Roux." He hoped she hadn't noticed his slight hesitation.

If she noticed she didn't let on. "Please take a seat, Monsieur Roux. I'll tell him you've arrived." She disappeared through a set of double doors.

The doctor, a short man with salt-and-pepper hair, appeared presently and motioned for Marcel to join him in an adjacent examining room. As soon as the door was closed, Dr. Billot shoved a piece of paper into Marcel's hands. In hastily scrawled letters it said, *Act like a patient. Assume that everything will be overheard.*

"So, Monsieur Roux," he said amiably once Marcel had seated himself on the examining table, "what seems to be the trouble?"

Marcel smiled at the irony of the situation. "It's my shoulder, doctor. It feels like one giant bruise."

❧   ❧   ❧

The sun was warm on his back as Marcel pedaled the green bicycle back through the busy heart of Lyons. He had altered his return route somewhat, in order to attract less attention as Pastor de Pury had suggested. He needn't have bothered, he told himself. What with all the traffic, no one was likely to pay him any attention, anyway. But it did permit him to see more of the city.

The appointment with Dr. Billot had not lasted long. He had given Marcel a poultice for his bruised shoulder, but only after some convincing that the injury was not part of the act. The doctor also gave him a small envelope, his hand signals making it clear that Marcel should deliver it to Pastor de Pury without delay. Then he had excused himself, saying that he needed to make his rounds at the hospital. He was pleasant enough, Marcel remarked to himself, but seemed rather in a hurry—so much so that he failed to collect his fee!

Marcel patted the breast pocket of the suit jacket he wore, just to reassure himself that the envelope was still there. The poultice, wrapped carefully and in a lower front pocket, would have to wait until later to work its healing magic. His shoulder felt increasingly sore and a bit stiff, but he was still able to grasp the handlebar without much difficulty. Tomorrow, he knew, was likely to be a different story. But tomorrow he would be home.

Home, however, hadn't been the same for several days, he mused with a wry smile. The arrival of Isabelle Karmazin had certainly had its effect on the Boussant family. He was even willing to admit that she was pleasant to be around in spite of his early misgivings—misgivings he hadn't entirely relinquished. She was beautiful, yes, but there was more to it than just that. There was something about her that made him want to be near her—and which kept him at a distance at the same time. But the more he thought about her, the more confused he felt.

For one thing, she was pregnant, though for the moment that fact certainly didn't detract from her beauty. He hadn't noticed at first because she was so thin that her clothes easily disguised the shape of her body. And he might still be unaware except that Françoise had told him. She had also told him that Isabelle had been married, which only added to his confusion.

What was it about this young Jewish widow who bore another man's child that intrigued him so? It made no sense at all, and yet she was seldom far from his thoughts. Trying to sort out his feelings had always been difficult, but now seemed harder than ever before. Was it pity he felt, or just some naïve infatuation?

A flurry of movement in the street ahead caught Marcel's eye and broke into his thoughts. From a distance he couldn't make out what it was, other than several people running about. He quickened his pace and soon was close enough to see that some sort of fight had erupted in the middle of the street. Closer still, he realized with a sick feeling in the pit of his stomach that it was not a fight at all, but three youths in turn kicking and punching a man, while a small crowd stood watching.

It wasn't just any man, either, Marcel was quick to note, but an old Jew, judging by the long beard and traditional garb. *Why doesn't someone stop this?* he wanted to shout. But no one made a move to help the man who by then was on hands and knees, trying to crawl away from his attackers. And suddenly, all Marcel could think of was Isabelle. What if it were *her* being beaten and abused? What if *she* were being hounded by these barbarians, simply for being a Jew?

Without another thought, Marcel raised up off the saddle and pedaled furiously, bearing down on the teenage thugs. When the nearest one dodged the speeding bike at the last second, Marcel's forearm caught him under the chin with a sickening crunch. The blow hurled him backward off his feet, but knocked the bike off balance in the process.

Leaping from the bike before it went down, Marcel kept his feet and charged back toward the remaining two. Caught completely off guard, the second one stood with his feet planted and swung wildly as Marcel lowered his head and butted him squarely in the solar plexus. The air exploded from the hooligan's lungs as Marcel's body weight and momentum slammed him to the pavement. Marcel rolled off the motionless body and clambered quickly to his feet, eyes searching the street for the last of the gang.

"What do you think you're doing here?" a faceless man in the crowd bellowed. "This is none of your business!"

"Leave them alone!" shrilled a woman from behind him. "It's just a stinking Jew! We should get rid of all of them."

Unable to spot the third assailant immediately, Marcel ignored the catcalls as best he could and helped the old man to his feet. Alert, but shaken, the old-timer just stared at him. So, this was the treatment Jews could expect! No wonder Isabelle was in hiding.

"Go on," he said to the man. "Go on home. These people are nothing but cowards." His whole body trembled with the adrenaline that surged through his veins.

As the old Jew limped awkwardly away, Marcel's eye caught a flash of motion to his left, an instant too late. He brought his left arm up protectively and threw his right fist across his body with every ounce of energy he could summon. His knuckles crashed full into the fleshy face of the third youth. His attacker crumpled from the force of the blow and dropped heavily to the street, a large knife falling from his hand to skitter uselessly across the pavement. Marcel stared at it numbly, his body still trembling. Had he seen a weapon earlier, he might not have— A sudden searing pain in his left forearm screamed for attention. Gritting his teeth he dropped his gaze to where a six-inch slash in the sleeve of the charcoal suit jacket was beginning to seep blood—his blood. The crazy fool had stabbed him!

Chapter 16

Armand Moreau sat on the edge of his hospital bed, absently stroking a scruffy growth of beard and staring out the fourth floor window. He was trying to enjoy the deep blue of the afternoon sky and the occasional puffy white cloud floating by. Other than the tops of several neighboring buildings, the sky was his only view of the outside world.

It hadn't always been that way. In the beginning, of course, he couldn't speak, or even sit up. Little by agonizing little, however, he had managed to regain much of his strength. Dr. Billot had seen to that. And by the end of the first week, after several days of the inspector's absence, Armand had begun to seriously consider making an escape. He had pried open the window and was on the verge of crawling out onto the ledge when his guard had entered the room unexpectedly. Now a handcuff chafed his wrist and linked him securely to the iron bed.

Dr. Billot had vigorously protested the handcuff, but to no avail. The event had, however, precipitated a visit from

Inspector Malfaire. For the first time, Malfaire had been physical with him. Repeated slaps to the face with his gloved hand reopened some of the cuts in Armand's mouth. But strangely, the inspector postponed his earlier threat to transfer Armand to St. Joseph's prison. All Armand could imagine was that Malfaire was up to something. He was definitely not the sort to make magnanimous gestures.

From the day they locked it on, Armand had explored ways to rid himself of the handcuff: soap on his wrist and hand, filing the cuff on the edge of the bedframe, picking the lock with any small object he could find. Nothing worked, however, and eventually he stopped trying. And since the guard searched Dr. Billot each time he came, there was little hope of outside help. So now Armand watched the sky, counted the two hundred sixteen floor tiles over and over, and mentally prepared himself for the inevitable transfer to prison.

Dr. Billot was late. At least it seemed that way to Armand. He had no way to tell time precisely, but he had come to know the clockwork of the hospital routine, and he was sure that Billot should have been there already. The doctor had been marvelous, coaching him as to how to get the most out of each injury in order to prolong his stay—that is until it became clear that Armand's recovery was not the only factor keeping him there. Even the doctor agreed that Malfaire was up to something.

In the meantime, the two had developed a rapport which Armand considered vital to his sanity. He had sensed early on that Billot could be trusted. The doctor's warning about Nurse Previn had proved too true. She had begun prying about Armand's "work" two days after he arrived, and had even confided that she knew his name was Pascal. When she got nothing out of him, she stopped coming 'round. A shame, Armand decided, in spite of the trouble she represented. She could have been such pleasant company.

Lately he and Billot had been having some interesting discussions about the doctor's relief work among Jewish refugees. Though Armand genuinely admired his new friend's humanitarian bent, he argued that an armed overthrow of the Nazi occupiers would be a lot more effective. That way problems like racism could be solved at their core—or so it seemed to him. Of course, he tried to choose his words carefully and well. He didn't wish to say—and hoped he hadn't already said—anything that might be repeated, and perhaps misinterpreted, however innocently. But the brief conversations with the amiable doctor had become a bright spot in his increasingly dreary existence.

Billot should have been here by now.

❦   ❦   ❦

"Traitor! France is for the French!"

"Jew-lover! Go to the devil—and take all these dirty Jews with you!"

The old Jew's assailants had hobbled off and the small crowd dispersed, yet some couldn't resist hurling a few last epithets in Marcel's direction. He heard them, but just barely. Cradling his wounded left arm close to his side, he paced the street in a confused circle, searching vainly for some clue as to where he was.

The pain in his arm had intensified, throbbing until it felt as though someone were pounding out a rhythm on it. He had drawn the sleeve tightly around the wound to try to stem the flow of blood, but he realized that he would have to get some medical attention soon. Still, he needed to deliver the doctor's note. He was certain that it contained some sort of encrypted message for Pastor de Pury, and he did not want, under any circumstances, to fail in this simple mission. But the pain was beginning to crowd everything else from his mind.

"Monsieur! Monsieur!" A young woman came running up to him with hands outstretched. "Please, monsieur, let me help you. You're bleeding!"

Marcel offered no resistance as she began to remove his jacket. He winced and groaned as she gingerly pulled the sleeve off over his tender wound. The once-white shirt underneath was bright crimson from the wrist to the elbow. With strong, nimble fingers the woman unbuttoned the cuff, then tore the sleeve completely off just above the elbow, exposing an ugly, gaping gash.

While Marcel watched dumbly, the unidentified woman removed her apron. Wrapping it carefully around his forearm, she secured the makeshift bandage firmly in place with the apron strings.

"There," she said as she tied the last knot. "It's not much, but it ought to get you as far as the hospital. *Allez,* go on, before those hoodlums return with some of their friends."

"My bicycle—"

"My husband is bringing it over," she said, turning to where a man approached, a grocer, judging by the way he dressed, pushing the green *vélo*. "Ah, here he is. Now go, *quickly!*"

The husband held the bicycle steady while Marcel swung his leg over the saddle. He would have to ride using only one hand, as his crudely bandaged left arm would be useless. The grocer's wife tucked his suit jacket into the rack that straddled the bike's rear wheel.

"Allez, mon brave," said the sturdy grocer, his brow furrowed with concern. He aimed a thick finger down the street. "The hospital is just two blocks ahead and then right a quarter kilometer. You'll be there in no time."

"Merci bien," Marcel grunted through clenched teeth as he pushed off. He was a little shaky with only one good arm, and the bike wobbled badly at first. But little by little he found his

rhythm, focusing all his energy on pedaling to the hospital. The envelope would just have to wait.

❧   ❧   ❧

Marcel's jaw was clenched so tightly it ached, and his forehead and upper lip were damp with perspiration. His eyes, squinting against the glare of the emergency ward lights, followed every tentative move the young medical intern made as he swabbed the wound clean. Marcel knew it would be over before too long, but so far the cure seemed worse than the cut. As if to confirm his misgivings, the cautious intern then applied a liberal quantity of iodine, leaving Marcel sucking in gulps of air and fighting back stinging tears.

"Aiiee!" he breathed through clenched teeth. "Can't you find a way to increase the pain?"

His sarcasm was apparently lost on the doctor, who continued silently, if slowly, with his work. Marcel wished he could hurry it up a little. In addition to the intensity of the pain, the room had seemed increasingly cool since his arrival, and he couldn't remember what he had done with his jacket. Maybe someone could find it for him. Or maybe they could bring him a blanket.

"I—I—I'm cold," he mumbled, finally. The doctor didn't look up. "Do you think someone could get my jacket for me?"

The response was as cool as the room temperature. "This is a hospital, monsieur, not a hotel—in spite of the name."

Marcel couldn't decide whether to smile or frown. The Hôpital Hôtel-Dieu, the sign out front had said. Was this intern a complete cad, or did he have a sense of humor after all?

"Let's put this over you," said a vaguely familiar voice. In the glare of the overhead lights Marcel was unable to see who it was that draped a wool blanket over him. "There," the man added when he had finished, "that ought to warm you up a little."

For the first time, the intern looked up. In fact, he almost stood up. *"Bonjour,* Dr. Billot," he said with obvious deference. "How are you this afternoon?"

"Somewhat better than your patient, from what I can see, doctor. Let's have a look."

Marcel felt what little color remained drain from his face. "Wh-what are you d-doing here, Dr. Billot?" he stammered. *What if he mentions the envelope?*

"I guess I must have gotten lost, Mr. Roux," the doctor replied drily, using the phony name Marcel had given at his office earlier. "Actually, I was making my rounds when I noticed your name on the admission list."

"Dr. Billot, if this is a patient of yours, perhaps you'd like to take over from here. I've cleansed and disinfected the wound and was just preparing to suture. Shall I assist you?"

"Thank you, no, doctor," said Billot. "That won't be necessary. Looks pretty straightforward to me."

The intern took his leave then, and Billot sat down in his place and began to suture the wound. "Pretty nasty gash, *mon ami,*" he said softly. "How did it happen?"

Marcel told him everything—except the part about not delivering the envelope yet—while Dr. Billot plied his needle and scissors.

"I just got so angry seeing those hoodlums terrorizing that old man," Marcel concluded. "Maybe too angry for my own good." He looked down at the even row of sutures that now closed the knife wound tightly.

"There is such a thing as righteous anger," said Billot, "and there is no reason to regret defending an old man," he looked around quickly and lowered his voice. "And all the more since he was a Jew. There aren't many people willing to do such an honorable deed for a Jew, you know."

"I couldn't very well have just stood by," Marcel protested. "He was just an innocent old man. But you would have thought he was some sort of ogre by the vicious way those people acted—even the bystanders. And that made me even more angry."

"I know just what you mean," said Billot. "I've seen it myself many times."

"What do you do about it?"

"Whatever is necessary."

Dr. Billot was silent for several moments. When at last he spoke again, he leaned in close, his voice a mere whisper. "Were you able to deliver the envelope?"

Marcel thought for a moment that he would be sick. What could he say? Eyes down, he slowly shook his head from side to side.

"Do you still have it?"

Marcel raised his head and looked into the doctor's anxious face. "I think so," he said softly. "It was in my jacket pocket. But after the fight—well, now I'm not even sure where my jacket is."

Billot's expression turned thoughtful and he patted Marcel's knee. "Maybe we can find another way. Wait here," he continued, smiling to himself. "I'll see if I can find you a decent shirt somewhere. I'd like you to visit a patient of mine, but I can't have you looking like a vagabond, now can I?" Without waiting for a reply he turned and strode from the room.

❦   ❦   ❦

The fourth floor corridor was quiet compared to the emergency ward. A gray-haired man in bedclothes and robe shuffled along with the help of a cane, while a couple of nurses scurried in and out of patient wards. Near the top of the stairs, a tired-looking woman with gnarled hands swabbed the floor tiles with a long-handled mop.

Marcel followed Dr. Billot as he turned right past the mop bucket and sauntered down the corridor. It seemed that the smell of antiseptic was stronger here. Perhaps he was just inhaling more deeply due to climbing the steps. Billot had said little, other than to point out the whereabouts of several of his patients as well as the ailments with which they suffered. Each time, of course, Marcel thought they had reached their destination, only to have the doctor continue on up the staircase.

As they approached the end of the corridor it looked deserted—all except for the policeman who slouched in his chair across from the last door on the left. *Strange,* thought Marcel. *What's a policeman doing here?* From a distance he looked like a raw recruit, and the closer they came the younger he looked. He must have been bored, as he balanced his semi-automatic pistol in first one hand, then the other. Only when Marcel and the doctor were within twenty feet did the sound of their footsteps catch his attention. The officer rose hastily to his feet, shoving the sidearm carelessly into his belted holster and straightening the *képi* on his head.

The look of alarm on his face turned almost instantly to one of embarrassment as he recognized Dr. Billot. "Ah, *monsieur le docteur,*" he said somewhat sheepishly, "I wasn't expecting anyone. You're here rather late, aren't you?"

"Yes, well, I've been rather busy seeing other patients. In fact," Billot turned to indicate Marcel, "this is one of them. He suffered an unfortunate knife attack this afternoon at the hands of some ruffians not far from here. I'm telling you, it's getting to where a person doesn't feel safe walking the streets anymore." He looked again at Marcel, concern etched on his face. "Show him what they did to you, Pierre."

Marcel stared dumbly at the doctor. Was he kidding? And if not, what was he trying to prove? Why would Billot, who had earlier passed him secret—and presumably illegal—information, now chat so freely with a policeman? Obviously, he was missing something.

"I—uh, well, I—" Marcel wanted to say something but nothing came readily to mind.

"Here," Billot jumped in, taking Marcel's wrist in his hand, "roll up your sleeve and let him see." There was an almost impatient edge to his voice.

Marcel obliged slowly, still dumbfounded by this unexpected drama. He winced as the sleeve caught on the ends of the first sutures, tugging painfully at his wound. Little by little, he uncovered the entire length of the puffy purplish incision.

The young police officer grimaced as he examined the thirty-three stitches. *"Punaise,"* he exhaled through clenched teeth, "that's one nasty slice you've got there. How did you—" He stopped short and clutched at his empty holster. The color drained from his face in one brief instant.

"Don't make a sound and do exactly as I tell you, monsieur, or you may soon require medical attention as well." While Marcel had unveiled his wound, Billot had moved around behind the guard and snatched the pistol from its unbuttoned holster. Now he prodded him toward the door of room 422, the room he had been guarding.

"Come on, before someone sees us!" hissed Billot when Marcel didn't follow immediately.

Marcel whirled to look down the long corridor. Only a couple of people were visible, neither of which were paying any attention to what was happening outside number 422. He darted in after Billot to find a third man, dressed only in a hospital gown and sporting a scruffy beard, handcuffed to the bed.

Finally, Marcel understood—and he was furious. The good doctor was using him to help a complete stranger escape from the Lyons police. The perfect end to an otherwise uneventful day. *What was he thinking?*

"Listen, Doctor, I don't think you understand—"

"Look, Pierre," the doctor said brusquely as he pushed the ashen-faced officer into the corner, "if we don't get this over with and get out of here quickly, we're all dead. That's what *you* need to understand." To the officer he added, "Take off your uniform and throw it on the bed."

The policeman stood frozen.

"Now!" Billot commanded as he raised the semiautomatic to point at the man's face.

This time Marcel froze as well. He was still fuming, but he had decided against doing anything foolish. Billot looked deadly serious.

Without saying a word, the officer began pulling at buttons, shedding first his shirt and then his boots and trousers. When he had finished, he stood shivering, dressed only in his skivvies and *képi*.

The bearded man quickly rifled through the trousers, grinning when he came up with the shiny piece of metal that would liberate him from his handcuff. He inserted the key, turned it, and nearly leaped off the bed in his excitement at being free.

"Come over here," he said, still smiling, and waggling a finger at the officer. "It's your turn."

"You'll never get away with this," the officer protested weakly, but shut up when Billot took a step toward him with the gun raised. Defeated, he sat down uneasily on the edge of the bed, allowing the bearded man in the hospital gown to snap the handcuff closed on his wrist. A look of relief spread over his face, however, when Billot lowered the gun.

Shedding his flimsy gown, the bearded man pulled on the uniform trousers and shirt, stepped into the boots, and buckled on the empty holster. Finally, he plucked the *képi* from the officer's head and placed it on his own.

"*Voila,*" he said, smirking and standing at attention. "I'm a regular *gardien de la paix.*"

"Not with a beard," Marcel blurted out. "You'll give yourself away for sure, looking like that." He had kept quiet until now, standing near the door, expecting the entire police force to break it down at any moment. But he wasn't about to let such an obvious *faux pas* go unnoticed.

"The boy is right," Billot said impatiently as he fished a pair of surgical scissors and a folding straight-razor out of his coat pocket. "Get rid of the beard."

Minutes later, the beard lay in pieces in the basin, and the man's face, though red and nicked in a place or two, looked much more in keeping with his uniform. And despite the uniform, it was a face Marcel knew he would recognize anywhere.

Chapter 17

I diot!"

Inspector Jean-Claude Malfaire saw it with his own eyes, yet he couldn't quite comprehend how it could be possible.

"You stupid fool! How could you let this happen?"

The guard didn't answer, even though the gag had been removed from his mouth. He looked pathetic sitting on the bed in his underwear, slowly coaxing the circulation back into his wrists and ankles. The handcuff that had tethered him to the head of the iron bedframe had been released. So had the strips of bedsheets that had tightly bound his other wrist to his feet.

Malfaire fought down the urge to slap him.

"What happened?" he screamed, pushing his face close to the cringing officer. "Answer me or I'll have your job!"

"There were two of them," the guard began in a weak voice. His hands trembled as he spoke.

"Speak up, Durand. I hate it when you whine."

"Dr. Billot, Inspector. He came just like he always does, only later. And he had another man with him. They pointed a gun at me—"

"What? You let that weasel Billot bring someone else in

here? Just what exactly were you thinking, Durand? Or were you too busy ogling the nurses again?"

"No, Inspector, I—"

"Shut up, Durand," Malfaire interrupted. He turned to one of the other two officers who seemed to be trying to stay out of his way. "Get some officers over to Billot's place immediately. I want him arrested. If he's not there," he added as the officer started for the door, "arrest his wife. That'll make him think twice about running."

Malfaire could feel his carefully laid plans crumbling beneath him. He had been on the brink of arresting Billot, waiting for the right moment. The terrorist Pascal remained in the hospital as bait, just to give the doctor a little more rope with which to tighten his own noose. And now they had both slipped from his grasp. If his superiors caught wind of this before he'd had a chance to rectify the situation, his never-fail reputation would be in serious trouble. He had to act quickly or risk losing some of the autonomy and status he had worked so hard to achieve.

"Durand," he said evenly, "you have one chance to redeem yourself. I want you to meet us at the Gare de Perrache as soon as you can find some clothes. We'll check all the trains leaving tonight. Unless I miss my guess, our friend Pascal will try to get out of the city tonight. In the meantime, I'll need to know exactly what this other man looks like."

He jotted a few details in a little notebook as Durand, still shaken, described the lanky, dark-haired accomplice as best he could remember, right down to the stitches on his left arm.

❦   ❦   ❦

Marcel took a deep breath before leading the way toward the *temple protestant* along a narrow side street near the Rue

Lanterne. He hoped someone would still be around at this late hour. Night was falling rapidly and he would need help if he were going to leave the city before morning. He didn't want to spend a minute more than necessary in Lyons after what had happened at the hospital.

He had to admit that Billot's plan had worked beautifully. His pride still smarted a little at being so thoroughly duped into participating, but discovering that the stranger from the *boules* game was alive and well—and now free—had taken some of the sting out of it. There was still a thing or two he would like to say to the doctor, but that would have to wait for another time and place. Dr. Billot had dropped him and the escapee in the neighborhood and sped off toward his office.

Trailing along behind Marcel was the man Dr. Billot referred to as Pascal. Dark like Marcel, but older, he was dressed in the uniform of a Lyons city policeman, *képi* on his head, holstered pistol at his waist. He seemed to be having trouble keeping up, and it was clear to Marcel that he was either uncomfortable impersonating a police officer, or the boots didn't fit him very well.

"Wait here," Marcel told him as they approached the side alley near the church. "I'll go in first to see if anyone is around. Stay out of sight."

Pascal complied without a word, and Marcel eased his lanky frame around the corner and into the shadowy darkness of the alley. He stopped to listen for a moment, but hearing nothing, he stepped tentatively forward. After ten paces he stopped to listen again. Still nothing. Again he moved forward, repeating the process. As he began the third time, Pepin the giant stepped out of the shadows and blocked his path.

"*Bon soir, petit,*" he said without humor. "What brings you back at this hour?"

"It's kind of a long story," Marcel replied, letting the *petit* remark pass unchallenged. "I need to see the pastor. Is he in tonight?"

Pepin ignored the question. "Why did you bring the police with you?"

Marcel was expecting that. "He's not a policeman. He just took the uniform to get out of the Hôpital Hôtel-Dieu. Really. I told you, it's a long story."

"Go get his gun and bring it to me—butt first, with the clip in your other hand."

Marcel knew he couldn't dissuade the big man. Slowly and deliberately, he retraced his steps to where Pascal crouched in an unlit doorway. "He wants the gun," he said when Pascal stood.

"You're crazy if you think—"

"Look, if we don't do what he says, we get nothing. You're still in a police uniform, and you've got neither money, proper identification, nor a way out of here."

"And if I do what he wants?"

"I already told you; I can't promise you anything. But I think they'll help. They'll at least give me back my things, and that will give you some civilian clothes to wear."

Pascal looked pensive for a minute before unholstering the pistol and dropping the ammo clip out of the handle. He handed both pieces to Marcel without a word, then crouched again in the doorway.

Pepin was visibly pleased. "Nice piece," he said approvingly as he hefted the semiautomatic. "Tell him to carry his hat and boots in his hands and come here."

Pascal complied, but grumbled all the way to where Pepin once more emerged from the shadows. Seeing the mountain of human flesh before him, he shut up and submitted meekly, if not happily, to a none-too-gentle frisking.

"Hugue," the big man called softly, "keep an eye on him. We're going in." He motioned for Marcel to follow him to the rear door of the church, then turned again to Pascal. "You, take off that uniform. We'll bring you some other clothes."

"Here?" Pascal looked incredulous. "It's getting cold out here."

"Eh, well, I don't make the weather. You'll have to take that up with God. Now give me the uniform."

Marcel wasn't sure whether to be amused or embarrassed. Pepin was really putting Pascal through the wringer. He couldn't help but feel a little sorry, but he was clearly in no position to intervene. So the uniform came off and Marcel followed Pepin inside, leaving Pascal to shiver in the chill night air under the watchful eye of the shadowy Hugue.

Pastor de Pury was still seated behind the same table. He just looked more tired than he had in the afternoon. A wan smile crossed his lips as Pepin issued Marcel into the room.

"So, you survived. How did it go?" de Pury asked, dispensing with any formalities. "Did you see our friend the doctor? Do you have a message for us?"

Marcel swallowed hard before answering. He wished he could simply lay out the whole story and let the pastor decide what to do next. At the same time, he didn't want to appear entirely incompetent.

"Yes, I saw him, and he gave me a small envelope for you." He paused, trying to decide what to say next. "Uh unfortunately, I no longer have it."

The thin smile disappeared from de Pury's face.

"What I do have," Marcel continued before de Pury could say anything, "is a man the police were holding prisoner at the Hôpital Hôtel-Dieu. Dr. Billot told me he thought you'd understand, and that perhaps you might be willing to help the man."

The pastor's smile returned. "A man called Pascal, perhaps?" he asked with a nod in Pepin's direction. Pepin's face fell.

"How did you know that?" Marcel was puzzled, and a little disappointed. "Do you know him?"

"I've never met him, as far as I know," said de Pury, whose smile remained. "But he's a very important man, and Dr. Billot has been planning his escape for days. I believe the message you were supposed to deliver was to tell us when and where to make contact with this Pascal in order to speed him on his way."

Marcel was speechless. So that was why Billot hadn't mentioned the message again. And why he had insisted that Pascal accompany Marcel when he had driven them to this *quartier*. He felt a twinge of disappointment that Billot hadn't trusted him enough to level with him.

"What happened to the message anyway?" de Pury wanted to know.

Marcel recounted the whole story from the time he left the *temple* in the afternoon to his return a few minutes earlier. The pastor listened without a word, occasionally nodding encouragement or furrowing his brow in consternation.

When he had finished, de Pury looked from Marcel to Pepin. "Am I to understand that Pascal is here *now?*"

Pepin looked as if he might choke. Marcel savored the big man's discomfort for a delicious moment before answering.

"He's waiting outside for a change of clothes. He had to borrow a police uniform when we, uh, that is, when he left the hospital."

"A police uniform? Well, if that isn't the most—Pepin, don't just sit there. Get the man some clothes. I'll get someone to work on an identity card. Let's get him in here for a photograph right away."

❧　　　❧　　　❧

Marcel whistled soundlessly as the newly transformed Pascal reentered the basement room where he sat alone, waiting.

Dressed in a stylish black suit and gray wool overcoat, and sporting wire-rimmed glasses and a false moustache, the man from Marseilles looked remarkably different. The light dusting of powder at the temples, as well as the fine leather valise he carried combined to temporarily endow him with age and wisdom. He pirouetted smartly as if on a runway in a Paris fashion show. Both smiled, but neither man said a word.

Marcel looked and felt like himself once again. His striped trousers and light blue shirt seemed more than comfortable, though pulling his arm in and out of shirt sleeves had reminded him pointedly of the freshness of his wound. He wondered how long it would take to heal.

After pulling on the black wool cap Pepin had brought him, he shrugged into his worn gray coat and immediately felt the bulk of the revolver against his chest. He reached inside the coat pocket and withdrew it, looking it over carefully. The last time he had held it in his hands, he had tried to use it. Tried and failed. *Did I actually pull the trigger,* he asked himself skeptically, *or did I only think I did?* Maybe he had left the safety on in the excitement of the moment in the alley. He checked and found that it was off. Of course, someone could have changed that easily enough while he was gone.

He spun the cylinder and counted the cartridges. Six. So, it was fully loaded. He swung the cylinder out, dropped out all the cartridges, and swung it shut again. Then he raised the pistol to eye level and aimed it at a photograph on the far wall.

"What do you think you're doing!" Pascal broke the silence. Click.

Marcel lowered the gun. "I'm just trying to decide if this old Lebel works or not. I pulled the trigger earlier today, or at least I thought I did, and nothing happened."

"Nothing?"

Marcel shook his head.

"What do you mean you *thought* you pulled the trigger? Did you or didn't you?"

"I did. I'm sure of it." He hoped it was true.

"Let me see it. I know these guns pretty well. They used to be standard army issue."

Marcel handed him the empty revolver.

"Where'd you get it?" asked Pascal as he turned it over in his hands.

"Remember the old man who beat you at *boules?*" Marcel couldn't help grinning just a little.

Pascal looked up with a frown, but went back to examining the gun without speaking.

"After the match," Marcel began, "I followed you out to where you were beaten up. I was too late. They must have seen me coming and they jumped me. Anyway, the next morning when I told the old man about it he gave me the gun. Said maybe I knew too much, and that I might need it to protect myself."

Pascal handed the gun back to Marcel. "This wouldn't protect you from a blind beggar. It's worthless. The firing pin has been removed."

Marcel grasped the gun in silence. His thoughts were spinning too fast for him to give voice to any one of them. *Why would someone remove the firing pin? Did Antoine know about it? Did he do it himself? Was I—am I—being set up?* He wanted to throw the gun down on the floor. Or against the stone wall. Or maybe he would just pitch it right through Antoine LeBoeuf's front window!

"Look, those people are cutthroats. They set me up. The dapper fellow, what's his name?"

"René Carlini."

"Carlini's a snake. I got the impression that the Resistance is not his only ambition. Some of the younger men go along because he talks a good line: 'down with the *boches*' and all that. But some of the others are right in step with him. They know the game and they share in the spoils."

"What do you mean? What game?"

"Black market. Selling information. Anything for a few more francs."

"The black market I can believe. Lots of people are buying and selling under the table. But what information? And where would they sell it?"

"Someone told a Lyons police inspector where to find me after I was beaten. Whoever told him where I was had to *know* where I was. Or he had to know where I was going to be. I figure it was this Carlini or one of his people. And I figure he was paid for it."

"But why?"

"Because if he'd just wanted me arrested, he'd have called the local *gendarmerie* or the Grenoble police. Either way he could have denounced me as a terrorist or some such thing and they would have happily put me in jail right there. Instead, he calls this big shot Inspector Malfaire from Lyons. Can you think of another reason, if not for money?"

Marcel couldn't think of any reason at all that would justify such an act. He was still stung by the thought that Antoine might have knowingly given him a faulty weapon. "Do you think the old man—"

"I think the old man wants to make sure you don't cause trouble for them. He wants you to think he's on your side, so he gave you the gun. But with *this* gun you can't hurt anyone. He figured he would gain your gratitude and loyalty, and at the same time ensure that you're more or less harmless. I'm telling you, the old man is as guilty as the rest of them."

De Pury came back into the room just then to announce that a car was ready to take them to the train.

❧   ❧   ❧

The Gare de Perrache was crowded when Marcel and Pascal arrived. The car, with Hugue at the wheel and Pepin beside him, had dropped them off two blocks away and they had taken separate routes. Marcel, with the unused portion of his round-trip ticket back to Domène still in his pocket, waited around on the street for several minutes before entering the *gare*.

From outside the front doors, he watched as Pascal stood in line at the ticket counter to purchase a one-way fare to Annecy. Once there, the smartly dressed southerner planned to connect with another group of armed *maquisards*. Hopefully, they would treat him better than the last group.

Policemen combed through the Perrache station, scanning the milling crowd. Few people seemed to pay them any attention. For Marcel, however, their very presence made him wonder if the train had been a wise choice. The knot in his stomach told him no.

Three minutes before the scheduled departure of the Grenoble train, Marcel entered the station, crossed the main concourse at a brisk walk, and looked for the sign for Quai 2. He had lost sight of Pascal, who would be taking the Culoz train and then on to Aix-les-Bains before connecting to Annecy. His train was scheduled to depart only minutes later from Quai 3.

Marcel followed the signs down the stairs and under the first set of tracks. By the time he resurfaced on Quai 2, the train was in the station and the arriving passengers were deboarding. Out of the corner of his eye he caught a glimpse of an approaching police officer. Almost instinctively, he pulled his cap low over his eyes. Thrusting his hands into his pockets and hunching his shoulders, he tried to make as little of his face visible as he could. He walked to where a dozen people packed together at an open passenger door, waiting for the last of the arrivals to exit. A quick glance over his shoulder confirmed that the officer was still moving in his direction. He held his breath and edged farther into the huddle of people.

Finally, all the arrivals were off the train and the little knot of waiting passengers inched forward. The policeman was only a few feet away now. Marcel could hear his heart pounding in his eardrums. Everything else seemed to have fallen silent as the woman in front of him stepped up onto the waiting train. He would be aboard in another few seconds.

"Hey! You there!" It must have been the policeman, but Marcel was afraid to turn around. "Stop!"

Marcel froze on the bottom step.

Suddenly, from the *quai* somewhere behind him, came the sounds of confusion. The shrill of a policeman's whistle mingled with the yelling of several men and a woman's scream. Marcel couldn't make out any of it, but unable to keep from looking, he turned just as the policeman ran back toward the stairs leading to Quai 3. Without another second's hesitation, Marcel plunged ahead into the car and quickly found a seat.

The train lurched as it began to pull away from the station. With his face pressed against the window glass, Marcel thought he saw the police leading a man away in handcuffs. The station was quickly disappearing from view, and he couldn't be sure, but it looked like the man was wearing a gray overcoat and wire-rimmed glasses.

The last thing Pascal had said before they parted echoed in Marcel's head as the train picked up speed. *Thanks to you and Dr. Billot, I'm free again. I owe you one.*

The trip back to Domène seemed to take an eternity.

Chapter 18

From her chair by the upstairs window, Isabelle parted the heavy drapes and looked out over the Boussant farm and into the woods beyond. Leaves, which had recently flaunted their crimson and gold from the safety of the trees, now began to scatter over the ground. Squirrels gathered food for the winter and carefully hid it. Frost remained on the ground just a little longer, as the sun rose later and set earlier each day.

She had seen the beauty of autumn before in the well-tended parks of Paris, but it wasn't the same. Here in the hills above Domène the sounds were clearer, the colors brighter. When the sunlight warmed the glen and sparkled on the rippling Domenon, she sometimes almost felt like dancing. And it had been a very long time since she had felt like dancing.

The farm animals both frightened and fascinated her. Luc had introduced her to each one, pointing out the Brown Swiss and proud Percherons. She had viewed cows and horses from a passing train, but never had she been so close, and she watched in amazement as Luc coddled and caressed the giant beasts without fear. Rabbits and chickens, of course, she had seen in the *marchés* of Paris, though for some reason their presence here affected her quite differently.

Luc seemed to enjoy having her around, though he never said so outright. Except when at school, or when his chores were required, he seldom wandered far away from Isabelle, hovering almost protectively. In the few short weeks since her stay had begun, she had come to feel genuinely fond of the boy, even if his constant presence was occasionally annoying.

This morning, however, Luc was still in bed. And it wasn't the animals, or even the glories of autumn that drew Isabelle to the window. She had awakened to the sounds of an axe splintering wood. Françoise was gone, probably downstairs preparing breakfast. With her robe pulled tightly about her, Isabelle sat in the chair and peered out toward the side of the barn where Marcel was splitting firewood.

He was handsome, she thought, even from a distance. And there was obvious strength in the arms that wielded the axe—the same arms that had carried her the day she arrived. He had seemed especially strong that day, and safe. Yet every day since, she had sensed an unseen barrier around him that she couldn't seem to penetrate. *Could it be that he still doesn't want me here?* she wondered.

Isabelle sighed as she rested her elbows on the windowsill and cupped her chin in her hands, watching the pile of uncut wood diminish. Marcel worked hard, she had noticed. Not just now, but at everything he did. She liked that about him. He seemed so responsible, and of course he had to be, what with his father gone and all.

She remained puzzled, though, by his activities away from the farm. Some days he left before light and returned late in the day. Other days he didn't return until everyone else had gone to bed. No one spoke about it and she hadn't wanted to seem impolite by bringing it up. Still, she couldn't help but wonder.

The sky was light, but the sun had not yet made its way over the Belledonne range to dispel all the shadows in the glen. Even so, Marcel had been working for some time and, apparently too warm, stopped to unbutton his shirt. He left the tails to hang freely and rolled up the sleeves. That's when Isabelle saw the scar for the first time. Even in the pale light, and from a distance, she couldn't help but notice the ugly line that traced at least six inches across his forearm. She saw him wince once when he bumped his arm on the axe handle and wondered how and when it had happened.

As she watched, she felt the child within her stir and kick. Her face grew warm and she pulled back from the window as if the infant were her conscience. Caught enjoying the sight of a man—a man who wasn't her husband, nor the father of her child—left her feeling somewhat ashamed. She hurried to get dressed, trying to put him out of her mind. She scolded herself for entertaining such admiring thoughts, however innocent they seemed. Adam hadn't yet been in the grave six months.

It had happened several times recently—the kicking of the baby, that is. At first it had unnerved and even frightened her, but the more it happened the more she began to envision a healthy, growing child inside her. The increasing roundness of her belly was very reassuring in that regard. As to what she would do once the child was born, she had no idea. But for now, she took comfort in the sense of safety and yes, even a glimmer of hope, that she felt in this place. Hope in what, she couldn't say. She only knew she couldn't go on if hope were dashed this time as it had been so many times before.

❧   ❧   ❧

The useless Lebel revolver had lain for days in Marcel's bureau drawer. He had avoided facing Antoine LeBoeuf, unsure as to just what he should say. He had rehearsed any number of times what he would *like* to say, but each time he had concluded that it wasn't quite right. Somehow, he wanted to convey the sense of hurt and anger he felt without sounding too sentimental. The fact was, if he'd had no strong feelings toward the grandfatherly old man, he could never have felt so completely betrayed.

If he hadn't tried to fire the gun himself, he would never have believed Pascal's accusation. But it made sense. Why would anyone, let alone someone he trusted, give him a weapon he knew wouldn't work? Something was wrong. Somehow, he'd have to look Antoine in the eye and ask him the hard questions.

Marcel swung the axe in an arc high over his head and drove it downward, splitting the piece of aging maple neatly in two.

Today would be the day, he decided as the wood tumbled from the stump he used for a chopping block. He couldn't put it off any longer, much as he would like to. He had to find out once and for all what Antoine knew about the gun. And he realized that he owed his old friend the chance to defend himself, though he couldn't imagine any justification for such a cowardly act. Still, it would be the right thing to do.

He wished he knew too what to do about Pascal. But Maurice Lambert had warned him against going back to Lyons any time soon. Besides, there was really nothing he could do. If it were Pascal the police arrested in the *gare,* they would take no chances this time. Pascal was probably locked in a cell in the St. Joseph Prison. And even the resourceful Dr. Billot couldn't arrange an escape from St. Joseph. According to

Lambert, Billot might be a prisoner there himself. No one had heard from him or his wife since the escape from Hôtel-Dieu.

The axe arced into the air and plunged downward again. This time the blade sank harmlessly into the heart of the broad chopping block and stopped. Marcel released his grip, leaving the axe-handle pointing toward the sun-drenched peaks of the Belledonne Range behind him.

Turning from the wood pile, he buttoned his shirt, rolled down his sleeves, and strolled back to the house. After breakfast he would get Maman to clip the sutures from his wound. It was healing nicely. Once that was over, he would take the revolver and walk down to the village to find Antoine.

❦   ❦   ❦

"Marcel?"

He stopped and turned around as Isabelle closed the door and descended the front steps.

"You really shouldn't be outside, you know," he said flatly, almost impatiently. "What if someone passing by should see you?"

"I know. I won't stay out long. I—I just need to ask you something." Isabelle never ventured out of doors during the day. She knew all too well the consequences of being seen by the wrong person. But something had been weighing on her mind since the day she arrived, and she couldn't hold it in any longer.

"Would you prefer that I find another place to stay?" she asked earnestly. "I know I must be a burden. Perhaps your pastor friend would be willing to—"

"Why would you say that?" he asked, his impatience suddenly replaced by surprise. "Maman doesn't consider you a burden at all. Why, even Françoise and Luc—"

"Yes, I know how *they* feel, Marcel," she interrupted softly. "I asked what *you* would prefer. Somehow, I have the impression that I'm in your way, that I've disrupted your plans. I'll go if that's what you want." She hadn't really intended to say that. It just slipped out.

"Aren't you happy here?" he asked in reply. "I mean, as much as possible, under the circumstances." He looked uncomfortable.

"I'd rather be home, if that's what you mean. But that's not possible right now. Anyway, I'm not so sure where home is anymore." He certainly wasn't making this easy. "But you still aren't answering my question, Marcel. Am I in your way, here?"

Marcel looked down and kicked at the dirt with the toe of his boot. "No," he said after a long pause, "You're not in my way. You're not in anyone's way."

"If you want me to go, all you have to do is tell me." Why she would say such a thing, she couldn't understand.

"No," he said again without looking up, "We—uh that is I—I want you to stay."

"Thank you." Isabelle's voice was hardly more than a whisper. The relief that flowed through her all at once caught her off guard. *Why did this suddenly get to be so important to me?* The distance she felt hadn't all melted away, yet she couldn't deny the sense that this conversation would change things for the better.

As Marcel turned to go, she thought she detected a softening of his features. "You'd better get back inside," he said. "I wouldn't want anyone to see you out here." This time he sounded as though he meant it.

❦   ❦   ❦

"What do you mean it doesn't work?"

Marcel stood with his hands on the kitchen table across

from Antoine LeBoeuf, who remained seated. The Lebel revolver lay in the center of the table, its 8mm cartridges scattered around it.

"Just that. I pulled the trigger and nothing happened."

"Who—or what—were you shooting at, anyway?" Antoine looked more than a little surprised.

"I don't think that's any of your business. The point is I tried to fire this worthless piece of metal and it failed!"

"Calm down, *mon ami*. Are you sure the safety catch was off?"

"Of course."

"And there was a cartridge in the chamber?"

"Yes!"

"Well, then, I wonder what the problem could be."

"I think you know very well what the problem is." Marcel had not intended to get overheated like this, but from the start it seemed to him that his old friend was being too coy. And that could only mean one thing.

"Perhaps you should just tell me, Marcel," the old man said. "Then I won't have to guess what you are talking about."

"I don't think you have to guess. The firing pin was removed."

"What?"

"The firing pin is missing."

Antoine looked skeptical. "How do you know the firing pin was removed? You don't know anything about guns!"

Antoine was half right. Marcel had often used his father's shotgun for hunting pheasants and quail, but he had never even held a pistol before this one. Still, the tone of the elder man's voice angered him.

Marcel didn't reply immediately, unable to decide how to answer. "I—I can't say," he mumbled finally. "I'd better go."

Antoine rose from his chair as Marcel turned to leave the

old man's kitchen. "You don't need to run away, Marcel. Why can't we talk about this? I'll make us some *tisane* and you can tell me what happened."

"There's nothing to talk about." Marcel strode quickly to the front door.

"Marcel?"

"Just leave me alone." He opened the door and stepped outside.

"Hey, Marcel—"

Marcel slammed the door behind him, passed through the gate, and walked as fast as he could up the street toward the village center. He didn't want to hear another word the old man had to say. And he never wanted to see him again if he could help it. Pascal was probably right. Antoine LeBoeuf was as guilty of the beating as René Carlini or Emile Bonet. They were all in this together, of course. Why he had ever thought otherwise suddenly seemed ridiculous.

It was clear that they wanted to keep him out of the way. He wondered if the gun had been Antoine's own idea, or if Carlini had put him up to it. Either way he had been completely duped, and perhaps more than anything else, that's what angered him so. It was bad enough to feel betrayed by someone he had trusted for years. But to be made a fool in the process—that was unforgivable! And he had certainly been made a fool.

Marcel continued his brisk pace through the center of Domène and trekked back up the hill toward home. It was probably only a matter of time before someone from Carlini's group came to find him. They would want to know more about his activities. But if he gave in and told them anything, he might compromise the relief networks. He couldn't imagine that René Carlini would be sympathetic to the harboring of illegal Jews. There wasn't enough money in it. But there might be a great deal of money in handing over the information to certain officials.

Marcel jumped at the sound of a short blast from a car horn. He had been so consumed with his thoughts that he hadn't heard the car pull up alongside him. The driver slowed to a full stop and rolled down his window.

"Are you going somewhere, or are you just sleepwalking?" It was Gilles Théron, grinning broadly. "I might have run you over and you'd never have known what hit you, *mon vieux.*"

Marcel felt sheepish. "I'm just glad it was you and not a German tank," he laughed. "Too much on my mind I guess."

"Anything I can help with?"

"No, not really," Marcel replied. "Say, what brings you all the way out here? Aren't you supposed to be in class or something?"

"Wake up, *mon ami.* It's Saturday. I don't have classes till Monday. I came to invite your family to dinner tomorrow after church. Maman says she hardly sees your mother anymore."

"That's very kind. I'll ask Maman and let you know what she says." It dawned on Marcel that Gilles would expect to come up to the house and perhaps even visit for a while. He would have no time to warn Maman and Françoise to hide Isabelle. This could be a disaster.

"Marcel, you don't have a telephone. How would you let me know before tomorrow? Besides, we're almost to your house. Climb in and I'll give you a lift home."

Marcel had to think of something fast. "I don't think that's such a good idea, Gilles. Maman is kind of busy these days, with the farm and all." It sounded lame even as he said it.

"All the more reason to get you home quickly," Gilles shot back good-naturedly. "Let's go."

Unable to think of anything to say that made any kind of sense, Marcel got in reluctantly and shut the door.

"So," Gilles began as he eased the car into gear, "is Françoise at home today?"

Marcel rolled his eyes. So that was what this was all about! Then perhaps this wouldn't be a disaster after all. If Gilles had eyes only for Françoise, Marcel might be able to keep Isabelle's presence a secret. It had to be kept a secret, now more than ever. After the confrontation with Antoine LeBoeuf, he knew he would be under suspicion. They would be watching more closely than ever. But no matter what they did to him, he couldn't risk her discovery.

And to think that just that morning she had offered to leave if he wanted her to. *Why did she think I would want such a thing?* He'd been reluctant to take her in at the beginning, it was true. But seeing the old man in Lyons being railed on and beaten simply because he was a Jew had changed all that. The scar on his arm was a constant reminder that if he hadn't acted, no one would have. Still a little surprised at having come to the aid of the grizzled old Jew, Marcel wondered to what lengths he would go to protect the beautiful one that shared his home.

He prayed he wouldn't have to find out.

❧   ❧   ❧

As Gilles pulled the car onto the narrow track that led to the Boussants' farmhouse, Marcel reached over and sounded the horn a couple of times. Almost immediately, Léo came bounding up from the barn to greet them. And by the time Gilles had braked the car to a complete stop, the rest of the family had gathered outside the front door. Relieved that Isabelle was nowhere in sight, Marcel was nonetheless nervous.

"*Bonjour,* Madame Boussant," Gilles said in his usual polite manner. "Is everything well with you?"

"*Bonjour,* Gilles." It was easy to see that she really liked the young man as she allowed him to kiss her cheeks. "Yes, everything is just fine. How is your mother?"

Marcel tried to catch his sister's eye while Gilles talked with Maman, but Françoise's eyes were glued on the fair-haired university student. It was still hard for Marcel to imagine his sister with a suitor, but he had to admit that she could have done far worse than Gilles. And, judging by what his friends said, she was pretty enough. Gilles obviously thought so. Because Françoise seemed so serious much of the time, he had assumed she wouldn't show much interest in young men. Maybe he really didn't know her as well as he thought he did.

"Hello, Françoise," Gilles said, having just conveyed his mother's invitation to Madame Boussant. "I hope you'll be able to come too."

"I'd like that very much, Gilles."

"Françoise, come help me prepare some lunch," suggested Evelyne. "This young man is probably hungry. You'll stay, won't you, Gilles?"

Gilles, of course, was only too happy to stay, and the two women soon disappeared into the house to make preparations. Luc began pestering their visitor with all sorts of questions about the university. He plainly admired Gilles, and Gilles seemed to find the little fellow entertaining. Marcel listened as long as he could before shooing his little brother off to finish some chore or other in the barn.

"Look, Gilles," he said when the two were finally alone, "I'm not sure we ought to come over to your house tomorrow after all."

"But your mother seemed all for it. What's the matter?"

"Well, I just think it's best that we stay close to home for a while, that's all."

"Don't be ridiculous. You leave home to come to church every Sunday. What's it going to hurt to come to dinner? I don't understand you, Marcel. What gives?"

Marcel was silent. He had no answers. He knew full well

that the excuses he was making were flimsy. He just hoped that perhaps somehow, Gilles would understand.

Gilles looked up toward the second story of the house. "Is it because you're hiding someone?" he said softly.

"What?" Marcel's voice sounded strained even to his own ears, and he felt the blood drain from his face.

"I saw the drapes move in the upstairs window when we drove up." He said it as calmly as if he were discussing the weather. "Your family was already outside." He paused. "Are you hiding Jews, Marcel?"

Once again, Marcel didn't respond. He didn't know what to say, and he wasn't about to lie to his friend. To say anything would be to confirm or deny Gilles' suspicions. And then what? Where would that lead? Either way it seemed to him, Isabelle would no longer be safe there. She would have to leave—and he suddenly realized how much he didn't want that to happen.

"Look, Marcel, I understand," Gilles was saying. "We have a family hiding in our basement."

Marcel wasn't sure which stunned him more—that Gilles knew someone was there, or that *his* family was hiding Jews too. Much as he loved his friend, he never expected the Thérons to risk everything to do the *righteous* thing. And in their case, everything really amounted to something.

"Do you hear me, Marcel? It's okay. We're on the same side."

"But—"

"I know what you're thinking. My family never took our faith as seriously as yours. Oh, we're good Protestants, and we've always said all the right things. But we only practiced what was convenient, or useful.

"Lately, though, I've been thinking about this 'convenient faith,' and I've come to the conclusion that it's really no faith at all. I told my parents that I believe God expects more from me than mere words, that it was time I demonstrated my faith by my actions.

"Marcel, you know my parents. It wasn't easy for them to hear that. But they agreed that what I was saying was right for all of us. Together, we decided to make a start by giving refuge to a Jewish family that Pastor Westphal told us about. We're a little scared, Marcel, but we know we're doing the right thing." He paused for a moment and then said with a grin, "Still worried about coming for dinner?"

Marcel could feel relief wash over him like the tide. He couldn't have imagined better news. To be able to share the struggle against injustice with his longtime friend was a gift too precious for words. Certainly, there were still dangers they would have to face, but at the moment he knew someone else would understand. And Isabelle would be safe there for a while longer.

"No, I'm not worried about dinner," he replied, trying to suppress a smile. "But I *am* worried just a little about my sister." Then he winked at his friend and they both laughed out loud. It felt good to finally let down his guard, even if only for a moment.

Chapter 19

The big Renault was parked on a dark street just off Grenoble's Boulevard Gambetta. The lights had been turned off, though the engine continued to idle. The driver had exited the car and was standing nearby, leaning against the stone front of an empty office building. Few people wandered by as the hour was late and the curfew would soon be in effect.

"What do you mean, 'do I still have him'?" Inspector Malfaire glared at his companion across the back seat. "Since when is what I do with my prisoners any of your business?"

"Of course, Inspector. I didn't mean to imply that you owed me any sort of explanation." René Carlini was suddenly defensive. As he spoke, long tendrils of smoke curled up from his cigarette and floated out into the night air through the partially opened window. Malfaire found himself wondering how he had allowed himself to get involved with the likes of this greedy vegetable vendor. The man could only be trusted if profit were involved—his profit.

"What then? Why are you asking about this Pascal fellow?" He might as well get to the bottom of it.

"Well, Inspector, as I've told you before, I know people who see things, who hear things. And these people talk to me sometimes—"

"Get on with it, Carlini."

"Well, I've heard a rumor from Lyons that Pascal is no longer in custody."

"Is that right?" Malfaire was noncomittal.

Carlini forced a laugh. "Of course it's just a rumor, you understand."

Malfaire didn't return his smile.

"But it would be troubling if it were true," Carlini said, nervously drawing on his cigarette. "He may try to return here. I don't mind telling you, I find that a bit unsettling. He has far too many connections to be taken lightly. Especially now that one of my own men may have turned against me."

"How is that?"

"It's a very long story, Inspector, but this man doesn't like the way the whole affair with Pascal was handled. It seems that one of his protégés was snooping about and got roughed up a bit in the process. Now he has discovered that a revolver I gave him has been tampered with. He's accused me of knowing it was faulty."

"And did you know?"

"Of course!" Carlini laughed wickedly. "There are several men in the network I don't feel I can trust. This is just my way of insuring that they never bite the hand that feeds them, if you know what I mean."

"And what do you intend to do about it?"

"The gun is not what worries me. I've dealt with disgruntled men before, and I can do it again. What worries me is the idea that this Pascal may have escaped custody at a time when things are, shall we say, complicated."

"That could be sticky," Malfaire replied thoughtfully. "Well, perhaps that fact will motivate you to snoop around a bit more diligently. I have reason to believe that one of the men who helped him escape may have fled in this direction. Perhaps one of your people knows him. If we can find the accomplice, we may be able to recapture Pascal."

"So he *has* escaped!" Carlini stiffened visibly. "Inspector, I may need your protection until this criminal is back in custody."

"I can only do so much without the proper information, Monsieur Carlini. Terrorists, Jews—I'll count on you to get me what you can. Keep in mind that it's in your best interest." He rapped on the window with his gloved hand and the driver opened Carlini's door. "But don't take too long or things might turn out rather unfortunately for you."

Carlini exited the car without a word, but the expression on his face radiated a blend of fear and frustration. Malfaire was satisfied. He knew well just how motivating such emotions could be—and he looked forward to reaping the benefits.

"Let's go home, Dominique," he said as the driver slid in behind the wheel. "And hurry. I promised my wife we'd go to early mass tomorrow, and I need my sleep." *Especially if I have to sit through another of Father Benoit's pitiful homilies about the plight of Jews,* he grumbled to himself.

"I'll do my best, Inspector," Dominique said as he eased the car into gear and headed for the highway back to Lyons.

❦　　❦　　❦

The afternoon sun spilled in through the window and Isabelle basked in its warmth. It felt good to be comfortable again. The fire Marcel had carefully laid in the fireplace had long since been reduced to a small pile of embers, and the house had grown chill. Except for Léo the shepherd, the house was silent and empty. The Boussants had gone into Grenoble to attend Sunday services, and would be dining afterward with Gilles Théron and his parents.

Sitting alone on the settee with her feet curled up under her to keep them warm, Isabelle deftly pushed and pulled a needle and thread through the yards of blue flowered cotton that lay in front of her. Evelyne Boussant had discovered the cloth in a trunk in the attic the day before, and she had insisted that Isabelle should have it for a new dress. It was hard to argue when anyone could see that the dress she had borrowed from Françoise no longer fit her comfortably.

The search of the attic's contents had come about rather unexpectedly. Gilles Théron had suggested it. He and his parents were sheltering an entire family in their basement. They were out of sight of passersby, and even visitors. And while the Boussants worried little about strangers, it still seemed wise that Isabelle be kept from prying eyes. So they had spent the better part of the afternoon preparing a place amid the clutter of the attic where she could hide at a moment's notice.

Isabelle had mixed feelings about the attic. She was grateful for a place to hide, of course, if the need should ever arise. But the only natural light came from a tiny diamond-shaped window at each end of the house, and there was no way to heat the cluttered room safely. On top of that, the floorboards creaked, making it all but impossible to move about quietly. She had helped quite willingly with the preparations, all the while hoping she would never need to ascend the ladder again.

The dress was coming along nicely. She had waited until the family left for church before beginning her work, and she hoped to have it completed by the time they returned. It was perhaps a lot to ask, especially without the machine to which she had become accustomed at Madame de la Court's. But she had become rather self-conscious about her expanding appearance, and she wanted to look as well as could be hoped under the circumstances.

It felt strange, though not unpleasant, to finally do something for herself. Perhaps that was what Evelyne had in mind when she offered the fabric. Not once did she suggest that she or Françoise would sew the new dress, and it was not because she knew that Isabelle was a seamstress. No one did. It had never occurred to Isabelle to tell them. Besides, dredging up the past inevitably reminded her of things she wanted desperately to blot from her memory—at least for now. Someday she would think about all that, and then she'd decide what to do about it all. But until then, the less said, the better.

Léo lifted his head from atop his front paws just then, his ears tilted forward, the thick fur on his neck and back bristling with apprehension. He gave a low growl, the same growl Isabelle had heard the evening she arrived at the Boussant's. Only this time his attention was riveted to the front door.

Isabelle could feel her pulse quicken as the dog rose from the floor and paced rapidly to the door, all the while growling and sniffing. A sharp rap on wood set the dog to barking in urgent, clipped tones. Isabelle uncurled herself from the settee and darted toward the stairs, the sound of her heart beating wildly in her ears. She cast a fleeting glance at the front door where Léo's barking was gaining intensity. The door was unlocked!

Teetering for an instant on the brink of indecision, Isabelle quickly abandoned any idea of securing the door. *What if the door opens before I can lock it?* she asked herself in desperation. There was no telling what might happen then. Rather than risk it, she bolted up the stairs as quickly as she was able, to where the attic ladder stood against the wall. It looked somehow taller and more precarious than it had the day before. Marcel had steadied it for her while she climbed, and Luc and Françoise had helped her into the attic once she had reached the ladder's top. Today she would have to do it her-self—and she would have to hurry.

The rapping on the door below had become more insis-tent, and she could hear someone—a man's voice—shouting. But over the sounds of Léo's barking and the pounding of her own heart, she couldn't make any sense out of his words. Her knees wobbled as she climbed the ladder one rung after the other. She was glad that the wood was worn smooth as she slid her sweaty hands upward, afraid to release her grip.

At the top, she nudged the hinged door open with her head, still unwilling to let go with even one hand. The air from above washed over her face and shoulders like cool water. Bracing herself, she reached up for a handhold in the dimly lit attic. The sound of frenzied barking far below spurred her on. Drawing a sharp breath, she scrambled up and onto the newly swept floor. Turning, she softly closed the door behind her, then pulled her knees to her trembling chin and waited. *If only Marcel were home,* she thought. *He'd know what to do, wouldn't he?* But he was gone, and all the old fears gnawed at her once again.

❧   ❧   ❧

Antoine LeBoeuf tapped the ground lightly with his walking stick as he ambled down the road toward Domène and home. The long walk up the hill had been an exercise in futility, he decided. Oh, it was good exercise, all right, if all he had been after was an excuse to stretch his legs. But unlike most Sunday afternoons, he'd had more on his mind than walking off the effects of a good meal. The Boussant farm was a little far for that sort of thing for a man of his age.

No, today he had waited until the Boussants had had plenty of time to return from the *temple protestant* in Grenoble before making the trek up the hill road toward Revel. He knew they were never home on Sunday mornings, and he needed to talk to Marcel before the situation with the revolver became irreparable. But it was nearly 3 o'clock in the afternoon by the time he had arrived, and still no one had answered the door.

Léo had certainly made his presence known. There was no mistaking that. But it seemed strange to Antoine that the Boussants had shut the dog up in the house, when normally he had the run of the place, whether the family was home or not. He recalled seeing Madame Boussant let the dog inside by the fire when the weather was cold. But the sun was out, and though the air was certainly brisk, it wasn't unusually cold. He just couldn't shake the feeling that someone had been home all along, yet for some reason had refused to come to the door. He could have sworn that he had heard footsteps on the stairs inside. It was very strange indeed.

Perhaps Marcel had meant it when he said he wanted to be left alone. Maybe he knew that it was Antoine at the door, and he had convinced his family to ignore his old friend—his former friend. Antoine grimaced at the thought. Marcel sure could be hotheaded at times. And he didn't always think things all the way through before acting on his impulses. At least that had been Antoine's experience. The boy was good-hearted enough. He just needed to temper his impulsiveness with a little common sense.

This mess with the pistol—now that was a real problem. He could almost understand why Marcel had become so angry. No one likes to be taken for a fool. Antoine slashed at a dried-up weed beside the road with his stick. *No one* likes to be taken for a fool.

The trouble was, while Marcel only *thought* he had been betrayed, Antoine *knew* without a doubt that *he* had been. If only he could talk to the boy, explain what happened, assure him that he had not known about the missing firing pin. Of course Marcel would have to be willing to listen, something he seemed to have little interest in so far.

Once back down the hill and into the village center, Antoine decided to stop in at the dingy Le Dauphin bar before going home. Some of the others in the network were likely to be there, and maybe he could find out if anyone else knew anything about faulty weapons.

"Salut, mon vieux!" hailed Georges from behind the bar. Unusually trim for a fifty-year-old career bartender, Georges Charrier was also the proprietor of Le Dauphin. He pushed his glasses higher on the bridge of his nose with one hand and held the other out to Antoine. "How goes it these days?"

"I can't complain," said Antoine, grasping the hand he had been offered. "And you?"

"Ah, well, now that you ask," replied the affable Georges, "aside from the fact that people have no money, and the trouble I have getting decent *pastis*, it's going pretty well."

Both men laughed as Antoine made himself comfortable on a stool at the bar. Without asking, Georges poured a demitasse of thick, black coffee and placed the cup in front of the older man. Antoine bent low over the tiny cup, inhaling the rich aroma. He looked up at the bartender, but Georges just smiled. Finally, Antoine placed the cup to his lips and took a tentative sip. Now it was his turn to smile.

"That's real coffee, *mon ami,*" he said softly. "Excellent, real coffee. Where'd you get it? You haven't had coffee that good in here for months."

Georges put his forefinger to his lips and leaned forward over the bar. "René Carlini got it for me," he whispered. "Claims he actually traded for it with some *boche* businessman."

"What did he have to give for it?" asked Antoine.

"Who cares? All I know is that if I keep my eyes and ears open, and keep him informed, I can get more—and at a fair price too. Trouble is," he laughed, "the stuff is so hard to come by, I may need to hire armed guards just to protect my supply!"

Antoine smiled, but inside he recoiled. So, Carlini had managed to buy off another man. Everyone has a price, or so the saying goes. It was just so disappointing to see that a man's head could be turned by nothing more than a couple of pounds of fine coffee.

Georges Charrier, by virtue of his occupation, knew a lot of people. And he was an integral part of the network. Antoine had been counting on him to help figure out if anyone else among them had been given one of Carlini's Lebel revolvers. Then he could try to uncover which, if any, might have been tampered with like his own. Now, however, he wasn't at all sure that broaching the subject with Georges was a good idea. Unless. . . .

"Georges, maybe you can help me." He motioned for the bartender to move closer and lowered his voice. "I need a good serviceable revolver, something ordinary like a six-shot Lebel. Do you have any ideas where I can get my hands on one?"

Georges looked a little puzzled. "Why? Surely you don't plan to, I mean, at your—"

"At my age I couldn't possibly need a handgun? Is that what you mean, Georges?" Antoine tried to sound insulted.

"No! No, it's just that—well, never mind." The bartender gave up.

"Well?"

Georges thought for a moment. "Well, I think René Carlini may still have some."

"Oh? What makes you say that?"

"Because he gave me one a while back. A Lebel, just like

you said."

"Is it any good?"

"I haven't shot anybody with it, if that's what you mean."

"Have you used it at all?"

"No. Why do you ask?"

"If it's in good condition I might be willing to buy it from you, that's all."

Georges was silent once more, rubbing his chin and thinking. "I don't think I want to sell it," he said finally. "I mean, I might need it myself someday. But I'll tell you what. I'll let you look at it. If you like it, you can borrow it for a few days while I try to find out about another one."

Antoine nodded his assent. Georges probably hadn't examined his pistol, just as Antoine hadn't really looked over the one he had received. He only hoped he was right about this. Otherwise, when Carlini caught wind of what he had done, as he surely would, he would have to find a very far corner of France in which to hide. And with the *boches* occupying sixty percent of the country, his options were limited.

Georges stepped around from behind the bar and motioned for Antoine to follow him into the back room. The three men who sat near the front playing cards looked up as the bartender headed toward the back, but no one said anything.

Antoine closed the door behind them and waited quietly while Georges opened a locked desk drawer and pulled out the revolver. From a distance it looked identical to the one Antoine had given Marcel Boussant. Carefully, almost ceremonially, Georges handed Antoine the gun with both hands.

Immediately, Antoine swung the cylinder away from the barrel and dumped the six 8mm cartridges onto the desktop. Then he turned the gun over and over in his hands, examining it carefully. Without saying a word, he picked up the cartridges, placed them in the cylinder, and swung the cylinder, shut. Then he raised the gun to shoulder height and pointed it directly at Georges Charrier's bobbing Adam's apple.

"A—A—Antoine!" he sputtered, the color suddenly gone from his face. "What are you doing? Please, Antoine, for the love of God, don't—"

Click!

Antoine placed the revolver on the desk. "It's completely harmless, Georges," he said flatly, "just like the one he gave me."

Georges stood still for a long while, his breathing labored, his face slowly regaining its natural hue. He stared at the top of the desk, unable to tear his gaze from the worthless Lebel. Slowly, he began shaking his head back and forth.

"I can't believe I could have been so stupid," he said at long last, his fists clenching and unclenching. "I'll kill the stinking—"

"I know how you feel, Georges. But don't do anything crazy. We've got to find out who else our friend Carlini is playing games with first."

"Don't do anything crazy, you say? Just what do you call pointing a gun at someone—and pulling the trigger! You could have killed me!"

"Not with this gun," Antoine said, grinning, "not a chance."

The bartender seemed to relax just a little. "What do we do next?"

"I'm not sure, Georges. But I do know we're going to have to be careful. Carlini knows that I know about the gun. He mustn't find out that you know too. Not yet. Not until we find out who else he gave faulty guns."

"Maybe if I ask around—discreetly, of course."

"Be very careful, my friend. In the meantime, see what you can do about getting us some weapons that actually work. We may need them."

❦   ❦   ❦

The sun was going down and the light was already starting to dim when Antoine stepped out of Le Dauphin and started for home, tapping his walking stick on the street as he went. A block away he heard the faint scuff of a boot behind him. He slowed his pace just a little, but didn't turn around. A little farther on he heard it again. This time he stopped dead in his tracks and turned slowly around. He saw no one.

"Let me save you some trouble," he said aloud, a little exasperated. "I'm an old man and I'm going home. I'll cook myself a little dinner, have a cup of *tisane,* read a book, and go to bed. Monsieur Carlini will probably do the same when he is old. *Bon soir.*"

With that he turned and walked casually toward home. He didn't hear the scuffing sound again.

Chapter 20

The sight of Isabelle huddled under a blanket in the dark of the attic wrenched Marcel's gut as he perched atop the ladder and pushed the trap door completely open. The light from the room below cast an eerie glow on her face. Her eyes stared back at him hopefully as he reached a hand out toward her.

"Isabelle?" he asked softly, almost afraid he might frighten her further if he spoke too loud. "Are you all right?"

"Is he gone?" she whispered.

"Who? Was someone here?" he didn't mean to startle her; his voice just seemed to rise involuntarily. *Who could have been here?*

"A man came and Léo began growling and barking. When I didn't answer the door, the man began pounding on it and shouting. So I came up here to hide."

"You must be freezing. How long have you been up here?"

"I don't know. I was afraid to come down, even after Léo

stopped barking."

"Could you see who it was?"

"I was afraid to look. I didn't want him to see me."

"Well, you did the right thing," Marcel soothed, holding out his hand once more. "Come, I'll help you down the ladder. You look like you need to spend some time next to the fire."

She said nothing in reply, but took his hand. As icy as her hand was, it felt to Marcel as though it belonged there, somehow. He clung to it as long as possible as he helped her down the ladder to where an anxious and unusually silent Luc stood waiting. The roaring fire Françoise had built was already chasing the chill from the *salon* when the three descended the stairs.

"Oh, Isabelle!" Françoise exclaimed as Isabelle entered the room with her two escorts. "We were so worried when we didn't see you. Marcel said you might go to the attic if you got scared. Are you freezing? Is everything all right? Come warm up by the fire. Maman is making some coffee."

Marcel smiled to himself. Françoise, normally quiet and thoughtful, was babbling like a child—a sure sign she was feeling relieved, or perhaps still giddy from the hours spent with Gilles. Maman would be out shortly with the coffee, a gift from the Thérons. On the drive home she had insisted that they use some right away, in spite of how rarely they had any, so that Isabelle could enjoy it with them. They had no way of knowing just how long she would stay, and Maman, for one, was growing quite fond of her. She wasn't alone.

Marcel's smile faded as he thought of Isabelle alone with no one but Léo to protect her. *Had someone really been here while we were gone?* It seemed highly unlikely that she would imagine such a thing. And yet, visitors were rare. *Who could it have been?* Perhaps he could probe a little more once things were back to normal. One thing was sure. They could no longer leave her alone for any extended period of time. He couldn't bear the thought of finding her huddled and trembling in the attic again.

❦   ❦   ❦

Before dawn the following Thursday morning, Marcel was out in the barn milking the cows by the light of a coal-oil lantern. When he had finished, he separated the cream and poured the milk into large, glazed, clay pots, which he covered and placed in the back of the old Peugeot. Next he loaded the meager quantities of butter and cheese that Maman had made, along with a few dozen eggs, some dried garlic, and onions. Lastly, he took six rabbits from their cages and placed them in small crates, which he set in the back seat.

Today was market day in Domène, and if he didn't get an early start he wouldn't have a good location for his stall in the tree-lined Place de la Mairie. He enjoyed the *marché* with its circus of sights, sounds, and smells. Virtually everyone in town passed among the colorful stalls at some point during the morning, exchanging gossip, debating politics, looking for bargains, shopping for the necessities of life.

On most *marché* mornings, Luc and Françoise rode down the hill with him. Once the stall was set up, they would head for school just the way Marcel had done after helping Papa each Thursday morning. But this morning he was alone. Today was Armistice Day, the day of the German surrender at the end of the Great War, and as part of a rather subdued celebration, many schools had quietly cancelled classes for the day.

When he arrived in the village, the space he normally occupied had already been claimed by a couple of Gypsies selling womens' underwear and silk hosiery. Too embarrassed to protest, Marcel reluctantly decided to set up in the only good location that remained—right next to Emile Bonet, the butcher. Bonet wouldn't be too thrilled at the prospect of plump live rabbits for sale next to his lean skinned ones, but he would have to make the best of it.

By the time Marcel had set the folding table and awning in place, unloaded the goods, and parked the car down the street by the primary school, people were already arriving. Wandering through the lanes between the stalls and examining the various wares as they went, basket-toting housewives called out greetings to one another. Men stood in smoky little clusters, excitedly debating the pros and cons of the three-day-old Allied invasion of French North Africa. There were signs of optimism in the air, the likes of which hadn't been seen in a long while.

Emile Bonet, busy exchanging war news and friendly banter with his clientele, seemed to ignore Marcel entirely until well into the morning. That suited Marcel just fine. He had tried to avoid the butcher as much as possible since the night he had run into his fist in the Rue des Contamines. The morning would pass quickly enough, he figured, if he just minded his own business—and if Bonet minded his.

It wasn't until there was a temporary lull in the bustle of activity that he heard the familiar voice.

"Hey, *jeune!*"

It wasn't as irritating as being referred to as *petit,* but Marcel found the reference to his age annoying nonetheless. He didn't turn around.

"Boussant!"

Marcel swiveled slowly around to look at the grinning Bonet, but offered no reply.

"Hey, how's the face?" the butcher asked, rubbing a huge hand over his jaw and chuckling out loud. "Nothing broken, I hope."

Marcel stiffened. "You underestimate me, Monsieur Bonet," he said evenly. He could feel his face growing warm as he spoke.

The man was a complete cad.

"Oh, now, let's not have any hard feelings, *mon ami.*" The butcher's tone sounded condescending. He took several steps closer. "A simple mistake, that's all," he continued, shrugging his shoulders and spreading his arms wide. "You surprised me." The playfulness went out of his voice. "And I don't like surprises."

"So, the mistake was all mine, is that it?" He looked the big man straight in the eyes.

Bonet stepped closer and jabbed a stubby finger into Marcel's chest. "Any time you decide to pry into Emile Bonet's business, it's a mistake. *Tu comprends?*"

Marcel was furious at being bullied this way, but he understood very well. *Stay calm,* he told himself. *Bonet could snap you in half like a dry twig if he chose to. There's no need to provoke a demonstration!*

"Well, Monsieur Bonet, I'll try not to surprise you in the future," he said, his eyes still fastened on Bonet's. He knew enough to bend, but he was not about to bow.

Bonet gave a loud laugh and clapped Marcel on the shoulder, nearly knocking him off balance. *"Bonne idée,"* he roared. "Don't surprise Bonet, and Bonet won't surprise you." As he said it, he grazed Marcel's chin with a feigned blow from his huge right fist, then turned and walked back to his stall laughing.

❦   ❦   ❦

From across the Place de la Mairie, near a cobbler's stall, René Carlini pulled deeply on a filterless cigarette and watched the exchange between Marcel Boussant and Emile Bonet. From this distance he couldn't tell what they were talking about, but it seemed odd to see the two of them together—especially after hearing how the butcher had belted the boy in the face several weeks ago. Antoine LeBoeuf had angrily demanded an expla-

nation the very next day. Didn't they have enough to worry
about without involving bystanders? And Emile had readily
admitted to teaching the nosy youth a lesson. The boy had no
business following him.

Now that Pascal had reportedly resurfaced, Carlini wondered if there were a connection. Perhaps the Boussant boy had
known about Pascal all along. As unlikely as it seemed, it
would explain why he followed Bonet. Could he possibly know
something about the fugitive's whereabouts now? For a farmer
he seemed to travel a lot lately, and one of his train trips had
been to Lyons, according to the stationmaster. Maybe he was
the one Malfaire was looking for.

The trouble was, Carlini couldn't go after the boy directly—
not as long as Antoine continued to command the respect of the
men in the network. The furor that would result might sink his
entire operation, and regardless of the pressure put on by
Inspector Malfaire, he couldn't risk that.

To complicate matters, the Americans and the British had
invaded French territory in North Africa, and that was likely to
provoke a reaction from Vichy, not to mention the Germans.
There was no telling what that might do to his own operation,
but any hope of Allied intervention on French soil would
undoubtedly give Pascal and his Gaullist friends a lot more
credibility. That could spell real trouble for his efforts to retain
control of the local network.

Carlini crushed the smoldering stub of his cigarette with
the heel of his shoe and strode toward Le Dauphin. Malfaire
would reward him handsomely for any information about
Pascal. And they would both sleep better once the rogue was
recaptured. But if the Boussant boy knew anything, he would
have to find a way to get to him without Antoine LeBoeuf
interfering. The old fool was beginning to pose more than his
share of problems.

⚜   ⚜   ⚜

Isabelle looked up from her sewing in surprise as Marcel burst through the front door. His face was flushed with color and his breathing was as labored as if he had run up the hill from the village.

"What is it, Marcel?" Evelyne Boussant had come into the *salon* the minute they heard the car door slam shut. Her brow was furrowed and she wiped her hands nervously on her apron. "Is something wrong?"

"The Germans," he said, trying to catch his breath. "They've broken the treaty."

"What do you mean?" Françoise, who had been doing homework in her room, had descended the stairs to see what was going on.

"They've crossed over the border into the free zone. They say they plan to occupy all of France."

Isabelle couldn't believe what she was hearing. *Germans? Here?* Memories flooded her thoughts unbidden—memories of what the Germans drove her father to do; what they did to Adam; what they would have done to her had she stayed in Paris. *Would they do it all over again—here?*

"Who told you this?" Evelyne was obviously shaken, as was Françoise, but she needed to hear more.

"The mayor, Monsieur Flandinet. He was supposed to give a speech for the Armistice Day celebration, but instead, he told us that because of the Allied invasion of North Africa, Germany and Italy decided to protect themselves by occupying the whole of France."

"Can't the marshal do something?" asked Evelyne, her voice strained. "Can't he make them at least honor the treaty?"

"Maman, Marshal Pétain is old and feeble. He couldn't do anything against Hitler even if he wanted to. Besides, the Nazis have ordered the French army disbanded. Monsieur Flandinet says if they resist, they'll be crushed."

Everyone was silent for several long moments. Finally, Isabelle spoke.

"When will they come here?" she asked softly without looking up. Her thoughts tumbled over one another so that she felt almost dizzy, but this one thing she had to know.

"I'm not sure," replied Marcel, "but it could be as early as this evening. At least that's what people were saying. I heard they've already occupied Lyons. But it won't be the Germans here."

Isabelle looked up quickly and put into words the question that was written on the faces of the other women. "Who then, if not the Germans?"

"According to the mayor, the Italians will control the southeast. And that includes us."

"The Italians?" Françoise was incredulous. "What gives them the right—"

"Hitler, apparently," Marcel cut in brusquely. "They obviously didn't ask *our* permission!"

An uncomfortable silence reigned once again. Isabelle looked from Marcel to his mother and then to Françoise. No one seemed to want to return her anxious gaze. There was a tear in Evelyne's eye, and her shoulders slumped as she turned and walked slowly back to the kitchen. A moment later Françoise disappeared quietly upstairs again, though it seemed doubtful she would get much homework done. Marcel remained a little longer, shifting his weight from one foot to the other and looking down at his shoe tops.

When at last she caught his eye, Isabelle opened her mouth to speak, but the lump in her throat prevented it. She held him in her gaze for a long moment, willing herself to believe that in the look on his face lay answers to the questions she longed to ask.

"I've got to find Luc and finish the chores," he said finally, breaking the spell. He started to leave.

"Marcel?" she said hoarsely, unwilling to let him go just yet. "This changes everything, doesn't it?"

He looked puzzled. "I don't know what you mean."

"The occupation. The Italians."

He thought for a moment. "Some things will be quite different, I'm sure," he said slowly, "but some things will never change." With that he opened the door on the late afternoon twilight and was quickly gone.

Isabelle stared after him for a long time.

Chapter 21

The park in the center of the Place de Verdun seemed more crowded than usual for a weekday afternoon. A week had passed since the Italian army had rolled its armor into Grenoble, and traffic into and out of the prefecture was heavy as local citizens vied with refugees, foreign businessmen, and low-level political representatives for the attention of whomever was in authority. As might have been expected, confusion reigned supreme as French officials grudgingly relinquished administrative control to the newly arrived Italian military.

As a result, lines were long, tempers flared frequently, and little was accomplished, leaving scores of people standing about in the square wondering what to do next. In addition, the sight of Italian troops and tanks in the heart of their city brought out the curious from blocks around. The initial shock of the occupation having worn off, they were gathered in tight little clusters, commiserating and offering their critiques of Marshal Pétain, Pierre Laval, and Mussolini to any who would listen.

Word was circulating that the old marshal had ceded virtually all power to Prime Minister Laval, a move apparently aimed at mollifying the Germans, but which shocked and angered many of the French. The swarthy Laval was well known for his willingness to collaborate with the Nazis.

Marcel listened to the animated, if idle talk as he strolled slowly toward the center of the tiny park. It was his third time through, though each time he had come from a different direction. Careful not to draw attention, he tried to appear aimless in his wandering. Hands stuffed into his coat pockets, and whistling a soundless tune, he allowed his gaze to drift from bench to bench in search of Professor Lambert.

Glancing quickly at his watch, he went over the instructions in his mind. Pastor Westphal had slipped him a note at the end of last Sunday's service asking him to meet the professor in the park on Friday at 3. It wasn't quite 3 o'clock yet, but Marcel was anxious to have this over with. Maybe too anxious, he decided. He found an empty spot on a nearby bench and sat down to wait.

He had started getting nervous while waiting in Domène for the bus into the city. He had spotted Antoine LeBoeuf and René Carlini through the open door of Le Dauphin, seated at the same table, obviously locked in an intense conversation. To make matters worse, Antoine had exited the bar just as the bus arrived and was the last passenger to board. Fortunately, the bus was crowded and Marcel had been able to avoid him. And when he got off at the Place de Verdun, Antoine remained onboard. Still, seeing the old man with Carlini had made him angry—and a little tense.

Gilles Théron smiled and held out his hand as he approached Marcel. Glad as he usually was to see his friend, Marcel stood and shook his hand quickly and silently, still scanning the park beyond for any sign of Lambert.

"Well, it's awfully good to see you too!" exclaimed Gilles, his voice dripping with sarcasm.

"I'm sorry, Gilles," Marcel felt like a schoolboy caught daydreaming in class. "I didn't expect to see you here. And I guess I've got a lot on my mind." He paused. "What are you doing here, anyway?"

"I just got out of a lecture across the street." He pointed behind him to one of the university buildings. "But mostly, I came looking for you."

Marcel was caught completely off guard. "What do you mean, you 'came looking for me'?"

"Just what I said." Gilles' smile broadened. "Come on. I'll take you to the professor."

Marcel followed without a word. So, Gilles was working with Professor Lambert too. He shouldn't have been surprised, he guessed. Not after learning that the Thérons were also hiding Jews. But he wondered how many more surprises Gilles had up his sleeve. He didn't have to wait long to find out.

"Marcel," began the fair-haired Gilles as they paused at the curb, "don't look now, but I think someone is watching us—or at least you."

Marcel felt his neck and shoulders tense. "Did you get a good look at him? What does he look like?" *Was Antoine right?* he wondered. *Did Carlini really have someone following him?*

"Maybe it's nothing, Marcel, just a wrinkled old man with snow-white hair. Does that sound like anyone you know?"

Marcel didn't answer. He took Gilles by the elbow and guided him across the street as quickly as possible without breaking into a run.

⚜   ⚜   ⚜

From behind the wheel of his sleek blue Talbot coupe, René Carlini watched as Marcel Boussant and an unknown youth strode quickly from the Place de Verdun. Parked near the museum on the Rue de la Liberté, Carlini had been just about to get out when the two came into view a block away. He slipped the Talbot into gear and eased away from the curb. If he could follow them, perhaps he would discover what, if any, was the boy's connection with the slippery Pascal.

A half-hour earlier, he had left Le Dauphin just as the bus for Grenoble was pulling out. Through the window, he saw young Boussant seated near the front. It had taken him only an instant to decide what to do. As far as he was able to tell, the boy hadn't wandered far from home lately. Perhaps this was his chance to catch him off guard. So he had followed the bus at a distance in his car.

Now, if he weren't careful, he could lose him simply because of the confusion of one-way streets. The boys appeared to be heading toward the Rue Condillac. He steered the Talbot right one block and then onto Condillac a hundred yards from where Boussant and his friend would next appear.

Only they never showed. Carlini waited as long as he could before advancing a block and turning left to where he had last seen the two. They were nowhere in sight. Instead, there was Antoine LeBoeuf leaning against the side of one of the old university buildings, near a side entrance.

Carlini pounded his fists against the Talbot's steering wheel. *LeBoeuf, the crazy fool! He'll ruin everything.* What was he doing there, anyway? Protecting Marcel Boussant? Or was *he* following him too? Either way, the boy surely must have something to hide. And sooner or later he would find out what it was. He would just have to be patient, that's all—and hope that Inspector Malfaire would be too. He also hoped that the presence of the Italians wouldn't complicate things too much.

❦   ❦   ❦

That night in the barn, Marcel sat on the milking stool, absorbed in his own thoughts as he milked first one cow and then the other. He could have done the milking with his eyes closed, by now. The cows, the barn, the routine—everything was so familiar that he gave no thought to what he was doing. Even the eerie, long shadows cast by the light from the coal oil lantern seemed familiar by the time he was finishing with the second cow. Perhaps that's why it startled him so to see Isabelle standing in the doorway, just beyond the full reach of the lantern's warm glow.

He stared at her for a moment in awed silence and wondered if she had ever been inside the barn—any barn. She hadn't since she had been there, as far as he knew. She looked so out of place there—almost too beautiful to be real, even in the dim light. Her fine, smooth features contrasted sharply with the rude, rough-hewn surroundings of the ancient barn.

She took a slow step forward into the light to reveal the blue dress she had recently sewn for herself. Marcel had been impressed from the first moment he saw her in it, and so had the rest of the family. It looked like something straight out of a Paris fashion magazine. And self-conscious as she was about her growing figure, Isabelle seemed to gain confidence once she put it on.

Now, the dress was visible in spite of the fact that she wore a coat, for the more she grew, the less she was able to fasten the coat. She hadn't seemed to mind, since she only rarely ventured outside the house. Still, it seemed a shame to Marcel that she didn't have a coat that fit her well.

"Hello, Marcel," she said softly, breaking into his thoughts. "May I come in for a minute?"

"Yes, of course." He rose so hurriedly from the wooden stool that he knocked it over backward in the process.

"Oh, don't let me interrupt you," she offered apologetically. "I'll just watch, if it's all right. I, uh—I've never seen anyone milk a cow before." A timid little smile crept across her lips. "It's not something you see every day in Paris."

"I suppose you're right about that." He returned the smile, still a little sheepish at his sudden clumsiness. "Actually, I'm about done here. But I'll walk you back to the house if you'd like, once I turn the cows out."

She nodded.

Quickly—much more so than usual—Marcel loosed the cows from their stanchions and shooed them toward the side door and into the small, fenced pasture with the other animals. The cows were in no particular hurry to go, and even seemed to resent being rushed out into the dark and chill of the night. Finally, after some coaxing and prodding, the lowing beasts lumbered out into the field and Marcel closed the wooden gate behind them. When he returned to Isabelle, he found her seated just inside the main barn door on the small wooden bench Papa had made.

"You must be tired," he said, reaching for the milk pails. "Perhaps we'd better go in."

"I'm fine. Really. And the fresh air feels good for a change, don't you think?"

Marcel set the pails down again and gave a little smile, but he really did not know what to say. He supposed that the air did feel good, but since he had been outside much of the day, it mostly felt cold. If she wanted to stay, though, it was fine with him, whatever the weather. He had begun to feel warmer just thinking about her.

The silence began to feel uncomfortable as Isabelle seemed to be waiting for him to say something. If he only had the courage, there were things he wished to say. But the last thing he wanted was to push her away. Deep down, he wanted to put his arms gently around her and whisper vows of devotion, protection. Would she understand? After all she had been through, all the loss and suffering, would she trust herself to him—or to anyone?

"Do you miss Paris?" he asked finally, taking the easy way out.

She gave him a strange look, half-sad, half-puzzled. "I don't know," she began slowly. "Perhaps the way it used to be. I certainly don't miss what it has become under the Nazis. There may not be any bomb craters in the streets, and the buildings are still standing, but the City of Lights I used to know is in ruins. Neighbors spying on each other, people starving, assassinations, reprisals, people arrested for no reason . . . I try not to think about it too much. It's too frightening."

"You're safe here, you know," Marcel said, trying to soothe her and make up for having evoked unhappy memories.

"I know," she said with a weak attempt at a smile, "but for how long? You said yourself that things would change now that the whole of France is occupied. I don't see how things will change for the better."

"Perhaps not," he replied quietly, "but maybe they won't get any worse, either."

"What do you mean?" Her smile dissolved. "Do you really think the Nazis won't be just as brutal here as in Paris?"

"The Nazis aren't here. The Italians are. Maybe they won't be as bad as the others. Maybe they'll be able to rein in the Vichy police." He had no reason to think so, but he wanted to sound hopeful.

"Do you think that means the police will stop hunting us down like animals?"

"I don't know." Marcel didn't venture a guess because he

didn't want to add to Isabelle's alarm. But Professor Lambert had said that everything the CIMADE had heard so far led them to believe that a change in the Vichy policy toward Jews was unlikely. The Italians controlled only ten departments, and even if they had a different Jewish agenda, it was unlikely to affect Vichy's desire to appease the Germans. For their part, the Germans were demanding more and more deportations of Jews. And since they held the power, it did not bode well for Isabelle. Marcel felt it keenly.

Lambert felt it too, which is why he had asked to meet with Marcel earlier in the day. The uncertainty of the occupation was forcing everyone hiding Jews to consider all their options. Giving assistance to Jews was swiftly and harshly punished under German occupation rules, and although the Italians hadn't spelled out their intentions, no one expected their rules to be any different. The professor wanted Marcel to be fully aware of the consequences, and to begin making plans to move Isabelle to a safer place—eventually Switzerland, if possible.

"I hope you feel safe here for now, anyway," he said after a long silence. He quickly avoided her gaze. He really didn't want to tell her that she would probably be leaving soon.

"Safer than I have felt in a long time," she replied softly. "I just hope I haven't been too much trouble."

He looked up at her in surprise. "You haven't been any trouble, Isabelle. We've enjoyed having you with us."

"*You* didn't always enjoy having me here," she teased, her smile returning.

Marcel felt his face flush. He felt trapped, and he was sure she knew it. "I, uh—well, I was afraid," he stammered weakly. Even as the words tumbled out he regretted the admission of weakness. *How could she possibly respect that?*

Isabelle's smile faded. "Afraid for me? Or afraid for your family?"

Marcel's eyes traced the mortar lines on the stone floor. His throat seemed to constrict as he spoke. "I guess I was afraid for myself, mostly," he said somewhat hoarsely. He swallowed quickly so he could continue before she asked him any more questions. "You see, I had this idea that I could serve my country—even God—by opposing the policies of the Vichy government. So I began to help friends who were aiding Jews. It seemed exciting, and important—and relatively easy."

"Easy?" Isabelle was skeptical. "But you could have been arrested. You know that don't you?"

"I mean easy in that I never actually saw or felt much suffering or injustice myself. I was just wrapped up in the idea. But it's different when you actually see people suffering. And even more so when the victims include someone you know personally. It's no longer just an idea, a concept. It becomes personal. You fight for the things and people you care for. And I guess I was afraid I wouldn't be up to it." It felt good to get it off his chest finally, but maybe he had gone too far, said too much. *What will she think of all of this babbling?*

"But when I arrived, I was a complete stranger to you." Isabelle's voice seemed strained. "Sometimes I think I still am. Maybe you worry too much about someone you hardly know."

Marcel looked directly into a face that glowed softly in the light of the lantern. "Do you really think so?" he asked, emboldened by the light in her eyes. "And if I knew you better—if you were no longer a stranger?"

"I—I'm not sure I understand." She looked away quickly.

Marcel's heart sank. He had spoken too soon. Being near her made him feel so confused sometimes, and now more than ever. Was he fooling himself? Or was what he felt more than just a passing infatuation? "I'm trying to do the right thing, Isabelle," he offered, trying to see into her eyes once more. "And every night I pray that God will help me."

Isabelle's mouth twisted a little at the corners, but she still wouldn't look at him. "Do you really think He—that any-one—is listening, Marcel?"

"Yes," he said simply, "I believe He is."

And I hope He answers soon, he breathed silently.

❦　　❦　　❦

"Do you think it's wrong for a Protestant to love a Catholic?" Isabelle asked Françoise later as they crawled into bed.

Françoise paused just as she was about to turn out the lamp. "What do you mean, 'wrong'?" she said, looking confused.

"I mean, would it be considered a sin in your religion?"

"It's never a sin to love someone, Isabelle. The Bible says we ought to love everyone—even our enemies—and do good to those who hate us."

"I could never do that!" Isabelle was incredulous. "Could you really love someone who hated you?"

"I don't know, Isabelle. I can't think of anyone who actual-ly hates me. I'd like to say I could love such a person, but I'm really not sure."

"Well, anyway, that's not the kind of love I meant," said Isabelle returning to her original question. She didn't want to think about the people who hated her. "I was thinking of the love of a man for a woman. Is that kind of love wrong?"

"You mean between a Protestant and a Catholic?"

"Yes."

"That depends."

"What do you mean?" Isabelle was puzzled. She had assumed that the answer would be unambiguous. These Christians could certainly be complicated.

"It shouldn't come as a surprise to you, Isabelle," Françoise began, "that many Catholics and Protestants are Christian in name only. They don't understand that true faith is not conferred by some rite in a church—no matter which church. For them, faith is just part of one's culture, a sort of honored tradition."

"But what if a person has 'true faith' as you call it?"

"Well, true faith, like love, is a matter of the heart. And I can't imagine opening my heart to someone who didn't share everything with me, including my faith. It seems to me that either my faith would be diminished, or my love would. I don't think I'd want to live that way."

Isabelle felt a knot in the pit of her stomach begin to grow. "Would you still care for Gilles if he were a Catholic?" she asked. This had gotten far more involved than she had expected, but she had to know.

Françoise blushed. "To be honest, I've never thought about it. I guess I'd have to say I'm not sure."

"And if he were Jewish?"

Bewilderment furrowed Françoise's brow. "Isabelle, where are you going with all of this? I'm afraid I don't understand. Are you worried that no one will care for you because you're Jewish?" She reached her arms out, almost instinctively it seemed, to pull Isabelle close. "You know we do!"

She doesn't understand. Isabelle stared unseeing over Françoise's shoulder, suddenly overcome by a deep sadness. Adam was gone, yet thoughts of him still tormented her. Sometimes she hated the fact that she couldn't seem to forget him. But just as often she was angry with herself for wanting to forget.

Now, she wanted to love a man who ultimately could not claim her—not, it seemed, without diminishing his faith. And while his faith was the part of him she found impossible to understand, she couldn't imagine him without it. She couldn't ask him to become less than he was, could she?

"I know you care, Françoise," she said, "and I've never felt reproached for being a Jew as long as I've been here."

"What is it then?"

Isabelle didn't answer right away. It was hard to admit even to herself that she could see clearly how Marcel felt. And it wasn't just wishful thinking, either. He hadn't needed to say it in so many words. It had been written in his eyes. When she finally spoke, her voice was barely audible. "Your brother cares too, Françoise. I know he does. But I'm scared—scared that he's blind to the consequences."

Françoise, eyes suddenly moist and penetrating, grasped her gently by the shoulders. "Is that what frightens you most, Isabelle?"

"I don't know. Sometimes I think I'm more afraid of never being loved at all. I'm so confused, Françoise, I don't know how I really feel."

Françoise said nothing. She just held her close for a long time.

It seemed like hours before Isabelle fell asleep. When at last she slumbered, she dreamed that she was running through a forest, deeper and deeper into its dense darkness. Behind her she could hear a voice calling her name, but she refused to answer. Instead, she hurried blindly on, fearful of the deepening gloom, but more frightened still by the insistent voice. At times it sounded like Marcel, other times like a voice she had never heard, still calling, still pursuing into the faint light of morning.

Chapter 22

Armand Moreau, sitting at the edge of the stone hearth in an old abandoned farmhouse, finished reading the one-page letter by the light of the fire. He examined the signature over and over, and satisfied that it was authentic, breathed a long, slow sigh of relief.

"Good news?" asked the man who had delivered the letter.

Armand smiled faintly in response. With nothing more than the dancing firelight to illumine the room, the delivery man looked a few years older than most of the others who sat huddled nearby, playing a game of cards. He wore his collar up and his hat down low over his eyes in spite of the dim surroundings. Of medium height and build, there was certainly nothing remarkable about his appearance. Somehow, though, Armand had a nagging sense that they had met somewhere.

He shrugged it off, leaned forward slightly, and placed the open letter in the flames, watching it dissolve into a crumple of charred ebony. Its contents, however, remained clearly etched in his mind. At last he had been granted his request for a change in mission, and Jean Moulin himself had given his approval, signing his *nom de guerre* "Max" as proof.

Armand had requested the change shortly after leaving Lyons. With his cover blown, he hadn't dared return to his original task of helping to align the various resistance networks for Moulin and de Gaulle. It had become far too risky for him to continue in that direction. But without official approval, he hadn't wanted to move too quickly in any other direction, either. He guessed it was probably his military training that made him that way. The chain of command was, after all, part of what made fighting men effective.

Effective, however, was not a word he would have used to describe the *maquis* with which he had fallen in. After his escape from the hospital in Lyons, Dr. Billot had directed him to Jean Soulain, a pastor in Annecy, who had in turn put him in touch with a local network. Operating out of the Bauges mountains, these *maquisards* were energetic, even enthusiastic, but from the very beginning it was clear that they were largely untrained and completely undisciplined.

They are all so young, Armand remarked to himself, and each time he saw them, whether by firelight or sunlight, it struck him anew. Could he possibly accomplish anything with such untested, undisciplined boys? He would have his chance soon enough, now, thanks to Moulin's reply.

"Can you drive me into Aix on your way back?" he asked the delivery man suddenly. The sooner he could meet with Hervé Chassin, the sooner he could begin to make a difference.

"Of course," the nondescript man replied, "but we'll need to hurry. I've already been gone too long."

Armand threw his coat on over his shoulders and followed the man outside to where a sleek black Renault sedan stood waiting. Two more youths stood in the shadows, keeping an admiring eye on the powerful machine.

"Don't wait up for me," Armand said jovially as he walked past the two and climbed into the car. "I should be back by this time tomorrow."

"Ready?" asked the driver as the Renault roared to life.

"Ready," replied Armand. "I'll give you directions once we get to the edge of town."

"No need," said the driver casually. "Hervé and I are old friends. I know the way to his house like I know the bottom of my pocket."

Armand watched out of the corner of his eye as the man handled the big sedan with ease down the winding road. Maybe he was just imagining it, but something about the shadowy messenger seemed familiar, though he couldn't decide what it was. "Have we met before?" he finally asked.

The driver didn't take his eyes from the road ahead. "Not exactly," he replied somewhat evasively, "but I know who you are."

They drove through the inky blackness for several miles in silence. It was obvious that the driver had no intention of volunteering his own identity, and Armand didn't ask. He knew better. But it bothered him that he couldn't remember where he had seen the man before. Perhaps Hervé would tell him something.

Armand had grown to appreciate Hervé Chassin over the last few weeks. Not that the stocky, somber stonemason who now found himself leading a *maquis* of nearly thirty men was easy to get to know. On the contrary, most of what Armand knew about Hervé had come from others. Having reached middle age, he was something of a father figure to many of the youths who followed him. And their devotion was evident in the stories they told about the silent man.

According to the boys in the *maquis* (for most could hardly be described otherwise), the once-gregarious Hervé and his wife

Babette raised three handsome sons in their modest home in Aix-les-Bains. The second son was born a brief ten months after the first, the third fifteen months later. As they grew toward adulthood, the boys were inseparable. In fact, they arranged to perform their military service together in late 1939. None of the three returned. The blitzkrieg which humbled France in six short weeks robbed the Chassin family of a generation.

Perhaps Hervé's silence was his way of grieving. One thing was sure, however. He had not withdrawn into self-pity. Armand himself could vouch for that. Both Hervé and Babette seemed determined not so much to make the Germans pay for the death of their sons, as to chip away at the Nazi system in France. It was an evil they chose to oppose, rather than see it devour the innocent sons and daughters of other families. And to that end they risked their own lives in the rescue of refugees, escaped prisoners-of-war, and even a few downed Allied airmen.

To expand this work, Hervé had begun recruiting local youths, many of whom had been friends of his sons. But molding them into something truly useful wasn't easy. Shortly after taking in Armand, the likable Chassin had seen in him the potential for whipping his ragtag little band into a force to be reckoned with. Armand agreed that his experience as an officer in the now-disbanded French army could once again serve him well—if he could get Moulin's permission. Tonight that permission had finally arrived. And tomorrow Armand would begin building Hervé Chassin's tiny army.

⚜   ⚜   ⚜

Jean-Claude Malfaire cursed under his breath and glared at the main lobby receptionist. How would he ever get anywhere when he was constantly having to put up with incompetence right there in the police department?

"I called his house, just like you said, Inspector," the receptionist said, her faced flushed with unconcealed anger. "His wife said that he was on his way. I don't know what else I can tell you."

Malfaire slammed his gloved fist down on the desk and walked back out the front door of Lyons' central police station. *It isn't like Dominique to be late,* he reminded himself, *but today of all days is no time to start a bad habit.* He glanced at his watch for the twelfth time in the past five minutes. Only ten minutes until his appointment with *Obersturmführer* Klaus Barbie. He could take a taxi, of course, but he wanted *Herr* Barbie to see the style in which he traveled. Still, it wouldn't do to be late for a meeting with the Gestapo's top man in Lyons.

Seconds later, Dominique pulled up in the black Renault.

"Where have you been?" Malfaire fumed aloud as he climbed in the back seat. He hadn't bothered waiting for Dominique to open the door for him. "Can't you see I'll be late for my meeting? Where have you been?" he repeated.

"Désolé, Inspector," Dominique offered apologetically as he pulled away from the curb. "I had a little trouble getting fuel this morning. You know, the *boches* are taking it all these days. Makes it rather hard on the rest of us."

"Didn't you just get fuel a couple of days ago?" demanded Malfaire. "Where does it all go? You're not selling it on the black market, are you?"

Dominique laughed, a little nervously it seemed to the inspector. "You know I'd never do that, Inspector. It's just that this beauty has a big appetite, that's all."

He's probably right, Malfaire decided. *No need to get into it now, in any case.* He had to concentrate on the meeting with Barbie. This could be his big opportunity. Though he wasn't overly fond of the idea, the Nazi occupation of France was a *fait accompli,* and he had determined to make the most of it.

For him that meant exploring ways to get his career moving ahead again. His skills would undoubtedly be of use to a man like Barbie, who would be a little out of his element here in France. Perhaps they would even find they had some things in common. He only hoped for his own sake that a passion for punctuality wasn't one of them.

The Hotel Terminus, a square box-like building made of granite, was a study in contrasts. While the hotel's exterior seldom got a mention in its guests' postcards home, the interior was quite a different matter. Marble floors, mirrored columns, *salons* paneled in finely carved wood, and frescoes depicting French country life, all contributed to a richly ornate look. The Hotel Terminus represented the best the city had to offer, and so it came as no surprise to Jean-Claude Malfaire that it had been claimed as headquarters for the Lyons SS.

Barbie was seated in the east dining room when Malfaire arrived at two minutes before 9. As he approached the *Obersturmführer's* table, the young Nazi rose politely and motioned for him to take a seat opposite. He wasn't as tall as Malfaire had expected, nor was he fair or blond. Only his bright-blue eyes hinted at some Aryan ancestry. And though he smiled easily, somehow it didn't put the inspector at ease.

"*Bonjour, monsieur l'inspecteur,*" Barbie said in excellent French. "I hope you are well this morning."

Malfaire had heard that the Gestapo chief's French was not bad, but he had to admit that he was impressed. Few Germans he had met thus far sounded this good. "Very well, thank you," he replied, warming to the man. "And you?"

Barbie sat down again. "Very well," he said, "and enjoying the hospitality of your beautiful city, I might add."

"Yes, well, I'm pleased to have the opportunity to meet you, Herr Barbie," said Malfaire, clearing his throat nervously, "and I hope we'll have occasion to work together."

"That depends entirely on what you have to say to me," said Barbie, suddenly all business. "I hear you have quite a reputation for tracking down criminals."

Malfaire felt his shirt pull tight across his swelling chest. "Yes, I have—"

"Then how is it that you haven't arrested more of these so-called resistance fighters—terrorists, I call them. According to my sources, the whole city is crawling with them." He paused for a brief second. "And Jews! Everywhere I go I see Jews. It's enough to make me sick. What are you doing about this, Inspector Malfaire?"

Malfaire was speechless. Here he was offering to help the Gestapo, and this little man with blue eyes was attacking his arrest record! *This is outrageous,* he said to himself, fuming.

"We—that is, I feel the same way as you do about these foul Jews, Herr Barbie," he finally managed aloud. He could feel his temperature begin to rise. "A-and I'm working on a terrorist case right now. A major case, I assure you."

"Any names?"

"Er—one man's name is Pascal, Herr Barbie."

"Pascal, eh? I know that name," said Barbie, stroking his chin. "He's a confederate of the one they call Max, I believe."

"Max?" Malfaire regretted the admission of ignorance the moment it escaped his lips.

"Yes, Max, you fool! If we can bring down Max we may bring down the entire terrorist network. Give me this Pascal, and I guarantee he'll lead us to Max." His blue eyes seemed to grow in intensity at the prospect.

"I'll do my best, Herr Barbie." Malfaire was growing warm and very uncomfortable by now. He was also kicking himself for ever dreaming he could work with the arrogant little tyrant.

"Do better than that, Inspector. I want this Pascal, and I want Jews, lots of Jews. And the people who help them. I want to put a stop to this foolishness. Do you understand?"

Malfaire was livid by the time he returned to his car. *So this is the thanks I get for offering my services. The pompous little jackal! Does he think I can produce miracles?* He jerked open the car door and slammed it shut again once inside. "Take me to a telephone, Dominique," he ordered. "It's time I put a little more pressure on our friend Carlini."

Chapter 23

Isabelle lay on her back, wide awake, staring into the darkness. For a couple of hours she'd been experiencing a growing discomfort in her lower abdomen. The muscles grew increasingly taut from time to time, only to relax a few moments later, ebbing and flowing like an intermittent tide. Except for her hands, instinctively reaching to soothe her tense muscles, she tried to lie still so as not to awaken the sleeping Françoise. *Could this be it?* she wondered in silence. Somehow, it didn't hurt like she had thought it would, though it was certainly uncomfortable. But if this were the real thing, she knew that it was likely to get worse before it was all over—far worse.

Each time her muscles relaxed and the tension subsided, she exhaled with relief and wondered just how long it would be before it started all over again. Up to now the discomfort had been rather erratic. It was probably just a false alarm. After all, she wasn't due yet for three more weeks, as nearly as she could tell. And given the stories she had been told of women whose first pregnancy went a week or more past term, she had just assumed that the child she carried would wait to make an appearance until close to the new year—maybe even the first week in January. The eighth of December was definitely too early.

Having convinced herself that what she was feeling was little more than a precursor of things to come in the weeks ahead, Isabelle drifted back to sleep—or nearly so. But then the tide of contracting muscles surged in again, more strongly than before, startling her so she nearly sat upright in the bed. *What's going on?* her mind raced. *This isn't supposed to be happening yet. It's too early. It's much too early!*

It seemed like the contraction would go on forever, but it eventually subsided, leaving Isabelle biting her lip to keep from crying. It wasn't pain that brought tears to her eyes. It wasn't really too painful—so far, at least. Rather it was the realization that today, or next week, or some time very soon, she would give birth to a fatherless child, a child with a fugitive mother, a child whose chances for a decent, happy life were remote at best.

For a moment she wished she had never become pregnant. The trouble she was in would only be aggravated by the presence of a child. She had been over this ground before, certainly, but not with the sense of urgency she now felt. How could I have been so careless? she chastised herself. *And Adam, how could he. . . .* She wanted to scream. *How could you leave me like this, Adam, with a child on the way—your child? Why didn't you just stay home that day? But no, you had to get yourself arrested and killed—all for the sake of your precious political views. Communism, fascism, what good is any of it now that you're dead? What about me, Adam? What am I supposed to do? And what about our baby?*

Hot tears scalded her cheeks as she vented her anger in silence. She lashed out with her thoughts at Adam, at her father, at the Nazis, at the surrounding darkness. So consumed

was she by her own grief and anger that she was caught completely off guard by Françoise's voice.

"Is everything all right, Isabelle?"

She didn't answer. She just sniffled and dabbed at her eyes.

"Isabelle?" Françoise wasn't going to give up easily.

Isabelle reached out for Françoise's hand, squeezed it hard
and felt Françoise respond in kind. It felt good to know that
she wasn't alone—especially now.

"What's the matter, Isabelle?"

"I think I'm having labor pains," she answered hoarsely.
That didn't explain the tears, of course, but then she couldn't
really expect her friend to understand all that was going on in
her mind.

"Does it hurt terribly?" Françoise soothed.

"It's not so bad," she replied. "Not yet, anyway."

"Are you scared?"

Isabelle paused before answering. "A little," she said finally.

Françoise moved to get out of the bed. "I'd better tell
Maman," she said excitedly. "She'll know what to do."

Isabelle hung onto her hand to keep her from leaving.
"Not yet," she said. "The pains have only just begun. Let's wait
awhile—until I'm sure. I don't want to bother your mother
with—"

She drew a sharp breath and gripped Françoise's hand
more tightly as the uncomfortable tide rolled in once more.
She couldn't tell how long it had been since the last one, but
she knew she should start keeping track of the intervals. There
was so much to think about, and she wanted desperately for
someone to tell her what to expect from this point on. So
when the contraction ebbed this time, she raised no objection
when Françoise renewed her offer to go get her mother.

⚜   ⚜   ⚜

"Marcel!"

Marcel, roused from a deep sleep, rolled onto his side where he could see the doorway to the bedroom he shared with Luc. Silhouetted in a dim light that seemed to come from somewhere down the hall, stood Maman.

"Are you awake, Marcel?" she asked in a hoarse whisper. Without waiting for an answer she added, "Get dressed and come downstairs. I need your help. Quickly!" Then she shut the door.

Fumbling in the near-total darkness for a match, Marcel eventually lit the lamp on the bedside table. He kept it turned down low while he dressed so as not to awaken his little brother. Then he extinguished the lamp and tiptoed out of the room. On the way by Françoise's room he heard voices. Isabelle and his sister were evidently awake too. Thinking little of it, he descended the stairs and joined his mother in the kitchen.

"Isabelle's labor has started," she said matter-of-factly, "and she's going to need a doctor." She handed him a demitasse of the precious coffee the Thérons had given her weeks ago.

Marcel was surprised by the cup of coffee almost as much as by the news. It was something Maman served sparingly, not knowing when or how they might obtain more. But coffee or no coffee, Isabelle couldn't really be having her baby. "Isn't this early?" he asked. "I thought you said the baby was due at the end of the year."

Maman smiled. "Babies come when they're ready, Marcel. And sometimes that means they arrive ahead of schedule. There's really nothing we can do about it but pray that mother and child will be all right."

Marcel took a sip of the steaming coffee. "What did you have in mind when you said you needed my help? The only babies I know anything about are the four-legged kind." He had watched lots of animals being born. He had even assisted a few.

"Not that kind of help!" Maman was not amused. "She's going to need a doctor, and I need you to bring him here."

"You mean Dr. La Forge?" La Forge was the doctor in Domène who had delivered all three of the Boussant children.

"No. We can't take that risk. We have no idea how he feels about Jews. What if he turned her in to the police? We'd all be arrested."

Marcel hated it when Maman told him things he already knew as if he were hearing it for the first time. "Who then?" he asked, trying to mask his annoyance. He didn't know any other doctors.

"Go to the presbytery," she said. "I'm sure Pastor Westphal knows a doctor we can trust. But hurry. I don't know how much time we have."

Marcel gulped down the last of his coffee and headed out the door toward the barn, buttoning up his coat as he went. It was still dark, and colder than it had been the previous few days. Winter was definitely on the way. Somehow, it just didn't seem like a great time to have a baby—especially when he knew that Isabelle might have to travel soon. It didn't seem right that anyone should have to take flight in the winter, much less with a newborn child.

The old Peugeot cranked over on the first try, and with high beams knifing through the darkness, Marcel urged her swiftly down the hill toward Domène and on to Grenoble, praying he wouldn't be stopped for breaking the curfew.

The eastern sky was just beginning to show a hint of light when he came to a stop in front of the old stone presbytery. The house was still shuttered tight, so it was impossible to tell whether anyone was up and about yet. But Marcel didn't have the luxury of waiting until a more appropriate hour before calling on his pastor. He was afraid he would be too late no matter what happened. He rapped his knuckles on the heavy wooden door.

"Marcel Boussant!" exclaimed Pastor Westphal a few moments later. "Is everything all right? What brings you into the city at such an hour?"

"May I come in, Pastor Westphal? It's not something we should talk about in the street."

"Of course. Where are my manners? I guess I'm not accustomed to receiving guests at this hour." Once Marcel was inside, Westphal closed the door. "Now then, tell me what this is all about, young man."

"It's Isabelle, Pastor, the Jewish girl. She's going to have her baby. She's not supposed to be due yet, and this being her first baby and all, we're kind of worried about her. Maman sent me to see if you know a doctor we can trust."

"Why yes, I believe I do, though he's not here in Grenoble."

"Where then?" Marcel's sense of urgency was suddenly heightened.

"He's in hiding. Resistance activity has made him a wanted man, so I arranged to keep him and his wife out of sight for a while. They're staying on a farm in the Chartreuse hills."

"Are you sure he can be trusted?"

"Absolutely. He's already saved scores of Jews from the Nazis, not to mention all the others he's helped. I would trust him with my life."

If Westphal trusted this doctor, then Marcel felt confident that he could as well. But other questions remained. "Do you think he'll be willing to come out of hiding long enough to help Isabelle?"

"I can't answer that, Marcel. You'll have to ask him yourself."

"Well, in that case, I guess I need to know how to find him so I can ask." The Chartreuse hills could be difficult to navigate even under the best of circumstances. But with winter approaching, ice and snow were common hazards on the narrow mountain roads. He hoped the directions wouldn't be too complicated. He had to get this over with quickly.

"I believe you know the Fontaine sisters, don't you?"

Marcel nodded. Everyone in the church knew the Fontaine sisters. Most people called them Tante Marthe and Tante Solange. Even Marcel's parents had always referred to them that way. And though the elderly sisters had no living relatives, they became "aunts" to everyone.

"He and his wife have been staying with the tantes for quite a while now. Do you know how to get there?"

"Of course," he replied, somewhat puzzled. "But why would anyone hide there now? Didn't you tell me that the reason you had to move Isabelle was that the police found out she was at the Fontaines'?"

"Oh, the police suspected, all right, but when they came they found nothing but two eccentric old ladies. Don't underestimate our dear tantes, Marcel. I doubt the police will return there anytime soon. Besides, we have people watching the road on the way to the farm. No one can get up there without us knowing about it."

Marcel shrugged. "Okay, Pastor," he said as he started toward the door. "I sure hope you're right."

It could take an hour to reach the tantes' farm, and even longer to get back home. Marcel hoped Isabelle would be able to delay the baby's arrival until he returned.

⚜   ⚜   ⚜

The fire of Isabelle's anger cooled considerably as her discomfort increased. With each contraction, an icy cloud of apprehension threatened to envelop her, leaving her with precious little energy to focus on what might have been. What was happening now was all that mattered, and it was all she could handle. *What's past is past,* she told herself in a feeble attempt to be brave. But bravery, she decided, was much easier to talk about than to practice—especially in the face of the pain she knew would only grow worse.

"Would you like me to read to you awhile?" asked Evelyne Boussant from her chair near the side of the bed. Evelyne and Françoise had been taking turns sitting with her, calming her with a sympathetic presence even when words failed. "It might make the time pass more pleasantly until the doctor arrives."

Isabelle tilted her head slowly toward the kindly voice, eyes searching the older woman's face, but made no audible response. It just didn't seem necessary. Anything would be better than the silent intervals between contractions that only seemed to heighten her fears.

"I hope you won't mind if I read from the words of a great Jewish king," said Evelyne without taking her eyes from Isabelle's face. "King David seemed to know a lot about the human condition, and I've always found his words to be quite comforting."

Isabelle turned her head back again to gaze at the ceiling. She too knew about the human condition, though it brought her scant comfort. Sometimes she wondered if escaping this human condition wasn't wiser than trying to understand it.

"O God, hear my cries," read Evelyne, "be attentive to my prayer."

So, it was going to be about God, this reading. All right. It couldn't do any more harm than listening in on the Boussant family Bible readings. But, really, the great King David praying, crying out to God? He had all kinds of wealth and power at his disposal. What would make him rely on the help of God? Of course, maybe there was something about it she was missing.

A time or two she had almost been tempted to pray herself; that's what the Boussants always did. It sounded so simple, and it seemed to give them perspective, to bring them calm. But of course, she had always stopped just short of anything so foolish. Like her father always said, only the silly and the weak resort to prayer; people with any common sense have no need to imagine an invisible Being hovering over them.

The problem with the Boussants was that they didn't fit her father's description very well. And silly and weak hardly seemed to describe the most revered king in Jewish history. So, what if Papa had been wrong and the Boussants knew something he didn't? Maybe it was his faith in humanity alone that *caused* him to give in to despair. With nowhere else to turn when men betrayed him, what else could he do?

She shuddered violently at the thought of her father taking his own life. Evelyne's voice fell silent, and Isabelle felt the gentle squeeze of a hand on her shoulder.

"Are you all right, Isabelle?"

Isabelle's gaze bored into the ceiling. She willed her eyes not to form tears. At the same time she dared not speak for fear that her voice would betray her. She nodded her head slowly, affirmatively. She would be all right—soon.

Evelyne continued reading but kept a hand on Isabelle's shoulder, stroking it softly.

> *The father of orphans,*
> *the defender of widows,*
> *is God in His holy dwelling place.*

Isabelle turned to see that Evelyne was actually reading the words and not simply making them up.

> *God gives a family*
> *to those who were abandoned,*

He delivers the captives and makes them happy.

A father to orphans . . . defender of widows . . . gives a family to those abandoned . . . delivers captives. . . . Isabelle felt as though someone had been watching her life, had broadcast all her secrets. How could that be? Her mind spinning, she no longer heard the words that Evelyne read. She no longer wanted to hear. It was too much. The sudden flood of thoughts threatened to overwhelm her in its path.

Just as suddenly, the river of her pain rushed in to dispel every other thought and sensation. Her belly tensed and strained, her muscles cried out for relief. The pain had intensified to a level she hadn't even imagined.

"Oh, God!" She moaned through clenched teeth. Alarmed by the sound of her own voice, she clamped her lips tightly to keep from saying anything more.

❧ ❧ ❧

"It's Isabelle, Tante Marthe. She's about to have her baby and she needs a doctor!" Marcel had dispensed with all formality as soon as a surprised Marthe Fontaine opened her front door.

"Why, Marcel Boussant, how nice to see you. Do come in." She closed the door behind him. "Now what's this about Isabelle? Isabelle who?"

"Tante Marthe," Marcel began, trying to hide his exasperation from the old woman, "I know Isabelle stayed with you because she told me so herself. I also know that you're keeping a doctor here because Pastor Westphal told me. Please, don't make this any harder than it already is. I have to see the doctor, Tante Marthe. Isabelle needs him badly."

"Sister, do you know anything about a pregnant girl named Isabelle?" she asked as Tante Solange appeared from the kitchen.

"We helped a girl named Isabelle, but I don't believe we've ever had a pregnant girl here, Sister," replied Solange, looking more confused than usual.

Marcel was getting impatient. "Please, Tante Marthe," he pleaded, "I know you're only trying to protect her, but if I don't get her some help soon, she may be in real trouble. You wouldn't want anything to happen to her would you?"

"Did you say her name was Isabelle?" asked a third voice.

Marcel stared slack-jawed as a familiar-looking middle-aged man with salt-and-pepper hair entered the room from the back of the house.

"It's all right, *mesdames,*" the man said to the alarmed tantes. "I know this man. And I think I know the girl he's talking about."

The man, Marcel realized, was Dr. Billot from Lyons. It hadn't occurred to him that he might be Pastor Westphal's mystery doctor. And he hadn't thought to ask. Now it made all kinds of sense. After helping Pascal escape, the police would certainly have come looking for him, which explained why he was hiding out. The surprise, however, had been complete, and he was speechless.

"You knew the girl was pregnant when she arrived here, didn't you?" Billot was saying to the equally speechless sisters.

"We had no idea," exclaimed Tante Marthe, once she'd found her voice. "The poor dear never said a word about it."

"Not a word, poor dear," echoed Tante Solange. "And she was so thin, who would have thought it?"

"Well, when I met her in the camp at Vénissieux she was about to be put on a train for Drancy. From there, they would have put her on another train to the east. She was in such poor condition she might not have survived the trip. I knew she was pregnant, but she wasn't far enough along to get an exemption. That's why we slipped her out of the camp and had her brought here."

"Will you help her again, Doctor? She needs you." Marcel was anxious to be on his way.

"I had no idea you knew the girl," said the doctor. "Roux, isn't it? Pierre Roux?

Marcel looked uncomfortably at the tantes who seemed anxious to hear how he would answer. "That's not my real name," he admitted.

"I didn't think so," said Billot, "but whatever your name is, I'd be glad to help. After all, you helped me once."

The room grew suddenly warm as Marcel recalled how the doctor had tricked him into aiding Pascal's escape. He wasn't sorry about the escape, but he still burned a little at the thought of having been duped. Avoiding Tante Marthe's curious gaze, he suppressed the urge to explain. "Shall we go, Doctor?" was all he said.

Chapter 24

Marcel stopped pacing the salon in mid-circle and stood motionless, his head cocked slightly to one side, straining to hear.

"What? What is it?" whispered nine-year-old Luc. He had been sitting in a chair pretending to read a book.

"Shhh!" hissed Marcel. "I can't hear."

There it was again, only louder this time. Marcel relaxed his hunched shoulders and released the air from his lungs. He turned toward his little brother and grinned broadly. "There, did you hear it?" he asked.

"Is that all the louder babies get?" Luc looked concerned.

Marcel laughed. "I'm afraid not, Luc. If Isabelle's baby is anything like you were, nobody will be getting any sleep around here for a week."

Luc brightened. "Can we go see her now?"

"Not for a while yet. Having a baby is a lot of hard work. I imagine she'll want to be alone for a while to rest and get used to being a mother."

Luc went back to reading his book, though he glanced over toward the stairs every few minutes as if he anticipated that Isabelle would soon descend with her tiny, squalling child.

Dr. Billot, in fact, was the first to come downstairs. He rolled his sleeves down and rebuttoned the cuffs as he spoke. "Well, my friend, we didn't arrive much too soon, as I'm sure you heard."

Marcel smiled and nodded. The infant's first tiny wail had come less than half an hour after the doctor climbed the stairs. "Is she all right?" he asked, a little catch in his voice.

"She'll be fine. She just needs to rest, that's all."

"And the baby?"

Luc burst in without waiting to hear the doctor's response. "Is it a girl or a boy?"

Billot chuckled and reached over to pat the boy on the shoulder. "It's a little boy," he said, "and I think he's going to be all right."

"You think?" Marcel wondered aloud.

"Well, he's rather small, as you'll soon see. He's early, of course, and Isabelle wasn't able to eat well for the first few months. I'll come back to check on them, but they should both be fine as long as they can stay put for a while."

"How long?" Marcel could feel a knot beginning to develop in the pit of his stomach.

"Just as long as possible, my friend, as long as possible." The sudden look of concern on Billot's face matched the way Marcel felt. He breathed a silent prayer that they wouldn't have to move Isabelle any time soon.

Neither of them said anything for several minutes, as though each were afraid to intrude on the other's thoughts. Finally, Luc broke the silence.

"What did she name it?"

"Him," Marcel corrected.

"I don't know," confessed Dr. Billot, "she didn't say. But there will be plenty of time for that later.

"Look, your mother will be down soon, young man," he continued, looking directly at Luc. "She'll be able to tell you all about it. In the meantime I have to get back. Can I count on you to look after things until Marcel returns?"

Luc drew himself up to his full height and then some. *"Oui,* monsieur," he said soberly, "you can count on Luc Boussant."

"Allez, mon brave!" The doctor chucked Luc gently on the chin and then turned to Marcel. "Ready when you are, *mon ami."*

❦   ❦   ❦

A handful of snowflakes fell lazily onto the windshield of the Renault sedan which idled at the curb near the east corner of Grenoble's Place Victor Hugo. A few yards in front of the car, the sparse afternoon traffic of the Boulevard Rey flowed past on its way to the quay along the Isère River. From the back seat, Jean-Claude Malfaire watched the cars and pedestrians pass by, bemused as usual by the noticeably slower pace of things here in the capital of the Dauphiné. Next to Lyons, Grenoble seemed rather provincial, almost quaint, he thought.

He would much rather have remained in Lyons today, but for the meeting he had planned with René Carlini. He had spoken briefly with Carlini by phone, but things were going so badly in his two key investigations that he needed to do things not possible over the wire, in an attempt to force his informant to be more productive. There would be no more carrots for the vegetable vendor, only a stick. If he didn't get what he wanted, and soon, Malfaire was quite prepared to expose Carlini for what he was—a politically ambitious crook.

Malfaire smiled to himself at the thought of Carlini having to choose the lesser of two unhappy fates. An arrest for alleged resistance activities would be easy to arrange with the Gestapo. On the other hand, if a rumor were to reach the ears of certain resistance leaders that Carlini was a police informant, they'd mete out their own justice. Either way, the dapper businessman would be dead.

But as much as that thought warmed him with satisfaction, Malfaire knew he would have to wait awhile before going that far. He wasn't yet convinced that Carlini had outlived his usefulness. Not only that, as far as the Grenoble area was concerned, Carlini was his only remotely reliable contact. For that reason alone, he had to keep him motivated, but he also had to keep from spooking him—at least for now.

He looked at his watch. "Carlini should have been here by now," he said, more to himself than to Dominique, the driver.

"Yes, Inspector. He's late again," replied Dominique as though the comment were directed at him. "Maybe it's this heavy traffic."

Malfaire looked up to see Dominique's sarcastic expression reflected in the rearview mirror. "But of course," he joined in the driver's joke. "Why didn't I think of that?"

Both men fell silent then, watching the spotty parade of cars, trucks, and the occasional Italian military vehicle. One such vehicle, an army transport truck, stopped suddenly just beyond the intersection, causing the cars behind it to halt as well. The uniformed driver got out and raised the hood, obviously having some sort of mechanical difficulty, but paid no attention to the distraction he had created. Cautiously skirting the vehicle, the civilian traffic was quickly reduced to a crawl.

"Ah, well, there you have it, Dominique." Malfaire's tone was derisive. "Leave it to the Italians to foul up a perfectly smooth traffic flow. Watch them bring in a couple of *carib-inieri* to direct traffic and mess it up even worse."

Dominique chuckled but said nothing.

Something in the crawling traffic ahead caught Malfaire's eye and made him forget all about the Italians. "Hey, look over there!" He leaned over the back of the Renault's front seat and pointed directly in front of them. "That looks like our friend Dr. Billot," he said excitedly.

"Where, Inspector?" asked Dominique. "I'm afraid I don't see him."

"Right there in front of us!" The inspector made no attempt to hide his impatience. "In that old green Peugeot. Follow him!"

Dominique turned in his seat toward Malfaire. "What about your meeting with Carlini?"

"Forget the meeting," snapped Malfaire, pointing again toward the green Peugeot. "Follow the car! If we can catch Billot, we won't need Carlini." Nothing would make him happier at the moment.

Dominique slipped the Renault into gear and lurched away from the curb, trying to force his way into the traffic while keeping the doctor in sight. It was slow going.

"Who's that with him?" asked Malfaire.

"I don't know, Inspector. I've never seen him before," Dominique replied as he edged his way deeper into the traffic. They were rounding the stalled army truck now, the green Peugeot three cars ahead of them. The traffic was picking back up to its normal pace, and Dominique gunned the engine to close the distance, passing two cars in the process.

Only one car remained between them when without warning, the Peugeot turned left at the next intersection. As the driver of the car in front slowed to make the same turn, Dominique swung the Renault wide to the right and sped on past. Braking hard at the last possible instant, he spun the wheel sharply to the left and jammed the accelerator to the floor. The big car slid almost sideways around the corner, tires squealing and clawing at the pavement for traction.

Malfaire clung white-knuckled to the passenger armrest in an effort to remain upright and seated as Dominique brought the car under control and urged it up the street. Fortunately for them, the snow still only amounted to a few haphazard flakes. The green car was in plain sight, though not yet close enough to see the registration plates clearly. It was obvious, however, that they were gaining on Billot and his companion and would soon overtake them.

Now Billot's car was turning again, this time to the right, back in the direction of the river. Again, Dominique braked hard, too hard it seemed, cranked the steering wheel hard to the right, and stomped on the accelerator. Again, the car careened around the corner, threatening once more to dislodge Malfaire from his seat. But this time the trajectory of the big Renault never quite straightened out.

Helpless, the inspector watched wide-eyed as they slid into the side of a parked car. The force of the impact threw him out of his seat and into the opposite door. The sounds of shattering glass and metal grinding on metal echoed and re-echoed in his ears for what seemed like minutes. Then all was silent—eerily silent. Only the ache in his shoulder and the throbbing pain in his head assured him that he was even conscious.

"*Désolé,* Inspector." It was Dominique's voice, though it sounded much too far away. "I think we lost them."

Malfaire swore viciously.

⚜   ⚜   ⚜

Somehow, Isabelle had always thought of motherhood in terms

of giving: giving food and comfort, giving attention, love, and protection in response to the needs of the child. It had seemed especially logical where infants were concerned, unable as they were to provide anything for themselves. And she was prepared—even anxious—to give whatever was necessary to this tiny little fellow who now aimlessly nuzzled her breast.

What had come as something of a surprise on holding her son for the very first time was the incredible sense she had of receiving. She had been given a gift—a priceless, irreplaceable treasure. It was almost as if she had been granted new life. And each moment she spent with him the feeling grew.

Tired and weak as she was after the hours of labor and the painful ordeal of delivery, she couldn't stop thinking how fortunate she was. True, things would not be easy in the days to come, but for the moment she was safe, surrounded by the affection of a good family, and gazing into the cherubic face of the most beautiful baby in the world.

"Isabelle?"

She looked up to see Françoise standing at the foot of the bed, smiling down on her.

"How's he doing?"

Isabelle looked down to see that the child had given up trying to nurse and was dozing off again. "Okay, I think," she said softly so as not to wake him. "I sure hope I'm doing this right."

"Maman says you're doing just fine," Françoise whispered back, striking a comical pose. "And she should know. Just look how I turned out!"

"Don't make me laugh, Françoise," Isabelle pleaded in mock seriousness. "I don't want to wake the baby."

"I'm sorry. I guess I'm still pretty excited about all this."

"Me too." Isabelle reached her free hand out to her friend. "Thank you," she said as Françoise came around beside the bed and grasped the hand she had offered.

"For what?"

"For being a friend. You and your family have been so kind. I don't know how I would have made it through all this without you."

"Really, Isabelle, it's the least we could do."

"I know," said Isabelle, smiling, "especially for a daughter of Abraham!"

They both laughed at that, remembering a similar conversation the day Isabelle arrived. When the laughter subsided they held hands in silence for a while, both staring at the sleeping baby. Isabelle knew that in the days and weeks ahead she was likely to need the closeness and kindness of Françoise and her family more than ever before. As happy as she felt tonight, the coming days would be difficult—for her *and* the baby.

"Got time for one more visitor?" Françoise asked suddenly.

Isabelle looked up at her friend. "Marcel?"

Françoise nodded.

Marcel had been gone so much of the day that he hadn't yet seen the child. Isabelle had hoped he would come before now, but had considered it inappropriate to say so, even to Françoise. He was probably feeling as awkward about it as she was.

"Does my hair look all right?" she asked, feeling self-conscious.

Françoise grinned. "Your hair looks fine, but you might want to close your robe. I'll go get him."

Isabelle felt herself blush and hurriedly arranged her bedclothes as Françoise left the room. Moments later, Marcel appeared in the doorway after knocking discreetly. He stood there without uttering a word for the longest time, eyes seeming to focus exclusively on Isabelle.

"Come say *bonjour* to little Alexandre," she said at last, breaking the silence.

Marcel took a few halting steps forward. "That's a fine

name," he offered. "I like it."

"It was my father's name," she explained.

"Your father would have been proud."

"Yes, I suppose he would."

Marcel was edging closer now, eying the sleeping Alexandre.

"Isn't he beautiful?" She wasn't so much asking as stating her opinion.

Marcel shifted his gaze to look at her. "Alexandre looks a lot like his mother," he said softly.

Isabelle felt as though her cheeks were on fire. Evelyne and Françoise had said the same thing earlier, but somehow it hadn't had the same effect. This man could be so unnerving. And yet she knew he didn't mean to be. Maybe it was just her. Maybe she just imagined that he paid special attention to her, that he was unusually tender toward her. Well, she couldn't think about all that. Not right now, anyway. She had a baby to care for.

"So, how is it that you know Dr. Billot?" she asked, steering the conversation to a less tender subject.

Marcel seemed to relax. "It's kind of a long story," he said. "I met him in Lyons once."

"He's the one who helped me escape the detention camp," she said.

"That's what he told me."

"And today he delivered my baby." She was really just thinking out loud at this point. "He's a good man," she concluded, "a really good man."

"Yes, he is," agreed Marcel.

"He said he would come back to check on us. Do you think he will?"

"I'm planning to go get him myself, when the time comes."

Isabelle stared silently at the baby for several moments before speaking again. "Marcel?" she began, then stopped for a second, afraid to look at him. "Before you go to sleep tonight, would—would you mind saying a prayer for little Alexandre?"

"Of course, Isabelle." He hesitated. "I'm—well, I'm—"

"Surprised?"

"Well, yes, a little. But I'm also honored that you would ask."

"This child means more to me than anything in the world, Marcel. Frankly, I'm not sure if there is a God. But if there is, I think He'll listen to you."

Marcel looked uncomfortable. "He's there, Isabelle," he said quietly, "and He'll listen to you too—if you ask."

For the first time since she could remember, Isabelle actually wanted to believe it. She wanted to believe for the sake of the baby, and because Marcel said it was so. But as Marcel slipped quietly out of the room, she wondered if she really could.

Chapter 25

René Carlini dusted a few flakes of snow from his hat and set it on the table by Le Dauphin's only window. There had been occasional flurries for three weeks now, but thankfully, no more than that. He shrugged out of his black wool overcoat, hung it on a hook behind the door, then straightened his jacket and tie before seating himself.

"Georges!" he called to the proprietor, "Bring me a glass of brandy. And pour one for yourself."

"Right away, Monsieur Carlini," Georges Charrier called back from behind the bar. "Celebrating Christmas a little early?"

"Even better than that," mumbled Carlini under his breath, smiling benignly back at Georges. It wouldn't do to elaborate at this point, especially with several other men in the café-bar. They would learn of his success soon enough, since most were in some way connected with his network. But they would have to wait until he had everything worked out— hopefully not more than a day or so.

He lit a cigarette with practiced ease as Georges set the drinks on the table. "Good Christmas Eve to you, monsieur," Georges said cheerily. "Can I get you anything else?"

Before Carlini had a chance to reply, Emile Bonet burst through the door, face flushed as usual, sputtering something about nearly being hit by a car.

"What's that you say, Emile?" asked Carlini, exhaling a long plume of smoke into the already hazy air and waving the muscular butcher to a chair. Georges left the drinks and retreated to the bar.

Bonet pulled off his coat, slumped into the chair he had been offered, and picked up the glass of brandy Georges had poured for himself. "That fool Boussant boy nearly ran me over in the street just now," he fumed. "I stepped off the curb and there he was. Why, if I hadn't jumped back onto the sidewalk when I did, I wouldn't be here talking to you."

"Boussant? Marcel Boussant?"

"Yeah, that's him. I should have clobbered him right then and there, but he had his whole family in the car." Bonet's lips curled into a sneer. "He even stopped to apologize. What a joke! I guess he's scared of me—just like everyone else."

"Wait," said Carlini, his mind sifting through Bonet's bluster. "Did you say that he had his whole family in the car?"

"Yeah, why?"

Carlini broke into a broad grin and tapped the cinders from his cigarette into the ashtray. "I'll tell you why, my friend. Remember the photograph I showed you the other day?" Inspector Malfaire had given Carlini the photo of a doctor from Lyons who he claimed was connected to the elusive Pascal, and who had been spotted in Grenoble. If Carlini could deliver the doctor, he could get Malfaire off his back and maybe even collect a favor or two in the process, not to mention what Pascal's capture would do for his own peace of mind.

Bonet sipped his brandy and nodded. "That's the guy you said was a Vichy spy posing as a doctor, right?"

Sometimes Carlini found it necessary to rearrange the facts a little when it came to Bonet. "I saw him earlier today with your friend Boussant," he told the butcher. "Now why do you suppose a spy would be interested in our young friend?"

Bonet leaned forward in his chair and arched his bushy eyebrows. "You think Marcel Boussant is working with a Vichy spy? I admit I don't like him much, but I find that hard to believe!"

"Look, Emile," Carlini said, lowering his voice, "the fact that he followed you the night you beat up Pascal ought to tell you something. And why is it that he's always taking the train here and there? Now today, I see him with a suspicious doctor from another city. I tell you, there's something going on *chez* Boussant besides farming."

Puzzled, Bonet sat back in his chair and released a long slow breath. "Maybe you're right. It *would* explain his strange behavior lately." He paused. "So, what do we do?"

Carlini smiled. Bonet was as strong as a team of oxen, but as easy to manipulate as a marionette—provided you knew which string to pull. And René Carlini knew all the right strings. "Let's drive up to the traitor's farm," he replied, tossing off the brandy that remained in his glass, "and find out for ourselves."

⚜   ⚜   ⚜

"Are you sure this is a good idea, Maman?" Marcel asked as he steered the old Peugeot through the dark streets of Grenoble.

"Marcel, we've been over this a dozen times." She was beginning to sound a little exasperated. "Sylvie Théron invited us over and there was no good reason to turn her down. I thought you wanted a chance to spend some time with Gilles, anyway."

"Of course I do. It's not that." He tried to keep his voice

down yet still be audible over the rumble of the engine. Luc, Françoise, Isabelle, and the baby were seated in the rear, and he preferred that they not hear what he was about to say. "I just got a funny feeling when we nearly ran over Emile Bonet, and I wonder if this is a good time to be gone from home."

"Oh, come now, you don't think he means us any harm do you? After all, you apologized. And it was as much his fault as yours. He wasn't watching where he was going."

"I know, Maman. I just have a strange feeling about him, that's all."

"Well, please try to relax. Christmas doesn't come along every day, and the Thérons were kind enough to invite us to spend it with them. Let's enjoy it!"

Marcel fell silent. It wasn't just the incident with Emile Bonet that had him upset. Earlier in the day, as he was driving Dr. Billot back to the tantes' house after his examination of Isabelle and Alexandre, he had seen René Carlini in Domène. Worse, he was pretty sure Carlini had noticed them too. And as distrustful as Marcel was of Carlini, it had made him uncomfortable.

For now, however, perhaps Maman was right. It was Christmas, the Advent of the Christ Child. And the laughter and music, good food and stories, ought to be enjoyed as an oasis in the desert. Maman, Françoise, and Luc were all looking forward to this. Isabelle too must be anxious to spend some time with the Jewish family sheltered by the Thérons. There was no good reason to spoil the holiday worrying about people like Emile Bonet and René Carlini.

❧   ❧   ❧

It was after 8 o'clock when Georges Charrier finally managed to push the last reluctant patrons out the front door of Le

Dauphin. *"Bonne Fête!"* he called after them. *"Joyeux Noël!"*

Hearing little more than indistinct mumbling in reply, he shuttered the windows and bolted the front door. All that remained before turning out the lights was to wash the half-dozen empty glasses which stood in disarray atop the deserted bar. He set about it quickly, using his large cotton apron as a towel the way he'd done a thousand times before. As soon as he was finished, he could head for home and forget about business for another day. In his line of work he didn't get many days off, and he was eager to begin the holiday celebration with his family.

Several of the men who had spent a part of their Christmas Eve in Le Dauphin weren't as lucky as Georges, and he felt a twinge of sadness for them. Naturally, some of his patrons whiled away the hours in front of a bottle precisely because they wished to avoid going home to wife and children. But several of them had no one to go home to. Some had not yet found a woman willing to marry them, like the burly Emile Bonet. Others, like Antoine LeBoeuf, had only their memories to warm the holidays.

Speaking of old Antoine, Georges thought suddenly, *I didn't see him in here all evening. Maybe I'd better go check in on him.* It was very unlike Antoine not to stop in at least long enough to wish everyone a happy holiday. Perhaps he wasn't well.

Then too, Georges wanted to see what Antoine would make of the snatches of conversation he had overheard between Emile Bonet and René Carlini. *Would they really go up to the Boussant's farm? For what?* He couldn't imagine how they could have been serious about such a thing, especially when everyone in town knew the Boussants to be kindhearted, patriotic people, even if they were Protestants. Not that Carlini would care about that. He made no pretense of being religious at all, and held in contempt all who were—Catholic and

Protestant alike.

A knock sounded at the back door just as Georges finished toweling the last glass dry. He pulled off his apron, turned off all but one light, and went to see who it was.

"Salut, Grandpère!" Ten-year-old Guy stood smiling up at him from the alley behind the café-bar. "Maman said I should come walk you home. Are you ready?"

Georges looked proudly down at the boy. He was growing up so quickly. "I'll just get my coat, *fiston,"* he said. "I won't be but a minute."

He took his coat down from its hook by the door, turned out the light, and stepped out into the dark alley, locking the door behind him.

"I'll race you, Grandpère!"

Georges hesitated. He really did want to check in on Antoine. Maybe he could stop by the old man's house in the morning. *"Allez!"* he said aloud. "You'll have to run hard to beat your old Pépé." And with that, Georges and his grandson sprinted side by side through the unlit streets of Domène toward home.

⚜   ⚜   ⚜

Christmas Eve dinner was not at all what Isabelle expected. Since this was the start of a Christian holiday, she had just assumed that she would visit quietly in the basement with the Jewish couple and their four small children, while the Thérons and the Boussants carried on their celebration upstairs. She really wouldn't mind so much. It might be interesting to meet the Thérons' guests, though she couldn't imagine that they had all that much in common with her—other than the fact that they were Jews, of course. But they were nowhere in sight as Gilles ushered his newly arrived guests into the foyer of the expansive home.

Madame Théron was apparently in no hurry to banish her young visitor to the basement. "Isabelle, dear," she said effusively as Gilles made the necessary introductions, "Gilles has told us so much about you. We're so glad you could come."

"Delighted to make your acquaintance," chimed in her suave husband. "Welcome to our home."

"Thank you," was all Isabelle could manage. She glanced at Evelyne Boussant, hoping for some reassurance. It was nice to be treated as a guest, even though in reality she'd had little choice but to tag along. Not that she minded, of course, but she wondered if it would be less awkward for everyone if she inquired about the as-yet-unseen refugee family. Perhaps then she would be shown downstairs, and the evening could take its natural course. Evelyne offered a smile in return.

"May we have a look at that darling child we've been hearing about?" Madame Théron tugged carefully at the corner of blanket that protected little Alexandre from the elements. "Oh!" she exclaimed as she gazed at his face, "he's beautiful. Absolutely beautiful. A little gift from God, wouldn't you say?"

Isabelle nodded. Alexandre did seem like a gift—a very special gift. And maybe he was from God. It seemed reasonable, if God were anything at all like the Boussants supposed Him to be. In any case, she was prepared to take her little "gift" down to the basement and spend the evening chatting with strangers.

Everyone took turns commenting on how handsome the peaceful, sleeping child was, how he favored his mother, how the boisterous conversation seemed not to faze him at all. Then, as the conversation hit a temporary lull, Monsieur Théron suggested they move into the dining room where dinner would begin shortly. Isabelle was swept along with the others, not quite sure what to do next.

The dining room seemed enormous, with its high ceiling and richly papered walls. Even more impressive, in Isabelle's mind, was the lacquered mahogany table, larger than any she had ever seen, and set with crystal, silver, and china enough for fourteen. It took only a moment to realize that the Thérons had apparently not envisioned a separation of Jews and Gentiles at all. At least they would all dine together.

In that moment a weight was lifted from her shoulders—only to be replaced by another. She was being spared an evening of superficial conversation with Jewish strangers. But she wasn't at all sure that she was prepared to be part of a Christian celebration with her Gentile friends, either. She didn't want to be rude; the Boussants had come to mean too much to her. She just didn't want to be a hypocrite.

Gilles, who had descended to the basement to lead the remaining guests to the table, burst suddenly back into the dining room, his handsome face suddenly ashen. "They're gone!" he said, his voice cracking.

"Gone?" His father was incredulous. "That can't be! Are you sure?"

"I've looked everywhere, Papa. They're not there. Come see for yourself."

Gilles turned and led the way out of the room again, followed closely by his father and Marcel. Luc would have gone too, but Evelyne restrained him.

Madame Théron sank wearily into her chair. "I don't understand," she said looking up at Evelyne in bewilderment. "Why would they leave? And why now? They're safe here, don't they understand that? And with winter coming on, and four little children. . . . Where do you suppose they would go, Eve?"

Evelyne sat down next to her friend and took her hand. "I don't know, Sylvie. But maybe the men can find them and persuade them to return."

I'm not so sure, Isabelle mused sadly and silently. *If they're desperate enough to believe that running is the best thing to do, it won't be easy to change their minds.* She could clearly remember feeling such desperation the night she plunged headlong down a winding mountain road in pitch darkness, away from the very people who could help her—who already *had* helped her. Only when she had come to the end of herself, physically and emotionally, had she been able to reconsider. And her guess was that unless the Thérons' guests came to that point soon, they were gone for good.

She shuddered involuntarily at the mere thought that she might ever be so utterly desperate again.

Chapter 26

I t just doesn't make sense!"

Marcel nodded. "I know, Gilles," he said numbly, "but there has to be a reason." His eyes nearly crossed from fatigue as he stared through the windshield of the Théron family's Citroën sedan.

They had been over and over the same ground perhaps a dozen times since they discovered that the Jewish family was missing. Gilles' father had compiled a list of all the likely places they might be found, and looked into half the possibilities himself while Gilles and Marcel pursued the other half. They had rendezvoused several times during the night to report their progress, but the sun was already rising, and they had yet to turn up a single clue. It was as if the six Jews had disappeared without a trace.

"Look, Gilles," Marcel said, suddenly realizing the futility of their efforts. "We've searched everywhere we can think of. I say we get some rest and start again later."

"I guess you're right," said Gilles, unable to stifle yet another yawn, "but I hate to just give up."

"I don't like it either, but maybe they don't want to be found."

"Yeah, maybe." Gilles didn't sound too convinced.

"So, why don't we go get some sleep?"

Gilles drove on in silence. When he spoke again, the unexpected sound of his voice jarred Marcel from his drowsiness. "Hey!" he said loudly, as if struck by a revelation, "weren't we supposed to go to your place this morning to check on the animals?"

"Aaiiee," Marcel groaned. He had forgotten all about the chores that couldn't be left undone. "That was before we spent all night looking for your friends. Maybe we could sleep a couple of hours and then go." At the moment, he wasn't sure he could stay awake long enough to milk one cow, let alone two.

"Let's just do it now and get it over with," said Gilles. "Then we can sleep all day if we want."

"You don't really think our families are going to let us sleep through Christmas Day, do you? Besides, you wouldn't be so anxious to visit our cows if you had to milk them 365 days a year like I do," Marcel protested, half in jest. "I ought to let you milk one just so you can see how much fun it really is."

"Try me," Gilles shot back with a grin. "If you can do it, it can't be all that hard." He aimed the Citroën toward Domène and they drove the rest of the way in sleepy silence.

❧   ❧   ❧

Marcel knew that something was wrong the moment Gilles turned off the engine. The farm looked just as it always did, as nearly as he could tell—except that Léo was nowhere in sight.

Sliding quickly out of the Citroën, Marcel strode straight

for the barn calling out as he went. "Léo! Come on, old boy. Where are you? Léo?!"

There was no response—no noise at all, other than a slow, rhythmic scraping sound that came from the other side of the barn. Marcel broke into a trot in the direction of the odd sound.

"Léo?—"

He stopped short just as he rounded the corner of the rustic stone building. Not fifty feet away was Antoine LeBoeuf, shovel in hand, apparently pushing and scraping a stony mound of earth into a shallow hole. The snowy-haired old man looked up at Marcel and hurriedly scooped in a few more shovelfuls.

"Ah, Marcel," he said, breathing hard and leaning on the shovel handle, "I was beginning to wonder where you'd run off to." He looked worn out. "I'm glad you're here."

"What are *you* doing here?" Marcel dispensed with all the good manners he had been taught since childhood. *And why are you digging a hole?* The question had no sooner crossed his mind, but then he knew the answer. "Léo!" he almost shouted as he rushed toward the nearly filled hole in the ground. Sadness and shock melded almost instantly into trembling, white-knuckled anger. "What have you done to my dog?" It was more an accusation than a question that he hurled at the subdued Antoine.

"Easy, Marcel." Gilles had followed him and now laid a restraining hand on his shoulder. "I'm sure he doesn't mean any harm."

Marcel shrugged off his friend's hand as well as his words. "Oh, doesn't he? Well, then maybe he can explain what he's doing burying my dog! That's what you're doing, isn't it Antoine?" He had never used LeBoeuf's first name before, given their age difference, but right now he was so angry he didn't care. Léo was gone, and the man who had betrayed him once before was standing over a fresh grave.

Antoine spoke slowly and carefully. "I don't blame you for getting angry, Marcel. I'd be furious if this had happened to my dog. But you've got to believe me, I didn't kill him."

"Then what are you *doing* here? I suppose you just happened to be passing by, is that it? Well, I thought I told you I didn't want you bothering me—"

"Marcel! Why don't you just listen to him?" pleaded Gilles. "Give him a chance to explain."

Marcel kicked at the rocky ground under his feet for a few seconds, then folded his arms across his chest and glared at Antoine. "All right," he said finally, grudgingly, "I'm listening."

Antoine moved closer before saying a word. When he spoke his voice was softer than usual. "Look, *mon ami,* I know how much Léo meant to you, and I'm sorry this happened. I buried him because I wanted to spare you the grief." He paused and took a deep breath. "The reason I came up here is that Georges Charrier came to see me early this morning about a conversation he overheard last night in the bar. It seems that our friends Messieurs Carlini and Bonet planned to pay a visit while you were away."

"What? Why would they come here?"

"That I don't know. But Georges said Carlini had referred to you as a traitor and said that he'd seen you with some Vichy spy yesterday."

Marcel thought for a moment that he was going to be sick. His face and neck suddenly felt clammy, and he could taste the bitter bile that rose in his throat. *So, Carlini saw me with Dr. Billot after all! Does he know the doctor, somehow? Does that mean he also knows about Isabelle?* He began to feel sweaty in spite of the chill morning air. He tried to say something, but no sound came out.

"Anyway," Antoine continued, "Georges thought I'd want

to know right away. For some reason he waited until morning, though, which is why I couldn't do anything to prevent this. I'm sorry, Marcel. I really am."

Marcel felt Gilles' hand on his shoulder once again, but this time Marcel did nothing to remove it. Gilles just stood there without saying a word, leaving Marcel to sort out his own thoughts.

"I don't understand," Marcel began, staring at the shallow grave. "Why would Carlini and Bonet come up here and kill Léo? Are they just trying to intimidate me, or does Carlini really believe that ridiculous story about me working with some Vichy spy?" What he didn't dare ask was how much they knew about Isabelle and the baby. That was something he wouldn't trust to anyone other than Gilles.

"It's hard to say what Carlini believes, Marcel," said Antoine. "But what I *can* say is that he'll use whatever means necessary to achieve his own ends. And that includes shooting your dog, or fabricating a story to get Emile Bonet to go along with him."

"It wouldn't take much," Marcel said with disgust. "Bonet doesn't like me as it is."

"He doesn't like anyone who gets in his way. That's where your trouble started in the first place. Don't you remember?"

Marcel didn't reply. He remembered all too well.

"There's something else, Marcel. Carlini has been watching you pretty closely for some time, now."

Marcel's anger had begun to ebb until he heard that. "Carlini?" he fumed. *"You're* the one who's been following me around lately! How do I know you're not still working for him? Especially after the gun you gave me!" He hadn't meant to bring that up again, but try as he might, he had never really forgotten it.

"Look, Marcel, I already tried to explain, but you wouldn't listen." Antoine's tone was almost stern. "After you stormed out of my house, I went to Carlini to confront him about the gun.

He claimed he didn't know anything about it, of course. But I found out I'm not the only one he gave a tampered gun. Georges Charrier got one as well, and I think there may be others. It's undoubtedly his way of making sure we never turn on him."

Charrier too? Maybe I was wrong about the gun, after all, Marcel thought, though he wasn't yet ready to admit it to Antoine.

"And as for me following you," Antoine continued, "somebody had to keep an eye on you. I caught Carlini watching you a couple of times, and it occurred to me that he was being too suspicious. You have to admit, you haven't exactly led the life of an ordinary farmer these past few months, what with all of your comings and goings. I wanted to make sure he didn't try anything, that's all."

"Try anything? What do you mean?" The fire was rapidly going out of Marcel's anger again, and he simply wanted to know.

Antoine turned and gestured toward the freshly dug grave. "That could just as easily be you, my friend. Anybody he doesn't control makes him nervous. He'd have had someone do it for him, of course, because he's essentially a coward. But you'd be just as dead, if that's what he wanted."

"You mean the way he had Pascal beaten and left for dead."

"Do you know him?"

Marcel hesitated before answering, trying to decide how much to divulge. "Yes," he said finally, "we've met. But he doesn't think Carlini intended to have him killed."

"What, then?"

"Well, he was arrested by a police inspector from Lyons, and taken back there. You have to wonder how the Lyons police would know where to find him, and why they would come all the way to Domène unless someone had tipped them off. Pascal thinks Carlini sold him."

"You might be on to something there." Antoine stroked the silver stubble on his chin and looked thoughtful.

"Could Carlini be working both sides?" Marcel knew that such a theory also cast doubts on Antoine himself, but he had to ask.

"Anything's possible. He's a ruthless man."

Marcel decided to push a step further. "Well, if he's so ruthless and knows he can't control you, then why doesn't he have *you* killed?"

"It's very simple," Antoine replied. "I've been around too long and I have too many friends, too many connections. He knows that if my death were to look like anything but old age or an accident, he'd lose half his men. And several of the wilder ones are not above exacting their revenge. Carlini may be a coward, perhaps even a traitor, but he's no fool."

"If you have so many friends, monsieur," Gilles broke in, "why do you continue to put up with this Carlini? Why don't you and your friends just get rid of him?"

"I'm not a barbarian, monsieur, as you might suppose," the old man sniffed, suddenly acting as though insulted. "I am an old man. What I can do best is influence, moderate, keep things from getting out of control. Beyond that, I'm afraid I must trust the fates to bring an end to Monsieur Carlini's reign of terror."

"And if he really is working both sides?"

"Then my advice to you is to leave immediately and don't come back. He killed your dog so he could have a look inside your house. Now, what he found there I have no way of knowing, but if it gives him evidence of any kind against you, he'll be back—and he won't be alone. He won't give a second thought to selling you to the police."

Marcel's mind reeled as Antoine's words began to sink in.

Leave and not come back? He didn't like to think about it, but he had always known that eventually Isabelle might have to be moved to a new location, though he hoped not too far away. It had never occurred to him, however, that *he* might have to leave. *And what of Maman, Françoise, and Luc? Could they never return either? Where would they go?*

He had to think, and quickly. Without a word to Antoine or Gilles, he turned and sprinted for the house. He didn't know what Carlini and Bonet thought he had been up to, but he needed to know what they had been looking for. Maybe they suspected him of distributing one of the underground papers, like *Temoignage Chrétien.* If that were the case they'd never find more than one copy, no matter how—*But of course! They wouldn't have to.* They could simply plant several copies in the house, call the police, and he would look as guilty as sin. Why hadn't he thought of that already?

Bounding up the steps to the front door, he turned the latch only to discover that it was broken, thanks to the brawny Emile Bonet no doubt. As he threw open the door, he could hear Gilles coming up the steps behind him.

"Keep him outside, Gilles," he called back over his shoulder. "He doesn't need to find out any more than he already knows." He ran upstairs without waiting for a reply.

What he saw stopped him as surely as if he had been kicked in the stomach. The attic door was ajar and the ladder leading to it was in place—the ladder Marcel had carefully stowed under his own bed just before leaving for Gilles' house. Françoise had even thought to put all the baby's things in the attic—just in case someone came snooping through the house. They had all dismissed such an event as too unlikely, but had put the clothes away just the same—just to be safe.

So, Carlini saw the room prepared for Isabelle to hide with little Alexandre. Did he suspect it all along? Or did he simply stumble onto it by sheer dumb luck? No need to worry about planting evidence once he's seen this. The only question now is how long before he returns.

Stumbling back down the stairs, Marcel crossed the *salon* to where the great old armoire stood. Papa's shotgun was kept inside. He would get it out and wait for Carlini to return. Then he would make him pay—for killing Léo, for plotting against Isabelle. *Especially for plotting against Isabelle.*

He groped around inside the armoire, clutching at first one object and then another. But the feel of polished wood and blued steel eluded his grasp. *The shotgun was gone.* Carlini had left nothing to chance. Deterred, at least for the moment, a strange kind of relief swept over Marcel as he sank exhausted to his knees, unable to hold back the tide of anger and frustration.

❦   ❦   ❦

"It's all set. You shouldn't have any problems, Inspector."

Jean-Claude Malfaire didn't respond right away to the voice on the telephone. He was trying to decide how to tell his wife and son that he had to go out on Christmas morning. It wouldn't be easy, but of course it had to be done. This was simply too important to wait any longer.

"Inspector?"

"Yes, I hear you. What else?"

"There's not much else to say. He's not armed, as far as I know, and there's no phone. And today being a holiday, they won't be expecting anything."

Not unless you've been sloppy, Malfaire thought. "I should be there in about two hours," he said aloud. "I'll meet you in front of that seedy bar in Domène and you can show me the way."

"Inspector, I don't think—"

"What's the matter, Carlini? Afraid it might not be so

trouble-free after all?"

"No. It's just that—"

"Be there in two hours or you get nothing out of this, my friend." Malfaire understood René Carlini's motives very well. "Understand?"

"I—I understand."

Malfaire set the receiver back in its cradle without another word, then lifted it again and dialed a local number.

"Dominique?" he said when the connection was made. "I'm sorry to interrupt your holiday, but I need you to bring the car around. Yes, it's very important. I think we may have found our lost Jew."

Chapter 27

Isabelle felt completely numb, almost paralyzed, as Marcel broke the news to her.

"We won't be safe at home any longer," he was saying urgently, "and we can't put the Thérons in jeopardy by staying here, especially after their guests' disappearance last night. We'll have to take the baby and go."

"I don't think I understand, Marcel," she said as the fog began to clear from her mind. "Go where? It's too soon to travel yet. Alexandre isn't even three weeks old." What she was unable to voice was just how alone she suddenly felt at the prospect of having to leave.

"We have no choice, Isabelle," he said gently, his eyes pleading. "We have to try to get you to someplace safe. I know it's not going to be easy, but Alexandre doesn't stand a chance if they send you back to the camp—and you may not, either."

He was right about that, of course. Just thinking about it made her shudder. "But what about you and your family? Where will you go?"

"Gilles is going to take Maman, Françoise, and Luc to my

grandparents' house in Ardeche. They'll be safe there, I think."

"And you?"

He looked down at the floor. "I'll stay with you," he said simply.

A sense of relief washed over her upon hearing that, and at the same time a kind of heaviness she couldn't explain. *Can I really mean that much to him,* she asked herself, *or is he just doing his duty?* She knew that the latter was a part of it, but more and more she'd had cause to wonder. There was something in his gaze and in the way he spoke to her that told her she was not the only one who dreamed of something more. She had reminded herself a hundred times over all the reasons why it could never work. And yet the feeling seemed to grow in her.

The stillness of the moment was broken as Gilles Théron burst into the room. "Marcel, I need a word with you. Will you excuse us for a minute, Isabelle?"

Without waiting for a reply, Marcel reached over and patted Isabelle's hand reassuringly, then rose to join his friend. They spoke in hushed tones and Isabelle only caught an occasional word, though she assumed that it had to do with plans to leave. Presently, however, Gilles turned to go and Marcel returned to sit beside her on the sofa. He took a deep breath before speaking.

"It looks like Geneva," he said slowly, softly. "We're going to try to make it over the border into Switzerland."

It's finally arrived, she thought, *my one chance for freedom. So, why am I so frightened?* Almost involuntarily, she reached over, grasped Marcel's hand, and bit her lip to keep back unexpected tears.

"It's all right," he whispered, squeezing her hand firmly, "I'll be right beside you."

❧   ❧   ❧

The Théron house was in an uproar. Everyone seemed to be talking at once, offering advice, consoling each other. The women packed a small suitcase with the barest of necessities for Isabelle and the baby, and then prepared lunch. No one seemed to be very hungry.

After talking with Professor Lambert by phone, Gilles took, and hastily developed, a photograph of Isabelle and one of Marcel with which he managed to forge ID cards. Marcel whistled in amazement as he watched his friend work magic with paper and ink.

"I had no idea, Gilles," he admitted freely. "You're really good at this."

"Where do you think all those documents came from that you took to Annecy?" Gilles replied, admiring his work. "Professor Lambert brings me photos and I create new identities for hundreds of people—maybe thousands." He blotted the ink dry and held up the new cards. "What do you think?"

It was hard not to be impressed. Every detail of his new card looked as authentic as the real one from which Gilles had copied. The only difference was that now Marcel and Isabelle would be traveling as Monsieur and Madame Rivier, though they had retained their first names to avoid any more confusion than necessary. Marcel clapped his friend on the shoulder and smiled his thanks.

The preparations were nearly finished. Monsieur Théron had siphoned enough fuel from his own cars to fill the tank of the Boussants' old Peugeot. Maman, Françoise, and Madame Théron had hurriedly arranged a basket of food from what had been left untouched at lunchtime. Marcel checked to see that the blankets he used to cover the car in the barn were dry and in place in the back. With the baby along, he was more than a little concerned about the car's temperamental heater. He hoped the blankets wouldn't be too dusty.

Outside the Thérons' carriage house, both families huddled close together against the chill wind as Marcel and Isabelle prepared to leave. No one seemed to have much to say as they all stared uncomfortably at one another.

"I'm sorry we couldn't find your friends last night," Marcel said awkwardly to Monsieur Théron.

"There's not much we can do about that now. We'll just have to trust that they're safe somewhere. Right now you need to concentrate on the safety of that girl and her baby. Do you have everything?"

"I think so." Marcel nodded in the direction of his family. "Are you sure you kept enough fuel for Gilles' trip?"

"They won't leave until tomorrow," Monsieur Théron replied. "Gilles can get some more in the morning."

"Don't worry, Marcel," added Gilles. "I'll see that they get to your grandparents' safely. I promise you that."

Marcel nodded and turned away to speak to his mother. "I'll join you when I can, Maman." He tried to keep his voice steady. "Or I'll send for you—just as soon as this is all over."

"I know you will, son," she said and drew him close in her embrace where she held him for several long moments. "God be with you," she added as she released him, tears marring her effort at a brave smile.

"I'm proud of you," Françoise whispered as she too threw her arms around his neck. "Take good care of her, Marcel. And please be careful."

Even Luc clung to Marcel briefly, but said nothing, which was not like him at all.

"Take good care of Maman and Françoise," Marcel urged him.

Luc just nodded in return.

Everyone hugged Isabelle and the baby, and they all cried together and told her they loved her and would miss her dearly. Then Gilles helped her into the car while Marcel started the engine.

"If you need to get word to us," Gilles said as he gripped Marcel's hand through the window, "let Pastor Jean Soulain know. He's expecting you tonight. He'll know how to reach us."

Marcel gave Gilles' hand one last squeeze, then eased the old Peugeot into gear and they were off. He kept his eyes on the road ahead, afraid to let Isabelle see the mist in them, and unable to bring himself to look in the rearview mirror until they were well out of sight of the Thérons' house.

⚜   ⚜   ⚜

He had always dreamed of retiring to a small farm, just like the one which nestled peacefully in the hollow in front of him. He could imagine himself tending a garden, raising a few animals, but mostly just taking in the fresh air and the tranquility of the country. Ah, that would be the life: no hustle and bustle, no lengthy investigations that seemed to go nowhere, no idiot stool pigeons, no Jews.

Sadly, however, it would be a good many years before Jean-Claude Malfaire could retire, and his work-a-day life seemed to require all of the above. Today, it also meant getting information out of a stubborn, white-haired old man they had found tending the animals.

"Look, *mon vieux,*" Malfaire began again for the third time, "Just tell us when this boy Marcel is coming back, and we'll go away and leave you alone."

"As I already told you," replied the old man, "I have no idea. He just said he wasn't going to be back for a while—those were his exact words, as near as I recall—and he asked me to look after his animals. I don't know anything else."

"He's lying! Can't you see that?" insisted René Carlini, and not for the first time. "Young Boussant has looked up to him for years. He knows exactly what the boy is up to."

Carlini had become unusually agitated the minute he saw the old man, as though he didn't want to be seen with Malfaire. The inspector just figured it was because he didn't want it known that he was feeding information to the police, even if it wasn't the local police. Malfaire rather enjoyed watching Carlini squirm. In any case, it didn't matter to him. He was through with Carlini, just as soon as he caught up to this Boussant boy. He guessed he had gotten all the useful information he could. Besides, it was beginning to be a little risky working the Italian zone so far from Lyons. As soon as he wrapped up the case, he'd stick closer to home.

"What do you know about the boy?" Malfaire asked the old man.

"Not much, really. He's just an ordinary, hardworking youth. There's not much to tell, as far as I know."

"You can't get away with that, LeBoeuf." Carlini was furious. "You know all about him!" He turned to Malfaire. "Why don't you arrest him, or something? He's obviously covering for the boy. Isn't that a crime?"

"He's an old man, Carlini, and he's of no value to me." Malfaire was tired of the whole conversation and decided that it just wasn't worth the effort. The old man probably knew that he had no real authority here. Besides, it was beginning to snow. "I think I have what I need, Carlini."

Carlini went pale. "But I can—"

"I have a name and a photo. I know what his car looks like and I can trace it. And if he's got Jews with him, I think I know where he's going." He opened his car door and started to climb in. "Oh yes, you said he was a Protestant, didn't you?"

"Yes, but I—"

"Good. That helps." He shut the car door. "Let's go, Dominique."

"What about Monsieur Carlini?" asked the driver.

"What about him?" snapped Malfaire. "He's pathetic. Leave him."

The inspector was only slightly tempted to look behind as Dominique guided the big Renault down the narrow track to the main road. He was already planning his next move. He would call Marie from Annecy to tell her he wouldn't be home tonight.

※　　　※　　　※

Antoine adjusted his collar against the soft falling snow and smiled at a pallid René Carlini. "You don't look too well, René," he said. "Maybe you should see a doctor."

Carlini fumbled in his coat pocket for a moment before producing a cigarette case. His fingers worked unsteadily as he pulled out a cigarette and poked it clumsily between his lips. He struck three matches before finally managing to light up, then drew deeply and exhaled a long, smoke-laden breath.

"What's the matter with you, Antoine?" he asked. "Why are you trying to protect the boy? He's not one of us."

"What do you mean, not one of us?" Antoine willed himself under control. "He's French, isn't he?"

"You know what I mean. He's not a part of our network."

"So that justifies making a sacrificial lamb of him?"

"It's not just that," Carlini insisted, taking another puff from his cigarette. "He's—well, he's a Protestant too."

"And you're an atheist! What do you care?" Antoine could feel his blood begin to boil. "Is that why you tried to get the inspector to arrest me, because I'm a Catholic?"

"I've got no quarrel with Catholics. But Protestants are

different and you know it, Antoine. They think they're better than everyone else, and they're too cozy with the Jews, if you ask me."

"Well, I think you did it for the money, René. That's the reason you do most things, the way I see it. What do you think, Georges?"

Carlini spun around to see that Georges Charrier was standing not twenty feet behind him. "Wha—what are you doing here, Georges?" he sputtered.

"Why don't you ask Emile, Monsieur Carlini," suggested the ever-polite Georges.

Carlini wheeled in the direction of the bartender's gaze to find Emile Bonet's burly form advancing on him. The butcher was clenching and unclenching his fists.

"You told me Marcel was a traitor," Bonet said sharply, his face even more flushed than usual. "But after what I just saw, I think maybe *you're* the traitor. Did you plan to sell me too?"

"Don't be crazy, Emile! The boy was spying. And he was helping Jews!"

"I don't really care about Jews, one way or the other," spat Bonet. "But I have no use for anyone who sells out to the Vichy police."

Carlini dropped his smoldering cigarette, and tearing at the buttons on his stylish coat, reached a hand inside.

"Don't touch the gun, Carlini, or you're a dead man," Antoine warned without moving an inch.

A wicked grin spread over Carlini's face. "I see you're not carrying a weapon, Antoine. And Bonet doesn't like guns. So who's going to stop me? Georges?" He laughed loudly and produced a pistol from inside his coat.

No sooner was the weapon out in the open than a sound exploded behind him and dirt kicked up from between his feet, splattering his well-shined shoes. Eyes wide in terror, he let his gun fall to the ground and stood motionless, slack-jawed.

"I forgot to tell you I bought a new pistol, Monsieur Carlini," said Georges mockingly. "It works a lot better than the one you gave me." He laughed out loud, but kept the gun aimed at Carlini's back.

Antoine picked up Carlini's piece and stuffed it into his own coat pocket. "I don't suppose you can convince the inspector to give up his search for Marcel." It wasn't really a question.

"You heard him, Antoine," said Carlini, his voice quavering. "He's got everything he needs. I can't do anything about it."

"I didn't think so," he said as he turned to leave. "Let's go Georges. I haven't had my Christmas dinner yet."

"Antoine, please, you can't just leave me here." The pitch of Carlini's voice rose as Emile Bonet approached menacingly. "Antoine! This is all a mistake. I can explain. *Please*, Antoine!"

Antoine LeBoeuf, with Georges Charrier at his heels, strode down the dirt track toward the main road and never once looked back. He winced at the pitiful sounds coming from the hollow, and hoped Bonet would be done with it quickly.

❦   ❦   ❦

The snow, which had been falling lightly and intermittently since just before noon, was beginning to pelt the windshield of the old green Peugeot with large, wet flakes, forcing Marcel to reduce his speed to a crawl in order to see. The vacuum-powered wipers struggled mightily to keep the windshield clear, losing ground each time the road rose steeply, making it up on the descents. The tires, adequate under normal conditions, slogged through the mounting white stuff with increasing difficulty, adding to Marcel's worries.

As he had feared, the Peugeot's heater could be coaxed to

work only briefly every few kilometers, and he had already needed to retrieve a couple of blankets from the back for Isabelle and the baby.

He had decided to avoid the main highway, even though it would have meant easier driving. There were few other cars on the narrow twisting backroads, this being Christmas. Each time they wound through a tiny village, or passed an isolated farm-house, he could imagine a family gathered in a warm parlor, telling stories, exchanging gifts, oblivious to the weather and consciously disregarding the Italian occupation. Each time he wished he could be home with his own family. And each time he would glance across at Isabelle, all bundled up with her child, staring at the road ahead, and know that he had to press on.

"Is he asleep?" he asked softly after they had been on the road for some time.

Isabelle nodded and offered a wan smile. She looked almost as tired as he felt.

"You've been awfully quiet," he said. "Are you all right?"

"I'll be okay, I guess. But what about you? You must be exhausted after being out all night."

"I'll be fine—just as soon as we get to Switzerland."

There was no response right away, only the low hum of the Peugeot's engine.

"Why didn't you take me to Switzerland in the very begin-ning?" she asked after what seemed like minutes of silence.

The hint of accusation in her voice surprised him. "I—I guess because it was too dangerous," he offered tentatively. "Is that what you would have preferred?"

"It might have been easier, that's all."

"Because of the baby?"

"He's part of it, of course. His presence will make it even more dangerous."

"Perhaps. But we really have no choice, do we?"

"I'm the one who has no choice, Marcel. You're free to do whatever you want."

"And what I want is to be with you." There, he had said it. And for the first time, he hadn't been paralyzed with fear over what she might think. If she felt the same way, then it was time they talked about it. If not, well, at least she would know where he stood.

But once again, all he could hear was the sound of the engine, laboring to crest yet another hill before easing into the valley beyond. As twilight fell, it struck Marcel that he too might be nearing the summit of a months-long climb. Whether or not he reached the other side would depend on how Isabelle responded to his declaration—if she responded at all.

The snow was deepening, and he slowed his descent to keep the car under control. Without warning, from around the curve at the base of the hill, twin beams of light stabbed out into the gathering darkness, momentarily blinding him. In spite of himself, his foot found the brake pedal, and by the time the other car had passed and he could see clearly again, his own headlights were no longer aimed at the road ahead. Instead they panned wildly from right to left as he fought the wheel in an effort to bring the car under control.

But just as the Peugeot entered the curve, the front wheels quit responding altogether. Marcel was unable to keep from drifting across the icy surface, and watched helplessly as the car skidded sideways off the road and into a drainage ditch filled with fluffy white snow.

Silence. The Peugeot's engine had died in the crash and there wasn't a sound to be heard. It took Marcel a few seconds to realize fully just what had happened. And then the stillness was shattered by the piercing wail of the baby.

"Is he hurt?" Marcel reached a hand out toward Isabelle.

"I don't think so," she replied quickly, her voice quavering, "just scared—like me." She tried to calm little Alexandre, but without much success.

"Stay here," Marcel commanded. "I'm going to see how bad it is, and find out if that other car stopped."

When he climbed back inside a few minutes later, he felt like giving up. The Peugeot was sitting in a ditch two feet below the level of the road, and the snow was piling higher and higher. The other car had apparently continued on over the hill, oblivious to their situation. On top of all that he was exhausted; he hadn't had any sleep for thirty-six hours. But there in the seat beside him sat the object of his affections, cooing to her frightened child. He couldn't give up. He had to try something.

Starting the engine once again, he tried to work the car out of the ditch under its own power. He pulled forward—a couple of feet. He tried reverse—not as far. Each time the car sank lower and lower into the ditch.

"What are we going to do?" Isabelle sounded anxious. The roar of the engine and the lurching of the car had disturbed Alexandre all over again, and he was in full voice.

"I don't know," was all Marcel dared say. He didn't want to vent his anger at Isabelle, especially when he was mostly mad at himself. If he hadn't braked so suddenly or so hard, this would never have happened, he reasoned. Still, it was all he could do to keep from banging the steering wheel with his fists, or shouting his frustration to the night sky.

"D—do you think," Isabelle stammered, her eyes lowered, "do you think God might be listening now?"

Marcel felt all the air go out of him like a punctured tire. She couldn't have asked a more humiliating question, though he knew it wasn't her intent. She, with all her doubts, stood on tiptoe, craning to catch a glimpse of a reason—any reason—to believe. And here he was, wrapped so tightly in his anger and frustration that he was blind to what for him should have been obvious.

"Of course," he said softly, a catch in his voice. "And He's probably wondering why I needed to be reminded." He bowed his head reverently without looking to see what Isabelle might say. "Dear God," he began, "I've tried everything I can think of to get out of this ditch. Everything, that is, but asking You for help, and I'm sorry for that. The truth is, we're a long way from where we need to be, with no way to get there. I know Isabelle is worried about little Alexandre, and I'm worried about both of them. We really need Your help, Lord. Amen."

No sooner had he raised his head than Isabelle exclaimed, "Oh, look! It's stopped snowing."

Indeed it had. At least they wouldn't be buried alive.

Chapter 28

Awakened by the urgent pleas of her hungry child, Isabelle peered into the darkness for signs of something familiar. It wasn't light enough to see anything, really. She could hear the rhythm of Marcel's breathing just a few feet away, but she could only vaguely make out his gray shape. And she felt, more than saw, little Alexandre, who pulled greedily at her breast.

The sweet smell of straw filled her nostrils, punctuated by the pungent odor of animal refuse. She hoped that Marcel had placed the blankets carefully enough to avoid the latter. It had felt so good to get out of the wet, cold snow that she hadn't given it a minute's thought when they arrived. But now the cold was beginning to creep back into her body; the night was dark and filled with strange sounds; the smells were decidedly unpleasant. She longed for daybreak.

Once they had decided to abandon the car, it seemed like they walked forever. Hoping to pass by a house or a village, they had found nothing but basic shelter in an old barn. Marcel had carried the food and as many blankets as he could from the car, and had fashioned a bed on the straw for her and Alexandre before curling up nearby and falling fast asleep. Unused as he was to the upheaval they'd been through, Alexandre followed suit. It had taken Isabelle a little longer, but in time she too had faded into unconsciousness.

Now, as she tended to the baby's needs, she shivered against the cold and tried to burrow deeper under the blankets for warmth. *God certainly has a strange way of answering a cry for help,* she mused. *The snow stopped, it's true. But we're no closer to the border, and we have no way to get there—unless Marcel can get the car unstuck in the morning.* It seemed unlikely, however, without help. And judging from what they had seen to this point, there wouldn't be much help available.

Am I expecting too much? she wondered. *Or is there something else going on that I can't see?* Evelyne Boussant had said as much when she explained how her faith had remained strong, even after her husband's disappearance. God's plans might not be obvious to everyone—or to anyone, for that matter—she had said, but that didn't mean He wasn't doing anything. Isabelle decided that she would just have to wait and see, and hope that things would be clearer in the morning light.

Alexandre was drifting back to sleep now that he'd had his fill, and Isabelle also soon found her eyelids growing heavy in spite of the gnawing cold.

⚜　　⚜　　⚜

Thin streaks of sunlight seeped through the cracks of the sagging barn door and fell across Marcel's face, beckoning him awake. He rubbed both sleep and sun from his eyes and tried to remember where he was. The odors that assaulted his nostrils immediately told him he was in a barn. But the feel of a soft, warm body pressed against his back, and warm breath on his neck, told him that he must still be dreaming.

Slowly, carefully, he turned his head to see Isabelle's face just inches from his, her eyes closed, her lips slightly parted. She lay on her back, her side touching his back, her tiny son clutched to her bosom. Marcel felt a sudden urge to turn and kiss her tenderly as she slept, but he didn't move for fear of disturbing her or the baby. Still, he couldn't help but wonder what it would be like to hold her in his arms. Too, he wondered what she would think if she truly knew what was in his heart.

He had tried to tell her last night before the accident. He really did want to be with her. It was as simple and as complicated as love always is, he imagined. It didn't make perfect sense. He knew that. But there was no longer any denying how he felt about her, and it seemed only right that she should know that. Perhaps her lack of response was her way of telling him that she didn't feel the same way. But waking up to her this way made it hard to believe that she felt nothing for him at all.

A shadow fell over Marcel just then, and he looked up to see an old man in work blues and a sheepskin coat standing at the edge of the makeshift straw bed, his arms folded across his chest.

"Imagine that," the old man boomed, a bemused look on his face, "I've been visited by the Blessed Virgin, Saint Joseph, and the baby Jesus! And right here in my own barn, of all places."

At the sound of the old man's voice, Alexandre flinched in his sleep, Isabelle awoke wide-eyed, and Marcel sat bolt upright. "I beg your pardon, monsieur," he hurried to say, "but our car slid into a ditch in the storm last night. We needed shelter and this was the only place we could find."

The farmer chuckled. "No need to apologize, young man. But if you'd walked another hundred meters or so around the edge of the hill, you'd have found my house. At least there you could have slept in front of the fire."

Marcel cast a sideways glance at Isabelle, half-expecting a reproachful look in return. Instead he saw only embarrassment. This was obviously as awkward for her as it was for him.

"Listen," the old man continued, "bring your wife and baby to the house and have something to eat while I get my horses."

"Horses?"

"You're going to need some help getting that machine unstuck, aren't you?"

"Well, yes, but—"

"It won't be the first time I've rescued city folk and their fancy machinery. Now go on, get your family over to the house before they freeze." The farmer pointed in the general direction of the house and then left abruptly after a polite nod to Isabelle.

Marcel didn't move. He just sat there hugging his knees, thinking. If the old man were able to get the Peugeot out of the ditch, so much the better. They'd be able to get to Annecy in less than an hour as nearly as he could figure. But it didn't seem likely that two horses could dislodge the heavy car from its predicament. And then what? How would they get to Annecy? On horseback? He snorted at the absurdity of it.

"Marcel?" He felt Isabelle's hand gently touch his back and turned to face her. "What are we going to do if he can't get the car out of the ditch?" she asked as if she had been reading his mind.

"I don't know," he said, "but I'll think of something." He forced a smile to reassure her. *Please, God, help me think of something.*

She returned his smile. "Maybe we should go eat," she suggested. "I have a feeling it's going to be a very long day."

"I'm sorry, I wasn't thinking. You're probably freezing too."

Isabelle blushed slightly. "I'm all right now. I—I was a little cold during the middle of the night, though. I hope you didn't mind."

He shook his head. He hadn't minded at all that she took refuge from the cold next to him. He was about to tell her so when she spoke again.

"Last night you told me," she began awkwardly, a little tremor in her voice, "well, you said that what you wanted was to be with me. Did you really mean that?"

"With all my heart."

She gazed up at him, a warm glow in her gray-green eyes. "It won't be easy for you," she said.

"Nor for you, but what that's worthwhile ever is?"

"What if we can't make it across the border?"

"But we will, Isabelle. God will help us." He wouldn't allow himself to think otherwise.

"Marcel," she said slowly, turning her eyes away, "I wish I could have such faith. I know how important it is to you. I'm just not sure I can."

"I understand," he said, "and I won't try to push you. But I believe you're a lot closer than you think."

She turned to give him a surprised look. "Then you won't give up on me?"

"Never," he grinned, shaking his head slowly from side to side. Then, as if to seal the promise, he leaned down and gently placed his lips on hers. He hadn't really planned it; it just happened. And Isabelle's warm and tender response made him glad it had.

Alexandre suddenly began to wriggle between them, breaking the spell. Marcel pulled away, but he couldn't take his eyes off her.

Isabelle returned his soft, steady gaze, then cleared her throat nervously and sat up, cradling the baby. "We'd better go eat," was all she said.

⚜   ⚜   ⚜

The sun had been up less than half an hour when Inspector

Malfaire slogged through the snowy shadows along Annecy's Rue de la Poste, on the way from his hotel to where Dominique waited with the car. The two had staked out the *temple protestant* on arriving late Christmas afternoon, hoping to find some answers, surmising that this would be as likely a place as any for Marcel Boussant to stop for help on his way to the border.

They had found the *temple* locked up tight. And after fruitless hours of waiting for anyone to show up, Malfaire had left Dominique to keep an eye on things while he retired to a nearby hotel to sleep.

"Here," he said to Dominique as he climbed into the back seat of the Renault, "I brought you a couple of croissants. They're quite good, really."

"*Merci,* Inspector," said the wan-looking driver as he reached over the backseat for the food. "Any coffee?"

"I've only got two hands," Malfaire replied, a little exasperated. "You'll have to get some later."

No sooner had Malfaire handed over the croissants than he looked up to see a tall, bespectacled young man getting out of a dilapidated old car in front of the *temple*. "Hey, someone's going inside!" he exclaimed. "Let's go!"

Leaping out onto the snow-covered sidewalk, he began walking briskly the two blocks to the *temple*. Dominique was right behind him. But before they had walked a half-block, the young man in glasses reemerged with a young woman, and they both got into his sorry-looking car.

"Come on!" Malfaire shouted as he raced back to the Renault. "Let's follow them."

"But what about the others, the Jew?" Dominique sounded out of breath as he took the wheel. "Shouldn't we wait here?"

"I've got a feeling this one will lead us to the others," said the inspector. The more he thought about it, the more confident he felt. *I may have underestimated our young farmer friend,* he mused, *but they all make mistakes. And when he makes his, I'll be waiting for him.*

❧   ❧   ❧

The soft crunch of the horses' hooves on the snow mingled with the steady whisper of crude wooden runners as the old farmer guided his rustic farm cart down the unplowed road. Wrapped in blankets, and surrounded by mounds of clean straw, Isabelle clutched Alexandre tightly and looked anxiously at Marcel, seated beside her. Not since leaving Poland years ago had she seen such an antique vehicle. And she had never had occasion to ride in one. She hoped it would hold together.

It wasn't that she was ungrateful for this outmoded transportation. On the contrary, she was glad to be moving toward the border and freedom—in spite of the tortoise-like pace. The farmer didn't have much use for "machines" as he called them. Couldn't trust them like you could a good strong Belgian or Percheron. So when the snow melted, he replaced the runners with wheels and used this old cart year 'round.

He and Marcel had managed to pull the car out of the ditch, thanks to these huge horses. But the front axle something-or-other was apparently damaged beyond repair, leaving them no option but to accept the farmer's offer to drop them at the train station in Rumilly, nearly ten kilometers away. They had traveled only a short way, and already Isabelle felt cold. She hoped the kilometers would pass quickly.

She leaned her head against Marcel's shoulder and closed her eyes. Neither said a word, but she couldn't help believing that their thoughts were linked. For her part, she couldn't get the morning's kiss out of her mind. There was a kind of promise in that brief moment she had never sensed before— ever. And she hoped with all her heart that Marcel sensed it too.

"Machine coming," the farmer sang out. "I'll pull over and let it pass."

Marcel twisted around to where he could look out between the cracks in the cart's weathered sideboards.

"Can you see anything?" Isabelle asked him.

"It looks like an old Peugeot—older than mine." He sounded surprised.

Now that the cart had stopped, Isabelle could hear the car's engine laboring up the hill, louder and louder as it approached. Then, just as it sounded like it had pulled alongside them, its labor ceased and it hummed quietly.

"Have you seen any other cars up this way?" a man's voice called out.

"I don't believe it!" Marcel whispered to Isabelle.

"No," she could hear the farmer lying, "haven't seen any other machines today. You looking for someone?"

"Don't believe what?" Isabelle whispered back. "What is it?"

Marcel stood without answering and jumped to the ground. "Jean?" he asked loudly, "is that you?"

Isabelle shed her blankets and tried unsuccessfully to dismount from the cart without waking little Alexandre. He was not at all happy about having his sleep disturbed and let her know about it—loudly. As she cuddled and rocked him and whispered assurances, a pretty young woman appeared at the rear of the cart, closely followed by Marcel and a tall man with round, wire glasses.

"Oh, he's so tiny!" exclaimed the woman. Then, holding out her hands toward Isabelle she added, "May I?"

Isabelle hesitated. *More strangers,* she thought, though Marcel apparently knew them. Were these the people who would guide them safely across the border? Could they be trusted? The woman didn't look much older than Isabelle. She looked at Marcel and hoped he had read her mind.

"It's all right, Isabelle," he soothed as if he understood. "This is Jean and his fiancée Anne. They were expecting us last night, and when we didn't show up they came looking for us."

Reluctantly, Isabelle handed the squalling Alexandre to Anne while Marcel helped her down out of the cart. Once on the snow-covered ground, she reached to take the child back, much to Anne's disappointment.

"Gilles said you would be avoiding the main highway, but we had no idea where to look beyond that. We just started praying and driving," said Jean. "Thank God we found you," he added, concern etching his face. "We were beginning to fear you'd been caught already."

Isabelle felt a knot develop in the pit of her stomach. *What did he mean "caught already"? Is it hopeless, then? Are Marcel and I just kidding ourselves, just prolonging the inevitable?* She hugged the pacified Alexandre tightly to her with one hand, reached out for Marcel's hand with the other, and vowed not to give up hope—not now, not without a fight.

⚜   ⚜   ⚜

The big black Renault lumbered steadily along through the snow, keeping pace with the battered old Peugeot, but at a discreet distance on the open road. There was no sense making a move too soon and alerting the Peugeot's occupants. The farm boy was supposedly unarmed, and although the tall young man in the glasses didn't look the part of a terrorist, it wouldn't do to be careless now.

Inspector Malfaire looked at his watch. Almost noon. No wonder his stomach was growling. Well, there was nothing he could do about it. He was going to show that arrogant little Nazi Lieutenant Barbie just how good he was. He would capture the young terrorist, break up this ring of Jew-lovers, and maybe even kill the Jew himself. On second thought, he'd get a reprimand for that, he guessed. He was supposed to take captured Jews to that disgusting pen at Vénissieux. That way the bigshots in Vichy got credit for turning them over to the Nazis.

"They're stopping, Inspector," Dominique said calmly as he applied the brakes. "We're just outside Annemasse."

"So I see." Malfaire peered ahead through a pair of binoculars to where the delapidated Peugeot had pulled onto a side lane and parked in front of an auto repair garage.

The garage doors swung open, the old Peugeot pulled inside, and two men closed the doors again. Malfaire didn't like the looks of this. More men, possibly armed, and he could no longer see what any of them was up to. He cursed his luck.

"Inspector?" Dominique turned toward the backseat. "There's a little *épicerie* across the road. How about if I run and get us something to eat while they're inside the garage. We may not get another chance for a while."

Malfaire looked up from his binoculars. "Yeah, that's a good idea. Just don't be gone long. We have no idea how long they'll stay in one place."

"Right." Dominique slipped out of the car and jogged across the road to the sad-looking little store.

Malfaire watched him go, hoping he'd bring back something palatable with which to fill his complaining stomach, then resumed his vigil. He hadn't been watching long when the garage doors reopened, and the old Peugeot backed slowly into the street.

"Come on, Dominique," Malfaire muttered under his breath, "let's go, before we lose them." He cast a quick glance at the *épicerie*. Dominique was nowhere to be seen.

To the inspector's surprise, the Peugeot turned onto the road and headed back in the direction from which it had come—directly toward him! He kept the binoculars trained on the advancing car, but sunk as low in the seat as possible to avoid being seen himself. As the car passed by, he saw clearly that its only occupants were the young man and woman he had first seen at the *temple* in Annecy.

His gaze reverted immediately to the garage. So, the couple had left the boy and the Jew inside. He still couldn't go after them. Not with the two men there as well. *What is keeping Dominique?* Even though he had done little but drive for the past few years, Dominique was a policeman. Maybe the two of them—

His thoughts were cut short as a late model Citroën sedan pulled out from behind the garage. From a distance, even with the binoculars, he couldn't make out any of the occupants for sure. But there was a woman at the wheel and someone in the back seat, but whether it was a man or another woman or more than one person, he couldn't tell.

The Citroën pulled onto the road leading into Annemasse without appearing to hurry at all. Malfaire was beside himself. *Where is that blasted Dominique? He should have been back long ago!* And who was in this car that was rapidly pulling out of sight? Was it a ruse? Did they know he was watching? He had no way of knowing for sure, but his instinct told him to follow.

He leaped out of the car and opened the driver's door. "Dominique!" he bellowed in the direction of the *épicerie*. No answer. He almost sounded the horn, but thought better of it as the Citroën wasn't out of earshot yet.

Furious, he jumped into the driver's seat and started the engine, lurching unexpectedly away from the curb and spinning the tires in the packed snow. "You'll pay for this, Dominique," he growled through clenched teeth. "I promise you that." He cursed long and violently as he fought to keep the Renault under control and the Citroën in sight. Clearly, they were headed toward the heart of Annemasse and the Swiss border.

Chapter 29

There wasn't as much snow in Annemasse as there had been south of Annecy, though the weather outside seemed just as cold. Maybe it was the fact that the morning's blue sky had turned slate gray that made it seem to Isabelle as though it might never warm up. It was hard to imagine spring on an afternoon like this, and try as she might, it was just as hard to imagine that the day of her deliverance had finally arrived—if all went according to plan.

The woman behind the wheel steered the powerful Citroën sedan onto the highway, and they soon left Annemasse behind, leaving Isabelle to wonder exactly what the plan was. They had been told little at the garage except that a change of vehicles was necessary. Jean and Anne and their old drafty Peugeot had been replaced by a nameless, mostly silent woman in her thirties, and this sleek, comfortable Citroën. Marcel assured her that the less they knew the better. That way, if they were caught, they would have little to offer that might jeopardize others. Still she wished she knew more.

Her shivering wasn't really due to the cold, she decided. For the past few months, until yesterday, her life had settled into a routine to which she had grown accustomed. True, she'd had to live in hiding, and she had known more than her share of fear. But now, with freedom looming on the horizon, she felt a new kind of fear—fear that somehow Marcel's affection would cool once the crisis was past.

Nestled close to him, she looked up into his youthful, unshaven face. How strong he seemed, and resolute, and yet so gentle. She loved the feel of his arm around her shoulders and hoped that he drew as much strength from her presence as she found in his.

The afternoon light began to fade as they sped past hamlets and farms, and by the time the driver turned off the highway onto a deserted-looking forest road, the sky was nearly dark. Isabelle strained to see the road ahead and wondered how the driver could keep up the pace without turning on her lights.

"We'll have to make a slight change in our plans," the driver announced suddenly, her voice matter-of-fact as she made eye contact with her passengers in the rearview mirror. "We're being followed."

❦　　❦　　❦

Trying to keep pace with the fleet Citroën was difficult enough without being spotted. But Jean-Claude Malfaire was finding it next to impossible to navigate the rutted forest road without the use of his headlights. Night had fallen, and if it weren't for the inch or two of snow that marked the edges of the muddy road, he would have long since plunged into the forest, wrecking the Renault beyond use.

Once the Citroën pulled off the highway, he had decided to close in. It wouldn't do to come this far only to let them slip through his fingers. He had to admit that he had expected them to make at least one more stop before the border. It was what he had expected, and it was what he had hoped for. If they got too close to the frontier before he caught up, he ran the risk of interference from the Italian *caribinieri*. Even though they didn't like illegal crossings, the Italians weren't about to let a French policeman operate within sight of the fences.

Sloshing around a tight corner, he cranked the wheel hard to keep from sliding into a tree, only to end up sideways in the road. And there, not fifty yards in front of him, sat the Citroën, brake lights ablaze, the driver and passengers silhouetted sharply against the glow of the headlights.

He slammed the Renault into reverse, and righting himself in the narrow roadway, switched on his own headlights and gunned the engine, throwing mud in every direction. But the moment he accelerated, the Citroën sped off, tires spinning, weaving from one side of the track to the other.

Sensing that he was gaining on his prey, Malfaire took one hand off the wheel and pulled his semi-automatic from the holster inside his coat, laying it on the seat beside him. Then he switched on his windshield wipers to fend off the mud spray from the fleeing Citroën.

The closer he came, the more erratic the Citroën's maneuvers. "This woman must be a lunatic," he muttered to himself. Why anyone would let a woman drive a car that powerful was beyond him anyway. No wonder she drove as if she were nearly out of control. It was just too much car.

Practically on top of her rear bumper as both cars slid around another tight corner, Malfaire noticed that the passengers' silhouettes had suddenly disappeared. He kept close, waiting for the pair to pop up again, but only the outline of the driver remained. Did they think he was about to fire on them? He grinned savagely. Of course! They were scared out of their minds. And when he caught up to them, he'd make them realize their worst fears.

Without warning, the Citroën spun out of control, turning broadside in the muddy ruts. And before he could slam on his brakes, Malfaire had plowed headlong into the rear quarter panel, spinning the Citroën even further around, propelling it backward. The grinding and scraping of metal, the shattering of glass, all ended in a dull thump as the Citroën came harshly to rest against the thick trunk of a pine tree.

Malfaire clutched at his pistol, shouldered the car door open, and advanced warily on the wrecked car. Its headlamps still shone, but its engine had gone silent, and no one inside moved to open a door and escape.

"You in the car!" he ordered loudly. "Come out with your hands in the air!"

There wasn't even the slightest sound in response.

"In the car!" he tried again. "Come out or I'll shoot!"

Still nothing.

He moved to the passenger side of the Citroën and, aiming his gun into the front seat, peered cautiously through the window. The driver had collapsed onto the front seat, unconscious, blood dripping from a cut on her head.

One down, he told himself, and took a step farther to look into the back seat. There, in a tangled heap on the floor, lay a pile of blankets. Blankets! The silhouettes he had seen had been nothing but old blankets propped up to look like people! Had there only been blankets here all along? Or had the fugitive pair somehow eluded him in the forest? Swearing furiously, he swung the butt of his pistol at the rear side window, shattering it into a thousand pieces.

So they wanted to play games, did they? Well, the game

was up, and they could forget about being arrested. When he caught them, he promised himself, he would take great delight in killing them.

※   ※   ※

Holding tightly to Alexandre, Marcel led the way through the woods at a trot in the direction the driver had indicated. Somewhere back here there was an abandoned farmhouse where a woman named Babette would be waiting for them. In the meantime, the woman who had brought them this far was going to attempt to keep occupied whoever had been following them. He prayed she would be successful—at least long enough to allow them to cross into Switzerland.

"There," he said to Isabelle, stopping to point out what looked like an old house. "That must be it."

She was out of breath from trying to keep up with him and only nodded that she saw it too. They approached at a walk, to let Isabelle catch her breath, and because Marcel had no way of knowing whether this were the only such house in the area.

There was no moon and it was hard to see anything clearly, except as dark shapes profiled against the snow. While that made the going difficult, Marcel took some comfort in knowing that the *caribinieri* would also be handicapped. And if Babette were as good as he had been told, the dark would surely be an advantage.

When they reached the house, Marcel handed the baby back to Isabelle. Then, standing to the side of the door with Isabelle behind him, he rapped softly. There was no answer. He waited and rapped again. This time the door opened inward just a crack.

Marcel could feel Isabelle pressing against his back. Should he knock again? Was the door simply ajar? He reached out and gave it a push. It swung open to reveal a completely dark interior. So, taking Isabelle by the hand, he proceeded to cross the threshold and closed the door softly after them. It was pitch black inside.

Marcel stopped cold at the sound of a revolver hammer being clicked into position. This was not what he expected.

"Who sent you?" asked a woman's voice.

Marcel swallowed hard. "She didn't tell us her name. She just told us to meet you here."

"Where is she? Why didn't she come with you?"

"She thought we were being followed. She wanted to decoy whoever it was while we came through the woods."

The room was silent again for a moment, and then a match was struck and a candle lit, revealing a middle-aged woman of medium height with short, light brown hair. She stood next to a sooty stone fireplace, with a pistol aimed at the middle of Marcel's chest.

So this was Babette.

Isabelle let out a gasp. "It's you!" she said barely above a whisper. "You and your friends rescued me from the camp. Oh, I can't believe it's you!"

Babette lowered the gun and visibly relaxed, almost to the point of smiling. "So," she said, "we meet again. I remember it well—well enough to know that you look in far better health this time."

"Much better, thank you."

"It's Isabelle, right? And this must be your baby." She turned down the edge of the blanket to get a look at Alexandre's face. "We'll need to make sure he stays quiet," she said gently.

"He's really very good," Marcel interjected.

Babette looked him over carefully. "I was told to expect a woman and child," she said. "Are you planning to go with them?"

Marcel looked at Isabelle. "Yes," he replied firmly. "Yes, I am."

"Then you'll have to follow my instructions. Is that clear?"

He nodded. He had no idea how to cross the border safely and was only too happy to take Babette's direction.

"It's very simple, really," she began. "If you can avoid the *caribinieri* patrols, cross a stream, and slip through the fence, you're in Switzerland. And I'll be with you every step of the way. I can't actually cross the frontier with you, but I can suggest where you might go for food and shelter—if the Swiss border guards let you through."

"You mean they might not?" Isabelle looked incredulous.

"It's a possibility, Isabelle," said Babette. "You can't take anything for granted. Legally, they don't have to let you in, and there are those who won't. We just have to trust God to intervene. That's all we can do."

She donned a pack then, and led them outside, directly behind the house where a stone path wended its way into the forest. Babette led the way, followed by Isabelle, who refused to let Alexandre out of her grasp. Marcel brought up the rear. No one said a word as they filed into the trees and out of sight of the house.

A tremor of excitement coursed through Marcel's body. Or it might have been fear. Whatever it was, his senses were heightened, alert to the crush of snow under his shoes, the snap of a twig, the scent of the pines. His eyes darted back and forth, scanning each tiny clearing for signs of danger.

A few minutes later, when Babette stopped and signaled for the others to do the same, Marcel could just make out what appeared to be a large, open field beyond the trees. The frontier was almost within reach.

"From here on out we won't have much cover," Babette whispered, "so do exactly as I tell you."

Marcel shuddered from a surge of nervous energy. This was it. If he were going to turn back, he would have to do it now. Halfway across the open field would be too late.

"We'll wait here until we've timed the passing patrols," Babette continued in a whisper, "and then we'll crawl one at a time across the clearing on our bellies. We should have ten to twelve minutes between patrols."

Isabelle looked at Babette, and then at Marcel, her eyes wide with fear. "But the baby!" she rasped. "How am I supposed to crawl on my belly while holding the baby?"

Marcel hadn't thought of that. He was wondering how far he could crawl before he froze to the ground.

"We'll tie him to your back like they do in Asia." Babette was matter-of-fact. "If all goes well, you won't actually be on the ground that long. Here," she reached into her pack and pulled out three white blankets. "Wrap yourselves in these, and you won't be so easily seen."

Babette produced another small blanket from the pack with which she fashioned a tricornered sort of pouch. Placing Alexandre inside, she then tied the two long ends around Isabelle's chest, effectively strapping him to her back. Then the three draped the blankets over themselves and crept to the edge of the broad clearing to await the passing patrols.

⚜   ⚜   ⚜

It didn't take Malfaire long to retrace his muddy course back to where he had first seen the Citroën stopped. It wasn't easy, since his left headlamp had been shattered in the crash, but he found it, and with an electric torch in one hand and 9mm pistol in the other, he began searching for signs to indicate whether the two fugitives ever really were in the car, and if so, where they might have fled.

If they were going to cross the frontier, then they had to rendezvous with someone who could take them across. Their flight had been too organized to this point for them to go it alone now. If he could get to the meeting place before they did, or at least before they got too close to the Italian patrols, he'd bring them down and no one would be the wiser.

Twenty feet from the side of the road he discovered the signs he was looking for. Footprints. Two sets of them, leading into the woods. He smiled to himself as he saw that they had made no attempt to hide their tracks. They probably thought he had fallen for their ruse and that he would be far away by now, chasing the elusive Citroën. Well, they had seriously underestimated him, if that's what they thought.

Much sooner than he expected, he came within sight of an old house. He quickly switched off his torch and cursed himself for leaving it on so long. He wanted desperately to maintain the element of surprise. Creeping carefully up to the house, he pressed an ear to the front door and listened. Not a sound came from inside. He tried the latch. It turned easily and the door creaked open.

Gun arm extended, he crouched low and shouldered his way inside, switching on his torch at the last second and panning the room rapidly. It was empty. He followed the same pattern in each room. Each time the result was the same. The house was empty. Completely empty, except for the candle on the mantle in the *salon*.

He grabbed the unlit candle, crushed it to bits in his hand, then hurled the pieces across the room. "Too late!" he bellowed like an enraged bull, hammering the mantle again and again with his fist. "All this time, all this work, and I'm too late!"

❧　　❧　　❧

Shivering from the cold, Marcel was almost ready to admit, at least to himself, that he was scared. Babette had crawled across the clearing first, and after dropping from sight as the next patrol passed by, reappeared just over the edge of the river-bank, beckoning for Isabelle to follow. Once she started, there would be no turning back.

"I'm scared," Isabelle whispered, her eyes glistening. "I don't know if I can do this."

"I'll join you in a few minutes," he rasped, trying to keep his own emotions under control. He even managed a little smile. "By midnight this will be all over and we'll be safe and warm."

She put a hand to her mouth to stifle a sob, and Marcel felt as though something were tearing at his insides. How he hated seeing her like this. It didn't seem fair. She had been through so much, yet without this next step, all would be in vain.

He placed his hands gently on her shoulders. "Think of Alexandre," he said, and his voice cracked. "He has no future unless you go. Please, before it's too late." He reached for her and enveloped her in his arms, holding her close for just a moment, feeling the love in her return embrace. He knew she would be strong when she had to be, and he told her so as he tenderly kissed away each fallen tear.

"Is Alexandre all right back there?" she asked between sniffles when he released her.

Marcel peeked carefully into the makeshift bundle on her back. "He's sound asleep," he replied, relieved. "Ready?"

Out across the open field a frantic Babette was waving her on. Isabelle nodded, pulled the white blanket over her, and crept to the field's edge. "Marcel," she called hoarsely over her shoulder, "promise you'll say a prayer for me."

"You know I will," he promised.

And then she was gone, snaking her way out across the snow-covered expanse. From the edge of the woods, he watched and waited, one eye on Isabelle's snail-like progress, the other on his watch. The luminous minute hand seemed to mock her efforts as it raced from one numeral to the next, and on to the next. Soon he could tell that she was wearing down, struggling for every meter of progress.

I knew I should have carried the baby! He shook his head slowly. He had tried to convince her, but she would have none of it. Letting him carry Alexandre from the car to the abandoned house was as much as she could bear. Maybe losing her husband had made her afraid she might somehow lose again.

Looking across the field, he saw the silhouetted Babette waving her arms again. He looked at his watch and began to tremble. Another patrol was due any moment and still a full third of the field remained for Isabelle to cross. *Come on, Isabelle,* he urged silently. *You don't have far to go, now.* He wanted to dash out into the field, scoop her and the baby into his arms, and run for cover. He had to force himself to stay where he was.

He wrapped the thin white blanket around his shoulders and tried to crouch down out of the wind. He still couldn't stop shaking.

Once again, Babette signaled. This time she seemed to be pointing at something. He looked to his left and immediately felt beads of sweat form on the back of his neck, in spite of the cold. The *caribinieri* were in sight! *Dear God, please—*

He didn't get to finish. Something hard struck his head just behind the left ear, and everything went black.

Chapter 30

Hot tears scalded Isabelle's cheeks as she clawed her way, inch by painful inch, toward the riverbank. Her fingers were numb from the snow, and the hard ground underneath had raised great bruises on her knees and elbows. The ice and snow were beginning to soak through her coat and shoes as she crawled, and the farther she crawled the colder she felt. She had begun to wonder if she would ever make it across the barren expanse of plowed field.

Only her back was warm, where little Alexandre rode bundled in a blanket and covered with another. If not for him, she might have been able to move faster, she admitted. But if not for him, she might not have ventured out onto the field in the first place.

Through misty eyes she could just make out the shadowy shape of Babette, arms extended, silently beckoning to her over the final few meters. The *caribinieri* must surely be approaching by now, she knew, but she dared not look. She was afraid to see how close they might be, afraid to know that they were bearing down on her. Unable to think of facing arrest again, she redoubled her efforts, and with all her remaining strength, surged over the edge of the embankment and into Babette's waiting arms.

"Get down!" the older woman whispered urgently, then added, "I was afraid you weren't going to make it."

Isabelle's sides heaved from her exertion and the damp, numbing cold of her clothing which clung to her legs and chest. Her wooden fingers fumbled as she tried to untie her blanket-bundle, and only with Babette's help did she finally succeed. She hugged Alexandre close to her as she crouched low in the protection of the embankment, absorbing the warmth and peace he exuded.

The embankment rose some four feet from the pebbly surface at the edge of the stream to the level of the plowed field that bordered it. In several places, the bank formed an overhang where the rising waters had cut away at it each spring. Beneath such an overhang, Isabelle and Babette waited unmoving, for fear of being detected by the advancing *caribinieri*.

Soon the sound of voices reached their ears—Italian voices. It might have been nothing more than idle conversation, but Isabelle knew few Italian words, too few to have any real idea about what was being said. The voices grew louder and louder until they were accompanied by the crunching sounds of boots in the snow. *They're practically on top of us!* she thought, afraid even to breathe.

The conversation continued unabated, but the crunching sounds stopped abruptly, just above the women's heads. Then the conversation halted, and all Isabelle could hear was the throbbing of her heartbeat in her ears. Was she visible from above? Had the *caribinieri* spotted the drag marks where she had heaved herself over the edge of the bank? She fought down the urge to leap up and run. That would mean certain capture.

Then, as quickly as it had stopped, the conversation started again, and the acrid smell of cigarette smoke filled the air. Soon, the soft crunch of boots in the snow resumed as well, and slowly the sound of Italian voices receded into the distance.

When all was silent once again, Isabelle let out a long, slow breath, relaxing her vise-like grip on Alexandre. Only when the boy began to cry softly did she realize just how tightly she had been holding on.

❧   ❧   ❧

A confusing jumble of sensations assaulted Marcel's brain as the warm, downy darkness that enveloped him began to recede. His fingers were leaden and his head throbbed a steady rhythm, while his body slid—or fell, he wasn't sure—over frigid, stony ground. Something unseen clutched at his throat, threatening to cut off his breathing, making it hard to focus on anything else.

Grunting with the effort, he reached his icy hands up to claw at whatever was choking him. Immediately the sliding stopped, the pressure on his throat eased, and he fell hard on his back to the ground. Gasping for breath, he rolled onto his side, just as a boot connected with his ribs.

"*Saligaud!*" a man's voice hissed. "Now that you're awake you can walk on your own two feet." Marcel felt the man's hot breath close to his ear. "And if you make a sound, you'll die for it. *Comprenez?*"

Marcel nodded weakly, unable to offer any resistance as his assailant jerked him roughly to his knees. Then cold metal was pressed rudely against his temple. Understanding dawned on him, in spite of the lingering fog in his head, as he rose unsteadily to his feet.

Blinking repeatedly to clear his vision, he tried to determine where he was. He couldn't tell exactly, but it was obvious he was no longer near the open field. The man must have dragged him through the woods—by his collar, judging from the feel of his throat.

"*Marchez!*"

The gun barrel moved from Marcel's temple to the base of his neck as the man prodded him to a slow walk along the narrow trail. Disoriented at first, he soon began to recover his balance and sense of direction, in spite of his pounding head. After advancing only a few yards, he was sure that they were headed back toward the abandoned house.

Isabelle! Marcel stopped in his tracks. She was still in the field when last he saw her. Had she made it to the river? Or had she too been caught? She must have made it, or whoever had him would have gotten her too.

The man shoved him roughly in the back, and he began plodding slowly forward again.

What will she think when I don't show up? he agonized, his thoughts swirling in a downward spiral. Perhaps Babette would call the whole thing off if she knew he had been caught. The women could hide out until he got free again. One way or another, he had to let them know they couldn't come back here though. But how?

Then, as if appearing out of nowhere, the abandoned farmhouse where he and Isabelle had encountered Babette loomed in front of him, and a cold shiver ran up his spine. If the man who held him was with the police, there would be others nearby. If he worked for the Italians, he wouldn't have insisted on silence. There would have been no need. So who was he? And why had they come back to this empty house?

Alert as never before, Marcel nevertheless complied as the unidentified man grabbed his coat collar and steered him toward the back door of the old house. The pistol—for that's what it surely must have been—was still pressed menacingly at the base of Marcel's skull. He didn't dare make a misstep for fear that the gun would go off.

At the door, a rough hand shoved him hard and he

tripped, landing heavily on the steps leading into the house. He twisted around to face his antagonist.

"So you want to help Jews, eh?" the man said aloud, but in a low, measured voice. It was hard to see his face clearly in the darkness, but the shape of the semiautomatic pistol aimed at Marcel's face was unmistakable. "And you want to be a terrorist like your friend Pascal?" He snorted in disgust. "Well, you are a complete fool to think that you can get away with such treachery. True Frenchmen are honorable, law-abiding citizens and patriots, not Jew-lovers and terrorists." He paused, and a wicked smile crept across his face as he moved closer to Marcel. "But since you insist on the latter, my friend, you must deal with me, Inspector Jean-Claude Malfaire," he enunciated slowly, "and I assure you that I will make you answer for your crimes."

Marcel felt an anger welling up inside him, unlike the fury that sometimes plagued him, almost as if it came from someplace other than himself. He looked the pompous Inspector Malfaire in the eye. "No true patriot could ever serve the Nazis," he said coldly, and felt his strength grow with each word. "And you, monsieur, make a mockery of honor when you hunt down innocent women and children. I will not answer to a man such as you!"

"*Embecile!* What do you know about anything? You only believe the propaganda of others." The inspector clearly did not intend for this to turn into a dialogue. He waved the pistol menacingly. "Get inside. Move!"

Common sense told Marcel that it was useless to refuse. He had no doubt that Malfaire would use the gun if necessary, and he had no wish to push him to it, exposed as he was. So he rose slowly, climbed the three steps and turned the latch on the door. It opened slightly, and he immediately felt the gun poking him in the small of the back. That was all the encouragement he needed to enter cautiously.

He peered inside where all was dark, just as before. He tried to recall the layout of the house, and whether he was entering the kitchen or a hallway. He decided it must be the kitchen. Grasping the edge of the door with his left hand, he opened it just enough to slide through into the house. Then with one quick movement, he wheeled and slammed the door back into Malfaire's face.

Just as he turned, there was a deafening explosion behind him as the gun fired, followed by a sickening moan, and the sound of something hard hitting the floor. Marcel leaned hard against the door, afraid to release it, yet unable to close it completely. It was all he could do to keep Malfaire at bay. And the vicious, animal sounds coming from the other side made him wonder if he were staving off a man or a demon.

A sudden confusing rush of footsteps and voices converged on Marcel from another room. Someone struck a match, and he could see dimly that Malfaire's right arm was crushed between the door and its frame. A moment later a lantern was lit, and then a man grabbed hold of Malfaire's trapped arm and kicked at the pistol that lay harmlessly on the kitchen floor, skidding it to the other side of the room.

"Open the door," the man said. "I've got a hold of him."

Marcel relaxed his hold on the door, and Malfaire, looking pale and in pain, was dragged into the room by his arm and slammed against the near wall.

❦   ❦   ❦

It didn't take Jean-Claude Malfaire long to identify two of the three men who had prevented him from executing the young Boussant.

"Pascal!" he heard the boy exclaim. "What are you doing here? I thought you'd been arrested again."

The dark fugitive grinned. "At the train station?" He laughed. "They grabbed the wrong man. I heard you might be in some trouble and I just couldn't stay away. I owe you one, remember?"

Malfaire had no doubt where Pascal had heard about the trouble. There, holding the lantern as calmly as you please, was Dominique. *The treacherous pig!* He wanted to spit on him, he was that disgusted. *After all the years we've spent together, and after all I've done for you, this is the thanks I get?* It was enough to make a man sick to his stomach. Well, if that's the way it was, then he would refuse to give the ingrate the satisfaction of even acknowledging his presence.

He didn't recognize the trio's third member, a short, stocky, middle-aged man, who now had a semiautomatic of his own pushed into the side of the inspector's face. He had a no-nonsense air about him, and his grip on the inspector's injured arm was still causing a good deal of pain.

"Hervé," Pascal said to the third man, nodding toward the Boussant boy, "this is the fellow who helped me escape from our friend the inspector, here. As you can see, he just can't seem to stay out of trouble."

"Apparently not," said Hervé with a wry smile. "I like that."

"What are you going to do with him?" Marcel asked Pascal, inclining his head in Malfaire's direction.

"I don't know yet," replied Pascal evenly. "Maybe we'll take him back to stand trial before a tribunal of *true* patriots."

"You can't do that; you have no legal authority!" cried Malfaire, suddenly finding his voice. Were these men crazy, thinking they could treat him this way with impunity?

"And what you were about to do here was legal?" Hervé didn't try to hide his disgust. "Your government became illegitimate the moment it became Hitler's puppet. You have no right to tell us what's legal and what isn't."

He pushed Malfaire to a sitting position on the floor, his back to the wall, and released his grip on the inspector's arm. Malfaire tried to massage the pain away with his other hand. This would never have happened had Dominique not betrayed him. Well, he was not through yet, he reminded himself. They would soon regret ever having crossed Inspector Malfaire.

The one called Hervé kept his pistol trained on Malfaire while the four men began to talk among themselves. The boy seemed upset about not being at the border with the Jew and her baby, while the others tried to assure him that she was in good hands. *What a fool to worry about a lousy Jew at a time like this,* Malfaire mused as he stretched a hand out slowly toward the top of his boot. *I'll give him something far greater to worry about.*

❦   ❦   ❦

Isabelle felt a sickening sense of panic welling up inside her. Babette, who had moved nearly thirty yards downstream from her to gain a better vantage point, was signaling furiously that the *caribinieri* were once again in sight. And still no sign of Marcel!

She had expected to see him crawling across the field as soon as the Italians disappeared the first time, but they had already come and gone since, and he hadn't shown. *What's keeping him?* she had asked herself a dozen times, but she hadn't come up with one good answer. Something had obviously gone wrong. Or had he simply backed out? After all, he couldn't claim refugee status in Switzerland the way she could, and maybe he had changed his mind.

She wouldn't allow herself to think that. It just wasn't possible.

Babette had now disappeared from view, and Isabelle knew instinctively that she too needed to get out of sight.

With one last look toward where she had last seen Marcel, she ducked down behind the embankment and held her breath.

The sound of voices, just like before, was joined by the sound of boots, approaching little by little, then receding just as slowly. And then, just when it seemed that the *caribinieri* were past, that she could relax for a few more minutes, it happened. Little Alexandre began to cry—not just a tiny whimper as before, but a full-throated squall!

Stunned by the sudden outburst, it took her a moment to recover and try to calm him. Her heart was pounding wildly and she couldn't think straight as she tried first her hand and then the blanket to muffle the piecing sounds. Nothing worked, and desperation nearly overwhelmed her. She wanted to scream, but didn't dare; to sob, but no tears came.

Suddenly, standing awkwardly in front of her was a man in uniform. It was too dark to tell what uniform, or even what color, but the sight of the machine gun he aimed at her belly made her feel faint. He didn't move. He just stared for a long moment, studying her face carefully.

"Signora?" he asked finally, tentatively. "What are you doing here?"

She didn't answer. Her throat was constricted with terror.

"Bambino?" When he reached out a hand toward Alexandre, Isabelle shrank back, fearful he would take the still-crying child from her. "Is this your baby?"

She nodded nervously.

"I have a baby too, *en Italia,"* he smiled proudly, *"Una bella bambina."*

Isabelle tried to force a smile in return. *What does he want?*

The sudden sounds of gunfire erupted in the still night air, and the young Italian jumped almost as much as Isabelle. Someone yelled something from the field above, and with a parting, almost sympathetic glance at Isabelle, the Italian hurried to scramble over the embankment to join his partner. Then both men raced for the far side of the field, in the direction of the shooting, which had now subsided.

Isabelle stared after them. They were running right past where Marcel should have been. *Is he all right? What is happening? Why didn't the caribinieri try to arrest me?* Her mind was spinning out of control, trying to grasp the meaning of this jumble of events.

"You've got to go, Isabelle!" It was Babette, who had appeared beside her, leading her toward the gurgling stream. "Please, you've got to go now, before they come back!"

⚜   ⚜   ⚜

Marcel saw the gun in Malfaire's hand a split second too late. Pulling a compact revolver from the top of his boot, the inspector rolled away from the others and began firing. Not one of the four saw it in time to do anything to stop him.

A scream died in Marcel's throat as Malfaire's gun erupted, sending Dominique sprawling backward and shattering the lantern. Flames immediately began licking at the coal oil that splattered across the floor and onto the wall. Dominique lay motionless where he fell amid the flames.

Marcel never saw where the next shot was aimed. But the explosion seemed to coincide with something clawing madly at his coat, and an intense burning sensation in his right shoulder. Knocked off balance, he felt himself spun halfway 'round and slammed into the wall behind him. Dazed, he sagged to the floor as Malfaire bolted for the door, turning to fire at Hervé and Pascal.

A chorus of loud blasts responded and the two men gave chase, though Marcel couldn't see what happened. More shots were fired outside, and then there was silence.

"Pascal?" he called. "Are you there?"

There was no answer.

The smoke was beginning to rise, and the flames looked as if they would soon engulf the room. He pushed himself up off the floor as best he could with his left arm and looked for a way to get Dominique outside. But the fire had spread too far and he couldn't even get close. His eyes burned and he began to cough as the smoke clogged the air in the small room.

He stumbled toward the door, gasping for breath, praying that Malfaire wasn't lurking just outside waiting for him. It almost didn't seem to matter, since he would soon be overcome with smoke anyway. Finding the opening, he lurched unsteadily down the outside steps into the cool darkness of the night as smoke billowed out of the house behind him.

Wiping at his stinging eyes, he looked up to see Pascal and Hervé standing together near the trees, some fifty feet away. As he approached he could see that at their feet lay the crumpled body of Inspector Jean-Claude Malfaire. He didn't know whether to feel revolted or relieved.

"Are you all right?" Pascal asked, coming over to take a cursory look at Marcel's shoulder.

Marcel nodded, but he couldn't stop staring at the man on the ground. He hadn't expected it to end like this. Somehow, he had never really believed that anyone would be killed. Arrested, surely. But not killed. And now two men were dead, and—

"Dominique!" Hervé exclaimed suddenly, as though waking from a dream. "We've got to get him out!"

"It's too late," Marcel blurted out, his voice breaking. "He's dead."

Both men stared at the house for a long moment as the flames began lapping at the exterior near the back door. It was Pascal who broke the silence.

"The *caribinieri* must have heard the shots. And they'll see the fire before long. We've got to get out of here!"

"But what about Isabelle?" Marcel's inner pain was more intense than the burning, throbbing sensation in his shoulder. "We can't just leave her! I've got to go to her!"

"You can't go anywhere until you get that wound patched up," said Hervé sternly. "Besides, Babette will see to Isabelle. She'll be fine. Don't you worry about that."

"But—"

The two men half-pushed, half-carried Marcel through the wooded path to their waiting car. Pascal took the wheel of the older Citroën sedan, while Hervé helped a rapidly weakening Marcel into the backseat. Marcel tried to remain seated upright, but he felt himself slipping into unconsciousness as Pascal gunned the Citroën onto the narrow road.

"O God," he murmured as the darkness closed in around him, "please protect her."

⚜   ⚜   ⚜

The *caribinieri* raced into the clearing in time to see flames leaping out of the windows throughout the first floor of the brittle old house. Machine guns at the ready, they made a careful sweep of the entire clearing, aided by the light of the roaring fire. Just as it appeared that they might abandon their search, they saw the blood in the snow.

Taking out their electric torches, they examined the spot carefully. There could be no doubt about it. The outline of a man's body was clear. Someone had been shot. But whoever he was, he was gone now.

The two Italians looked up at the sound of branches rustling in the trees beyond. They glanced at each other, and then one fell in behind the other as they followed the man's bloody trail into the woods.

❧   ❧   ❧

Isabelle's feet were in the icy water now, little ripples tugging at her ankles. *Marcel should be here. He said he'd be here!* Babette was still urging her on, but she no longer heard the words. Unthinking, unfeeling, she plunged ahead as the water lapped up over her knees.

Holding Alexandre high to keep him from getting wet, she plodded deeper and deeper until the water swirled around her waist. *Marcel, I need someone and you aren't here. What am I supposed to do?* Her clothes grew heavy with water and she felt as though she were being dragged down into the current. Her feet slipped on the smooth stones on the stream bottom. *O dear God,* she breathed, *I need Your help.*

And then the ground under her feet began to rise, and in another twenty feet she walked out onto the snow-covered Swiss shore. Dripping water, and trembling violently from the numbing cold, she managed to worm her way through the barbed-wire fence. Teeth chattering, she turned to look back to France, where Babette retreated across the open field. *Thank you, Babette,* she wanted to say, but her lips wouldn't form the words.

Her eyes searched the distant tree line where she had last seen Marcel. She could almost feel his arms about her once again, the touch of his lips on her cheek, hear his soft, strong voice. *Please,* she pleaded silently, *please don't let him die.* And somehow, she knew that if he were still alive, he would be thinking of her—and saying a prayer of his own.

A single tear rolled unchecked down Isabelle's cheek as she turned and carried her tiny son into Switzerland. Weary and cold, she was safe at last.

Epilogue

January 1943, Aix-les-Bains

The days had passed slowly for Marcel since he had last seen Isabelle Karmazin. While his shoulder was healing, he'd had a lot of time to think—too much, it seemed some days. He had relived every moment of their last day together, over and over, as if by doing so, he could turn back the hands of time. There was so much he still wanted to say, so much he wanted to hear.

Hervé and Babette had nursed him back to health in the days following the shooting, and Marcel had grown quite fond of them. In some small way, he filled in for the sons they had lost in the war. As his recovery progressed, they encouraged him to join them in their rescue efforts, as well as to frustrate the occupation authorities wherever possible. They had built quite a network, he had to admit. He just wasn't sure he was ready to put his heart on the line again.

"Marcel, you'll never guess who I saw today," gushed Babette, arriving home with Hervé from one of their late-night meetings. Without waiting for a reply, she went on. "Gilles Théron brought us some documents. He asked about you, and said to tell you that your mother sends her love, as do Françoise and Luc. They miss you, but they're doing fine."

"When did he last see them?" Marcel hadn't heard anything for a couple of weeks.

"He went to Ardeche for the weekend. He doesn't like going too long without seeing Françoise, you know." Hervé smiled mischievously. "Your sister must really be something."

Marcel too smiled. "Yes, she is," he replied. It would be good to see the family again, but he knew it wouldn't be possible for a while yet. It was simply too risky.

"There's something else," Babette said, and her voice softened so noticeably that Marcel wondered what was wrong. She handed him a plain white envelope.

He took it, and then just stared at it without saying a word.

"Well, open it," Hervé urged. "It has your name on it."

That it did, though there was no other marking on the entire envelope. "Who could—?" he began.

"One of our Swiss couriers brought it."

He felt unusually warm, and his clammy hands trembled as he tore it open. Inside was a single sheet of paper on which a letter was written in a delicate female hand. A lump rose in his throat as he unfolded the paper.

"Don't just sit there. Read it!" Babette was beginning to sound like Maman! He just frowned up at her.

Dearest Marcel, he read. *I don't know if this will reach you, or when, but I have to try. I want you to know that Alexandre and I are quite safe. Some people found us wandering near the border and took us in. You'll be pleased to know that they too share your faith in God. I often have the feeling that Someone's looking out for me, though I'm not sure why.*

I never had the chance to thank you for my life! You and your friends are truly a legion of honor. You risk yourselves for others, knowing that the reward may be arrest or death. No one will pin a medal on your chest, dear Marcel, for what you did for me. But you have my eternal gratitude, and if God is anything like I imagine Him to be, He must be smiling too.

I miss you terribly. I'm sure you know that. But it was naïve to think you could come with me. The Swiss are very strict about their laws, and even I cannot stay here long. Perhaps it was not meant to be.

Some relief workers are here from America. There is a possibility that I can go there with them when they return, though nothing is certain yet.

Give your family my love. Please don't be sad. Think of me often as I shall of you.

Yours faithfully, Isabelle.

Marcel read and reread each carefully written line until the words began to blur.

"Is everything all right?" Babette's soft voice broke the silence.

"Yes," he replied slowly, huskily. "She's going to be just fine."

Historical Note

The beginning of substantial underground activity on behalf of the Jews in France is traced by some to the July 16, 1942 roundup of Jews in Paris. Of the more than 12,000 arrested that day by the French police, 4,000 were children. None of the children survived the concentration camps to which they were sent, and fewer than 400 adults made it out alive. All told, about 100,000 of France's 300,000 Jews did not survive the horrors of World War II.

French Protestants were among the first to speak out against the repressive anti-Jew policies of the Nazis as well as their own government. Many Protestant families and churches actively participated in the rescue and hiding of Jews. Perhaps the most celebrated case is the small village of Le Chambon-sur-Lignon which was responsible for the rescue of some 5,000 Jews during the war. Most such activities, however, were carried out on a much smaller scale.

Protestants and Catholics cooperated through organizations such as Amitié Chrétienne (Christian Friendship), and through underground publications such as Témoignage Chrétien (Christian Testimony) whose first edition warned that France was in danger of "losing its soul."

A few of the characters in this book are actual people: the pastors Charles Westphal and Roland de Pury, Monsignor Théas of Montauban, Cardinal Gerlier, and Klaus Barbie. The depiction of the pastors is not based on specific knowledge of their words or acts but on their known involvement in the rescue movement, and their vehement preaching and teaching against the mistreatment of the Jews. The pastoral letter credited in the story to Monsignor Théas is real and accurately attributed. Barbie and the Cardinal, though not political figures, strictly speaking, are well known and their actions well documented.

All other characters in the book, with the exception of political figures, are of the author's own creation. Any similarity, real or imagined, to persons living or dead is purely coincidental.

Enter a medieval world of ancient secrets, an evil conspiracy, and a mysterious castle called Magnus.

The year is 1312. The place, the remote North York Moors of England. Join young Thomas as he pursues his destiny—the conquest of an 800-year-old castle that harbors secrets dating back to the days of King Arthur and Merlin.

You'll find *Magnus* at your local
Christian bookstore.

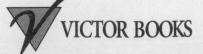

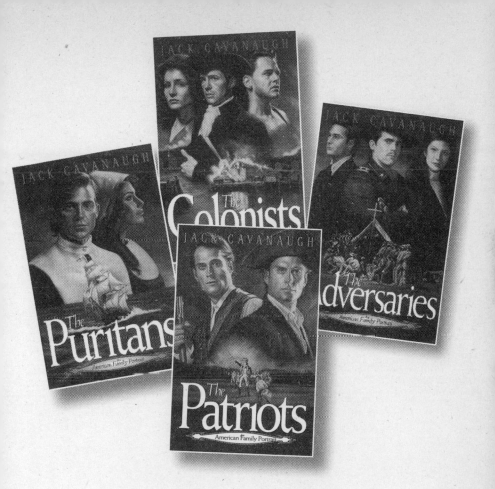

Don't miss a single book from the American Family Portrait Series!

Jack Cavanaugh's epic of faith, love, and sacrifice follows the Morgans through the years, chronicling the triumphs and tragedies of one of America's first families of faith.

Look for *The Puritans*, *The Colonists*, *The Patriots*, and *The Adversaries* in your local Christian bookstore.

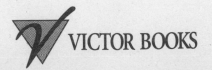

VICTOR BOOKS